Karen Rose was introduced to suspense and horror at the tender age of eight when she accidentally read Poe's *The Pit and the Pendulum* and was afraid to go to sleep for years. She now enjoys writing books that make other people afraid to go to sleep.

Karen lives in Florida with her husband of twenty years and their children. When she's not writing, she enjoys travelling, karate and, though not a popular Florida pastime, skiing.

By Karen Rose

I'm Watching You
Nothing to Fear
You Can't Hide
Count to Ten
Die For Me
Scream For Me

SCREAM FOR ME

KAREN ROSE

headline

First published in Great Britain in 2008 by
HEADLINE PUBLISHING GROUP

First published in paperback in Great Britain in 2009 by
HEADLINE PUBLISHING GROUP

9

Cataloguing in Publication Data is available from the British Library

ISBN 978 0 7553 3712 5

Typeset in Palatino by Avon DataSet Ltd, Bidford-on-Avon

Printed and bound in Great Britain by Clays Ltd, St Ives plc

Headline's policy is to use papers that are natural, renewable and recyclable products and made from wood grown in sustainable forests. The logging and manufacturing processes are expected to conform to the environmental regulations of the country of origin.

HEADLINE PUBLISHING GROUP
An Hachette Livre UK Company
338 Euston Road
London NW1 3BH

www.headline.co.uk
www.hachettelivre.co.uk

To Martin, because the sun shines brighter whenever you're with me. Of course, living in a very sunny state doesn't hurt, but you get my drift. I love you.

To Kay and Marc. Your friendship is without price.

And to my editor, Karen Kosztolnyik, and my agent, Robin Rue.
Thank you.

Acknowledgments

Danny Agan for answering all my questions on police procedure.

Doug Byron for answering all my questions on forensic chemistry.

Marc Conterato for all things medical.

Martin Hafer for information on hypnosis and for sliding dinner under my office door when I'm on deadline.

Jimmy Hatton and Mike Koenig for being such a great team all those years ago. I couldn't help but give you an encore performance.

Terri Bolyard, Kay Conterato, and Sonie Lasker for listening when I get stuck!

Shannon Aviles for your support and all the buzz.

Beth Miller for all your enthusiasm!

All mistakes are my own.

Prologue

Mansfield Community Hospital, Dutton, Georgia
Thirteen years ago

A bell dinged. Another elevator had arrived. Alex stared at the floor and wished to be invisible as a strong perfume tickled her nose.

'Violet Drummond, come *on*. We've still got two patients to visit. What are you *doing*? Oh.' The last was uttered on an indrawn breath.

Go away, Alex thought.

'Isn't that . . . *her*?' The whisper came from Alex's left. 'The Tremaine girl that lived?'

Alex kept her eyes fixed on the fists she clenched in her lap. *Go away*.

'Looks like,' the first woman answered, dropping her voice. 'My goodness, she looks just like her sister. I saw the other one's picture in the paper. Spittin' images, they are.'

'Well, they are twins. Identical, even. Were, anyway. God rest her soul.'

Alicia. Alex's chest closed up and she couldn't breathe.

'Shame, it was. Pretty thing like that found dead in a ditch without a stitch on. God only knows what that man did to her before he killed her.'

'Dirty no-good drifter. I hope they fry him alive. I heard he'd . . . *you* know.'

Screaming. *Screaming*. A million voices were screaming in her head. *Cover your ears. Make them stop*. But Alex's hands stayed clenched in her lap. *Shut the door. Shut the door*. The door in her mind closed and the screaming abruptly stilled. There was quiet again. Alex dragged in a breath. Her heart was racing.

'Well, *that* one in the wheelchair there tried to kill herself after she found her mama dead on the floor. She took every pill Doc Fabares prescribed for her mother's nerves. Luckily her aunt found her in time. The girl, of course. Not the mother.'

'Well, of course not. You don't get up after shootin' yourself in the head.'

Alex flinched, the crack of the single shot echoing through her mind, again and again and again. And the blood. *So much blood. Mama*.

I hate you I hate you I wish you were dead.

Alex closed her eyes. Tried to make the screams go away, but they wouldn't stop. *I hate you I hate you I wish you were dead*.

Shut the door.

'Where's she from, the aunt?'

'Delia at the bank says the aunt's a nurse from Ohio. She and the girl's mama are sisters. Were anyway. Delia says when the aunt walked up to her window she nearly had heart failure. Lookin' at the aunt was just like looking at Kathy – spooked her good.'

'Well, I heard Kathy Tremaine used the gun that belonged to that man she was livin' with. What an example to set for those girls of hers, livin' with a man, and at her age.'

Panic began to well. *Shut the door*.

'Hers *and* his. He has a daughter, too. Bailey's her name.'

'They were wild, wild girls, all three of 'em. Somethin' like this was bound t'happen.'

'Wanda, please. It's not that girl's fault some homeless man raped and killed her.'

Alex's breath was backing up in her lungs. *Go away. Go to hell. Both of you. All of you. Just leave me alone and let me finish what I started*.

Wanda scoffed. 'Have you seen the way these girls dress today? Just askin' for a man to drag them off and do God-knows-what. I'm just glad *she's* being taken away.'

'She is? The aunt's takin' her back to Ohio?'

'That's what Delia at the bank told me. I say it's a blessing that she won't be going back to the high school. My granddaughter goes to that school, in the tenth grade, same as the Tremaine girls. Alexandra Tremaine would have been a terrible influence.'

'Terrible,' Violet agreed. 'Oh, look at the time. We still have to visit Gracie and Estelle Johnson. Push the elevator button, Wanda. My hands are full with these violets.'

The button dinged and the two old women were gone. Alex was shaking from inside her body out to her skin. Kim was taking her to Ohio. Alex didn't really care. She didn't plan on making it to Ohio anyway. All she wanted was to finish what she'd started.

'Alex?' Footsteps clacked on the tile and she smelled a new perfume, clean and sweet. 'What's wrong? You're shaking like a leaf. Meredith, what happened? You were supposed to be watching her, not sitting on that bench with your nose in a book.'

Kim touched her forehead and Alex wrenched back, keeping her eyes on her hands. *Don't touch me.* She wanted it to be a snarl, but the words echoed only in her own mind.

'Is she okay, Mom?' It was Meredith. Alex had a vague memory of her cousin, one big girl of seven playing Barbies with two five-year-olds. *Two little girls. Alicia.* Alex wasn't part of two anymore. *I'm alone.* Panic began to well again. *For God's sake shut the door.* Alex drew a breath. Focused on the darkness in her mind. Quiet darkness.

'I think so, Merry.' Kim knelt in front of the chair and tugged on Alex's chin until she lifted her face. Her eyes met Kim's and instantly skittered away. With a sigh, Kim stood and Alex breathed again. 'Let's get her to the car. Dad's bringing it up to the door.' The elevator door dinged once again and Alex's chair was pulled into the elevator backward. 'I wonder what upset her? I was only gone for a few minutes.'

'I think it was those old ladies. I think they were talking about Alicia and Aunt Kathy.'

'What? Meredith, why didn't you say something to them?'

'I couldn't really hear them. I didn't think Alex could hear them either. Mostly they were just whispering.'

'I'll just bet they were, old busybodies. Next time, come get me.'

The elevator dinged and the chair was pushed into the hall. 'Mom.' Meredith's voice took on a warning tone. 'It's Mr Crighton. And he's got Bailey and Wade with him.'

'I was hoping he'd do the right thing for once. Meredith, run out to the car and get your father. Have him call the sheriff, just in case Mr Crighton gives us any trouble.'

'Okay. Mom, don't make him mad, please.'

'I won't. Now go.'

The wheelchair came to a stop and Alex stared hard at the hands in her lap. Her own hands. She blinked hard. They looked different. Had they always looked this way?

'Dad, she's taking her. You can't let her take Alex away.' Bailey. It sounded like she was crying. *Don't cry, Bailey. It's better this way.*

'She's not taking her anywhere.' His boots stopped shuffling on the tile.

Kim sighed. 'Craig, please. Don't make a scene. It's not good for Alex or your own kids. Take Wade and Bailey home. I'm taking Alex with me.'

'Alex is my daughter. You can't have her.'

'She's not your daughter, Craig. You never married my sister, never adopted her children. Alex is mine and she leaves with me, today. I'm sorry, Bailey,' Kim added, her voice gentling. 'But this is the way it needs to be. *You* can come visit her any time.'

Scuffed black work boots stopped next to Alex's own feet. She pulled her feet back. Kept her eyes down. *Breathe.*

'No. That girl lived in my house for five years, Kim. She called me "Daddy."'

No, that Alex had never done. She'd called him 'sir.'

Bailey was crying now, hard. 'Please, Kim, don't do this.'

'You can't take her. She can't even look at you.' There was desperation in Craig's voice and truth in his words. Alex couldn't look at Kim, not even now that she'd changed her hair. It was a nice try and Alex knew she should be grateful for Kim's sacrifice. But Kim couldn't change her eyes. 'You cut and dyed your hair, but you still look like Kathy. Every time she looks at you, she'll see her mama. Is that what you want?'

'If she stayed with you, she'd see her mama dead in the living room every time she came downstairs,' Kim snapped. 'What were you thinking, leaving them alone?'

'I had to go to work,' Craig snarled back. 'It's what keeps bread on my table.'

I hate you. I wish you were dead. The voices screamed in her mind, loud and long and angry. Alex bent her head low and Kim's hand brushed the back of her neck. *Don't touch me.* She tried to pull away, but Craig was too close. So she stayed frozen.

'Damn you and damn your work,' Kim said bitterly. 'You left Kathy alone on the worst day of her life. If you'd been home, she might be alive and Alex wouldn't be here.'

The boots came closer and Alex pulled her feet back further.

'Are you saying *I* caused this? That *I* made Kathy kill herself? That *I* made Alex swallow a bottle of pills? *Is that what you're saying?*'

The silence between them was tense and Alex held her breath, waiting. Kim wasn't saying no and Craig's hands were now fisted as tight as Alex's were.

The doors swished open, then closed and there were more footsteps on the tile floor. 'Kim, is there a problem?' Kim's husband, Steve. Alex let out the breath she held. He was a big man with a kind face. Alex could look at his face. But not now.

'I don't know.' Kim's voice trembled. 'Craig, is there a problem?'

Another few beats of silence and Craig's fists slowly

relaxed. 'No. Will you at least let me and the kids say good-bye?'

'I suppose that would be okay.' Kim's perfume grew faint as she moved away.

Craig was coming closer. *Shut the door.* Alex squeezed her eyes closed and held her breath while he whispered in her ear. She concentrated hard, keeping him out of her mind, and finally, finally he stepped away.

She sat hunched over while Bailey hugged her. 'I'll miss you, Alex. Whose clothes will I steal now?' Bailey tried to laugh, but choked on a sob. 'Write to me, please.'

Wade was last. *Shut the door.* Again she held herself rigid as he hugged her good-bye. The voices screeched. It hurt. *Please. Make it stop.* She focused, hands on the door, shoving it closed. Finally Wade stepped away and she could breathe once more.

'Now we'll leave,' Kim said. 'Please let us go.' Alex held her breath again until they reached a white car. Steve scooped her up and settled her on the seat.

Click. Steve fastened her seat belt, then cupped her face in his hand.

'We'll take care of you, Alex. I promise,' he said softly.

He slammed her car door and it was only then that Alex let herself unclench her fist. Just a little. Just enough to see the bag she held. Pills. A lot of tiny white pills. Where? When? It didn't matter where or when.

What mattered was she could now finish what she'd started. She licked her bottom lip and forced her chin up.

'Please.' She flinched at the sound of her own voice. It was rusty from lack of use.

In the front seat both Steve and Kim jerked around to look.

'Mom, Alex talked!' Meredith was grinning.

Alex was not.

'What is it, honey?' Kim asked. 'What do you need?'

Alex dropped her eyes. 'Water. Please.'

Chapter One

Arcadia, Georgia, Present day
Friday, January 26, 1:25 A.M.

He'd chosen her with care. Taken her with relish. Made her scream, long and loud.

Mack O'Brien shivered. It still gave him goose bumps. Still made his blood race and his nostrils flare as he remembered how she'd looked, sounded. Tasted. The taste of pure fear was like nothing else. This he knew. She'd been his first murder. She would not be his last.

He'd chosen her final resting place with equal care. He let her body roll off his back and drop to the soggy ground with a muted thud. He squatted next to her and arranged the rough brown blanket in which he'd wrapped her like a shroud, his anticipation growing. Sunday was the annual cross-county bicycle race. One hundred cyclists would be passing this way. He'd placed her so that she'd be visible from the road.

Soon she would be found. Soon *they* would hear of her demise.

They'll wonder. And they'll suspect each other. They'll all be afraid.

He stood, satisfied with his handiwork. He wanted them to be afraid. He wanted them to shake and tremble like girls. He wanted them to know the true taste of fear.

Because he knew that taste, just as he knew hunger and fury. That he knew all those flavors so intimately was their fault.

He looked down, nudged the brown blanket with his toe. She had paid. Soon, every one of them would suffer and they would pay. Soon they'd know he'd returned.

Hello, Dutton. Mack is back. And he wouldn't rest until he'd ruined them all.

Cincinnati, Ohio, Friday, January 26, 2:55 P.M.

'Ow. That hurt.'

Alex Fallon glanced down at the pale, sullen teenage girl. 'I suppose it does at that.' Quickly Alex taped the IV needle in place. 'Maybe you'll remember this the next time you're tempted to skip school, eat an entire hot fudge sundae, and end up in the ER. Vonnie, you have diabetes and denial won't change that. You have to follow—'

'My diet,' Vonnie snarled. 'I know already. Why can't everybody leave me alone?'

The words echoed in Alex's mind, as they always did. Gratitude to her family mixed with the sympathy for her patient, as it always did. 'One of these days you're going to eat the wrong thing and end up . . . downstairs.'

Vonnie gave her best shot at belligerence. 'So? What's downstairs anyway?'

'The morgue.' Alex held the girl's startled gaze. 'Unless that's what you want.'

Abruptly, Vonnie's eyes filled with tears. 'Some days it is.'

'I know, honey.' And she understood more than anyone outside her family imagined. 'But you're going to have to decide which it's going to be. Live or die.'

'Alex?' Letta, their charge nurse, poked her head into the examination room. 'You've got an urgent call on two. I can take over in here.'

Alex squeezed Vonnie's shoulder. 'I'm done for now.' She gave Vonnie the eye. 'I don't want to see you in here again.' She handed the chart to Letta. 'Who is it?'

'Nancy Barker from Fulton County Social Services down in Georgia.'

Alex's heart sank. 'That's where my stepsister lives.'

Letta lifted her brows. 'I didn't know you had a stepsister.'

Technically Alex didn't, but the story was too long and her relationship with Bailey too convoluted. 'I haven't seen her in a long time.' Five years, in fact, when Bailey had shown up on Alex's Cincinnati doorstep higher than a kite. Alex had tried to get Bailey into rehab, but Bailey had disappeared, taking Alex's credit cards with her.

Letta's brow creased with concern. 'I hope everything's okay.'

Alex had been both expecting and dreading this call for years. 'Yeah. Me, too.'

It was one of those sad ironies, Alex thought as she hurried to the phone. Alex had been the one to attempt suicide all those years ago and Bailey was the one who'd ended up an addict. Family had made a huge difference. Alex had had Kim and Steve and Meredith to get her through. But Bailey's family . . . Bailey had no one.

She picked up line two. 'This is Alex Fallon.'

'This is Nancy Barker. I'm with Fulton County Social Services.'

Alex sighed. 'Just tell me, is she alive?'

There was a long pause. 'Who, Miss Fallon?'

Alex winced at the 'Miss.' She still wasn't used to not being 'Mrs Preville.' Her cousin Meredith said it would be just a matter of time after her divorce, but a year had passed and Alex felt no closure. Perhaps it was because she and her ex still crossed paths several times a week. Right at this moment, as a matter of fact. Alex watched Dr Richard Preville reach next to the phone for his own messages. Carefully not meeting her eyes, he bobbed an awkward nod. No, sharing shifts with her ex was not speeding her along the road to relationship recovery.

'Miss Fallon?' the woman prompted.

Alex wrenched her focus back. 'Bailey. That is who you're calling about, isn't it?'

'Actually I'm calling about Hope.'

'Hope.' Alex repeated it blankly. 'I don't understand. Hope what?'

'Hope Crighton, Bailey's daughter. Your niece.'

Alex sat down, stunned. 'I didn't know Bailey had a daughter.' *That poor child.*

'Oh. Then you didn't know that you're listed as the emergency contact on all of Hope's registration forms at her preschool.'

'No.' Alex drew a bolstering breath. 'Is Bailey dead, Ms Barker?'

'I hope not, but we don't know where she is. She didn't show up for work this morning and one of her coworkers went to her house to check on her. The coworker found Hope curled up in a little ball in a closet.'

Sick dread settled in Alex's gut, but she kept her voice calm. 'And Bailey was gone.'

'The last anyone saw her was last night when she picked Hope up from preschool.'

Preschool. The child was old enough for preschool and Alex had no idea she'd even existed. *Oh, Bailey, what have you done?* 'And Hope? Was she hurt?'

'Not physically, but she's scared. Very scared. She's not talking to anyone.'

'Where is she?'

'Right now she's in emergency foster care.' Nancy Barker sighed. 'Well, if you're not going to take her, I'll line up a permanent foster family for her.'

'I'll take her.' The words were out of Alex's mouth before she even knew she planned to say them. But once said, she knew it was the right thing to do.

'You didn't even know she existed until five minutes ago,' Barker protested.

'It doesn't matter. I'm her aunt. I'll take her.' *Like Kim took me. And saved my life.* 'I'll get there as soon as I can arrange leave from my job and buy a plane ticket.'

Alex hung up, turned, and walked into Letta, whose brows were nearly off her forehead. Alex knew she'd been listening. 'Well? Can I have the leave?'

Letta's eyes were filled with worry. 'Do you have vacation saved up?'

'Six weeks. I haven't taken a day in more than three years.' There hadn't been reason to. Richard never had time to go anywhere. He'd always been working.

'Then start out with vacation,' Letta said. 'I'll get somebody to cover your shifts. But, Alex, you know nothing about this child. Maybe she has a disability or special needs.'

'I'll cope,' Alex said. 'She has no one, and she's family. I won't abandon her.'

'Like her mother did.' Letta tilted her head. 'Like your mother did you.'

Alex fought the wince, keeping her face impassive.

Her past was only a few clicks away from anyone with Google. But Letta did mean well, so Alex made her lips curve. 'I'll call you when I get down there and find out more. Thanks, Letta.'

Arcadia, Georgia, Sunday, January 28, 4:05 P.M.

'Welcome back, Danny boy,' Special Agent Daniel Vartanian murmured to himself as he got out of his car and surveyed the scene. He'd only been gone two weeks, but it had been an eventful two weeks. It was time to get back to work, back to his life. Which in Daniel's case meant the same thing. Work was his life, and death was his work.

Avenging death, that was. Not causing it. He thought of the past two weeks, of all the death, all the lives destroyed. It was enough to drive a man insane, if he let it. Daniel didn't intend to let it. He'd go back to his life, finding justice for one victim at a time. He'd make a difference. It was the only way he knew to . . . atone.

The victim this day was a woman. She'd been found in a ditch on the side of the road, which was now lined with law enforcement vehicles of all shapes and functions.

The crime lab was already here, as was the ME. Daniel stopped at the edge of the road where someone had strung yellow crime scene tape and peered down into the ditch where the body lay, a tech from the ME's office crouched by her side. She'd been wrapped in a brown blanket that had been pulled away just enough to do the exam. Daniel could see she had dark hair and was perhaps five foot six. She was nude and her face was . . . damaged. He'd lifted one leg over the tape when a voice stopped him.

'Stop, sir. This area is off limits.'

Straddling the tape, Daniel looked over his shoulder to where a young, earnest-faced officer stood, one hand on his weapon. 'I'm Special Agent Daniel Vartanian, Georgia Bureau of Investigation.'

The man's eyes widened. 'Vartanian? You mean – I mean—' He took a breath and straightened abruptly. 'I'm sorry, sir. I was just surprised, that's all.'

Daniel nodded, giving the young man a kind smile. 'I understand.' He didn't like it, but he did understand. The name Vartanian had gotten quite a bit of publicity in the week since his brother Simon's death, none of it good, all of it deserved. Simon Vartanian had taken seventeen lives in Philadelphia – two of those victims his own parents. The story had made every newspaper in the country. It would be a long time before the name Vartanian could be said without a wide-eyed response. 'Where can I find the sheriff?'

The officer pointed about forty feet down the road. 'That's Sheriff Corchran.'

'Thanks, Officer.' Daniel pulled his leg back over the tape and started walking again, conscious of the officer's eyes following him. In two minutes everyone here would know a Vartanian was on the scene. Daniel hoped he could keep the hubbub to a minimum. This wasn't about him or any other Vartanian, it was about that woman lying in the ditch wrapped in a brown blanket. She had family somewhere, people who would be missing her. People who would need justice and closure to get on with their lives.

Daniel had once thought justice and closure to be the same thing, that knowing a perpetrator had been caught and punished for his crimes closed the book on a painful chapter in the lives of the victims and their families. Now, hundreds of crimes, victims, and families later, he understood that every crime created a ripple effect, touched lives in ways that could never be measured. Simply knowing evil had been punished wasn't always enough to allow one to move on. Daniel knew all about that, too.

'Daniel.' It was a surprised greeting from Ed Randall, head of the crime lab team. 'I didn't know you were back.'

'Just today.' It was supposed to have been tomorrow, but having been away for two weeks, Daniel was next in the barrel for an assignment. When this call had come in, his boss had called him back in early. He stuck out his hand to the sheriff. 'Sheriff Corchran, I'm Special Agent Vartanian, GBI. We'll provide any support you request.'

The sheriff's eyes widened as he shook Daniel's hand. 'Any relation to . . . ?'

God help me, yes. He made himself smile. 'I'm afraid so.'

Corchran studied him shrewdly. 'You ready to be back?'

No. Daniel kept his voice level. 'Yes. If it's a problem, I can request someone else.'

Corchran seemed to consider it and Daniel waited, keeping his temper carefully locked down. It wasn't right, wasn't fair, but being judged by his family's deeds was his reality. Finally Corchran shook his head. 'No, you don't need to do that. We're good.'

Daniel's temper settled and again he made himself smile. 'Good. So can you tell me what happened? Who discovered the body and when?'

'Today was our annual Cycle Challenge and this road is part of the course. One of the cyclists noticed the blanket. He didn't want to lose the race, so he called 911 and kept cycling. I have him waiting at the finish line if you need to talk to him.'

'I'll want to talk to him, yes. Did anyone else stop?'

'No, we got lucky,' Ed Randall said. 'We had an undisturbed scene when we got here and no crowd watching – they were all at the finish line.'

'That doesn't happen very often. Who was first on the scene from your department, Sheriff?' Daniel asked.

'Larkin. He lifted only a corner of the blanket to see her face.' Corchran's stony face flinched, a telling sign. 'I immediately called you guys. We don't have the resources to investigate a scene like this.'

Daniel acknowledged the final statement with a nod. He appreciated sheriffs like Corchran who were willing to bring in the Georgia Bureau of Investigation. So many were territorial, viewing any GBI involvement as . . . a swarm of locusts descending on their town. Yes, that's how the sheriff of Daniel's hometown had put it only two weeks ago. 'We'll work with you in whatever capacity you choose, Sheriff.'

'For now, take it all,' Corchran said. 'My department is at your disposal.' His jaw squared. 'We haven't had a murder in Arcadia in the ten years since I've been in office. We want to see whoever did *that* go away for a long time.'

'We do, too.' Daniel turned to Ed. 'So what do you know?'

'She was killed somewhere else and dumped here. Her body was found wrapped in a brown blanket.'

'Like a shroud,' Daniel murmured and Ed nodded.

'Just like. The blanket appears to be new, it's some wool blend. Her face was beaten badly and there was bruising around her mouth. The ME can give you more on that. There's no sign of struggle down there and no footprints up or down the slope.'

Daniel frowned and looked down into the ditch. It was a drainage ditch and the water ran down to the storm sewer about a hundred yards away. The sides were smooth mud. 'Then he must have walked through the water to the storm sewer, then up to the road.' He considered it a moment. 'This bike race. Was it widely publicized?'

Corchran nodded. 'This is a big fund-raiser for the local youth clubs, so the boosters put flyers in towns fifty miles away. Besides, we've had this race on the last Sunday in January for more than ten years. We get bikers from up north who want to ride where it's warmer. It's a pretty big deal.'

'Then he wanted her to be found,' Daniel said.

'Daniel.' The ME techs came over the crime scene tape. One of them went straight to their rig and the other stopped next to Ed. 'Good to see you back.'

'Good to be back, Malcolm. What do you know?'

Malcolm Zuckerman stretched his back. 'That it's going to be fun getting the body out of that ditch. The incline's steep and the mud's slick. Trey's gonna jerry-rig a crane.'

'Malcolm,' Daniel said with exaggerated patience. Malcolm was always complaining about his back or weather conditions or something. 'What do you know about the victim?'

'Female, Caucasian, mid-twenties most likely. She's been dead about two days. Cause of death appears to be asphyxiation. Bruising on her buttocks and inner thighs indicates sexual assault. Her face has been beaten with a blunt object. Don't know what yet, but it caused significant damage to her facial structure. Nose, cheekbones, jaw are all broken.' He frowned. 'The beating of her face may have been postmortem.'

Daniel lifted a brow. 'So he wanted her to be found, but not identified.'

'That's what I'm thinkin'. I'm betting we won't find her prints in the system. There is a pattern of bruises to the side of her mouth, could be from her assailant's fingers.'

'He held his hand over her mouth until she smothered,' Corchran muttered, his jaw clenched. 'Then pounded her face to pulp. Sonofabitch.'

'That's what it looks like,' Malcolm said, sympathy in his voice, but a weariness in his eyes Daniel more than understood. Too many bodies, too many sonsofbitches. 'We'll get more once the doc does the examination. You done with me, Danny?'

'Yeah. Call me when you do the autopsy. I want to be there.'

Malcolm shrugged. 'Suit yourself. Doc Berg will probably start after Three-M.'

'What's Three-M?' Corchran asked as Malcolm went back to the ME rig to wait.

'Morgue morning meeting,' Daniel told him. 'That means Dr Berg will probably start the autopsy at nine-thirty or ten. You're welcome if you want to watch.'

Corchran swallowed. 'Thanks. I will if I can.'

Corchran looked a little green and Daniel didn't blame him. It wasn't easy to watch the MEs do their thing. The sound of the bone saws still made Daniel queasy after years of autopsies. 'That's fine. What else, Ed?'

'We got shots of all the area around the body and on both sides of the ditch,' Ed said. 'Video and still. We'll search this side of the ditch first so Malcolm won't destroy anything getting her out of here, then we'll set up the lights and search the rest.' He waved at his team and they headed over the tape. Ed started to follow, then hesitated before drawing Daniel aside. 'I'm sorry about your parents, Daniel,' he said quietly. 'I know there's nothing I can say. I just wanted you to know.'

Daniel dropped his eyes to the ground, caught off balance. Ed was sorry Arthur and Carol Vartanian were dead. Daniel wasn't sure he could be. Some days Daniel wasn't sure his parents hadn't brought a large measure of their doom on themselves. Simon had been evil, but his parents had enabled his brother, in their own way.

The people Daniel felt truly sorry for were Simon's other victims. Still . . . Arthur and Carol had been his parents. He could still see them lying in the Philadelphia morgue, dead at the hand of their own son. That hideous picture mixed in with all the others that haunted him, awake or asleep. So much death. So many lives destroyed. *Ripples*.

Daniel cleared his throat. 'I saw you at the funeral. Thanks, Ed. It meant a lot.'

'If you need anything, you know where to call.' Ed gave Daniel's shoulder a hard clap, then followed his team. Daniel turned back to Corchran, who'd been watching.

'Sheriff, I'd like to talk to Officer Larkin and have him take me down to the body the same way he approached earlier. I know he'll do a thorough report, but I'd like to get his memory and impressions straight from him.'

'Sure. He's stationed down the road, keeping curiosity seekers back.' Corchran radioed Larkin and in less than five minutes the officer had joined them. Larkin's face was still a little pale, but his eyes were clear. In his hand he held a piece of paper.

'My report, Agent Vartanian. But there is one other thing. I just remembered it when I was driving back here. There was a murder just like this not far from here.'

Corchran's brows shot up. 'Where? When?'

'Before you got here,' Larkin replied. 'It was thirteen years ago this April. A girl was found in a ditch just like this. She was wrapped in a brown blanket, and she'd been raped and suffocated.' He swallowed. 'And her face had been beaten in, just like this.'

Daniel felt a chill race down his spine. 'You seem to remember it clearly, Officer.'

Larkin looked pained. 'The girl was sixteen, same age as my own daughter at the time. I don't remember the girl's name, but it happened outside of Dutton, which is about twenty-five miles east of here.'

The chill spread and Daniel clenched his body against a shiver. 'I know where Dutton is,' he said. He knew Dutton well. He'd walked its streets, shopped in its stores, played Little League on its team. He also knew that evil had lived in Dutton and had borne the Vartanian name. Dutton, Georgia, was Daniel Vartanian's hometown.

Larkin nodded as he put Daniel's name with current events. 'I expect you do.'

'Thank you, Officer,' Daniel said, managing to keep his voice level. 'I'll look into it as soon as possible. For now, let's go take a look at Jane Doe.'

Dutton, Georgia, Sunday, January 28, 9:05 P.M.

Alex closed the bedroom door, then leaned against it, drained. 'She's finally asleep,' she murmured to her cousin Meredith, who sat on the sofa in the adjoining sitting room of Alex's hotel room.

Meredith looked up from her study of the pages and pages of the coloring books four-year-old Hope Crighton had filled since Alex had taken custody of her niece from the social worker thirty-six hours before. 'Then we need to talk,' she said softly.

There was concern in Meredith's eyes. Coming from a paediatric psychologist who specialized in emotionally traumatized children, this only intensified Alex's dread.

Alex sat down. 'I appreciate you coming. I know you're busy with your patients.'

'I can get someone to take care of my patients for a

day or two. I would have been here yesterday had you told me you were coming, because I would have been sitting on the plane right next to you.' There was frustration and hurt in Meredith's voice. 'What were you thinking, Alex? Coming down here all by yourself. Of all places . . . *here*.'

Here. Dutton, Georgia. The name made Alex's stomach churn. It was the last place she'd ever wanted to come back to. But the churning in her stomach was nothing compared to the fear she'd felt when she'd first looked into Hope's blank gray eyes.

'I don't know,' Alex admitted. 'I should have known better. But Mer, I had no idea it would be this bad, but it is as bad as I think, isn't it?'

'From what I've seen in the last three hours? Yes. Whether her traumatizing event was waking up to find her mother gone on Friday or the years that came before that, I can't say. I don't know what Hope was like before Bailey disappeared.' Meredith frowned. 'But she's nothing like I expected her to be.'

'I know. I'd prepared myself for a dirty, malnourished child. I mean, the last time I saw Bailey, she was really bad, Meredith. High and dirty. Track marks on both arms. I've always wondered if I could have done something more.'

Meredith lifted an auburn brow. 'So here you are?'

'No. Well, maybe it started that way, but as soon as I saw Hope, all that changed.' She thought of the little girl with the golden curls and Botticelli angel face. And empty gray eyes. 'I thought for a moment they'd brought me the wrong child. She's clean and well-fed. Her clothes and shoes were like new.'

'The social worker would have given her clean clothes and shoes.'

'Those were the clothes the social worker took from Hope's preschool. Hope's teacher said Bailey always kept a clean set in Hope's cubby. They said Bailey was a good mom, Mer. They were shocked when the social worker told them Bailey had disappeared. The school director said Bailey would never leave Hope alone like that.'

Meredith lifted her brows. 'Does she suspect foul play?'

'Yeah, the preschool director did. She told that to the cops.'

'So what do the cops say?'

Alex clenched her teeth. 'That they're following every lead, but that junkies disappear every day. It was a standard "leave us alone" response. I couldn't get anywhere with them on the phone. They just ignored me. She's been gone three days and they haven't declared her a missing person yet.'

'Junkies do disappear, Alex.'

'I know that. But why would the preschool director lie?'

'Maybe she didn't. Maybe Bailey was a good actress or maybe she had a good spell of sobriety but went back on the juice. For now, let's focus on Hope. You said the social worker told you she'd been coloring all night?'

'Yes. Nancy Barker, she's the social worker, said it was all Hope had done since they'd taken her from the closet.' The closet in Bailey's house. Panic began to well, as it did every time she thought of *that* house. 'Bailey still lives there.'

Meredith's eyes widened. 'Really? I thought it would have been sold years ago.'

'No. I checked the property records online. The deed's still in Craig's name.' The pressure in Alex's chest increased and she closed her eyes, focusing on quieting her mind. Meredith's hand closed over hers and squeezed.

'You okay, kid?'

'Yeah.' Alex shook herself. 'Stupid, these panic attacks. I should be past this.'

'Because you're superhuman,' Meredith said blandly. 'This place was the site of the worst disaster of your life, so stop beating yourself up for being all too human, Alex.'

Alex shrugged, then frowned. 'Nancy Barker said the house was a mess, piles of trash on the floor. The mattresses were old and torn. There was rotten food in the fridge.'

'That I would expect from a junkie's house.'

'Yes, but they found no clothes for Hope or Bailey. None. Clean or dirty.'

Meredith frowned. 'Based on what the preschool

said, that is surprising.' She hesitated. 'Did you go to the house?'

'No.' The word shot from Alex's lips like the crack of a bullet. 'No,' she said more evenly. 'I haven't. Yet.'

'When you do, I'll go with you. No arguments. Is Craig still there?'

Focus on the quiet. 'No. Nancy Barker said they tried to locate him, but nobody's heard from him in a long time. I was listed as the emergency contact at the preschool.'

'How did the social worker know where Hope went to preschool?'

'Bailey's coworker told her. That's how they found Hope – Bailey hadn't shown up to work and her coworker was worried and went to check on her during her break.'

'Where does Bailey work?'

'She's a hairdresser, apparently in a pretty upscale salon.'

Meredith blinked. 'Dutton has an upscale salon?'

'No. Dutton has Angie's.' Her mother used to go to Angie's every other Monday. 'Bailey worked in Atlanta. I got the coworker's phone number, but she hasn't been home. I left messages.'

Meredith picked up one of the coloring books. 'Where did all these come from?'

Alex eyed the stack. 'Nancy Barker found one in Hope's backpack. She said Hope was staring into space, but when she gave her the coloring book and crayons, Hope started to color. Nancy tried to get her to draw on blank paper, hoping Hope would tell her something through her pictures, but Hope kept grabbing the book. She ran out of coloring books early last night and I had to pay the bellboy to go to the store and buy more. More crayons, too.' Alex stared at the box that had held sixty-four crayons, when new. It now held fifty-seven – every color except red. Every redlike crayon was gone, used down to a half-inch nub.

'She likes red,' Meredith observed.

Alex swallowed hard. 'I don't even want to consider the implications of that.'

Meredith lifted a shoulder. 'It may mean nothing more than that she likes red.'

'But you don't think so.'

'No.'

'She's holding a red crayon now. I finally gave up and let her take it to bed with her.'

'What happened when she ran out of red crayons last night?'

'She cried, but she never said a single word.' Alex shuddered. 'I've seen thousands of children cry in the ER, in pain, in fear . . . but never like that. She was like . . . a robot the way she cried – no emotion. She never made a sound. Not a word. Then she went into what looked like a catatonic state. She scared me so badly that I took her to the clinic in town. Dr Granville checked her out, said she was just in shock.'

'Did he run any tests?'

'No. The social worker had told me she'd taken Hope to the ER after they found her hiding in the closet on Friday. They ran tox screens and titers to check her immunization record. She's had all her childhood immunizations and everything else was in order.'

'Who is her family doctor?'

'I don't know. Granville, the doctor here in town, said he'd never seen Hope or Bailey in "a professional capacity." He seemed surprised Hope was so clean and well cared for, as if he'd seen her dirty before. He wanted to give her a shot, to sedate her.'

Meredith's brows lifted. 'Did you let him?'

'No, and he got a little huffy, asking why I'd brought her at all if I didn't want him to treat her. But I didn't like the idea of drugging a child if you don't need to. She wasn't violent and there seemed no danger of her hurting herself, so I didn't want her drugged.'

'I agree. So all this time Hope never said a word? Are we sure she can speak?'

'The preschool says she's very talkative, big vocabulary. In fact, she can even read.'

Meredith looked taken aback. 'Wow. She's what, four?'

'Barely. The preschool said Bailey read to Hope every night. Meredith, none of this feels like a junkie abandoning her child.'

'You think foul play, too.'

Something in Meredith's voice rubbed Alex wrong. 'Don't you?' she demanded.

Meredith was unperturbed. 'I don't know. I know you've always given Bailey the benefit of the doubt. But now this isn't just about Bailey, it's about Hope and what's best for her. Are you going to bring her home? To your home, I mean?'

Alex thought of the little apartment she only slept in. Richard had kept the house. Alex hadn't wanted it. But her apartment was big enough for herself and one small child. 'That's my intent, yes. But Meredith, if something did happen to Bailey . . . I mean, if she has changed and she's met with some harm . . .'

'What will you do?'

'I don't know yet. I couldn't get anywhere with the police over the phone and I couldn't leave Hope alone to go in person. Can you stay with me for a few days? Help me with Hope while I check this out?'

'I had all the appointments with my most critical patients moved to Wednesday before I left. I have to fly back late Tuesday night. It's the best I can do for now.'

'It's a lot. Thank you.'

Meredith squeezed her hand. 'Now go get some sleep. I'll sleep here on the sofa. If you need me, wake me up.'

'I'll sleep in there with Hope. I'm just praying she sleeps through the night. So far she hasn't slept more than a few hours at a time, then she wakes up and colors. If she needs you, I'll let you know.'

'I wasn't talking about Hope needing me. I was talking about you. Now go to sleep.'

Chapter Two

Atlanta, Sunday, January 28, 10:45 P.M.

'Daniel, I think your dog is dead.' The voice came from Daniel's living room and it belonged to fellow GBI investigator Luke Papadopoulos. Luke was also quite possibly Daniel's best friend, despite his being the reason Daniel owned the dog to begin with.

Daniel slid the last plate into the dishwasher, then went to the doorway to his living room. Luke sat on the sofa, watching ESPN. Riley the basset hound lounged at Luke's feet, looking like he normally did. Which, Daniel had to agree, was like a dog who'd gone on to meet his Maker. 'Offer him a pork chop, he'll perk up.'

Riley opened one eye at the mention of a pork chop, but closed it again, knowing he probably wouldn't get one. Riley was a pessimistic realist. He and Daniel got along well.

'Hell, I just offered him some of the moussaka, and he still didn't perk up,' Luke said.

Daniel was able to visualize the results of such an irresponsible action all too well. 'Riley can't have your mom's cooking. It's way too rich and that's bad for his stomach.'

'I know. He got into some leftovers while you were gone up north and he was staying with me.' Luke winced. 'It wasn't pretty, trust me.'

Daniel rolled his eyes. 'I'm not paying your carpet-cleaning bill, Luke.'

'It's okay. My cousin owns his own carpet-cleaning business. I got it taken care of.'

'If you knew, then why for God's sake did you try to feed him tonight?'

Luke gently nudged Riley's butt with the toe of his boot. 'He always looks so sad.'

'Sad' in Luke's family meant 'feed me.' Which explained Luke's showing up on Daniel's doorstep tonight with a full Greek meal when Daniel knew full well he'd had to break a date with his on-again-off-again flight attendant girlfriend to do so. Mama Papadopoulos had been worried about Daniel since he'd returned from Philadelphia the week before. Luke's mama had a kind heart, but Mama Papa's food did not agree with Riley, and Daniel did *not* have a cousin with his own carpet-cleaning business.

'He's a damn basset hound. They all look that way. Riley's not sad, so stop feeding him.' Daniel sat in his recliner and whistled. Riley trotted over and plopped at his feet with a huge sigh, as if the four-foot trek had tired him out. 'I know how you feel, boy.'

Luke was quiet a moment. 'I hear you pulled a tough one tonight.'

Daniel's mind immediately conjured the victim in the ditch. 'You could say that.' Abruptly he frowned. 'How did you hear about that already?'

Luke looked uncomfortable. 'Ed Randall called. He was worried about you. Your first day back and you pull a case like the Arcadia woman.'

Daniel swallowed his irritation. They all meant well. 'So you brought me food.'

'Nah, Mama had that all prepared before Ed called. She's worried about you, too. I'll tell her you ate a second helping and that you're doing all right. So, *are* you all right?'

'I have to be. There's work to be done.'

'You could have taken more time off. A week's not that much, considering.'

Considering he'd had to bury his parents. 'When you add in the week I was in Philly looking for them, I've been out for two weeks. That's long enough.' He leaned over to scratch Riley's ears. 'If I don't work, I'll go crazy,' he added quietly.

'It wasn't your fault, Daniel.'

'No, not directly. But I knew what Simon was a long time before now.'

'And you thought he was dead for the last twelve years.'

Daniel conceded the point. 'There is that.'

'If you ask me, I'd say your father carried most of the blame. After Simon, of course.'

Seventeen people. Simon had taken seventeen lives, with one old woman still holding on in cardiac intensive care in Philadelphia. But Daniel's father had not only known Simon was evil, he'd known Simon was *alive.* Twelve years ago Arthur Vartanian had banished his younger son and told the world he'd died. He'd even buried a stranger in the family plot and erected Simon's tombstone, leaving Simon free to roam, doing whatever he wished, as long as it wasn't under the Vartanian name.

'Seventeen people,' Daniel murmured, and wondered if they weren't the tip of the iceberg. He thought of the pictures that were never far from the front of his mind. The pictures Simon had left behind. The faces flashed before his eyes like a slide show. All female. Nameless victims of rape.

Just like the victim today. He had to see that the Arcadia victim got a name. That she got justice. It was the only way he'd stay sane. 'One of the Arcadia officers mentioned a similar murder thirteen years ago. I was working on checking it out when you got here. It happened in Dutton.'

Luke's brows came way down. '*Dutton?* Daniel, you grew up in Dutton.'

'Thanks. I'd forgotten that fact,' Daniel said sarcastically. 'I looked in our database back at the office when I filed my report earlier tonight, but GBI didn't investigate, so it wasn't there. I called Frank Loomis, the sheriff in Dutton, but he hasn't returned my call yet. And I didn't want to call one of the deputies. If it hadn't been anything, I would have added fuel to the fire. Bastard reporters are crawling all over the damn place.'

'But you did find something,' Luke pushed. 'What?'

'I searched online and found an article.' He tapped the laptop he'd set on the coffee table when Luke had arrived with the food. 'Alicia Tremaine was found murdered in a ditch outside Dutton on April 2, thirteen years ago. She was wrapped in a brown wool blanket and her facial bones were broken. She'd been raped. She was sixteen.'

'Copycat killer?'

'I was thinking that. With all the news about Dutton the past week, maybe somebody found that article and decided to re-create it. It's a theory. Trouble is, these old online articles don't have pictures. I was trying to find a photo of Alicia.'

Luke shot him a long-suffering glance. A computer expert, Luke was often appalled at Daniel's lack of what he considered basic computer skills. 'Give me the laptop.' In less than three minutes Luke sat back with a satisfied, 'Got it. Take a look.'

Daniel's heart thudded to a stop. *It couldn't be*. It was his tired eyes playing tricks. Slowly he leaned forward and blinked hard. But she was still there. 'My God.'

'Who is she?'

Daniel jerked a glance back to Luke, his pulse now racing. 'I know her, that's all.' But his voice sounded desperate. Yes, he knew her. Her face had haunted his dreams for years, along with the faces of all the others. For years he'd hoped they'd been faked. Posed. For years he'd feared they were real. That they were dead. Now he knew for sure. Now one of the nameless victims had a name. *Alicia Tremaine.*

'You know her from where?' Luke's voice was firmly demanding. 'Daniel?'

Daniel calmed himself. 'We both lived in Dutton. It makes sense that I knew her.'

Luke's jaw went hard. 'Before you said you "know" her, not "knew."'

A spurt of anger burned away some of the shock. 'Are you questioning me, Luke?'

'Yes, because you're not being honest with me. You look like you've seen a ghost.'

'I have.' He stared at her face. She'd been beautiful. Thick hair the color of caramel spilled over her shoulders and there had been a sparkle in her eyes that hinted at mischief and fun. Now she was dead.

'Who is she?' Luke asked again, his voice quieter. 'An old girlfriend?'

'No.' His shoulders sagged and his chin dropped to his chest. 'I've never met her.'

'But you know her,' Luke countered cautiously. 'How?'

Straightening his spine, Daniel walked behind the bar in the corner of his living room, pulled the *Dogs Playing Poker* painting from the wall, revealing a safe. From the corner of his eye he saw Luke's brows go up. 'You have a wall safe?' Luke asked.

'Vartanian family tradition,' Daniel said grimly, hoping it was the only tendency he shared with his father. He dialed the combination and pulled out the envelope he'd stored there on his return from Philly the week before. He picked Alicia Tremaine's picture from the stack of the others just like it and handed it to Luke.

Luke flinched. 'My God. It's her.' He looked up, horrified. 'Who is the man?'

Daniel shook his head. 'I don't know.'

Luke's eyes flashed fire. 'This is sick, Daniel. Where the hell did you get this?'

'My mother,' Daniel said bitterly.

Luke opened his mouth, then closed it again. 'Your mother,' he repeated carefully.

Daniel sat down wearily. 'I got the pictures from my mother, who'd left—'

Luke held up his hand. 'Wait. *Pictures*? What else is in that envelope?'

'More of the same. Different girls. Different men.'

'This one looks like she's been drugged.'

'They all do. None of them are awake. There are fifteen of them. That doesn't count the pictures that are obviously cut from magazines.'

'Fifteen.' Luke blew out a breath. 'So tell me how your mother gave them to you.'

'More like she left them for me. My father had the pictures first and—' Luke's eyes widened and Daniel sighed. 'Maybe I should start from the beginning.'

'That would be best, I think.'

'Some of this I knew. Some my sister Susannah knew. We didn't put it together until last week, after Simon was dead.'

'So your sister knows about these, too?'

Daniel remembered Susannah's haunted eyes. 'Yes, she does.' She knew much more than she'd told, of that Daniel was certain, just as he was certain that she'd suffered at Simon's hand. He hoped she'd tell him in her own time.

'Who else?'

'Philly PD. I gave Detective Vito Ciccotelli copies. At the time I thought they were part of his case.' Daniel leaned forward, elbows on his knees, his eyes on Alicia Tremaine's face. 'Simon was the first owner of the pictures. First that I know of, anyway. I know he had them before he died.' He glanced over at Luke. 'The first time he died.'

'Twelve years ago,' Luke supplied, then shrugged. 'Mama read it in the paper.'

Daniel's lips thinned. 'Mama Papa and millions of her closest friends. It doesn't matter. My father found these pictures and threw Simon out of the house, told him if he ever came back he'd turn Simon over to the police. Simon had just turned eighteen.'

'Your father. The judge. He just let Simon go.'

'Good old Dad. He was afraid if the pictures became public, he'd lose the election.'

'But he kept the pictures? Why?'

'Dad didn't want Simon ever coming back, so he held the pictures as insurance, blackmail. A few days later my father told my mother that he'd received a phone call, that Simon had died in a car crash in Mexico. Dad went down there, brought the body home, had it buried in the family plot.'

'But it's an unidentified man almost a foot shorter than Simon.' Luke shrugged again. 'It was a good article – had lots of details. So how did your mother get these?'

'The first time she found them in Dad's safe. That was eleven years ago, a year after Simon "died." She found the pictures and some drawings Simon had made from them. My mother rarely cried, but she cried about those pictures. I found her that way.'

'And you saw the pictures.'

'Only a glimpse. Enough to suspect at least some of them were real. But my father came home then and was so angry. He had to admit he'd had them for a year. I said we should turn them over to the police, but my father refused. He said it would be bad for the family name and Simon was already dead, so what was the point?'

Luke was frowning. 'The point? Like, the victims? That was the point.'

'Of course it was. But when I tried to take the pictures to the police, we got into it.' Daniel clenched his hands into fists, remembering. 'I almost hit him. I was so mad.'

'So what did you do?' Luke asked quietly.

'I left the house to cool down, but when I came back, my father had burned the photos in the fireplace. They were gone.'

'Obviously not gone.' Luke pointed to the envelope.

'He must've had copies somewhere else. I was . . . stunned. My mother was telling me it was for the best and my father was standing looking so smug and superior. I lost it. I hit him. Knocked him down. We had a terrible fight. I was on my way out the front door when Susannah came in the back. She'd missed the reason for the fight and I didn't want her to know. She was only seventeen. Turned out she knew more than I thought. If we'd talked then . . .' Daniel thought of the seventeen bodies Simon had left behind in Philadelphia. 'Who knows what we might have averted?'

'Did you tell anyone?'

Daniel shrugged, disgusted with himself. 'Tell them what? I had no proof and it was my word against that of a judge. My sister hadn't seen any of it and my mother would never have crossed my father. So I said nothing and I've regretted it ever since.'

'So you left home and never came back.'

'Not until I got the call from the Dutton sheriff two weeks ago that they were missing. It was the same day I found out my mother had cancer. I just wanted to see her once more, but she'd already been dead for two months.' Killed by Simon.

'So how did you get these pictures now?'

'This past Thanksgiving my parents found out Simon was still alive.'

'Because the blackmailer up in Philly had contacted your father.'

Daniel's eyes widened. 'Wow, that really was some article.'

'Got that off the Internet. Your family's hot news, boy.'

Daniel rolled his eyes. 'Wonderful. Well, Dad and Mother went up to Philly to find Simon. Mother wanted to bring him home, certain he'd been some amnesia victim or something. Dad wanted to reinforce his blackmail, so he took the pictures with him to Philly. Eventually Mother realized Dad was never going to let her see Simon.'

'Simon would have told her that your father had known all along that he was alive.'

'Exactly. Then Dad disappeared. He must have found Simon because Simon killed him and buried him in a deserted field with all his other victims. Simon contacted my mother and she was planning to meet him. She knew she could be walking into a trap but she didn't care.'

'Because she was dying of cancer and had nothing more to lose.'

'Yes. She opened a mailbox for me at one of those mailbox stores. Inside the box were these pictures. She'd left them in the event Simon did kill her.'

'You said Ciccotelli up in Philly had copies. Does he know you kept the originals?'

'No. I made the copies I gave him.'

Luke's eyes widened. 'You copied these at a regular copy machine?'

'No,' Daniel scoffed. 'After I found the pictures at the mailbox store, I bought a copier-scanner. I had a few hours before Susannah arrived from New York, so I went back to my hotel room, set the scanner up to my laptop, and made the copies there.'

'You set up a scanner all by yourself?'

'I'm not completely inept,' Daniel said dryly. 'The guy in the store showed me how.' He looked back at the picture of Alicia's assault. 'I've had nightmares about these girls for years. Since I got the pictures back a week ago, I've been memorizing their faces. I promised myself that I'd find out what part Simon had in getting these pictures, then I'd find the girls and tell them Simon was dead. I never dreamed the first ID would be dumped in my lap this way.'

'So you didn't know Alicia Tremaine at all?'

'No. She was five years younger than me, so I never would have known her at school and I was away at college when she was murdered.'

'And none of these guys in the pictures are Simon?'

'No. All the men have both their legs. Simon was an amputee. Plus Simon was a good bit taller than any of these guys. I haven't seen any tattoos or any other identifying features or marks on any of the pictures.'

'But now you have one of the victims' names, which is more than you had before.'

'True. Now I'm wondering if I should tell Chase about the pictures.' Chase Wharton was Daniel's CO. 'If I do, he could take the Arcadia case away from me, along with any investigation of these pictures. I really want to solve both of these cases. I need to.'

'It's atonement,' Luke murmured and Daniel nodded.

'Yes.'

Luke lifted a brow. 'You're assuming no one was ever arrested for Alicia's murder.'

Daniel straightened abruptly. 'Can you check?'

Luke was already typing into the laptop. 'Police arrested Gary Fulmore a few hours after they found Alicia's body.' He typed again, his keystrokes rapid. 'Gary Fulmore was found guilty of sexual assault and murder in the second degree the following January.'

'It's January now,' Daniel said. 'Coincidence?'

Luke shrugged. 'That's what you need to find out. Look, Danny, it's pretty cut-and-dried that Simon didn't kill that woman in Arcadia. He's been dead himself a week.'

'And this time I watched him die myself,' Daniel said grimly. *In fact, I helped*. And he was glad that he had. He'd done the world a service in ensuring Simon was dead.

Luke's eyes flickered in sympathy. 'And they caught the man who murdered Alicia. Who knows, maybe this is Fulmore.' He pointed to the rapist in the picture. 'And most important, you aren't solving the murder of Alicia Tremaine. You're solving the murder of the woman in the Arcadia ditch. If it was me, I wouldn't mention the pictures just yet.'

Viewed logically, Luke's argument made perfect sense. Or maybe he just needed it to. Either way, Daniel blew out a sigh that was mostly relief. 'Thanks. I owe you one.'

Luke raised a brow. 'For this, you owe me a lot more than one.'

Daniel looked down at Riley, who hadn't moved a muscle the entire time. 'I took your dog and saved your sex life. That's good for one hell of a lot, Papa.'

'Hey, it wasn't my fault that Denise wouldn't live with Brandi's dog.'

'Which Brandi only got because of you.'

'Brandi thought a detective should have a bloodhound.'

Daniel rolled his eyes. 'Clearly Brandi's assets were not in her brain.'

Luke grinned. 'Nope. But in her defense, my apartment has a weight limit. A bloodhound would have been too big. We settled on Riley there.'

'I should have given him back to you when Denise split,' Daniel grumbled.

'Which was two years and six girlfriends ago,' Luke pointed out. 'I think you've developed an attachment to good old Riley.'

Which of course Daniel had. 'All I know is you'd better not be feeding him any more of your mama's food or you will get him back. Then you'll be praying that your next girlfriend likes basset hounds *and* that your mama likes your girlfriend.'

Luke's revolving door of girlfriends was a constant source of angst for poor Mama Papa. Most of them she didn't care for, but she had never given up hoping Luke would settle down with one of them and give her grandchildren.

'I'll just remind her you haven't had a date in years,' Luke said smugly, getting up from the sofa. 'She'll be so busy finding you a nice Greek girl that she won't have time to worry over me.' He opened the door, then turned back, his expression serious. 'You didn't do anything wrong, Daniel. Even if you'd reported those pictures ten years ago, no one could have done anything without the evidence.'

'Thanks, man. That helps.' It really did.

'So what are you going to do next?'

'Now, I'm gonna walk Riley. Tomorrow, I'll follow

the evidence on the Arcadia homicide like normal. And I'm going to check out Alicia Tremaine, see if any of her family or friends remember anything. Who knows, it might turn up something. Tell Mama Papa thanks for the food.'

Dutton, Sunday, January 28, 11:30 P.M.

'I'm sorry I haven't come before,' Mack murmured as he sat on the cold ground. The marble at his back was even colder. He wished he could have come here during the daytime when it was warm and sunny, but he couldn't be seen next to her headstone. He didn't want anyone to know he was back, because once they knew, they'd know all – and he wasn't ready for that yet.

But he'd needed to come to her, just once. He'd owed her so much more than he'd given her. It was his greatest regret. He'd failed her in nearly every way. And she'd died, without him by her side. It was his greatest fury.

The last time he'd stood here had been under a blazing summer sun, three and a half years ago. He'd worn shackles and a suit that didn't fit. They hadn't let him out to sit at her deathbed, but they had allowed him one afternoon for her funeral.

'One fucking afternoon,' he said quietly. 'Too damn late.'

He'd had everything stolen from him – his home, his family's business, his freedom, and finally his mother – and all he'd been allowed was one fucking afternoon, too damn late to do anything but simmer in his rage and vow his retribution.

Across his mother's grave his sister-in-law had stood crying, holding one of her little boys by the hand and the other on her hip. His jaw clenched just at the thought of Annette. She'd cared for his mother in her final days while he'd been locked up like an animal, and for that he'd always be beholden. But for years his brother Jared's wife had harbored a secret that should have been the ruin of those who'd ruined their family. For years Annette had *known the truth*, but she'd *never said a word*.

He vividly remembered the explosion of rage when just nine days ago he'd found and read the journals she'd kept so carefully hidden. At first he'd hated her, adding her to his retribution list. But she'd cared for his mother, and one of the lessons he'd learned in his four years behind bars was the value of loyalty and the karma of a good deed done. So he'd spared Annette, allowing her to go on living her miserable little life in that miserable little house.

Besides, she had to take care of his nephews. Their family name, such as it was, would live on through his brother's sons.

His own name would soon become inextricably linked to murder and revenge.

He would exact his revenge and then disappear. How to disappear was one of the other things he'd learned in prison. Disappearing wasn't as easy as it once was, but it still could be done, if one had the right loyal contacts, and if one was patient.

Patience was the most important thing he'd learned while inside. If a man bided his time, a solution would become clear. Mack had bided his time for four long years. In that time he'd followed the Dutton news while he'd plotted, schemed, and studied. He'd strengthened his body and his mind. And his rage had continued to simmer and stew.

When he'd walked through the prison's front gates a free man one month ago, he'd known more about Dutton than any of its residents knew, but he still didn't know how to best punish those who'd ruined his life. A bullet to their heads was too fast, too merciful. He'd wanted something painful and lasting, so he'd bided his time a little longer, lurking about town like a shadow, watching them, charting their movements, their habits, their secrets.

And then, nine days ago, his patience had paid off. After four years of simmering, his plan had come together in minutes. Now, the curtain had risen. He was on his way.

'There are so many things you never knew, Mama,' he said softly. 'So many people you trusted who'd already betrayed you. The pillars of the town are more evil than you ever contemplated. The things they've done are far worse than anything I'd ever dreamed of doing.' Until now. 'I wish you could see what I'm about to do. I'm about to stir up the dirt in this town, and everyone will know what they did to you and to me and even to Jared. They'll be ruined and humiliated. And the people they love will die.'

Today they'd found the first one, at the bike race, just as he'd planned. And the lead investigator was none other than Daniel Vartanian himself. Which added a whole new layer of meaning to the game.

He lifted his eyes and peered through the shadows to the Vartanian family plot. The police tape was gone now and they'd filled in the grave that until nine days ago everyone had thought held the remains of Simon Vartanian. Now the Vartanian family plot had two new graves.

'The judge and his wife are dead. The whole town came out for the double funeral on Friday afternoon, just two days ago.' The whole town, as opposed to the sad little group that had gathered at his mother's graveside. *Annette, her boys, the reverend, and me.* And the prison guards, of course. Couldn't forget about them. 'But don't fret. Not many came out of respect for the judge and Mrs Vartanian. Most of them really came to gawk at Daniel and Susannah.'

Mack, on the other hand, had watched the double service from far enough away so he could watch the whole town. They had no clue what was coming.

'Daniel was back to work today.' Which had been his fondest hope. 'I thought he'd take more time off.'

He ran his hand over the blanket of grass that covered her. 'I guess family means more to some people than others. I couldn't have gone back to work so fast after your funeral. Of course, *I* wasn't given the choice,' he said bitterly.

He lifted his eyes again to the Vartanian plot. 'The judge and his wife were killed by Simon. We thought he was dead, all these years. Remember, you made me and Jared come and stand by his grave. I was only ten, but you said we had to show respect for the dead. But Simon wasn't dead. Nine days ago they dug him up and Simon wasn't buried in Simon's tomb. That was the day we heard Simon had killed his parents.'

It had also been the day he'd finally figured out how to exact his revenge. The day he'd found the journals Annette had kept hidden for so long. Nine days ago had been a very good day, all in all.

'Simon really is dead now.' It was too bad that Daniel Vartanian had beaten him to it. 'But no worries, the empty grave won't go to waste. Soon a Vartanian son will be buried in the family plot.' He smiled. 'Soon, a lot of people'll be gettin' buried in Dutton.'

How fast the cemetery got filled would depend on how smart Daniel Vartanian really was. If Daniel hadn't yet linked today's victim to Alicia Tremaine, he soon would. Add an anonymous tip to the *Dutton Review* and by tomorrow morning everyone in town would know what he'd done. Importantly, the ones *he* wanted to know, would. They'd wonder. Sweat. *Fear*.

'Soon they'll all pay.' He stood and took a last look at the headstone that bore his mother's name. If all went well, he'd never be able to come back. 'I'll get justice for us both if it's the last thing I do.'

Monday, January 29, 7:15 A.M.

'Alex. *Wake up*.'

Alex opened the bedroom door at Meredith's hiss. 'No need to be quiet. We're both awake.' She pointed to Hope, who sat at the bedroom desk, her bare feet swinging inches from the ground, her bottom lip between her teeth in concentration. 'She's coloring.' Alex sighed. 'With red. I got her to eat a little cereal.'

Meredith stayed in the doorway, dressed in her running clothes and clutching a newspaper in one hand. 'Good morning, Hope. Alex, can I see you out here?'

'Sure. I'll be just outside the door, Hope.' But Hope gave no indication she'd heard. Alex followed Meredith into the sitting room. 'When I woke up she was sitting at the desk already. I have no idea how long she'd been awake. She didn't make a sound.'

'I wish I didn't have to show you this.' Meredith held out the newspaper.

Alex took one look at the headline, then sank onto

the sofa as her legs gave out. Background noise faded until all she could hear was her own pulse pounding in her ears. MURDERED WOMAN FOUND IN ARCADIA DITCH. 'Oh, Mer. Oh, no.'

Crouching, Meredith met her eyes. 'It might not be Bailey.'

Alex shook her head. 'But the timing's just right. She was found yesterday and had been dead two days.' She made herself breathe, made herself focus on the rest of the article. *Please, don't be Bailey. Be too short or too tall. Be a brunette or a redhead, just don't be Bailey.* But as she read, her pounding heart began to race. 'Meredith.' She looked up, panic shooting like a geyser. 'This woman was wrapped in a brown blanket.'

Meredith grabbed the paper. 'I only read the headline.' Her lips moved as she read. Then she looked up, her freckles standing out against her pale cheeks. 'Her face.'

Alex nodded numbly. 'I know.' Her voice was thin. The woman's face had been beaten beyond recognition. 'Just like . . .' *Just like Alicia.*

'My God.' Meredith swallowed. 'She was . . .' She looked over her shoulder to where Hope sat, coloring as furiously as before. 'Alex.'

She'd been raped. Just like Alicia. 'I know.' Alex stood up, willing her knees not to buckle. 'I told the Dutton police something terrible had happened, but they wouldn't listen.' She straightened her spine. 'Can you stay with Hope?'

'Of course. But where are you going?'

She took the newspaper. 'This article says the investigation is being led by Special Agent Daniel Vartanian, GBI. GBI's the state crime bureau and they're in Atlanta, so that's where I'm going.' She narrowed her eyes, back in control. 'And by God, this Vartanian better not even consider ignoring me now.'

Monday, January 29, 7:50 A.M.

He'd expected the call ever since he'd picked his paper up from his front porch this morning. Still, when the phone rang, he was angry. Angry and afraid. He snatched the receiver, his hand trembling. But he kept his voice neutral. Even a little bored. 'Yeah.'

'Did you see?' The voice on the phone was as unsteady as his own hand, but he wouldn't allow the others to see his fear. One sign of weakness and the others would fall like dominoes, starting with the one who'd taken a stupid risk in calling him like this.

'I'm looking at it right now.' The headline had grabbed his attention. The article had grabbed his gut and squeezed, leaving him nauseated. 'It's nothing to do with us. Say nothing and it will just go away.'

'But if somebody starts asking questions . . .'

'We say nothing, just like we did then. This is just some copycat. Act naturally and everything will be fine.'

'But . . . this is really bad, man. I don't think I can act naturally.'

'You can and you will. This has nothing to do with us. Now stop whimpering and get to work. And don't call me again.'

He hung up, then read the article again. He was still angry and afraid. He wondered how he could have been so very stupid. *You were just a kid. Kids make mistakes.* He picked up the photo on his desk, staring into the smiling face of his wife with their two children. He wasn't a kid any longer. He was an adult with far too much to lose.

If one of them broke, if one of them told . . . He pushed away from his desk, went to the bathroom, and threw up. Then pulled himself together and got ready to face his day.

Atlanta, Monday, January 29, 7:55 A.M.

'Here. You look like you need this more than I do.'

Daniel smelled the coffee and looked up as Chase Wharton sat on the corner of his desk. 'Thanks. I've been looking at these missing persons printouts for an hour and I'm starting to see double.' He gulped down a swallow, then winced when bitter dregs slid down his throat. 'Thanks,' he repeated, far less sincerely, and his boss chuckled.

'Sorry. I had to clear the bottom of the pot before I

made a fresh one and you really did look like you needed it.' Chase looked at the stack of printouts. 'No luck?'

'No. We got no hits on her prints. She's been dead two days, but that doesn't mean that's when she disappeared. I've gone back two months and nobody stands out.'

'She might not be from around here, Daniel.'

'I know. Leigh's requesting missing person reports from departments in a fifty-mile radius.' But so far their clerk hadn't found anything either. 'I'm hoping she's only been gone the two days and nobody's missed her, since it was the weekend. It's Monday morning. Maybe somebody will report her today when she doesn't show up for work.'

'We'll cross our fingers. Are you going to have an update meeting today?'

'At six tonight. By then Dr Berg will have done the autopsy and the lab will be finished with the crime scene.' He drew a breath. 'Until then, we've got other problems.' From under the stack of printouts, he pulled the three pages that had been waiting for him on the fax machine when he'd arrived that morning.

Chase's face darkened. 'Sonofabitch. Who took that picture? What paper is this?'

'The guy that took the picture is the same one that wrote the article. His name is Jim Woolf and he owns the *Dutton Review*. You're looking at today's headline.'

Chase looked startled. 'Dutton? I thought this victim was found in Arcadia.'

'She was. You might want to sit down. This could take a few minutes.'

Chase sat. 'All right. What's going on, Daniel? Where did you get this fax?'

'From the sheriff in Arcadia. He saw it when he stopped to get his coffee this morning. He called at six a.m. to let me know, then faxed me the article. From the angle of the picture, he's thinking Jim Woolf was sitting in a tree watching us the whole time.'

Daniel studied the grainy photo and his anger surged again. 'Woolf has got all the details in there that I would have held back – the victim's broken face, her being found wrapped in a brown blanket. He didn't even have the decency to wait until they'd finished zipping her body bag. Luckily Malcolm's blocking most of his shot.' Her body was hidden, but her feet were visible.

Chase was grim. 'How the hell did he get through your barricade?'

'I don't think he got through, not if he was sitting in the tree Corchran thinks. There's no way we wouldn't have seen him climbing that tree.'

'So he was there before you got there.'

Daniel nodded. 'Which at a minimum means that somebody tipped him off. Worst case, it could mean he tampered with the scene before we got there.'

'Who called this in? I mean initially?'

'Biker in the race. He said he called 911 without ever getting off his bike. I already filed a warrant to check his cell phone records to see if he called anyone else first.'

'Vultures,' Chase muttered. 'Call this Woolf guy. Make him tell you who told him.'

'I've called him four times this morning, but there's no answer. I'll drive to Dutton today to question him, but I'm betting he'll hide behind the First Amendment and won't reveal his source.'

'Probably. Hell.' Chase flicked the fax like it was a bug. 'This Woolf guy could have been the one to put her there.'

'That's occurred to me, although I have to doubt it. I went to high school with Jim Woolf and knew his family. He and his brothers were always quiet, nice kids.'

Chase glared at the photo. 'I think it's safe to say he's changed.'

Daniel sighed. Hadn't they all? There was something about Dutton, Georgia, that brought out the worst in people. 'I guess so.'

Chase held up his hand. 'Wait. I still want to know why Dutton? If this crime happened in Arcadia, why tip off this Woolf guy in Dutton?'

'The victim yesterday was found in Arcadia, in a ditch, wrapped in a brown blanket. A similar crime happened in Dutton thirteen years ago.' Daniel showed him the article on the murder of Alicia

Tremaine. 'Her killer is now serving life in Macon State.'

Chase grimaced. 'God, I hate copycat killers.'

'I don't like the original ones too much either. At any rate, I'm thinking somebody saw the body earlier, remembered the Tremaine connection, and leaked the Arcadia story to Jim Woolf. It could have been the biker or anybody else on that race course. I talked to the race officials when I was trying to figure when the body had been put in the ditch to begin with and one of them said he'd ridden the course Saturday and hadn't seen anything. I believed him because the guy wore glasses with Coke-bottle lenses.'

'But if he was riding earlier, others might have been, too. Dig deeper.' Chase frowned. 'But what's this about the Tremaine connection? I don't like you being on a case that involves Dutton. Not right now.'

Daniel had been ready for the argument. Still, it left his palms clammy. 'Simon didn't kill this woman, Chase. There's no conflict here.'

Chase rolled his eyes. 'Hell, Daniel. I know that. I also know the names Dutton and Vartanian together make the brass real nervous.'

'That's not my problem. I haven't done anything wrong.' And maybe someday he'd believe his own words. For now, he just needed Chase to believe them.

'Okay. But as soon as you hear a whisper of a bad Vartanian, you're gone, okay?'

Daniel smiled wryly. 'Okay.'

'What are you going to do next?'

'Identify this woman.' He tapped the photo of the victim. 'Find out who told Jim Woolf what and when, and . . . follow up on Alicia Tremaine. I've left a few messages with the sheriff down in Dutton. I want to get a copy of the police report from the Tremaine case. Maybe there's something in it that can help me now.'

Chapter Three

Atlanta, Monday, January 29, 8:45 A.M.

Alex paused outside the office for the Investigative Division of the GBI and prayed Agent Daniel Vartanian would be more helpful than Dutton's Sheriff Loomis. 'Check Peachtree and Pine,' Loomis had snapped when she'd called his office for the fifth time on Sunday morning, trying to get someone to give her information on Bailey. She'd googled and found Peachtree and Pine was the location of several homeless shelters in Atlanta. If she was wrong . . . *God, please let me be wrong* . . . and this victim wasn't Bailey, Peachtree and Pine would be her next stop.

But the years had made Alex a realist and she knew the chances were good that the woman found in Arcadia was Bailey. That she'd been found the same way as Alicia . . . A shiver of apprehension ran down her back and she took a moment to compose herself before opening the office door. *Focus on the quiet. Be assertive.*

At least she was confident in her clothes. She'd

dressed in the black suit she'd brought in case she needed to appear in court to get custody of Hope. Or if Bailey was found. She'd worn the suit to more than a few funerals over the years. Praying she wouldn't be attending another, she steeled herself for the worst and opened the door.

The counter held a nameplate that said Leigh Smithson, Clerk. The blonde behind the counter looked up from her computer with a friendly smile. 'Can I help you?'

'I'm here to see Agent Vartanian.' Alex lifted her chin, daring the woman to refuse.

The blonde's smile dimmed. 'Do you have an appointment?'

'No. But it's important. It's about a newspaper article.' She'd pulled the *Dutton Review* from her satchel when the woman's eyes flashed fire.

'Agent Vartanian has no comment for your paper. You reporters . . .' she muttered.

'I'm not a reporter and I don't want information on Agent Vartanian,' Alex snapped back. 'I want information on this investigation.' She swallowed hard, appalled when her voice broke. She controlled it, lifting her chin. 'I think this victim is my stepsister.'

The woman's expression instantly changed and she lurched from her chair. 'I'm so sorry. I assumed that you . . . What is your name, ma'am?'

'Alex Fallon. My stepsister is Bailey Crighton. She disappeared two days ago.'

'I'll tell Agent Vartanian you're here, Ms Fallon. Please have a seat.' She pointed to a row of plastic chairs and picked up a phone. 'He should be with you any moment.'

Alex was too nervous to sit. She paced, looking at the wall covered with childish renderings of cops, robbers, and jails drawn by schoolchildren. Alex thought of Hope and her red crayons. What had that baby seen? *Could you even handle it if you knew?*

She stopped midstep, the taunt catching her off-guard. Could she handle it? She'd have to, for Hope's sake. The child had no one. *So you have to handle it this time, Alex*. Although in the quiet of her mind she knew she hadn't handled it well so far.

She'd dreamed *the dream* last night. Dark and pierced with a scream so long and loud that she'd woken in a cold sweat, trembling so hard she thought she'd wake Hope. But the child never stirred. Alex had wondered if Hope dreamed, and what she saw.

'Miss Fallon? I'm Special Agent Vartanian.' The voice was rich and deep and calm. Still her heart raced. *This is it. He'll tell you it's Bailey. You have to handle this.*

She slowly turned and had a split second to stare up into a ruggedly handsome face with a broad forehead, unsmiling lips, and eyes so piercingly blue she caught her breath. Then those eyes widened and Alex watched them flicker wildly for just a moment before his unsmiling lips fell open, and the color drained from his face.

It was *Bailey, then*. Alex pursed her lips hard, willing her legs to hold her up. She'd known what the answer would be. Still, she'd hoped . . . 'Agent Vartanian?' she whispered. 'Is that woman my stepsister?'

He stared at her face, his color returning. 'Please,' he said, his voice now low and taut. He held out his arm, gesturing for her to go in front of him. Forcing one foot in front of the other, Alex complied. 'My office is through this door,' he said, 'on the left.'

It was a stark office. Government-issue desk and chairs. Maps on the wall, along with a few plaques. No pictures, anywhere. She sat in the chair he pulled out for her, then he took his seat behind his desk. 'I have to apologize, Miss Fallon. You look like someone else. I was . . . startled. Please, tell me about your stepsister. Miss Smithson said her name is Bailey Crighton and she's been missing for two days.'

He was staring at her with an intensity that left her unnerved. So she stared back, finding it helped keep her focused. 'I got a call from Social Services on Friday afternoon. Bailey hadn't come to work and a coworker found her daughter alone in her house.'

'So you came to take care of the daughter?'

Alex nodded. 'Yes. Her name is Hope. She's four. I tried to talk to the sheriff down in Dutton, but he said Bailey had probably just taken off.'

His jaw tightened, so infinitesimally that she might have missed it had she not been staring at him as hard as he was staring at her. 'So she lived in Dutton?'

'All her life.'

'I see. Can you describe her, Miss Fallon?'

Alex clenched her fingers in her lap. 'I haven't seen her in five years. She was using then and she looked hard and old. But I've heard she's been sober since her daughter was born. I don't know exactly what she looks like now and I don't have any pictures of her.' She'd left them all behind when Kim and Steve took her away thirteen years ago, and later . . . Alex hadn't wanted any pictures of the drugged-out Bailey. It was too painful to watch, much less capture on film. 'She's about my height, five-six. Last time I saw her she was very thin, maybe one-twenty. Her eyes are gray. Then, her hair was blond, but she's a hairdresser, so it could be any color.'

Vartanian was taking notes. He looked up. 'What color blond? Dark, golden?'

'Well, not as blond as yours.' Vartanian's hair was the color of cornsilk, and so thick it still held the ridges from where he'd shoved his fingers through it. He looked up, his lips bending in a small smile, and she felt her cheeks heat. 'I'm sorry.'

'Don't be,' he said kindly. Even though he still stared at her with that same intensity, something had changed in his demeanor and for the first time Alex let herself hope.

'Was the victim blond, Agent Vartanian?'

He shook his head. 'No. Did your cousin have any identifying marks?'

'She has a tattoo on her right ankle. A sheep.'

Vartanian looked surprised. 'A sheep?'

Alex's cheeks heated again. 'A lamb actually. It was a joke between us. Bailey and my sister and me. We all got them . . .' She cut herself off. She was rambling.

His eyes flickered once more, just barely. 'Your sister?'

'Yes.' Alex glanced at Vartanian's desk and saw a copy of the headline from this morning's *Dutton Review*. Suddenly his extreme reaction on meeting her made sense and she wasn't sure if she should be relieved or annoyed. 'You've already read the paper, so you know about the similarities between my sister's death and the woman you found yesterday.' He said nothing and Alex decided she was annoyed. 'Please, Agent Vartanian. I'm tired and scared to death. Don't play games with me.'

'I'm sorry, Miss Fallon. I don't mean to play games with you. Tell me about your sister. What was her name?'

Alex sucked in her cheeks. 'Alicia Tremaine. For God's sake, you must have seen her picture. You looked at me like you'd seen a damn ghost.'

Again his eyes flickered, this time in an annoyance of his own. 'There is a strong resemblance,' he said mildly.

'Considering we were identical twins, I'm somehow not surprised.' Alex managed to keep her voice level, but it took effort. 'Agent Vartanian, is that woman Bailey or not?'

He toyed with his pencil in a way that made Alex want to leap across his desk and rip it from his hands. Finally he spoke. 'She isn't blond and she doesn't have a tattoo.'

The relief left her light-headed and Alex fought to quell the tears that suddenly threatened. When she was back in control, she slowly exhaled and looked at him. But he didn't look as relieved as she felt.

'It can't be Bailey, then,' she said evenly.

'Tattoos can be removed.'

'But there will be some physical scarring left behind. Your ME can check this.'

'And I'll make sure that she does,' he said in a way that told Alex his next words would be a promise to call her when he knew something. She didn't want to wait.

Alex lifted her chin. 'I want to see her. The victim. I need to know. Bailey has a child. Hope needs to know. She needs to know her mother didn't just abandon her.' Alex suspected Hope knew exactly what had occurred, but she kept that to herself.

Vartanian shook his head, although his eyes had softened to something approaching sympathy. 'You can't see her. She was badly beaten. She isn't recognizable.'

'I'm a nurse, Agent Vartanian. I've seen dead bodies before. If it's Bailey, I'll know. Please. I need to know one way or the other.'

He hesitated, then finally nodded. 'I'll call the ME.

She was supposed to start the examination at about ten, so we should be able to catch her before she begins.'

'Thank you.'

Monday, January 29, 9:45 A.M.

'This is our viewing room.' Dr Felicity Berg stood aside as Daniel followed Alex Fallon through the door. 'If you'd like to sit down, please do.'

Daniel watched Alex Fallon take in the room with a sweeping glance. Then she shook her head. 'Thank you, but I'll stand,' she said. 'Is she ready?'

She was a cool one, Miss Alex Fallon. And she'd given him the shock of his life.

It's her, was all he'd been able to think when she'd looked up into his face. He felt lucky he hadn't embarrassed himself more than he had. When she'd said he looked like he'd seen a ghost, she'd hit the nail on the head. His heart was still unsteady when he looked at her, but he couldn't seem to stop himself.

When he really looked at her, he could see she was different from the smiling photo of her sister. She was thirteen years older, but that wasn't it. There was something different in her eyes. They were whiskey-colored, identical to her sister's, of course. But the laughter he'd seen in Alicia Tremaine's eyes was nonexistent in Alex Fallon's.

She'd been through trauma, thirteen years ago and again now, so perhaps her eyes had once held mischief and fun. But now Alex Fallon was cool and collected. He'd witnessed brief spurts of emotion – fear, anger, relief, all quickly controlled. Watching her stand before the curtained window, he wondered what was going through her mind.

'I'll go check,' Felicity said and closed the door behind her, leaving them alone.

Alex stood quietly, her arms at her sides. But her hands were clenched into fists and Daniel fought the urge to pry her fingers apart.

She was a beautiful woman, he thought, finally able to look at her without her watching him in return. Her eyes had rattled him, as if she'd seen more than he'd wanted her to. Her lips were full but unsmiling. She was slender, but her sensible black suit still hinted of curves beneath. Her hair was the same dark caramel color as her sister's and it fell midway down her back in waves, thick and sleek.

Because the thought of touching her hair, of caressing her cheek . . . because the thought had actually entered his mind, Daniel shoved his hands into his pockets. She flinched when he moved. She'd been aware of him, even if she hadn't been looking at him. 'Where do you live, Miss Fallon?'

She turned, just enough so that she could see over her shoulder. 'Cincinnati.'

'Where you're a nurse?'

'Yes. I work in the ER.'

'Tough job.'

'As is yours.'

'You don't use the name Tremaine.'

A muscle moved in her throat as she swallowed. 'No. I had it changed.'

'When you got married?' he asked and realized he was holding his breath.

'I'm not married. I was adopted by my aunt and uncle after my sister died.' Her tone dared him to push further, so he turned the conversation a different way.

She wasn't married. It didn't matter. But it did. Deep down, he knew that it mattered very much. 'You said your stepsister has a child. You called her Hope.'

'Yes. Hope is four. Social Services found her hiding in a closet Friday morning.'

'The locals think Bailey abandoned her daughter?'

Her jaw tightened, as did her fists. Even in the dim light, he could see her knuckles whiten. 'That's what they think. Hope's teachers said Bailey would never have left her.'

'So you came straight down to take care of the child?'

She did look at him then, straight and long, and he knew he wouldn't have been able to look away if he'd tried. Alex Fallon had an inner strength, a purpose . . . whatever it was, it demanded his attention. 'Yes. Until Bailey's found. One way or another.'

He knew it was a bad idea, nevertheless he took

her hand and uncurled her fingers. Her neat, unpolished nails had left deep gouges in the tender flesh of her palm. Gently he rubbed the creases with his thumbs. 'And if Bailey's never found?' he murmured.

She looked down at his hands holding hers, then back up to meet his eyes, and his nerves fired in a chain reaction that seemed to singe his skin. There was a connection here, a tie, an affinity that he'd never experienced before. 'Then Hope will be my child and she'll never be alone and afraid again,' she said quietly but resolutely, leaving no doubt in his mind that she would keep her promise.

And suddenly he was swallowing hard. 'I hope you get closure, Miss Fallon.'

The grim line of her mouth softened, not a smile, but still softer. 'Thank you.'

He held her hand another few seconds, then released her as Felicity came back in.

Felicity glanced from Daniel to Alex Fallon, her eyes narrowing slightly. 'We're ready, Miss Fallon. We won't show you her face, all right?'

Alex Fallon nodded. 'I understand.'

Felicity pulled the curtain about two-thirds of the way across. Malcolm Zuckerman was on the other side of the glass. Felicity leaned into the speaker. 'Let's begin.'

Malcolm pulled the sheet to the side, revealing the right side of the victim.

'Agent Vartanian said your stepsister had a tattoo,'

Felicity said quietly. 'I checked myself and saw no scarring. There's no evidence there was ever a tattoo on that ankle.'

She nodded again. 'Thank you. Can he show me the inside of her arm?'

'I didn't see evidence of needle scarring, either,' Felicity said as Malcolm complied.

Her shoulders finally relaxed and she trembled visibly. 'It's not Bailey.' She met Daniel's eyes and in hers he saw a raging combination of sympathy, regret, and relief. 'You still have an unidentified victim, Agent Vartanian. I'm sorry about that.'

He smiled, but sadly. 'I'm glad it's not your stepsister.'

Felicity pulled the curtain back over the window. 'I'll be starting the autopsy in a few minutes, Daniel. Should I wait for you?'

'If you wouldn't mind. Thanks, Doc.' He waited until Felicity was gone, then stood up and put his hands in his pockets. Alex Fallon still trembled and he was tempted to pull her against him and hold her until she put her public face back on. 'Are you all right, Miss Fallon?'

She nodded unsteadily. 'Yes. But Bailey's still missing.'

He knew what she was asking. 'I can't help you find her.'

Her eyes flashed. 'Why not?'

'Because the GBI doesn't just take cases from the locals. We have to be invited.'

Her jaw tightened and her eyes went cold. 'I see.

Well, then, can you tell me how to get to Peachtree and Pine?'

Daniel blinked at her. 'Excuse me?'

'I said Peachtree and Pine.' She enunciated it. 'Sheriff Loomis, the Dutton sheriff, said that's where I should look for her.'

Damn you, Frank, Daniel thought. *That was insensitive and irresponsible.* 'I'd be glad to give you directions, but you might have more luck after dark, and that I wouldn't recommend. You're from out of town and don't know the safe areas.'

She lifted her chin. 'I don't seem to have much choice. Sheriff Loomis won't help me and you can't.'

He didn't think so, but chose to keep his opinions to himself. He looked down at his shoe, then back up at her. 'If you can wait until seven, I'll take you.'

Her eyes narrowed. 'Why?'

'Because I have a six o'clock meeting that's not done till seven.'

She shook her head. 'Don't play games with me, Vartanian. Why?'

He decided to tell her some small sliver of the truth. 'Because that victim was found just like your sister, and on the same day my Jane Doe died, your stepsister disappeared. Whether I have a copycat killer or not, this is too much of a coincidence for me to ignore. And . . . you're here, Miss Fallon. Has it occurred to you that you might be a target of a copycat killer, too?'

Her face paled. 'No.'

'I don't mean to scare you, but I'd rather see you scared than lying in there.'

She nodded shakily and he could see he'd made his point. 'I appreciate it,' she murmured. 'So where should I meet you at seven?'

'How about back here? Don't wear that suit, okay? It's too nice.'

'Okay.'

The need to put his arm around her swamped him again, but he shoved it away. 'Come on, I'll walk you up to the front.'

Monday, January 29, 10:45 A.M.

I'm still alive. She struggled to wake up and squinted, unable to open her eyes fully. But it didn't matter, it was so dark that she couldn't have seen anything anyway. It was daytime, but she knew that only because she could hear the birds.

She tried to move and groaned when pain streaked everywhere. She hurt so bad.

And she didn't even know why. Well, technically she knew part of it, maybe even all of it, but she didn't let herself acknowledge that she held the information in her brain. In her weaker moments she might tell him and then he'd kill her.

She didn't want to die. *I want to go home. I want my baby.* She let herself think of Hope and winced as the tear burned on its way down her cheek. *Please, God, take care of my baby*. She prayed someone knew she was gone, that someone had come for Hope. *That someone is looking for me*. That she'd be important to someone.

Anyone. *Please*.

Footsteps approached and she drew a shallow breath. He was coming. *God help me, he's coming. Don't let me be afraid*. And she forced herself to go blank, to clear her mind of everything. *Everything*.

The door swung open and she winced at the dim light from the hall.

'Well, now,' he drawled. 'Are you ready to tell me where it is?'

She gritted her teeth and prepared for the blow. Still she cried out when the end of his boot kicked her hip. She looked up into black eyes that she'd once trusted.

'Bailey, darlin'. You can't win here. Tell me where the key is. Then I'll let you go.'

Dutton, Monday, January 29, 11:15 A.M.

It was still there, Alex thought as she stared up at Bailey's house from the street.

So go in. Check it out. Don't be such a coward. But still she sat, staring, her heart beating hard and fast. Before she'd been afraid for Bailey. She'd been terrified of Bailey's house. Now, thanks to Vartanian, she was afraid for herself, too.

He might be totally wrong, but if he was right . . . She needed protection. She needed a dog. A big dog. And a gun. She started up the rental car and was ready to pull away from the curb when a knock at her car window had her screaming.

Her gaze flew up to the window where a young man in a military uniform stood smiling. He hadn't heard her scream. Nobody ever did. Her screams were only in her mind. Drawing an unsteady breath, she rolled down the window a crack. 'Yes?'

'I'm sorry to bother you,' he said pleasantly. 'I'm Captain Beardsley, US Army. I'm looking for Bailey Crighton. I thought maybe you might know where I could find her.'

'Why are you looking for her?'

Again his smile was pleasant. 'That's between me and Miss Crighton. If you see her, could you tell her Reverend Beardsley stopped by?'

Alex frowned. 'Are you a captain or a reverend?'

'Both. I'm an army chaplain.' He smiled. 'Have a nice day.'

'Wait.' Alex grabbed her cell phone and dialed Meredith while the man stood outside her window. He did wear a cross on his lapel. Maybe he was really a chaplain.

And maybe he wasn't. Vartanian had her paranoid. But then again, Bailey *was* missing and that woman was dead.

'Well?' Meredith demanded without preamble.

'It's not Bailey.'

Meredith sighed. 'I'm relieved and at the same time . . . not.'

'I know. Listen, I came by Bailey's old house to see if I could find anything—'

'*Alex*. You promised to wait until I could go with you.'

'I didn't go in. I just needed to see if I could.' She glanced at the house and her gut began to twist. 'I can't. But as I was sitting here on the street, this guy came up.'

'What guy?'

'Reverend Beardsley. He says he's looking for Bailey. He's an army chaplain.'

'An army chaplain is looking for Bailey? Why?'

'That's what I'm going to find out. I just wanted someone to know I was talking to him. If I don't call you in ten minutes, call 911, okay?'

'Alex, you're scaring me.'

'Good. I was getting too full of fear myself. Need to spread it around. How's Hope?'

'The same. We need to get her out of this hotel room, Alex.'

'I'll see what I can do.' She hung up and got out of her car.

Captain Beardsley looked concerned. 'Has something happened to Bailey?'

'Yes. She disappeared.'

Beardsley's concern became shock. 'When did Bailey disappear?'

'This past Thursday night, four days ago now.'

'Oh, dear. Who are you?'

'My name is Alex Fallon. I'm Bailey's stepsister.'

His brows went up. 'Alex Tremaine?'

Alex swallowed. 'That's my old last name, yes. How do you know that?'

'Wade told me.'

'*Wade?*'

'Bailey's older brother.'

'I know who Wade is. Why would he tell you about me?'

Beardsley tilted his head, studying her. 'He's dead.'

Alex blinked. 'Dead?'

'Yes. I'm sorry. I assumed you'd been notified. Lieutenant Wade Crighton was killed in the line of duty in Iraq about a month ago.'

'We're not really blood relations, so I guess the government wouldn't have contacted me. Why are you looking for Bailey?'

'I sent her a letter her brother dictated to me just before he died. Lieutenant Crighton was injured in a raid on a village outside Baghdad. Some called it a suicide mission.'

A sense of satisfaction stole through Alex, making her ashamed. 'Was the mission accomplished?' she asked very quietly.

'Partly. At any rate, Wade was hit by mortar fire. By the time the medics got to him, it was too late. He asked me to hear his confession.'

Alex's brows knit. 'Wade wasn't Catholic.'

'Neither am I. I'm a Lutheran pastor. A lot of men who ask me to hear their final confessions aren't Catholic, and clergy other than priests can hear them.'

'I'm sorry. I knew that. We have all kinds of clergy come through our ER. I was just surprised Wade would confess anything. Do you visit all the families of the deceased?'

'Not all. I was up for R&R and just came into Fort Benning. It was on my way, so I thought I'd stop on my way home. I still have one of Wade's letters, you see. He asked that I write three letters, one to his sister, one to his father, and one to you.'

The screaming took up in her head and Alex closed her eyes. When she opened them Beardsley was watching her with a concern she ignored. 'Wade wrote to *me*?'

'Yes. I mailed his letters to Bailey and his father to this address, but I didn't know where to find you. I was looking for Alex Tremaine.' From the portfolio he carried under his arm, Beardsley pulled an envelope and his card. 'Call me if you need to talk.'

Alex took the envelope and Beardsley started to walk away. 'Wait. Wade sends Bailey a letter. She disappears, the same day a woman is killed and left in a ditch.'

He blinked at her. 'A woman was killed?'

'Yes. I thought it was Bailey, but it's not.' She ripped open the envelope and scanned the letter Wade had dictated. She looked up. 'There's nothing in this letter that will tell me where Bailey's gone. It's just a letter asking for forgiveness. He doesn't even say what he's asking forgiveness for.' Although Alex was pretty sure she knew. Still, it wasn't anything that Bailey would have been abducted over. 'Did he tell you?'

'He didn't say in the letter.'

Alex noticed the tightening of Beardsley's jaw. 'But he did say in his confession. Trust Wade to screw up. You won't tell me what he said, will you?'

Beardsley shook his head. 'I can't. And don't say I'm not Catholic. The sanctity of a confession is just as critical to me. I won't tell you, Miss Fallon. I can't.'

First Vartanian and now Beardsley. *I can't*. 'Bailey has a little girl. Hope.'

'I know. Wade told me about her. He loved that little girl.'

That Alex found hard to believe, but she didn't argue with him. 'Then tell me something that can help me get Hope's mother back to her. Please. The police won't help me. They say Bailey's just a junkie and probably ran away. Did Wade say anything outside the confession?'

Beardsley looked down, then into her eyes. '"Simon."'

Alex shook her head in frustration. 'Simon? What is that supposed to mean?'

'It's a name. Just as he died he said, "I'll see you in hell, Simon." I'm sorry, Miss Fallon. That's going to have to be enough. I can't tell you any more.'

Chapter Four

Atlanta, Monday, January 29, 12:15 P.M.

Dr Felicity Berg looked up at Daniel through her goggles. She was standing on the other side of the autopsy table, bending over what remained of their Jane Doe. 'You want the good news or the bad news first?'

Daniel had watched in silence as Felicity had taken Jane Doe apart with deliberate care. He'd watched her do autopsies more than a dozen times, but he never failed to wonder how she kept her hands so steady. 'The bad news, I guess.'

The mask covering her face moved and he imagined her wry smile. He'd always liked Felicity Berg, even though she was called 'The Iceberg' by most of the men. He'd never seen her as cold, just . . . careful. There was a difference, as Daniel well knew.

'I can't definitively identify her. She was about twenty. She had no blood alcohol, and doesn't have any obvious diseases or defects. Cause of death was asphyxia.'

'And the blows to her face? Were they pre- or postmortem?'

'Post. As was this bruising around her mouth.' She pointed to four fingertip-sized bruises.

Daniel frowned. 'Wouldn't those bruises be from the hand that killed her?'

Her brows lifted. 'That's what he wanted you to think. Remember the fibers I pointed out in her lungs and in the lining of her cheeks?'

'Cotton,' Daniel said. 'From the handkerchief he shoved in her mouth.'

'Exactly. I'm guessing he didn't want any of his own DNA in her teeth in the event she bit him. There are bruises on her nose that were put there before she was dead, you just can't see them because of the beating. But after she was dead, somebody's fingers were pressed to the side of her mouth. The distance between the finger bruises indicates it was a man's hand, small in size. He went to considerable trouble to make this happen, Daniel. He was careful when hitting her face to leave this area around her mouth untouched. It's almost like he wanted the finger bruises to show.'

'I wonder if Alicia Tremaine had finger bruising around her mouth.'

'That's for you to find out. I can tell you this woman's last meal was Italian, with sausage, pasta, and some kind of hard cheese.'

'Only about a million Italian restaurants in the city,' he said glumly.

She picked up the woman's left hand. 'She has thick calluses on her fingertips.'

Daniel leaned closer to see. 'She played a musical instrument. Violin maybe?'

'Or something in the string family, something with a bow, I think. The other hand is soft, no calluses, so it's probably not a harp or a guitar.'

'Was that the good news?'

Her eyes glinted in mild amusement. 'No. The good news is that even if I can't tell you who she was, I think I can tell you where she'd been twenty-four hours before she was killed. Come here, to this side of the table.' Felicity ran a black light wand over the victim's hand, revealing the remnants of a fluorescent stamp.

He looked up and met Felicity's satisfied eyes. 'She'd been to Fun-N-Sun,' he said. The amusement park stamped the hands of anyone leaving and planning to return the same day. 'They get thousands of visitors every day, but maybe we'll get lucky.'

Felicity placed the woman's arm at her side with gentle care and respect, elevating her in Daniel's regard. 'Or maybe someone will finally miss her,' she said quietly.

'Dr Berg?' One of her assistants came into the room, carrying a sheet of paper. 'This woman's urine tox came back positive for flunitrazepam, one hundred micrograms.'

Daniel frowned. 'Rohypnol? He used a date-rape drug? That's not a lethal dose, is it?'

'That's not even enough to knock her out. It's barely enough to show up on the test. Jackie, can you run the test again? If I get called before a grand jury, I'm going to want a verification of your results. No offense.'

Unperturbed, Jackie nodded. 'None taken. I'll do it right now.'

'He wanted us to find the drug, but he didn't want her completely incapacitated,' Daniel mused. 'He wanted her awake and aware.'

'And he knows his pharmacology. It wouldn't have been simple to achieve that low level of flunitrazepam. Again, he went to some trouble.'

'So the presence of Rohypnol is one more thing I need to check on the murder of Alicia Tremaine. I need to get that police report.' And so far, Dutton Sheriff Frank Loomis still hadn't called him back. So much for professional courtesy. Daniel was going to Dutton to get that report in person. 'Thanks, Felicity. As always, it's been fun.'

'Daniel.' Felicity had stepped back from the body and was pulling off her mask. 'I wanted to tell you that I was sorry to hear about your parents.'

Daniel drew a breath. 'Thank you.'

'I wanted to go to the funeral, but . . .' A self-deprecating smile bent her lips. 'I got to the church, but I couldn't go inside. Funerals make me queasy. Believe it or not.'

He smiled at her. 'I believe you, Felicity. And I thank you for trying.'

She nodded briskly. 'I had Malcolm request the autopsy report on Alicia Tremaine after Miss Fallon left. When we get it, I'll let you know.'

'Again, I appreciate it.' And as he walked away, he felt her watch him go.

Atlanta, Monday, January 29, 1:15 P.M.

When Daniel got back to his office, Luke was sitting in one of his chairs, a laptop in his lap and his feet up on Daniel's desk. He looked up, studied Daniel's face, then shrugged. 'You're making it damn hard for me to lie to my mama, Daniel. I can tell her you're all right all I want, but those dark circles under your eyes tell a different tale.'

Daniel hung his jacket behind his door. 'Don't you have a job?'

'Hey, I'm working.' Luke held up the laptop. 'I'm running a diagnostic on the chief's machine. It's been running "buggy."' He quirked the air with his fingers, a smile on his face, but Daniel heard the tension in his friend's voice.

He sat at his desk and did some studying of his own. There were no dark circles under Luke's eyes, but within them was a bleakness few got to see. 'Bad day?'

Luke's smile disappeared, and closing his eyes, he swallowed audibly. 'Yeah.' The single word was harsh and filled with a pain few truly understood. Luke was on the GBI's task force against Internet crime, and for the last year he'd been focused on crime involving children. Daniel thought he'd rather watch a thousand autopsies than look at the obscenities Luke was forced to view every day. Luke drew a breath and opened his eyes, control restored even if serenity was not.

Daniel wondered if any cop ever got to serenity.

'I needed a break,' Luke said simply, and Daniel nodded.

'I just came from the morgue. My Jane Doe went to Fun-N-Sun on Thursday and plays the violin.'

'Well, the violin might narrow it down some. I brought you something.' Luke pulled a thick stack of papers from his computer bag. 'I ran a deeper search on Alicia Tremaine and came up with all these articles. She had a twin sister.'

'I know,' Daniel said wryly. 'Too bad you didn't tell me before she walked in here this morning and scared the ever-livin' shit outta me.'

Luke's dark brows shot up. 'She was *here*? Alexandra Tremaine?'

'She calls herself Fallon now. Alex Fallon. She's an ER nurse from Cincinnati.'

'So she lived then,' Luke said thoughtfully and Daniel frowned.

'What do you mean?'

Luke handed the stack of papers over the table. 'Well, the story didn't stop with Alicia's murder. The day Alicia's body was found, Kathy Tremaine, that's their mother, shot herself in the head. She was apparently discovered by her daughter Alexandra, who then took all the pills the doctor had prescribed for the mother, who was hysterical after having to identify her daughter's body.'

Daniel thought of Jane Doe on the table at the morgue and of a mother having to identify her child looking like that. Still, suicide was the coward's way out . . . and for Alex to have discovered her that way. 'My God,' he murmured.

'Kathy Tremaine's sister had come down from Ohio because of Alicia and discovered them both. Her name was Kim Fallon.'

'Alex said she'd been adopted by her aunt and uncle, so that makes sense.'

'There's more in the stack, obits and articles about the trial of Gary Fulmore, the man they charged with the murder. But there was no other mention of Alexandra after the article on Fulmore's arrest. I guess Kim Fallon took her to Ohio after that.'

Daniel leafed through the pages. 'Did you see mention of a Bailey Crighton?'

'Craig Crighton, yes, but not Bailey. Craig was the man Kathy Tremaine was living with at the time of her death. Why?'

'That's why Alex Fallon came to see me today. Her stepsister Bailey went missing Thursday night and she thought she was the Arcadia woman.'

Luke whistled softly. 'Well, that had to have been a shock.'

Daniel thought of the fists she'd squeezed nearly bloodless, and the way her hand felt in his. 'I imagine it was, but she held herself together well.'

'I was actually talking about it being a shock for you.' Luke swung his feet off the desk and stood up. 'I've got to be getting back now. Break's over.'

Daniel narrowed his eyes. 'You gonna be okay?'

Luke nodded. 'Sure.' But there was little conviction in his voice. 'I'll see you later.'

Daniel lifted the papers. 'Thanks, Luke.'

'Don't mention it.'

Ripples, Daniel thought as he watched him go. They changed the lives of the victims and their families. *And sometimes they change us. Usually they change us.* With a sigh he turned to his own computer to look up the number for Fun-N-Sun. He had a victim to identify.

Dutton, Monday, January 29, 1:00 P.M.

'Here's all the stuff.' Alex dumped it on the sofa in her hotel room. 'Play-Doh, Legos, Mr Potato Head, more crayons, paper, and more coloring books.'

Meredith was sitting next to Hope at the little dinette table. 'And the Barbie head?'

'In the bag, but they were out of Barbies. You got Princess Fiona from *Shrek*.'

'But she has hair we can cut? I'm thinking since Bailey was a hairdresser they might have played that way together.'

'Yep. I checked. And I got Hope some clothes. Man, kids' clothes are expensive.'

'Get used to it, Auntie.'

'You moved her from the desk in the bedroom.'

'Had to. Wasn't room for both of us to color in there and I needed a change in scenery.' Meredith chose a blue crayon from a pile. 'Hope, I'm picking periwinkle this time. Periwinkle sounds like a happy color, like it's winking at me.'

Meredith continued to chatter as she colored and Alex could see this had been going on for some time while she'd been gone. There was a stack of pages with ragged edges that Meredith had torn from Hope's coloring book. All were colored with blue.

'Can we talk while you color?'

Meredith smiled. 'Sure. Or you can sit down and color with us. Hope and I don't mind, do we, Hope?'

Hope didn't appear to even hear her. Alex dragged the chair from the bedroom desk up to the dinette and sat down, meeting Meredith's eyes over Hope's head. 'Anything?'

'Nope,' Meredith said cheerfully. 'There are no magic wands, Alex.'

Hope's hand stopped abruptly, still clutching the red crayon in her small fist. She kept her eyes on the coloring book, but she'd gone completely still. Alex opened her mouth, but Meredith shot her a warning glance and Alex remained silent.

'At least not in that sack from the store,' Meredith went on. 'I like magic wands.' Hope didn't move a muscle. 'When I was little, I used to pretend celery stalks were magic wands. My mom would get so mad when she'd go to make a salad and all the celery was gone.' Meredith chuckled and kept coloring with her periwinkle. 'She'd fuss, but she'd play with me. Celery was cheap, she'd say, but playtime was precious.'

Alex swallowed hard. 'My mom used to say that, too. "Playtime is precious."'

'Probably because our moms were sisters. Did your mom say that, too, Hope?'

Slowly, Hope's crayon began to move again, then faster, until she colored with the same focus as before. Alex wanted to sigh, but Meredith was smiling.

'Baby steps,' she murmured. 'Sometimes the best therapy's just in being there, Alex.' She tore a page from her coloring book. 'Try it. It's really very relaxing.'

Alex drew a deep breath, steadying herself. 'You did that for me. Sat with me, when I first came to live with you. Every day after school and all that summer. You'd just come into my room and read a book. You never said a word.'

'I didn't know what to say,' Meredith said. 'But you were sad and you seemed happier when I sat with you. Then one day you said, "Hi." It was days later before you said any more and weeks before you were carrying on any conversation at all.'

'I think you saved my life,' Alex murmured. 'You and Kim and Steve.' The Fallons had been her salvation. 'I miss them.' Her aunt and uncle had died the year before when Steve's little plane had crashed into an Ohio cornfield.

Meredith's hand faltered and her throat worked as she swallowed hard. 'I miss them, too.' She rested her cheek on Hope's pretty curls for a brief moment. 'That's a very nice caterpillar, Hope. I'm going to use the periwinkle on the butterfly.' She chattered on for another few minutes, then casually turned the topic. 'I would love to see some butterflies. Did you find a park where we can take Hope, Alex?'

'Yes, there's a park not too far from the elementary school. I picked up one of those real estate booklets when I was out. There's a furnished house near the park that we might rent for a while.' *Until I find Bailey*, she added silently.

Meredith nodded. 'Got it. Oh, and you know what? When we go to the park we can play Simon Says.' Her auburn brows lifted meaningfully. 'I found instructions online. You'll find them fascinating. I left the page open on my laptop. It's in the bedroom.'

Alex stood up, her heart tripping. 'I'll go check.' She'd called Meredith right back after Captain-Reverend Beardsley had driven away, and relayed the conversation, especially the line, 'I'll see you in hell, Simon.' Apparently Meredith had done some searching while Alex had bought out the toy section of the local Wal-Mart so that Meredith could do play therapy with Hope.

Alex clicked the page Meredith had been reading and sucked in a startled breath as her memories began to fall into place. *Simon Vartanian.*

Vartanian. Daniel's name had been naggingly familiar, but she'd been too worried about Bailey to dwell on it at the time. Then, waiting to view that woman's body . . . he'd held her hand and she'd felt an awareness that had heated her from the inside out. But there had been more. A closeness, a kinship, a . . . comfort, as if she'd known him before. Maybe she had.

Vartanian. She remembered the family now, vaguely. They'd been rich. The dad was important. He'd been a judge. She remembered Simon, also vaguely. He'd been a big, hulking, frightening boy. Simon had been in Wade's class at school.

She sat down to read the article, immediately engrossed in a story so evil . . . Simon Vartanian had died just one week ago after murdering his parents and a lot of other people. Simon had been killed in Philadelphia by a detective named Vito Ciccotelli.

Simon was survived by his sister Susannah Vartanian. *I remember her*. She'd been a cultured girl in expensive clothes. Susannah had been her age, but had gone to the expensive private school. She was now an ADA in New York.

Alex released the breath she held in a slow hiss. Simon was also survived by his brother, Daniel Vartanian, a special agent with the GBI. Alex replayed in her mind the moment they'd met, the utter shock on Daniel's face. He'd known about Alicia and Alex had attributed his shock to that only. But now . . . *I'll see you in hell, Simon*.

She pressed her knuckles into her lips, staring at the picture of Simon Vartanian on Meredith's screen. There was some small resemblance between the brothers. Both had the same body type, tall and broad, and they shared the same piercing look around the eyes. But Simon had a harsh look to him while Daniel had looked . . . sad. Weary and very sad. His parents had been murdered, so that explained the sadness, but what explained his shock at seeing her face? What did Daniel Vartanian know?

I'll see you in hell. What had Simon done? Alex could read what he'd done recently – and it had been inhuman. But what did he do back then?

And what had Wade done? *I know what he did to*

me . . . but what did he do with Simon? What was Wade's connection to Simon Vartanian? And what did it have to do with Bailey? And Alicia? And what about the poor woman they'd found in the ditch yesterday evening, killed just like Alicia? Could Wade have . . . ?

Alex's pulse began to pound in her ears and it was suddenly as if all the air were sucked from the room. *Calm. Focus on the quiet.* Slowly she began to breathe again, to think rationally again. Alicia's murderer was rotting in jail, where he belonged. And Wade . . . no. Not murder. No. Whatever it was, she knew it wasn't that.

What she did know was that she was meeting Special Agent Daniel Vartanian tonight and he *would* tell her what he knew. Until then, she had things to do.

Atlanta, Monday, January 29, 2:15 P.M.

Daniel looked up from his computer when Ed Randall came into his office looking generally disgusted. 'Hey, Ed, what do you know?'

'That this guy was careful. We haven't found so much as a hair so far. We took mud from around the entrance to the storm sewer and we're checking it in the lab now. If he came down from the road by the storm sewer, maybe he dropped something.'

'What about the brown blanket?' Daniel asked.

'The labels have both been cut away,' Ed said. 'We're trying to match the fabric to manufacturers. We might get lucky and trace it to a point of purchase. Are we any closer to an ID on the victim?'

'Yeah, actually. Felicity also found a stamp on the victim's hand from Fun-N-Sun.'

'So you get a trip to the amusement park and I get to play in the mud. No fair.'

Daniel smiled. 'I don't think I need to go down to the park. I spent most of the afternoon on the phone with their security. They were able to patch me into their network so that I could view their security tapes from my desk.'

Ed looked impressed. 'Ain't technology grand. And?'

'And we found a woman standing in line at the Italian food kiosk. The victim had eaten pasta as her last meal. She was wearing a sweatshirt saying *Cellists Do It With Strings Attached* – the victim has calluses on her fingertips. The park is going through their receipts to see if she paid for her lunch with a credit card. I'm waiting for them to call back. Cross your fingers.'

'I will. We did find one thing of interest.' Ed put a small jar on Daniel's desk. 'We found hair and skin in the bark of one of the trees about fifty feet back from the ditch.'

Daniel looked at the headline Corchran had faxed that morning. 'The reporter?'

'That's what we're thinking. If you find this Jim Woolf person, we can put him at the scene before we got there.'

'How did he get away without being seen?'

'My team was there till after eleven last night and back again this morning. Between eleven and six we had a unit patrolling. We found shoeprints along the road about a quarter mile from here. I think the reporter waited until we were all gone, climbed down and stayed low until he got a quarter mile away, then caught a ride.'

'There's no cover along the road. He must have slithered on his belly to get away.'

Ed's jaw tightened. 'Slithered is about right. Guy's a snake. He gave away everything we've got in that article. I heard you went to school with him.'

Ed sounded slightly accusatory, as if Daniel were to blame for Jim Woolf's behavior. 'I was a V and he was a W, so he always sat in back of me. He seemed nice enough then. But as Chase so astutely observed, he appears to have changed. I guess I'm about to go see how much.' He pointed to his computer screen. 'I was just checking him out. He was an accountant until his dad died a year ago and left him the *Review*. Jim's pretty new at this reporter stuff. Maybe he can be persuaded to talk.'

'You got a flute?' Ed asked sourly.

'Why?'

'Isn't that what those snake charmers use?'

Daniel grimaced at the image. 'I hate snakes almost as much as reporters.'

Ed broke into a good-natured grin. 'Then you're going to have a fun afternoon.'

Dutton, Monday, January 29, 2:15 P.M.

'It's a thousand a month,' the realtor said, a gleam in her eye as if she sensed a done deal. In her mid-fifties, Delia Anderson had a bouffant-do that dynamite couldn't budge. 'First and last month's rent payable on signing.'

Alex looked around at the bungalow. It was homey, had two bedrooms and a real kitchen – and was less than a block from a really nice park where Hope could play. If they were ever able to get her to drop the crayons. 'Furnishings all stay?'

Delia nodded. 'Including the organ.' It was one of the older models that synthesized every instrument in the orchestra. 'You can move in tomorrow.'

'Tonight.' Alex met the woman's eagle eyes. 'I need to move in tonight.'

Delia smiled cagily. 'I think that can be arranged.'

'Does it have an alarm?'

'I suppose not.' Delia looked unhappy. 'No, it doesn't have an alarm.'

Alex frowned, thinking of Vartanian's caution before she'd left the morgue viewing room. She wasn't a big fan of guns, but fear was a great motivator. She'd tried to buy a gun in the sporting goods department of the store where she'd bought all the toys for Hope's play therapy, but the clerk told her that she couldn't buy a gun in Georgia if she wasn't a resident. She could prove residency with a Georgia driver's license. She could get a driver's license with a rental contract. *So let's get this done.*

Still, she was practical. 'If it doesn't have an alarm, then can I have a dog?' A dog was a better deterrent to an attacker. She lifted a brow. 'An alarm will cost the owners money. I'd pay an extra security deposit if I got a dog.'

Delia bit at her lip. 'Maybe a little dog. I'll check with the owners.'

Alex swallowed her smile. 'You do that. If I can have a dog, I'll sign right now.'

Delia took her cell phone outside and two minutes later she was back, as was her cagey smile. 'Darlin', we have a deal and you have a house.'

Dutton, Monday, January 29, 4:15 P.M.

Daniel felt like he was channeling Clint Eastwood as he walked Dutton's Main Street. As he passed, conversations stilled and people stared. All he was missing was the poncho and the eerie music. Last week he'd been to the funeral home, the cemetery, and his parents' home out past the city limits. With the exception of the funeral and the graveside, he'd managed to stay out of the public eye.

But not now. He met the eyes of each staring person. Most of them he knew. All of them had aged. It had been a long time since he'd been back. Eleven years since he'd fought with his father over the pictures and left Dutton for good, but he'd left in spirit the day he'd left for college, seven years before that. He'd changed a lot in those years.

Dutton's Main Street, however, had not. He walked past the curious eyes peering from the windows of the bakery, the florist, the barbershop. Three old men sat outside the barbershop on a bench. Three old men had always sat outside on that bench, ever since Daniel could remember. When one went on to the Great Beyond, another took his place. Daniel had always wondered if there was some kind of formal waiting list for the bench, as there was for box seats at Braves' games.

He was surprised when one of the old men stood up. He couldn't recall ever having seen any of the old men stand up before. But this one stood and leaned on his cane, watching Daniel approach. 'Daniel Vartanian.'

Daniel recognized the voice instantly and was a little amused to find himself standing straighter as he stopped in front of his old high school English teacher. 'Mr Grant.'

One side of the old man's bushy white mustache lifted. 'So you do remember.'

Daniel met the old man's eyes. '"Death, be not proud, though some have called thee mighty and dreadful, for thou art not so."' *Odd that that would be the first quotation to enter his mind.* Daniel thought about the woman lying in the morgue, unidentified and as yet unreported as missing. *Or maybe not so odd.*

The other side of Grant's mustache lifted and he bobbed his white head in salute. 'John Donne. One of your favorites, as I recall.'

'Not so much anymore. I guess I've seen too much death.'

'I suspect you have at that, Daniel. We're all sorry about your parents.'

'Thank you. It's been a difficult time for all of us.'

'I was at the funeral and the grave. Susannah looked pale.'

Daniel swallowed. That his sister had. She'd had good reason. 'She'll hold up.'

'Of course she will. Your parents raised good stock.' Grant winced when he realized what he'd said. 'Hell. You know what I meant.'

To his surprise, Daniel found his lips curving. 'I know what you meant, sir.'

'That Simon was always bad news.' Grant leaned forward and dropped his voice, although Daniel knew every eye in town was watching them. 'I read what you did, Daniel. It took courage. Good for you, son. I was proud of you.'

Daniel's smile faded and he swallowed again, this time as his eyes stung. 'Thank you.' He cleared his voice. 'You got a seat on the barbershop bench, I see.'

Grant nodded. 'Only had to wait for old Jeff Orwell to pass.' He scowled. 'Old man held on for two long years, just because he knew I was waiting.'

Daniel shook his head. 'The nerve of some people.'

Grant smiled. 'It's good to see you, Daniel. You were one of my best students.'

'You were always one of my favorite teachers. You and Miss Agreen.' He lifted his brows. 'You two still an item?'

Grant coughed until Daniel thought he'd have to do CPR. 'You knew about that?'

'Everybody did, Mr Grant. I always thought you knew we knew and didn't care.'

Grant drew a deep breath. 'People think their secrets are so damn safe,' he murmured, so quietly Daniel almost didn't hear. 'People are fools.' Then he whispered under his breath, 'Don't be a fool, son.' Then he looked up, his smile reappearing, and he rocked back on his cane. 'Good to see you. Don't be a stranger, Daniel Vartanian.'

Daniel studied his old teacher's eyes, but there was no hint of what had seemed a dire warning just a few seconds before. 'I'll try. Take care, Mr Grant. Give the next guy on the waiting list for the barbershop bench a very long wait.'

'That I will.'

Daniel walked on to the office of the *Dutton Review*, the real reason for his visit. The *Review* sat across the street from the police station, which would be Daniel's next stop. The inside of the newspaper office was stuffy and packed floor to ceiling with boxes. A small space had been carved out for a desk, a computer, and a phone. At the desk sat a plump man with a pair of glasses resting on his balding head.

Four large bandages covered his left forearm, looking like sergeant's stripes, and an angry red welt peeked from his shirt collar. It looked as if the man had tangled with something and lost. Perhaps a tree. *Hello*, Daniel thought.

The man looked up and Daniel recognized the boy who'd sat behind him from kindergarten through high school. Jim Woolf's mouth curved in something just shy of a sneer. 'Well. If it isn't the man himself. Special Agent Daniel Vartanian. In the flesh.'

'Jim. How are you?'

'Better today than you are, I suspect, although I have to say I'm flattered. I thought you'd send a flunkie to do your dirty work, but here you are, back in little old Dutton.'

Daniel sat on the edge of Woolf's desk. 'You didn't return my phone calls, Jim.'

Jim's fingers resting lightly on his rounded stomach. 'I didn't have anything to say.'

'A newspaperman with nothing to say. That has to be a first.'

'I'm not telling you what you want to know, Daniel.'

Daniel abandoned the polite path. 'Then I'll arrest you for impeding an investigation.'

Jim flinched. 'Wow. You pulled off the gloves there, real fast.'

'I spent the morning in the morgue watching that woman autopsied. Tends to suck the joy right out of a man's day. Ever seen an autopsy, Jim?'

Jim's jaw squared. 'No. But I'm still not telling you what you want to know.'

'Okay. Get your coat.'

Jim sat up straight. 'You're bluffing.'

'No, I'm not. Someone clued you in to that crime scene before the cops arrived. No telling how long you had to poke around that body. No telling what you touched. What you took.' Daniel met Jim's eyes. 'Maybe you even put her there.'

Jim turned red. 'I had nothing to do with that and you know it.'

'I know nothing. I wasn't there. You, on the other hand, were.'

'You don't know that I was. Maybe I got the pictures from somebody else.'

Daniel leaned across the desk and pointed to the Band-Aids on the man's forearm. 'You left part of yourself behind, Jim. Crime scene guys found your skin in the bark of that tree.' Jim paled a little. 'Now I can take you in and get a warrant for a DNA sample or you can tell me how you knew to be up that tree yesterday afternoon.'

'I can't. Beyond the constitutional aspects, if I tell you, I'll never get another tip.'

'So you got a tip.'

Jim sighed. 'Daniel . . . If I knew I wouldn't tell you, but I don't know who it was.'

'An anonymous tip. Convenient.'

'It's the truth. The call came through on my home phone, but the number was blocked. I didn't know what I'd see when I got there.'

'Was the caller male or female?'

Jim shook his head. 'No. Not gonna tell you that.'

Daniel considered. He'd already gotten more than he thought he would. 'Then tell me when you arrived and what you did see.'

Jim tilted his head. 'What's in it for me?'

'An interview, exclusive. You might even sell to one of the big guys in Atlanta.'

Jim's eyes lit up and Daniel knew he'd plucked the right chord. 'All right. It's not complicated. I got the call yesterday at noon. I got there at about one, climbed the tree, and waited. About two the bikers came through. A half hour later Officer Larkin showed up. He took one look at the body, climbed back up the bank to the road, and threw up. Pretty soon you state boys showed up. After everybody left I climbed down and went home.'

'Once you climbed down, how exactly did you get home?'

Jim's lips thinned. 'My wife. Marianne.'

Daniel blinked. 'Marianne? Marianne Murphy? You married Marianne Murphy?'

Jim looked smug. 'Yes.'

Marianne Murphy had been the girl voted most likely to do . . . everybody. 'Well.' Daniel cleared his throat, not wanting to visualize Jim Woolf with the buxom and very generous Marianne Murphy. 'How did you get there?'

'She dropped me off, too.'

'I'll want to talk to her. To confirm the times. And I want the pictures you took while you were sitting there. All of them.'

Glaring, Jim popped his memory card from his camera and tossed it. Daniel caught it with one hand and slipped it into his pocket as he stood up. 'I'll be in touch.'

Jim followed him to the door. 'When?'

'When I know something.' Daniel opened the door, then stopped, his hand still on the doorknob. And stared.

Behind him he heard Jim's soft gasp. 'Oh my God. That's . . .'

Alex Fallon. She stood at the bottom of the police station stairs, a satchel over one shoulder. She still wore her black suit. Her shoulders abruptly stiffened and she turned slowly until she met his eyes. For a long moment they stared at each other across Main Street. She didn't smile. In fact, even from this distance Daniel could see her full lips go thin. She was angry.

Daniel crossed the street, his eyes never breaking away from hers. When he stood before her she lifted her chin, as she'd done that morning. 'Agent Vartanian.'

His mouth went dry. 'I didn't expect to see you here.'

'I'm here to see the sheriff about filing a missing person report on Bailey.' She looked over his shoulder. 'Who are you?'

Jim Woolf stepped around him. 'Jim Woolf, *Dutton Review*. Did I hear you say you were filing a missing person report? Perhaps I can be of assistance. We can print a photograph of Bailey, did you say? Bailey Crighton is missing?'

Daniel looked down at Jim and frowned. 'Go away.'

But Alex tilted her head. 'Give me your card. I may wish to talk with you.'

Again smug, Jim gave her a card. 'Any time, Miss Tremaine.'

Alex flinched as if he'd struck her. 'Fallon. My name is Alex Fallon.'

'Any time, Miss Fallon.' Jim gave Daniel a salute and was gone.

Something had changed and Daniel didn't like it. 'I'm going to the station, too. Can I carry your bag?'

The way she searched his face made Daniel

uncomfortable. 'No thank you.' She started up the stairs, leaving him to follow.

He could see her hunch one shoulder from the weight of her bag, but it didn't seem to affect the sway of her slim hips as she hurried. Daniel thought her bag was a far safer thing on which to focus. He caught up to her easily. 'You're about to topple over. What are you carrying in here? Bricks?'

'A gun and lots of bullets. If you must know.'

She started up the stairs again, but Daniel grabbed her arm and pulled her around to face him. *'Excuse me?'*

Her whiskey eyes were cool. 'You said I might be in danger. I took you seriously. I have a child to protect.'

Her stepsister's daughter. Hope. 'How did you buy a gun? You're not a resident.'

'I am now. You want to see my new driver's license?'

'You got a driver's license? How did you do that? You don't live here.'

'I do now. You want to see my rental contract?'

Bowled over, he blinked. 'You rented an apartment?'

'A house.' She really was staying a while.

'In Dutton?'

She nodded. 'I'm not leaving until Bailey's found, and Hope can't live in a hotel.'

'I see. Are we still meeting at seven?'

'That was my plan. Now if you don't mind, I still have a lot to do before then.' She'd run up a few more stairs before he called her name.

'Alex.' He waited until she stopped and turned again.

'Yes, Agent Vartanian? What is it?'

He ignored the ice in her voice. 'Alex. You can't take a gun into the police station. Even in Dutton. It's a government building.'

Her shoulders sagged and her frosty expression melted away, leaving exhaustion and vulnerability in its place. She was afraid and doing her damndest to hide it. 'I forgot. I should have come here first. I wanted to get my driver's license before the DMV closed. But I can't leave a gun in the car. Somebody might steal it.' A ghost of a smile flitted across her unpainted lips, tugging at his heart. 'Even in Dutton.'

'You look tired. I'm going to see the sheriff. I'll ask him about Bailey. Go back to your house and get some sleep. I'll meet you at seven in front of the GBI building.' He eyed her satchel. 'And for God's sake, make sure the safety is on on that thing and you put it in a lockbox so Hope can't get to it.'

'I bought a lockbox.' She lifted her chin, a gesture he was coming to anticipate. 'I've coded enough children in the ER who've played with guns. I won't put my niece in any more danger. Please call me if Loomis refuses to file Bailey as a missing person.'

'He won't refuse,' Daniel said grimly, 'but give me your cell phone number anyway.' She did, and he committed it to memory as she started back down the stairs, her steps weary. When she got to the street she looked back up at him.

'Seven o'clock, Agent Vartanian.'

Somehow the way she said it made it seem more like a threat than the confirmation of a meeting. 'Seven o'clock. And don't forget to change your suit.'

Dutton, Monday, January 29, 4:55 P.M.

Mack pulled the earpiece from his ear. *How the plot thickened,* he thought as he watched Daniel Vartanian watch Alexandra Tremaine drive away. Oh, wait. Alex *Fallon*. She'd changed her name.

It had been a surprise to hear she'd come back. That was one of the good things about a small town. No sooner had she stepped into Delia Anderson's real estate office than the word began to spread. *Alexandra Tremaine is back. The sister who lived.*

Her stepsister Bailey Crighton was missing. He had a good idea where Bailey might have been taken. And why. But that was not his business at the moment. Should it become important, he'd act. Until then, he'd watch and listen.

Alex Tremaine was back. And Daniel Vartanian was interested. This, too, he'd watch. It could be useful later. He smiled. What a kickoff that would have been, to kill the identical twin and leave her in the same exact place. *I wish I'd thought of it*. But he'd kicked it off with a target of his own choosing. She'd deserved everything she got, but Alex Tremaine would have been a most excellent first victim. Now it was too late.

For a first victim. His brows lifted as he considered it. *But what about his last?* It would make quite the grand finale. It would complete the circle. He'd consider it.

For now, he had work to do. Another lovely with whom to deal. He already had her picked out. Very soon the cops would find another body in a ditch and the *pillars of the community* would find another skeleton dumped on their doorstep. He had it on good authority that they'd all been practically pissing themselves all day. Who would break? Who would tell? Who would tear their idyllic little world asunder?

He chuckled, just picturing it. Pretty soon the first two he'd targeted would get their letters. He was starting to enjoy himself.

Chapter Five

Dutton, Monday, January 29, 5:35 P.M.

'This is really nice!' Meredith explored the bungalow with a delighted smile.

Hope sat at the table. Alex took the red Play-Doh under her nails as a good sign.

'It is nice,' Alex agreed. 'And there's a park not even a block away with a carousel.'

Meredith looked impressed. 'A real carousel? With horses?'

'With horses. It's been there since I was a kid.' Alex sat on the arm of the sofa. 'This place was here then, too. I'd pass by when I was walking home from school.'

Meredith sat next to Hope, but her eyes stayed on Alex's face. 'You sound wistful.'

'I was, then. I always thought this was like a dollhouse and the people that lived here were so lucky. They could go on the carousel any time they chose.'

'And you couldn't?'

'No. We didn't have money for things like that after my dad died. Mama had trouble scraping enough together for us to eat.'

'Until she moved in with Craig.'

Alex winced and slammed the door in her mind before the first scream took hold. 'I'm going to change and run out for some groceries. Then I'm going out again.'

Meredith frowned. 'Why?'

'I'm going to search. I've got to try, Mer, because nobody else cares enough to.'

Not entirely true. Daniel Vartanian had offered to help. *We'll see how helpful he is.*

'I've got to go back to Cincinnati tomorrow night, Alex.'

'I know. That's why I'm trying to get all this done now. I'll be back later and you can show me all the wonderful games you and Hope play so I can take over tomorrow.'

Alex went into the bedroom, closed the door, and took the gun from the satchel. It was still in its box, and willing her hands to steady, Alex took it out and looked it over again. She loaded the magazine like the store owner had shown her and set the safety with care. She'd need a bigger purse, because she intended to keep the gun with her. It would do her no good locked in its lockbox when she was elsewhere. For now, the satchel would have to do.

'My God, Alex.' Alex whipped around in time to see

a furious Meredith close the bedroom door with a hard snap. 'What the fucking hell is that?' Meredith hissed.

Alex pressed her free hand against her racing heart. 'Don't do that.'

'Don't *do* that?' Meredith's hiss was shrill. 'You're telling me not to *do* that when you're standing there holding a goddamn *gun*? What the hell are you *thinking*?'

'That Bailey's missing and another woman is dead.' Alex sat on the edge of the bed, breathing again. 'And that I don't want to end up the same way.'

'Dammit, girl, you don't know anything about guns.'

'I don't know anything about searching for missing people, either. Or caring for traumatized little girls. I'm kind of learning as I go here, Mer. And don't scream at me.'

'I'm not screaming.' Meredith sucked in a breath. 'I'm whispering loudly, which is different.' She sagged against the closed door. 'I'm sorry. I shouldn't have reacted that way, but seeing you with that *thing* was a shock. Tell me why you bought the gun.'

'I went to see the dead woman today in the morgue.'

'I know that. Agent Vartanian was with you.'

He hadn't told her the whole truth, of that Alex was certain. But there was a kindness in his eyes and a comfort in his touch that she couldn't ignore. 'He doesn't think Bailey's disappearance is a coincidence. If whoever killed that woman is copying Alicia's murder, I'm the other original player who's returned to the stage.'

Meredith paled. 'Where are you going tonight, Alex?'

'The Dutton sheriff told me to check out the homeless shelter in Atlanta if I wanted to find Bailey. Vartanian said it wasn't safe to go alone, that he'd go with me.'

Meredith narrowed her eyes. 'Why? What's in it for Vartanian to go with you?'

'That's what I'm going to find out.'

'Will you tell him about what Wade said to the army chaplain?'

I'll see you in hell, Simon. 'I haven't decided yet. I'm playing it by ear.'

'You call me while you're out,' Meredith said fiercely. 'Every half hour.'

Alex slid the gun into the satchel. 'I saw the Play-Doh under Hope's fingernails.'

Meredith's brows winged up and down again in a facial shrug. 'I stuck her fingers in a ball of it, hoping to engage her, but no deal. You might want to pick up some more red crayons when you go to the grocery store.'

Alex sighed. 'What happened to that baby, Meredith?'

'I don't know. But somebody needs to check out Bailey's house. If you can't make the local cops do it, maybe Vartanian can.'

'Don't think so. He said he couldn't get involved unless he was invited by the sheriff, and so far, Sheriff Frank Loomis hasn't been too helpful.'

'Maybe this girl's death will change that.'

Alex shrugged out of her suit coat. 'Maybe. But I won't hold my breath.'

Atlanta, Monday, January 29, 6:15 P.M.

Daniel was still frowning as he exited the elevator and headed toward the team room. Frank Loomis had been too busy to see him and finally Daniel had to leave.

He sat down at the team table where Chase and Ed were waiting. 'Sorry I'm late.'

'Why were you?' Chase asked.

'I tried to call you from the road, Chase, but Leigh said you were in a meeting. I'll explain. I promise.' He pulled out his notebook. 'But first, let's debrief. Ed?'

Ed held up a plastic evidence bag triumphantly. 'A key.'

Daniel squinted at it. It was about an inch tall and silver and had a muddy string threaded through the ring hole. 'Where did you find it?'

'In the mud we took from around the storm sewer. It's a brand new key. It still has the marks from the key cutter. I don't think it's ever been used.'

'Fingerprints?' Chase asked.

Ed scoffed. 'We should be so lucky. No fingerprints.'

'It could have been dropped by anyone before the body was left there,' Chase said.

Ed was undaunted. 'Or he could have dropped it.'

'What about the blanket?' Daniel asked. 'Do you know where it came from?'

'Not yet. It's a camping blanket sold in sporting goods stores. The wool is water resistant. It kept the victim fairly dry given the rain we had on Saturday.'

'So this murder thirteen years ago, the girl in Dutton,' Chase said. 'Was that also a wool camping blanket?'

Daniel rubbed his forehead. 'I don't know. I haven't been able to get the old police report yet. I'm running into a brick wall I don't understand.' And it was disturbing. 'But we do have a lead on the victim, maybe even her face.' Daniel told Chase about his work with the Fun-N-Sun security team. 'The security guy e-mailed me this still photo. It's grainy, but you can see her face. She's the right height and body type.'

'Slick,' Chase murmured. 'This came off the park's security tape?'

'Yep. The cellist slogan on her sweatshirt caught my eye. Park Security called me while I was driving back. They couldn't find a credit card receipt, so they think she paid cash for her meal. They're going to review the tapes from the front gate and FedEx copies of the tapes to us, too. She may have paid her park admission with a credit card. If we haven't tracked her by morning I'll release this photo to the news services.'

'Sounds like a plan,' Chase said. 'So your trip to Dutton was a bust?'

'Not entirely.' Daniel put the memory card from Jim Woolf's camera on the table. 'The reporter got an "anonymous" call telling him where to go and when to get there.'

'You don't believe him?' Chase asked.

'Not entirely. He lied about a few things and left a few things out altogether. Woolf said he got the call at noon, got to the tree at one, and the bikers passed by at two.'

'It's only a thirty-minute drive from Dutton to Arcadia,' Ed said. 'He had time.'

'It's normally a thirty-minute drive,' Daniel said. 'But they had a five-mile section of that road blocked off before nine yesterday morning. It was local traffic only and they checked IDs and wrote down tag numbers. Woolf told me his wife dropped him off, but I called Sheriff Corchran on my way back and she's not on his list of cars that passed through their checkpoint.'

Chase nodded. 'So either Woolf got there before nine yesterday morning, or his wife dropped him off a couple miles from the crime scene and he had a two- or three-mile hike. He still would have had time to climb the tree by two, but just barely and only if he ran the whole way.'

'Jim doesn't seem like the running type. Hell, I was kind of surprised he even managed to get up in the tree at all. Add to that, that the call came into 911 at two-oh-three,' Daniel said. 'The biker who called it in came in sixty-third, so he was in the back of the pack. I checked with the race officials. The biker who came in first passed by there at quarter to two.'

Ed frowned. 'Why would the reporter lie about something you could check?'

'I don't think he wanted to admit he'd been at the ditch a lot longer than a few minutes. It gives him time to contaminate the scene. And maybe if he told me what I wanted to know, I'd go away. I called Chloe Hathaway in the SA's office on my way in. She's going to try to get a warrant for his phone records at the *Review* office and at home as well as his cell. I'm betting he got a call early Sunday morning.' Daniel sighed. 'Then when I got done with Jim Woolf, I went across the street to the police station. Alex Fallon was on her way in.'

Chase's brows went up. 'Interesting.'

'She said she was trying to get her stepsister's missing person paperwork filed. She'd called repeatedly over the weekend, but was told her stepsister had probably just taken off somewhere. She's convinced her stepsister's disappearance and the Arcadia murder are no coincidence. I'm inclined to agree.'

'I'm not inclined to disagree,' Chase said. 'So?'

'So I told her I was going to see the sheriff and I'd check it for her.' Daniel fought the urge to squirm when Chase's brows went higher. 'I was going in there anyway, Chase. I thought I could talk to Frank Loomis, maybe find out if there was something they weren't telling Alex, some reason why they were so sure Bailey had just run away.'

'But?' Chase asked.

'But his clerk kept telling me it would be just a few minutes more. Finally, I left. Either Frank wasn't there at all, or he was refusing to see me and the clerk didn't want to be upfront about it. Either way, I was being stonewalled and I don't like it.'

'Did you request the Tremaine police report?' Ed asked.

'Finally, yes. Wanda, she's Frank's clerk, said it was in "storage" and would take some time to find. She said she'd get back to me in a few days.'

'It *is* thirteen years old,' Chase noted, but Daniel shook his head.

'This is Dutton we're talking about. It's not like they have warehouses full of records. All Wanda had to do was go to the basement and get a box. She was putting me off.'

'So what are you gonna do, Daniel?' Chase asked.

'When I talked to Chloe about the warrant for Jim Woolf, I asked her about getting this report quickly. She said if I didn't get a response by Wednesday morning to get her involved. I know Frank Loomis doesn't like outsiders, but it's not like him to just blow me off like this. I'm starting to get really worried, like maybe *he's* a missing person.'

'What about the Fallon woman's stepsister?' Ed asked. 'Did they file her?'

'Yes, but Wanda said they're not pursuing it with any resources. She said Bailey Crighton had a record for possession and public intoxication. She'd been in and out of rehab. She was a junkie.'

'Then maybe she did run off,' Chase said gently. 'For now focus on our victim.'

'I know.' But Daniel wasn't going to mention his planned trip to Peachtree and Pine with Alex Fallon. 'Felicity said the bruising around her mouth was put there after the fact, so I think we were meant to see it. Rape kit found evidence of assault, but no fluids. She died sometime between ten p.m. Thursday and two a.m. Friday, and she had just enough Rohypnol in her system to show up on the test. The old newspaper articles on Alicia Tremaine's murder said they found GHB in her system. So both victims were given date-rape drugs.'

Chase blew out a breath. 'Damn. He's copying it all.'

'Yeah, I know.' Daniel checked his watch. Alex would be getting here soon. He couldn't get rid of the worry that she'd been brought back here for a reason. At least he could keep her safe while she searched for Bailey in the hellhole of Peachtree and Pine. 'That's all I have for now. Let's meet tomorrow, same time.'

Atlanta, Monday, January 29, 7:25 P.M.

Alex had no sooner parked her car at the curb in front of a small two-story house in a quiet Atlanta suburb than Daniel Vartanian appeared at her window. She rolled it down and he crouched, his face level with hers. 'I won't be long,' he said. 'Thanks for following me home. You can leave your car here and not have to drive so far later.'

His eyes were bright blue and completely focused on her face, and Alex found herself staring too closely. His nose was sharp and his lips firm, but all in all, his features worked together to make him a very ruggedly handsome man. She remembered him holding her hand, then remembered he most likely knew more than he'd let on. 'I appreciate you being willing to come with me.'

One side of his mouth lifted, softening the harshness of his features. 'I have to change and walk my dog. You can come in or sit out here, but it's getting cooler.'

It was, actually. Now that the sun had gone down, there was a hard chill in the air. Still, prudence prevailed. 'It's okay. I'll wait.'

He lifted one blond brow. 'Alex, you're trusting me to take you to Peachtree and Pine. My living room is a good bit safer, that I can assure you. But it's up to you.'

'Put that way . . .' She rolled up her window, grabbed her satchel, and locked up her car. She looked up to find Vartanian eyeing the satchel dubiously.

'I don't want to know if you're carrying anything nasty in there, because unless you have a permit to carry a concealed, you'd be breaking the law.'

'That would be bad of me,' Alex said, blinking her eyes, and his lips twitched.

'Now if you were to leave the satchel in my private residence . . . that would be okay.'

'No kids in your house?'

He took her elbow and led her up the sidewalk. 'Just Riley, but he doesn't have opposable thumbs, so he's safe.' He unlocked his front door and disengaged his alarm. 'That's him.'

Alex laughed as a droopy-looking basset hound sat up and yawned. 'Oh, he's cute!'

'Yeah, well, he has his moments. Just don't feed him anything.' And with that cryptic advice, Vartanian jogged up the stairs, leaving Alex alone in his living room. It was a nice enough living room, more comfortable than the one she'd left behind in Cincinnati, which wasn't hard to accomplish. The super-size flat-screen TV was the centerpiece of the room. A pool table dominated his dining room and in the corner was a shiny mahogany bar, complete with stools and a *Dogs Playing Poker* painting.

She chuckled again, then started when something poked her calf. She hadn't heard his dog approach, but there Riley stood, gazing up soulfully. She'd crouched to scratch behind the hound's ears when Vartanian reappeared, looking completely different in faded jeans and an Atlanta Braves sweatshirt, carrying a leash.

'He likes you,' Vartanian said. 'He won't walk across the room for just anyone.'

Alex stood up when Vartanian leaned down to snap the leash on the dog's collar. 'I'm going to get a dog,' she said. 'It's on my list of things to do tomorrow.'

'That makes me feel a whole lot better than the thought of you depending on a gun.'

Her chin went up. 'I'm not stupid, Agent Vartanian. I know a barking dog is a greater deterrent to intruders than a poorly handled handgun. But I'd rather hedge my bets.'

He grinned and stood up, tugging Riley toward the door. 'You might have a point there, Alex. You want to come with us? I think Riley wants you to.'

Riley had dropped to his belly, ears splayed straight out, nose pointed straight at Alex. Drowsily he blinked up at her and Alex had to chuckle again. 'What a ham. But I think I'd need a more active dog. More of a watchdog.'

'Believe it or not, this boy can move when he wants to.'

Riley padded between them as Vartanian led them out his front door and back down to the sidewalk. 'Well, he's moving now,' Alex said. 'But he's still no watchdog.'

'No, he's a huntin' dog. He's won awards.' They walked in companionable silence for a time and then Vartanian asked, 'Does your niece like dogs?'

'I don't know. I just met her two days ago and she hasn't been very . . . engaged.' Alex frowned. 'I don't know if she's scared of dogs or even if she's allergic. I don't have her medical history. Damn, that's one more thing to add to the list.'

'Before you buy a dog, see how she does around Riley. If she's afraid of *him*, any other dog might be too much.'

'I hope she likes dogs. I'd like to snag her interest in something.' Alex sighed. 'Hell, I'd just like to see her do something besides color all day.'

'She colors?'

'She's obsessed.' And before she knew it, Alex had spilled the whole story and they were back in his living room. 'I just wish I knew what she's seen. It terrifies me.'

Riley flopped to the floor with a dramatic sigh, and as one they crouched to scratch the dog's floppy ears. 'It doesn't sound good,' he said. 'What are you going to do when your cousin goes home tomorrow?'

'I don't know.' Alex looked into Daniel Vartanian's kind eyes and felt the connection once again, even though he hadn't touched her. 'I have no idea.'

'And that scares you,' he said softly.

She nodded tightly. 'I seem to be scared a lot lately.'

'I'm sure our department psychologist could recommend a specialist for children.'

'Thank you,' she murmured, and as she stared at his

face, something between them shifted. Settled. And Alex drew her first easy breath all day.

Vartanian swallowed, then stood, ending the moment. 'Your jacket's still too fancy for where we're going.' He went to his coat closet and began moving hangers around with more force than he probably needed to. Finally he emerged with an old high school letter jacket. 'I was skinnier then. This might actually not swallow you whole.'

He held it out and she shrugged out of her jacket and into his. It smelled like him and Alex fought the urge to sniff the sleeve with all the finesse of Riley. 'Thank you.'

He nodded but said nothing, setting his alarm and locking his door behind them. When they got to his car, she looked up again and caught her breath. His eyes were piercing as always, but there was something more now, a hunger that should have scared her, but with which she found herself fascinated instead.

'You've been nice to me, Agent Vartanian. Nicer than you needed to be. Why?'

'I don't know,' he said, so quietly she shivered. 'I have no idea.'

'And . . . that scares you?' she asked, purposely repeating his line.

One side of his mouth lifted in a wry gesture she was coming to appreciate. 'Let's just say it's . . . unfamiliar ground.' He opened her car door. 'Let's go to Peachtree and Pine. It's still cold enough at night that a good number of the city's homeless head for the shelters. The shelters are pretty well filled by six, so by the time we get there, they should be finished serving supper. Looking for Bailey will be easier that way.'

She waited until he'd slid behind the wheel. 'I wish I had a current picture of her. I know they'd have one at the salon where she works – on her cosmetologist's license. But I got so busy I forgot to call and they're closed now.'

He pulled a folded sheet of paper from his shirt pocket. 'I ran her driver's license before I left the office. It's not glamorous, but it's recent.'

Alex's throat closed. In the photo, a clear-eyed Bailey smiled. 'Oh. Bailey.'

Vartanian shot her a puzzled sideways glance. 'I didn't think she looked bad.'

'No. She looks good. I'm so relieved and . . . sad at the same time. She was so out of her mind the last time I saw her. I kept wishing I could see her look like this again.' Alex pursed her lips. 'Now she might be dead.'

Vartanian gave her shoulder a quick squeeze. 'Don't think it. Think positive.'

Alex took a deep breath, her shoulder tingling from his touch. This was something to think about that was positive. 'All right. I'll try.'

Atlanta, Monday, January 29, 7:30 P.M.

She was married now, to some rich stockbroker she'd met in college. She'd gone to college, while he'd . . . *While I rotted in a cell.* His payback list had become quite long during his unfortunate incarceration. She was right up there near the top.

Her heels clacked on the concrete floor as she came out of the elevator to the parking garage. She was dressed to the nines tonight. She wore mink and some perfume that probably cost four hundred dollars an ounce. The pearls at her neck gleamed in the dome light as she settled herself behind the wheel.

He waited patiently for her to shut her door and start the engine. Then quick as a whisper he slipped the knife to her throat and shoved a handkerchief in her mouth.

'Drive,' he murmured, and he chuckled when, wide-eyed, she obeyed. He told her where to go, where to turn, enjoying the terror in her eyes every time she looked up into her rearview mirror. She didn't recognize him, and while this was advantageous in the everyday, he wanted her to know exactly who now controlled her life. And death.

'Don't tell me you don't know me, Claudia. Think back to the night of your senior prom. It wasn't so long ago.' Her eyes flared wide and he knew the reality of her fate had fully sunk in. He laughed quietly. 'You know that I can't let you live. But if it's any consolation, I wouldn't have anyway.'

Monday, January 29, 7:45 P.M.

Bailey blinked, slowly coming awake. The floor was cold against her cheek. She heard footsteps out in the hall. He was coming. *Not again*.

She braced herself for the light. For the pain. But the door never opened. Instead, she heard another door open and the sick thud of dead weight as someone was thrown into the cell next to her. A voice moaned in pain. It sounded like a man.

Then from the hall *he* spoke, his voice shaking with rage. 'I'll be back in a few hours. Think about what I said. What I did. How much you hurt right now. And think about the right way to answer my questions the next time.'

She clenched her jaw, so afraid she'd cry out, that she'd call attention to herself in some way. But the door in the next cell swung shut and there was only silence.

She'd been spared, for now. For now, there would be no beating, no punishment for her insolent refusal to tell him what he wanted to hear. The voice next door moaned again, so pitifully. It would appear he'd caught another fly in his web.

No one was coming for her. Nobody was even looking for her. *I'll never see my baby again*. Tears squeezed from her eyes and ran down her cheek. It was no use to even scream. Anyone who could hear her was locked inside, too.

Atlanta, Monday, January 29, 9:15 P.M.

'Bailey Crighton?' The woman who'd introduced herself as Sister Anne put a tray full of dirty dishes on the kitchen counter. 'What about her?'

In front of him Alex Fallon stood clutching Bailey's driver's license picture that she'd already shown at four other shelters. 'I'm looking for her. Have you seen her?'

'Depends. You a cop?'

Alex shook her head. 'No,' she said and Daniel noticed she said nothing about him.

Watching Alex Fallon in action had been an educational experience. She'd never outright lied anywhere they'd gone, but was quite adept at telling only as much as she needed to tell and letting people believe what they would. But she was tired and discouraged and now he could hear a tremble in her voice that made him want to make it better somehow. Any way he could.

'I'm a nurse. Bailey's my stepsister and she's missing. Have you seen her?'

Sister Anne cast a suspicious glance at Daniel.

'Please,' he mouthed silently and her eyes softened.

'She comes here every Sunday. Yesterday was the first day she'd missed in years. I've been worried.'

It was the first time anyone had admitted to having seen Bailey, although Daniel could tell a few of them had seen her and had been too skittish to admit it.

'She comes here on Sundays?' Alex asked. 'Why?'

Sister Anne smiled. 'Her pancakes are the best around.'

'She makes happy-face pancakes for the kids,' another woman said as she brought in another tray of dirty dishes. 'What's wrong with Bailey?'

'She's missing,' Sister Anne said.

'She volunteers here, then?' Daniel asked, and Sister Anne bobbed her head.

'For five years now, ever since she's been sober. How long has she been missing?'

'Since Thursday night.' Alex straightened her spine. 'Do you know Hope?'

'Of course. That doll-baby can talk a blue streak and I love hearing every word.' She frowned abruptly, glancing at them through narrowed eyes. 'Is Hope missing, too?'

'No, she's been staying with me and my cousin,' Alex said quickly. 'But she's not well. She hasn't said a word since I got here on Saturday.'

Sister Anne looked perplexed. 'That's very wrong. Tell me what happened.'

Alex did and Sister Anne started shaking her head. 'There is *no* way that Bailey would ever abandon that child. Hope was her life.' She sighed. 'Hope saved her life.'

'So Bailey was a regular here before she got sober?' Daniel asked.

'Oh, yeah. Here and at the methadone clinic up the

street. But that was then. I've seen junkies come and go for thirty years. I can tell who's gonna make it and who's not. Bailey was gonna make it. Coming here every week was her way of keeping her head straight, of making her remember what she was so she wouldn't go back. She was making a life for herself and that baby of hers. There is no way she gave up on Hope.' She bit at her lip, hesitating. 'Did you talk to her daddy?'

'Hope's daddy?' Alex asked tentatively.

'No.' Sister Anne looked at Alex shrewdly. 'Bailey's daddy.'

Alex stiffened and Daniel sensed what had been discouragement was now fear.

'Alex?' he murmured behind her. 'Are you okay?'

She jerked a nod. 'No, I haven't talked to her father.' Her voice was cool, careful, and Daniel knew by now that meant she was scared. 'Do you know where he is?'

Sister Anne heaved a giant sigh. 'Out there somewhere. Bailey never gave up hope that he'd turn from the life and come home. I know she spent hours pokin' her head in every godforsaken corner of this town, lookin' for him.' She gave Alex a sideways look. 'She still lives in that old house in Dutton, hoping he'll come back.'

Alex grew even stiffer, more afraid. Daniel gave in to the urge to touch her that he'd been fighting since she'd met his eyes back in his living room. He needed to connect with her again, needed her to know he was there, that she wasn't alone and didn't need to be afraid. So he covered her shoulders with his hands and pulled gently until she leaned against him.

'I hate that house,' she whispered.

'I know,' he whispered back. And he did. He knew what she meant by 'that house' and what had happened there. Daniel had read the articles Luke had downloaded and now he knew about Alex's mother, how she'd put a .38 to her head to end her life, how Alex had found her body. All on the same day Alicia's body had been found.

Sister Anne was studying Alex intently. 'Bailey hates that place, too, honey. But she stays, hopin' her daddy will come home.'

Alex was trembling and Daniel tightened his hold. 'Did he come home?' he asked.

'No. Leastways she never told me.'

Alex straightened her shoulders and pulled far enough away that she no longer leaned against him. 'Thank you, Sister. If you hear anything, will you call me?' She tore a corner from the copy of Bailey's driver's license photo and wrote her name and cell phone number. 'And could you talk to Hope? We haven't been able to get through.'

Sister Anne's smile was sympathetic and sad. 'You couldn't stop me. I don't drive anymore, though, so it'd be hard for me to get down to Dutton.'

'We'll bring her to you,' Daniel said, and Alex twisted back to look at him, surprised gratitude on her face. 'If it wasn't safe for you,' he murmured, 'it's certainly not safe for you and Hope.'

'It was safe for Bailey and Hope,' she protested.

'Bailey knew her way around. You don't. When's a good time, Sister?'

'Pick any time. I'm always here.'

'It'll be tomorrow night then.' Daniel squeezed Alex's shoulders lightly. 'Let's go.'

They'd gotten to the door when a young woman stopped them. She couldn't have been more than twenty, but like all the other women there, her eyes were far older. 'Excuse me,' she said. 'Somebody heard you in the kitchen. Are you a nurse?'

Daniel felt her change. She'd put her fear aside and was instantly focused on the woman who stood before her. She nodded, her eyes assessing. 'Yes. Are you sick?'

'No, it's my little girl.' The young woman pointed to a cot in the middle of a sea of cots where a child lay, curled in a ball. 'She's got some kind of rash on her foot and it's hurting her. I was at the clinic all day, but if you don't get here by six all the beds get filled.'

Alex put her hand on the woman's back. 'Let's take a look.' Daniel followed, curious to see her in action. 'What's your name?' she asked the mother.

'Sarah. Sarah Jenkins. This is Tamara.'

Alex smiled at the girl, who looked about four or five. 'Hi there, Tamara. Can I look at your foot?' She was efficient but gentle as she examined the child. 'It's not serious,' she said, and the mother relaxed. 'It's impetigo. Looks like it might have started with a cut, though. Has she had a tetanus S-H-O-T recently?'

Tamara's eyes widened with fear. 'I have to get a shot?'

Alex blinked. 'You're pretty smart, Tamara. Well, Mom, has she had one?'

Sarah nodded. 'Right before Christmas.'

'Then you don't need one,' she said to Tamara, who looked relieved. Alex looked up at Sister Anne. 'Do you keep any ointments here?'

'Only Neosporin.'

'This is pretty inflamed. Neosporin won't do too much. When I come back I'll bring something stronger. Until then, wash it and keep it covered. You have gauze?'

The nun nodded. 'A little.'

'Then use it and I'll bring you some more of that, too. And no scratching, Tamara.'

Tamara's lip pushed out in a pout. 'It itches.'

'I know,' she said softly. 'You're just going to have to tell yourself it doesn't.'

'You mean lie?' Tamara asked, and Alex made a face.

'Well . . . more like a trick. You ever see a magician put someone in a closet and make them disappear?'

Tamara nodded. 'On a cartoon.'

'That's what you have to do. You have to imagine all your itchiness going in a closet and you pushhh the door cloooosed.' She pushed with her hands, demonstrating. 'Then your itch is trapped in the closet and not on you anymore. A girl smart enough to spell "shot" should be able to trick the itch into the closet.'

'I'll try.'

'You might have to try a few times. The itch won't want to go in the closet. You have to concentrate.' She sounded as if she spoke from experience. 'And keep your fingers out of your eyes. That's important, too.'

'Thank you,' the mother said when Alex stood up.

'It was nothing. She's a smart girl.' But she'd eased the mother's mind, and Daniel thought that was a great deal more than nothing. Plus, in helping the woman she'd put her own fear aside. 'Sister, I'll see you tomorrow.'

Sister Anne nodded. 'I'll be here. I'm always here.'

Dutton, Monday, January 29, 10:00 P.M.

The carousel horses were beautiful in the moonlight. He'd always enjoyed this park as a child. But he was no longer a child and the innocence of the park now mocked him as he sat on the bench, reeling from the twisted direction his life had taken.

The bench on which he sat jiggled, then settled with the weight of another. 'You're a fool,' he whispered, keeping his eyes fixed on the carousel horses. 'It was one thing to call me this morning, but meeting here like this. If somebody sees us . . .'

'Dammit.' It was a frightened hiss. 'I got a key.'

He sat up straighter. 'A real one?'

'No. A drawing. But it looks like it could match.'

It did. He'd laid his key on the drawing. It matched perfectly. 'So someone knows.'

'We'll be ruined.' His whisper was shrill. 'We'll go to prison. I can't go to prison.'

Like any of them could? *I'll die first*. But he injected calm certainty into his voice. 'Nobody's going to prison. We'll be fine. He probably just wants money.'

'We need to talk to the others. Come up with a plan.'

'No. Say nothing to the others. Keep your head down and your mouth shut and we'll get through this.' Talking was unhealthy. One of them had talked and that one had been stopped. Permanently. It could and would be done again. 'For now, stay calm, stay quiet, and stay away from me. If you freak out, we're all dead.'

Chapter Six

Atlanta, Monday, January 29, 10:15 P.M.

Vartanian brought his car to a stop in his driveway. 'Are you all right?' His voice was deep and calm in the darkness of his car. 'You've been very quiet.'

She had, in fact, been silent as she struggled to process all the thoughts and fears that warred in her mind. 'I'm fine. I've just been thinking.' She remembered her manners. 'Thank you for going with me tonight,' she said. 'You've been very kind.'

His jaw was tight as he came around to open her door. She followed him up to his house and waited while he disarmed the alarm. 'Come in. I'll get your jacket.'

'And my satchel.'

His smile was grim. 'I didn't think you'd forgotten about it.'

Riley sat up, yawning again. He padded across the room and plopped down at Alex's feet. Vartanian's lips twitched. 'And you're not even a pork chop,' he murmured.

Alex bent over to scratch Riley's ears. 'Did you say "pork chop"?'

'It's a private joke, mine and Riley's. I'll get your coat.' He sighed. 'And satchel.'

Alex watched him go, shaking her head. Men were not creatures she'd ever fully understood. Not that she'd had much practice. Richard had been her first, if she didn't count Wade, which she never did. So that would be . . . one. And wasn't Richard a sterling example of her finesse with members of the opposite sex? That would be . . . no.

Thoughts of Richard always depressed her. She'd failed at their marriage. She'd never been able to be what he needed or the kind of wife she'd wanted to be.

But she wouldn't fail Hope. If nothing else, Bailey's child would have a good life, with or without Bailey. Now both depressed and terrified, she looked around Vartanian's living room for a distraction and found it in the painting over his bar. It made her smile.

'What?' he asked, holding her jacket draped over one arm like a maître d'.

'Your painting.'

He grinned, making him look younger. 'Hey, *Dogs Playing Poker* is a classic.'

'I don't know. Somehow I took you for a man with more sophisticated taste in art.'

His grin dimmed. 'I don't take art too seriously.'

'Because of Simon,' she said quietly. Vartanian's brother had been a painter.

What was left of his grin disappeared, leaving him sober and haunted. 'You know.'

'I read the articles online.' She'd read about the people Simon had killed, including Daniel's parents. She'd read how Daniel assisted in Simon's capture and death.

I'll see you in hell, Simon. She needed to tell him. 'Agent Vartanian, I have information you need to know. When I left the morgue today, I drove to Bailey's house. While I was there I met a man. A reverend. And a soldier, too, I guess.'

He sat on a bar stool, dropping her jacket and satchel to the bar and focusing his piercing blue eyes on her face. 'A reverend and a soldier came to Bailey's house?'

'No. The reverend *was* a soldier, an army chaplain. Bailey had an older brother. His name was Wade. He died a month ago in Iraq.'

'I'm sorry.'

She frowned. 'I'm not sure I am. I guess you think that's pretty rotten of me.'

Something moved in his eyes. 'No. I don't, actually. What did the chaplain say?'

'Reverend Beardsley was with Wade when he died. He heard Wade's last confession and wrote three letters Wade dictated, to me, his father, and Bailey. Beardsley mailed Bailey's and her father's to the old house where Bailey's still living. He didn't mail mine because he didn't have my address, so he gave it to me today.'

'Bailey would have received the letters a few weeks ago. The timing is interesting.'

'I told Beardsley that Bailey was missing, but he wouldn't divulge what Wade had said in his last confession. I begged him for anything that could help me find Bailey, anything that wasn't privileged. Before he died, Wade said, "I'll see you in hell, Simon." '

She blew out a breath and watched as Vartanian paled. 'Wade knew Simon?'

'Apparently so. Just like you know something you haven't told me, Agent Vartanian. I can see it in your face. And I want to know what it is.'

'I killed my brother a week ago. If nothing showed on my face, I wouldn't be human.'

Alex frowned. 'You didn't kill him. The article said that other detective did.'

His eyes flickered. 'We both fired. The other guy just got lucky.'

'So you're not going to tell me.'

'There's nothing to tell. Why are you so sure I know something?'

Alex narrowed her eyes. 'Because you've been way too nice to me.'

'And a man always has an ulterior motive.' He said it darkly.

She shrugged out of his letter jacket. 'In my experience, yes.'

He slid off the stool and stood toe-to-toe with her, forcing her to look way up. 'I've been nice to you because I thought you needed a friend.'

She rolled her eyes. 'Right. I must have "stupid" tattooed on my forehead.'

His blue eyes flashed. 'Fine. I was nice to you because I think you're right – Bailey's disappearance is connected to that woman we found yesterday and I'm ashamed at how the Dutton sheriff, who I thought was my friend, hasn't lifted a goddamn finger to help either of us. That's the truth, Alex, whether you can accept it or not.'

You can't take the truth. As it had that morning, the taunt sprang from nowhere and Alex closed her eyes, quelling the panic. She opened her eyes to find him still staring, every bit as intently as before. 'All right,' she murmured. 'That I can believe.'

He leaned closer. Too close. 'Good, because there's another reason.'

'Do tell,' she said, her voice cool despite the way her heart now pounded.

'I like you. I want to spend time with you when you're not scared to death and vulnerable. And because I respect how you've held up now . . . and back then.'

Her chin lifted. 'Back then?'

'You read my articles, Alex, and I read yours.'

Heat flooded her cheeks. He knew about her breakdown, about her suicide attempt. She wanted to look away, but she refused to be the first to do so. 'I see.'

He searched her eyes, then shook his head. 'No, I

really don't think you do. And maybe that's for the best right now.' He straightened and took a step back and she sucked in a deep breath. 'So Wade knew Simon,' he said. 'Were they the same age?'

'They were in the same class at Jefferson High.' She frowned. 'But you have a sister who's the same age as I am and she went to Bryson Academy.'

'So did I and so did Simon at first. My father went there, too, as did his father.'

'Bryson was an expensive school. I imagine it still is.'

Daniel shrugged. 'We were comfortable.'

Alex's smile was wry. 'No, you were rich. That school cost more than some colleges. My mother tried to get us in on a scholarship, but our kin hadn't fought alongside Lee and Stonewall.' She injected a drawl into her voice and his smile was equally wry.

'You're right. We had financial wealth. Simon didn't graduate from Bryson,' he said. 'He got expelled and had to go to Jefferson.'

To the public school. 'Lucky us,' Alex said. 'So that's how Wade and Simon met.'

'I assume so. I was away at college by then. What was in Wade's letter to you?'

She shrugged. 'He asked my forgiveness and wished me a good life.'

'What was he asking forgiveness for?'

Alex shook her head. 'It could have been any number of things. He wasn't specific.'

'But you've got it narrowed to one,' he said, and she lifted her brows.

'Remind me not to play poker with you. I think Riley's dog pals are more my speed.'

'Alex.'

She huffed a breath. 'Fine. Alicia and I were twins. Identical twins.'

'Yeah,' he said dryly. 'I got that this morning.'

She grimaced in sympathy. 'I truly had no idea you'd be so startled.' He was still hiding something, but for now she'd play his game. 'You've heard all the twin stories about switching places? Well, Alicia and I did that more than a few times. I think Mama always knew. Anyway, Alicia was the party animal and I was the practical one.'

'No,' he said, deadpan, and she chuckled, in spite of herself.

'A few times we'd switch places for tests, until the teachers wised up. I felt so guilty, cheating like that, so I told them and Alicia was so mad. I was a "downer", no fun at the parties, so Alicia started going alone. She had a string of boyfriends from Dutton to Atlanta and back and a couple times she double-booked. Once, I stepped in.'

Daniel became suddenly serious. 'I don't like the direction this is going.'

'I went to this B-list party – the one she didn't want to go to, but didn't want to get excluded from the next time around. Wade was there. He was never an A-list party kind of guy, although he always wanted to be. He . . . put the moves on Alicia. Me.'

Daniel grimaced. 'That's disgusting.'

It had been. No one had ever touched her there before and Wade hadn't been gentle. It still made her sick to her stomach to remember. 'Well, yes, but technically we weren't related. My mother never married his father, but it was still gross.' And terrifying.

'So what did you do?'

'I slugged him, on pure reflex. Broke his nose, then kneed him in the . . . you know.'

Vartanian winced. 'I know.'

She could still see Wade lying on the floor, in a cursing, bleeding fetal ball. 'We were both shocked. Then he was humiliated and I was still shocked.'

'So what happened? Did he get in trouble?'

'No. Alicia and I got grounded for a month and Wade walked away whistlin' Dixie.'

'That wasn't fair.'

'But that was life in our house.' Alex studied his face. There was still something . . . But he was a far better poker player than she. 'I never thought I'd get a deathbed apology. I guess you never know what you're gonna do when the Reaper knocks.'

'I guess not. Listen, do you have that chaplain's contact information?'

'Sure.' Alex dug it out of her satchel. 'Why?'

'Because I want to talk to him. The timing's too convenient. Now, about tomorrow.'

'Tomorrow?'

'Yeah. Your cousin leaves tomorrow, right? How about I bring Riley to meet your niece tomorrow night? I can bring some pizza or something, then we can see if Hope likes dogs before we take her to talk to Sister Anne.'

She blinked, a little stunned. She'd never thought he'd been serious. Then she remembered his hands on her shoulders, supporting her when her knees wanted to buckle. Maybe Daniel Vartanian was really just a very nice man. 'That will work. Thank you, Daniel. It's a date.'

He shook his head, his expression changing, almost as if he was daring her to disagree. 'Not hardly. A date doesn't typically involve children or dogs.' His eyes were totally serious and sent a shiver down her spine. A nice shiver, she thought. The kind she hadn't had in a very long time. 'And it definitely does not involve nuns.'

She swallowed hard, certain her cheeks were red as flame. 'I see.'

His hand lifted to her face, hesitating a moment before his thumb swept across her lower lip and she shivered again, harder this time. 'Now I think you finally do,' he murmured, then flinched. He pulled his cell phone from his pocket where it had apparently buzzed him out of what was becoming a very interesting mood.

'Vartanian.' His face went expressionless. It was his

case, then. Alex thought of the woman on the table in the morgue and wondered who she was. If someone had finally missed her. 'How many tickets did she buy?' he asked, then shook his head. 'No, I don't need you to spell it. I know the family. Thanks, you've been a big help.'

He hung up and stunned her once again by pulling his sweatshirt over his head and jogging toward the stairs. On his way he balled the sweatshirt and shot it basketball style at a laundry chute in the wall. He missed, but didn't stop to try again. 'Stay there,' he called over his shoulder. 'I'll be back.'

Wide-eyed and open-mouthed, she watched him disappear up the stairs. The man had a beautiful back, broad and well-muscled and covered with smooth, golden skin. The glimpse of his chest hadn't been half bad either. *Hell*. There was nothing half bad about that man. Alex realized she'd reached out to touch. *Ridiculous*. She considered the look in his eyes just before his cell had gone off. *Maybe not so ridiculous after all*.

She drew a shuddering breath and picked up the sweatshirt, indulging the urge to sniff it before stuffing it down the chute. *Be careful, Alex*. What had he called it? *Unfamiliar ground*. She cast a wistful look up the stairs, knowing he'd probably pulled off the jeans when he'd reached the top. *But damn fine unfamiliar ground it was*.

In less than two minutes he was thundering back

down the stairs, dressed in his dark suit, tugging his tie into place. Without slowing down, he picked up her satchel and kept walking. 'Get your jacket and come on. I'll follow you back to Dutton.'

'That's not necessary,' she started, but he was already out the door.

'I'm going there anyway. I'll bring Riley to your house by six-thirty tomorrow night.' He opened her car door and waited till she'd buckled up before closing her door.

She rolled down the window. 'Daniel,' she called after him.

He turned to face her, walking backward. 'What?'

'Thank you.'

His steps faltered. 'You're welcome. I'll see you tomorrow night.'

Dutton, Monday, January 29, 11:35 P.M.

Daniel got out of his car and looked up at the house on the hill with a wince. This was not going to be good. Janet Bowie had used a credit card to buy her own admission ticket to Fun-N-Sun and the tickets of seven other people, a group of kids.

Now he got to tell state congressman Robert Bowie his daughter was thought dead. With heavy steps he climbed the steep driveway to the Bowie mansion and rang the bell.

The door was opened by a sweaty young man wearing running shorts. 'Yes?'

Daniel pulled out his shield. 'I'm Special Agent Vartanian, Georgia Bureau of Investigation. I need to talk with Congressman and Mrs Bowie.'

The man narrowed his eyes. 'My parents are asleep.'

Daniel blinked. 'Michael?' It had been nearly sixteen years since he'd seen Michael Bowie. Michael had been a skinny fourteen-year-old when Daniel had gone away to college. He wasn't skinny any longer. 'I'm sorry, I didn't recognize you.'

'You, on the other hand, haven't changed a bit.' It was said in a way that could just as easily be taken as a compliment or as an insult. 'You need to come back tomorrow.'

Daniel put his hand on the door when Michael started to close it. 'I need to talk to your parents,' he repeated quietly but firmly. 'I wouldn't be here if it weren't important.'

'Michael, who's calling at this time of night?' a booming voice thundered.

'State police.' Michael stepped back and Daniel stepped into the grand foyer of Bowie Hall, one of the few antebellum mansions the Yankees hadn't managed to burn.

Congressman Bowie was tying the belt of a smoking jacket. His face was impassive, but in his eyes Daniel saw apprehension. 'Daniel Vartanian. I heard you'd come into town today. What can I do for you?'

'I'm sorry to bother you at this time of night, Congressman,' Daniel began. 'I'm investigating the murder of a woman found in Arcadia yesterday.'

'At the bike race.' Bowie nodded. 'I read about it in today's *Review*.'

Daniel drew a quiet breath. 'I think the victim may be your daughter, sir.'

Bowie drew back, shaking his head. 'No, it's not possible. Janet is in Atlanta.'

'When did you last see your daughter, sir?'

Bowie's jaw hardened. 'Last week, but her sister talked to her yesterday morning.'

'Can I talk to your other daughter, Mr Bowie?' Daniel asked.

'It's late. Patricia's asleep.'

'I know it's late, but if we've made a mistake, we need to know so we can keep searching for this woman's identity. Somebody is waiting for her to come home, sir.'

'I understand. Patricia! Come down here. And make sure you're properly dressed.'

Two doors opened upstairs and both Mrs Bowie and a young girl came down the stairs, the girl looking uncertain. 'What's this about, Bob?' Mrs Bowie asked. She recognized Daniel and frowned. 'Why is he here? Bob?'

'Calm down, Rose. This is all a mistake and we're going to clear it up right now.' Bowie turned to the young girl. 'Patricia, you said you talked to Janet yesterday morning. You said that she was sick and not driving down for supper.'

Patricia blinked innocently and Daniel sighed inside. *Sisters covering for each other*.

'Janet said she had the flu.' Patricia smiled, trying for sophisticated. 'Why, did she get a parking ticket or something? That's just like Janet.'

Bowie had grown as pale as had his wife. 'Patricia,' he said hoarsely, 'Agent Vartanian is investigating a murder. He thinks Janet is the victim. Don't cover for her.'

Patricia's mouth fell open. 'What?'

'Did you really talk to your sister, Patricia?' Daniel asked gently.

The girl's eyes filled with horrified tears. 'No. She asked me to tell everybody she was sick. She had somewhere else to go that day. But it can't be her. It can't.'

Mrs Bowie made a panicked sound. 'Bob.'

Bowie put his arm around his wife. 'Michael, get your mother a chair.'

Michael had already done so and helped his mother sit while Daniel focused on Patricia. 'When did she ask you to cover for her?'

'Wednesday night. She said she was spending the weekend with . . . friends.'

'This is important, Patricia. Which friends?' Daniel pressed. From the corner of his eye he watched Mrs Bowie sink into a chair, visibly shaking.

Patricia looked miserably at her parents, tears

streaming down her cheeks. 'She has a boyfriend. She knew you wouldn't approve. I'm sorry.'

Ashen, Bowie looked at Daniel. 'What do you need from us, Daniel?'

'Hair from her brush. We'll need to fingerprint the room she uses when she's here.' He hesitated. 'The name of her dentist.'

Bowie blanched, but swallowed and nodded. 'You'll have it.'

'Oh, God. We never should have let her have that apartment in Atlanta.' Mrs Bowie was crying, rocking, her hands covering her face.

'She has an apartment in Atlanta?' Daniel asked.

Bowie's nod was barely perceptible. 'She's with the orchestra.'

'She's a cellist,' Daniel said quietly. 'But she comes home on weekends?'

'Sunday evenings, mostly. She comes home for supper.' Bowie tightened his jaw, struggling for composure. 'Not so much lately. She's growing up. Away. But she's only twenty-two.' He broke, dropping his chin to his chest, and Daniel looked away, giving him privacy in his grief.

'Her room is upstairs,' Michael murmured.

'Thank you. I'll have a CSU van out here as quickly as possible. Patricia, I need to know everything you know about Janet and her boyfriend.' Daniel put his hand on Bob Bowie's arm. 'I'm so sorry, sir.'

Bowie jerked a nod and said nothing.

Dutton, Tuesday, January 30, 12:55 A.M.

'What's going on here?'

Daniel stopped short. A wave of anger swept through him and he tamped it back. 'Well, if it isn't the elusive Sheriff Loomis. Let me introduce myself. I'm Special Agent Daniel Vartanian and I've left you six messages since Sunday.'

'Don't get sarcastic with me, Daniel.' Frank scowled at the small army that had descended on Bowie Hall. 'Goddamn GBI has overrun my town. Like locusts.'

In truth, only one car and one van belonged to GBI personnel. Three of the police cars were from Dutton's small force and one was from Arcadia. Sheriff Corchran himself had come, offering his condolences to the Bowies and his help to Daniel.

Deputy Mansfield, Loomis's second in command, had arrived shortly after Ed's crime scene van had pulled into the drive, outraged at not having been the one to process Janet's bedroom, in direct contrast to Corchran's helpful attitude.

Of the other cars that lined the drive, one belonged to Dutton's mayor, two others to Congressman Bowie's aides. Still another belonged to Dr Granville, who was currently overseeing the near-hysterical state of Mrs Bowie.

One of the cars belonged to Jim Woolf. The Bowies had given him no comment and Daniel had held him off with the promise of a statement when the ID was confirmed.

It had been, just minutes before. One of Ed's techs had brought a card bearing the victim's fingerprints with him and had almost immediately matched the prints to those taken from a crystal vase next to Janet Bowie's bed. Daniel himself had confirmed the news to Bob Bowie and Bowie had just climbed the stairs to his wife's room.

Shrieking from the upstairs bedroom told Daniel that Bowie had told his wife. Both he and Frank looked toward the upstairs, then back at each other. 'Do you have something to say, Frank?' Daniel asked coldly. 'Because I'm a little busy right now.'

Frank's face darkened. 'This is my town, Daniel Vartanian. Not yours. You left.'

Again Daniel tamped down his temper, and when he spoke, it was evenly. 'It may not be my town, but it's my case, Frank. If you really wanted to be of some help, you might have returned any of the messages I've left on your voicemail.'

Frank's gaze never faltered, becoming almost belligerent. 'I was out of town yesterday and today. I didn't get your messages until I got back tonight.'

'I sat outside your office for nearly forty-five minutes today,' Daniel said quietly. 'Wanda said you couldn't be disturbed. I don't care if you needed to get away, but you wasted my time. Time I could have been looking for the man who killed Janet Bowie.'

Frank finally looked away. 'I'm sorry, Daniel.' But the apology was stiffly delivered. 'The last week has been difficult. Your parents . . . they were my friends. The funeral was difficult enough, but the media . . . After dealing with reporters all week, I needed some space. I told Wanda not to let anybody know I was gone. I should have called you.'

A little of Daniel's anger melted away. 'It's okay. But Frank, I really need that police report – the one on Alicia Tremaine's murder. Please get it for me.'

'I'll get it for you first thing in the morning,' Frank promised, 'when Wanda comes in. She knows how everything's filed in the basement. You're sure it's Janet?'

'Her fingerprints match.'

'Dammit. Who did this?'

'Well, now that we know who she is, we can start investigating. Frank, if you needed help, why didn't you call me?'

Frank's jaw squared. 'I didn't say I needed help. I said I needed space. I went up to my cabin to be alone.' He turned on his heel and headed for the door.

'Okay,' Daniel murmured, trying not to feel stung. 'Frank?'

Frank looked back. 'What?' It was very nearly a snap.

'Bailey Crighton. I think she really is missing.'

Frank's lip curled. 'Thanks for your opinion, *Special Agent Vartanian*. Good night.'

Daniel shook off the hurt. He had work to do and couldn't afford to worry about Frank Loomis. Frank was a grown man. If and when he needed help, Daniel would be there for him.

Ed came up behind him. 'We're dusting her room. I found a few old diaries in a drawer. A few matchbooks. Not much else. What did you find out about the boyfriend?'

'His name is Lamar Washington, African-American. He plays in a jazz club. Patricia didn't know where.'

Ed held out a baggie filled with matchbooks. 'Could be one of these places.'

Daniel took the bag. 'I'll write down the names, then give them back. Patricia said Janet made it sound like a fling, that Janet never intended to bring him home.'

'That could make a man mad enough to beat a woman's face in,' Ed said. 'But it doesn't explain copying the Tremaine scene.'

'I know,' Daniel said. 'But it's all I have for now. I'm going to check out the jazz clubs once I'm done here.'

'We're going to check out Janet's apartment.' Ed held up a key ring. 'Janet's brother Michael got us the key to her place.'

When Ed was gone, Daniel went into the sitting room, which was standing room only. Michael Bowie was the only family member in the room. He'd changed into a black suit and his face was haggard in his grief, but he was ever the politician's son. 'Can you give them a statement so they'll go?' Michael murmured. 'I just want them all to go.'

'I'll make it fast,' Daniel murmured back, then cleared his throat. 'Excuse me.' He'd already introduced himself when he'd taken their statements and whereabouts at the time of Janet's death Thursday night. A few postured, but all complied. 'We've tentatively identified the body found in Arcadia Sunday afternoon as that of Janet Bowie.' No one was surprised at this point. 'We'll run confirmatory DNA testing and I'll schedule a press conference when we have definitive findings.'

Jim Woolf stood up. 'What was the official cause of death?'

'I'll have an official statement as to cause of death tomorrow.' Daniel checked his watch. 'I mean later today. Probably after noon.'

The mayor smoothed his tie. 'Agent Vartanian, do you have any suspects?'

'We have some leads, Mayor Davis,' Daniel said. *That* title felt odd. He'd played football with Garth Davis in high school. Garth had been a thickheaded jock back then, one of the last people Daniel would have expected to run for mayor, much less win. But Garth did come from a long line of politicians. Garth's daddy had been Dutton's mayor for years. 'I'll have an official statement tomorrow.'

'Toby, how is Mrs Bowie?' Woolf asked, directing his question to the town's doctor.

'Resting,' Toby Granville said, but everyone knew that meant 'sedated.' Everyone had heard the poor woman's shrieks when her husband told her the ID was official.

Daniel gestured toward the door. 'It's very late. I'm sure everyone here means to offer their support, but you all need to go home. Please.'

The mayor held back as everyone exited. 'Daniel, do you have any suspects?'

Daniel sighed. The day was catching up to him. 'Garth . . .'

Davis leaned closer. 'I'm going to have all the residents of Dutton calling me as soon as the *Review* hits their front porches. They're going to be worried about the safety of their families. Please give me something more to tell them than you've got leads.'

'That's all I can tell you because it's all we know. We've only just identified her in the last two hours. Give us a day, at least.'

Frowning, Davis nodded. 'You'll call my office?'

'I promise.'

Finally everyone was gone and it was just Daniel and Michael and Toby Granville. 'I thought they'd never leave,' Michael said, his shoulders sagging wearily.

Granville tugged on his tie. 'I'm going to go check on your mother before I head out. You call me if she needs anything during the night.'

Daniel shook both men's hands. 'If there's anything you or your family needs, Michael, please call me.' He stepped through the Bowies' front door and was immediately hit by a strong gusty wind. A storm was blowing in, he thought as he looked down the big hill to the street where three additional news vans had now congregated. The reporters swarmed from the vans when they spied him up on the stoop. *Like locusts*, Daniel thought with an inner wince. He could kind of see Frank's point, in the smallest of ways.

He steeled himself for the onslaught as he made his way down the hill past a Mercedes, two BMWs, a Rolls-Royce, a Jag, and a Lincoln Town Car to where he'd left his own state-issued vehicle. Reporters from the news van had been interviewing Garth, but they swarmed toward him as he passed by.

'Agent Vartanian, can you comment . . .' Daniel lifted his hand, silencing them.

'We've identified the Arcadia victim as Janet Bowie.' Lights flashed as they took their pictures and rolled their video and Daniel put on his best press face.

'Has the congressman been notified?'

Daniel fought the urge to roll his eyes. 'Yes, or I wouldn't be telling you now. No more comments for tonight. I'll be scheduling a press conference for tomorrow. Call the PR hotline at GBI headquarters for the time and venue. Good night.'

He started walking and one of the reporters followed. 'Agent Vartanian, how does it feel investigating a murder in your hometown just a week after your brother's murder?'

Daniel stopped and blinked at the young man holding the microphone. Simon hadn't been *murdered*. To use that word was an affront to victims and their families everywhere. Simon had been *exterminated*. But that word was inflammatory in its own right. So Daniel said only, 'No comment.' The man opened his mouth to push and Daniel gave him a look so cold the reporter took a physical step back.

'No more questions,' the man said in answer to the threat Daniel had left unvoiced.

It was a look Daniel had learned from his father. Freezing men with a single look was one of Arthur Vartanian's many skills. Daniel didn't employ the skill often, but when he did, it was effective. 'Good night.'

When he got to his car, Daniel closed his eyes. He'd dealt with grieving families for years, and it never got easier. But it was Frank Loomis's behavior that bothered him the most. Frank had been the closest thing Daniel had had to a real father. God knew Arthur Vartanian hadn't filled that role. To be the object of Frank's . . . scorn. It stung.

However, Frank was human, and learning of Arthur Vartanian's duplicity in Simon's 'first death' must have been hard to take. It made Frank look foolish, and the press had exacerbated it all, making Frank appear a hokey hometown sheriff who couldn't tie his shoes without help. It was no wonder Frank was angry. *I'd be angry, too.*

He pulled away from the news vans headed toward

Main Street. He was exhausted and he still had to find Lamar Washington's jazz bar before he finally got to sleep.

Dutton, Tuesday, January 30, 1:40 A.M.

They were leaving, Alex thought, standing at the window of the bungalow, watching all the cars come down the hill. Wondering from whose house they'd come. She pulled her robe closer, fighting a chill that had nothing to do with the thermostat.

She'd dreamed again. Thunder and lightning. And screams, jagged piercing screams. She'd been at the morgue and the woman on the table had sat up and stared through sightless eyes. But her eyes were Bailey's, her hand Bailey's as she reached out, her flesh waxy and . . . dead. And she'd said, 'Please. Help me.'

Alex had woken in a cold sweat, shaking so hard she was sure she'd wake Hope. But the child slept heavily. Unsettled, Alex had come out to the living room to pace.

And to worry. *Where are you, Bailey? And how do I take care of your baby girl?*

'Please, God,' she whispered. 'Don't let me mess this up.'

But there was no return whisper in the dark and Alex stood, watching car after car come down the hill.

Then one slowed and stopped in front of her bungalow.

Her stomach tightened in fear and she thought about the gun in the lockbox until she recognized the car and its driver.

Daniel's car rolled down Main Street, past the park with the carousel, stopping outside Alex's rented bungalow. He'd lied to her tonight and it was eating him up.

She'd asked him straight out what he knew and he'd told her there was nothing to tell. Which, he averred, was not a total lie. He didn't have anything to tell her yet. He certainly wouldn't show her the pictures of her sister being violated. Alex Fallon had been through enough without seeing that.

He thought about Wade Crighton. *I'll see you in hell.* Her stepbrother had known Simon, and that could never be good. Wade had tried to rape Alex and for that alone Daniel was glad he was dead. Alex thought she'd kept her story light, but Daniel had seen the truth in her eyes.

And if her stepbrother had tried to molest her once thinking she was Alicia, maybe he'd done so again. Maybe it was Wade in the picture with Alicia Tremaine. The man had two legs, so Daniel was positive it was not Simon, but if they'd known each other . . .

And who were the other girls? It had been nagging him. Maybe they were local girls. Maybe they'd gone to the public school. Daniel wouldn't have known them, but Simon might have. Daniel wondered if there were any other small-town murders he just hadn't heard about yet. He wondered if the other girls in the pictures were dead, too.

Give the pictures to Chase. The thought had been circling his mind for a week. He had turned the pictures over to the Philly police, which was the only thing that was letting him get any sleep at all. But Daniel was sure Vito Ciccotelli hadn't had time to do anything with the envelope full of pictures he'd given him less than two weeks ago. Vito and his partner were still up to their asses cleaning up the mess Simon had left behind.

I'll see you in hell, Simon. Daniel wondered what messes Wade and Simon had left behind, although any crimes they'd committed would be more than ten years old. He had a brand-new crime. He owed his concentration to Janet Bowie. He needed to find out who hated her enough to kill her in such a way.

Then again, Janet Bowie might have simply been a convenient target and not the object of any rage or revenge. Or . . . Daniel thought of Congressman Bowie. The man had taken some tough stances on controversial issues. Maybe somebody hated *him* enough to kill his daughter. But why the tie to Alicia? Why now? And why leave a key?

He'd put his car in gear when the bungalow door opened and Alex stepped onto the porch and his breath caught in his throat. She wore a sensible robe that covered her from her chin to her toes. It should have made her look dowdy and plain, but all he could think about was what lay underneath. The wind had kicked up, tossing her glossy hair, and she scooped it back with one hand to stare at him across the tiny front yard.

There was no smile on her face. The thought registered as he killed his engine and crossed her yard, single-minded in his intent. To leave her, to drive on by, never entered his mind, only to have now what he'd wanted earlier, what the call from the Fun-N-Sun security chief had kept him from taking. He needed to see that wide-eyed wonder again, the look in her eyes when she'd finally understood what he wanted from her. He needed to see that she wanted him, too.

Without slowing for a greeting, he took the porch stairs in one step, took her face in his hands, covered her mouth with his, and took what he needed. She made a hungry sound deep in her throat and leaned up on her toes, trying to get closer, and the kiss exploded into motion and heat.

She let go of her hair and her robe to clutch at the lapels of his coat, propelling her mouth into his. Daniel let go of her face to pull her arms around his neck. He splayed his hands across her slender back and pulled until her body was flush against him and he took what he wanted as the wind whistled and screamed around them.

It had been too long, was all he could think, all he could hear over the wind and the pounding of his own pulse in his ears. Too long since he'd felt like this. Alive. Invincible. Too damn long. Or maybe never.

Too soon she slid back down until her heels hit the porch, ending the kiss and taking her warmth with her. Needing more, he ran his lips over her jaw and buried his face in the curve of her shoulder. He shuddered, breathing hard as her hands stroked his hair, soothing. And as his pulse slowed, his mind returned and his cheeks heated in embarrassment at the depth of his need. 'I'm sorry,' he murmured, lifting his head. 'I don't normally do things like that.'

She traced his lips with her fingers. 'Neither do I. But I needed it tonight. Thank you.'

Annoyance bubbled up through him. 'Stop thanking me.' It was almost a snarl and she flinched as if he'd struck her. Feeling about an inch tall, he bowed his head and caught her hand, bringing her fingers back to his lips when she tried to pull away. 'I'm sorry. But I don't want you thinking I'm doing this for any other reason than that I wanted to.' *Needed* to. 'I wanted to,' he repeated. 'I wanted *you*. I still do.'

She drew a breath and he could see her pulse throbbing at the hollow of her throat. The wind was whipping her hair and once again she scooped it back out of her face. 'I see.' Her lips curved to lighten her words, but her eyes were stark. Haunted, even.

'What happened?' he demanded.

She shook her head. 'Nothing.'

Daniel clenched his jaw. 'Alex.'

She looked away. 'Nothing. I just had a bad dream, that's all.' She looked back and met his eyes. 'I had a bad dream, so I got up. And there you were.'

He pressed his lips to her palm. 'I stopped here because I was thinking about you. And there you were. And I couldn't stop myself.'

She shivered and he glanced down as she shifted, covering one totally bare foot with the other. He frowned. 'Alex, you're not wearing any shoes.'

Her lips curved, sincerely this time. 'I wasn't expecting to stand out on my porch kissing you.' She leaned up and into his mouth, kissing him a good deal more softly than he'd kissed her. 'But I liked it.'

And it was suddenly as simple as that. He smiled down at her. 'Go back into your house and lock your door and cover your feet. I'll see you tomorrow night. Six-thirty.'

Chapter Seven

Dutton, Tuesday, January 30, 1:55 A.M.

Alex closed the door and leaned against it, eyes closed. Heart still racing. She brought her hands to her face, smelling his scent that lingered on her palms. She'd almost forgotten how good a man could smell. With a sigh she opened her eyes, then pressed her hands to her mouth to muffle a shriek.

Meredith sat at the table choosing a hat for Mr Potato Head. She grinned as she plugged the hat in the hole meant for the feet because lips already protruded from the top of the head. 'I thought I was gonna have to bring you your shoes.'

Alex ran her tongue over her teeth. 'You were sitting there the whole time?'

'Mostly.' Her grin widened. 'I heard the car stop outside, then heard you open the door. I was afraid you'd decided to test your new . . . thing.' She lifted a brow.

'Hope's asleep. You can call it a gun.'

'Oh,' Meredith said, blinking innocently. 'That, too.'

Alex laughed. 'You're so bad.'

'I know.' She waggled her brows. 'So was he? Bad, I mean. It sounded bad.'

Alex shot her a guarded look. 'He's very nice.'

'Nice is not nice. Bad is nice. She'll tell me all,' she said to the potato-head, which looked more like a Picasso-head with every feature out of place. 'I have my ways.'

'You scare me sometimes, Mer. Why are you playing with this? Hope's asleep.'

'Because I like to play with toys. You should try it, Alex. It might relax you a little.'

Alex sat down at the table. 'I am relaxed.'

'She lies. She's wound tighter than a corkscrew,' Meredith said to the potato-head. Then her eyes grew sober. 'What are you dreaming, Alex? Still the screams?'

'Yes.' Alex took the toy, aimlessly twirling an ear. 'And the body I saw today.'

'I should have gone instead.'

'No, I needed to see for myself that it wasn't Bailey. But in my dream it is. She sits up and says, "Please. Help me."'

'Your subconscious is a powerful force. You want her to be alive, and so do I, but you have to come to terms with what happens if she's not, or if you never find her at all. Or maybe worse, if you find her and can't fix her.'

Alex gritted her teeth. 'You make me sound like some Dr Roboto control freak.'

'You are, honey,' Meredith said gently. 'Just look.'

Alex looked at the toy in her hands. Meredith's Picasso-head was no more, every feature now properly placed in the right slot. 'This is just a toy,' she said, annoyed.

'No, it's not,' Meredith said sadly, 'but you keep on thinking that if you need to.'

'All right. I like control. I like to have everything neatly labeled. That's not bad.'

'Nope. And sometimes you get a wild hair and buy a *thing*.'

'Or kiss a man I just met?'

'That, too, so you aren't without hope.' Meredith winced a little. 'No pun intended.'

'Of course not. But I think that's exactly why Bailey gave her that name.'

'I agree. These toys are important, Alex. Don't discount them. Play takes our minds to a place where our guard comes down. Remember that when you play with Hope.'

'Daniel's bringing his dog over tomorrow to see if Hope likes animals.'

'That's nice of him.'

Alex raised a brow. 'I thought nice wasn't nice.'

'Only when it comes to sex, kid. I'm going back to sleep. You should try, too.'

Tuesday, January 30, 4:00 A.M.

Someone was crying. Bailey listened hard. It wasn't the man in the next cell. She wasn't sure he was even conscious anymore. No, the weeping came from farther away. She looked up at the ceiling, expecting to see speakers. She saw none, but it didn't mean they weren't there. *He* might try to brainwash her.

Because she hadn't told him what he wanted to know. Not yet. *Not ever.*

She closed her eyes. *Or maybe I'm just losing my mind.* The weeping abruptly stopped and she looked up at the ceiling again. And made herself think of Hope. *You're not losing your mind, Bailey. You can't. Hope needs you.*

It had been the mantra she'd chanted when Hope was a baby, when Bailey had wanted a fix so bad she thought she'd die. *Hope needs you.* It had gotten her through and would continue to do so. *If he doesn't kill me first.* Which was a definite possibility.

Then in the next cell she heard a noise. She held her breath and listened as the sound became a scraping. Someone was scraping at the wall between the two cells.

She pulled herself to her hands and knees, grimacing when the room spun around her. She crawled toward the wall, a few inches at a time, then breathed. And waited.

The scraping stilled, but a tapping took its place, the

same rhythm again and again. Code? Dammit. She didn't know any codes. She hadn't been a Girl Scout.

It could be a trap. It could be *him*, trying to trick her.

Or it could be another human. Tentatively she reached into the dark and tapped back. The tapping on the other side stopped and the scraping began again. She'd been wrong. The scraping wasn't on the wall, it was on the floor. Wincing at the pain in her fingertips, Bailey pushed at the old concrete floor and felt it crumble.

She drew a sharp breath, then let it out, dizzy in her disappointment. It didn't matter. Whoever was scraping was digging a tunnel to another cell. A tunnel to nowhere.

The scraping stilled once again and Bailey heard footsteps in the hall. *He was coming*. God help her, she prayed he was coming for the other guy, the scraper. *Not me. Please not me*. But God didn't listen and the door to her cell swung open.

She squinted at the light, weakly raising one hand in front of her face.

He laughed. 'It's playtime, Bailey.'

Tuesday, January 30, 4:00 A.M.

He was a fortunate man to live in a county with so many drainage ditches. He leaned to one side and let the blanket-wrapped body fall to the ground. She'd died so beautifully, begging his mercy as he'd done his worst. She'd been so prissy and full of contempt when she'd held the power. Now the power was his. She'd paid for her sins.

So would the four *pillars of the community* who remained. He'd gotten the attention of his first two targets with the first note, with his tracing of the key that would exactly match their own. He'd get some of their money with the second, due to be delivered to the same two some time later today. It was time to begin to divide and conquer. He'd take down the first two, and by the time he was finished they'd be ruined, every last one of them. *And I?* He smiled. *I get to watch it all crumble and fall.*

He pulled the blanket away from her foot and gave a final nod.

The key was there. In the *Review*'s picture of Janet, she hadn't been wearing her key, so the first one must have gotten lost somewhere. Disappointing, but he'd made sure this one was tied on extra tight. The threat would be delivered. *Take that, Vartanian.*

Dutton, Tuesday, January 30, 5:30 A.M.

A loud creak woke her and Alex snapped her head up, listening. She'd fallen asleep on the sofa after Meredith had gone to bed. She heard the creak again and knew she hadn't dreamed it. Something or someone was on her front porch. Thinking of the gun in the lockbox, she quietly grabbed the cell phone she'd left on the end table instead.

Hell of a lot of good a locked-up gun did her now, but at least she could call 911. Although that wouldn't do a hell of a lot of good either, if Sheriff Loomis's response to Bailey's disappearance was his norm. She slipped into her kitchen and chose the biggest butcher knife in the drawer, then crept to the window and peeked out.

Then let out the breath she'd been holding. It was just the paperboy, who looked like he was closer to college-aged. He was filling out a form on a clipboard, the small flashlight clenched between his teeth giving his face an unearthly glow. Just then he looked up and saw her. Startled, he let the flashlight fall from his teeth to the porch with a clatter. Eyes wide, he stared, and Alex realized he could see the knife in her hand.

Lowering the knife, she cranked the window open a crack. 'You scared me.'

His swallow was audible in the predawn stillness. 'You scared me worse, ma'am.'

Her lips quirked and tentatively he smiled back. 'I didn't order the paper,' she said.

'I know, but Miz Delia said she'd rented the bungalow. The *Review* gives a free week to folks new to the neighborhood.'

She lifted her brows. 'You get many new people to the neighborhood?'

He grinned shyly. 'No, ma'am.' He handed her the paper and the form he'd been filling out. She had to crank the window a little wider to take it from him.

'Thank you,' she whispered. 'Don't forget your flashlight.'

He picked up the light. 'Welcome to Dutton, Miss Fallon. Have a nice day.'

She cranked the window closed as he got back into his van and drove to the next house on his route. Her pulse nearing normal, she opened the paper to the front page.

And her pulse started to race again. 'Janet Bowie,' she murmured. Alex had only a vague recollection of Congressman Bowie, but his wife she remembered clearly. Rose Bowie and her negative, very public assessment of Alex's mama's character had been the reason they'd stopped going to church on Sundays. Most of the women in Dutton had shunned Kathy Tremaine after she'd moved in with Craig Crighton.

Alex rubbed at the sudden pain in her temples and put Craig from her mind. The memory of her mother wasn't so easily dismissed. There were the good years, when her father had been alive and her mother had been happy. Then the hard years, when it had just been the three of them, *Mama, Alicia, and me*. Money was tight and her mama had worried all the time, but there had still been some happiness in her eyes. But after they'd moved in with Craig, her happiness had been extinguished.

The last memories she had of her mother weren't good ones. Her mother had lived with Craig to give them a place to live and food to eat. And women like Rose Bowie had shunned her for it and made her cry. That was hard to forgive. For years Alex had hated all the whispering biddies. Now, as she stared down at the headline, she had to wonder who'd hated Janet Bowie enough to kill her that way.

And why her killer had resurrected Alicia's ghost after all these years.

Dutton, Tuesday, January 30, 5:35 A.M.

Mack got back into his van and rolled up to the next house. Old Violet Drummond came tottering out of her house to get her paper as she did every day. The first time she'd done it, he'd nearly freaked, but she hadn't recognized him. He'd changed in the years since he'd left Dutton, in many ways. Old Violet was not a threat, but a great source of information, which she readily provided. And she was friends with Wanda in the sheriff's office, so her information was usually pretty good.

He handed her her paper through his window. 'Mornin', Miz Drummond.'

She nodded briskly. 'Mornin', Jack.'

Mack looked over his shoulder at the bungalow. 'Got yourself a new neighbor.'

Violet's old eyes narrowed. 'That Tremaine girl is back.'

'I don't know her,' he lied.

'Girl's no good. She shows up in town and this starts happenin' all over again.' Violet thumped the front page on which Jim Woolf had described Janet Bowie's demise in great detail. 'Doesn't even have the decency to behave properly.'

His brows lifted. 'What's she done?' His surveillance told him that Alex Fallon was single-mindedly determined to find her stepsister, but she'd done nothing improper.

'Kissin' that Daniel Vartanian. Right on the front porch, for all the world to see!'

'That's disgraceful.' *That's fascinating*. 'Some people have no class.'

Violet huffed. 'No, they don't. Well, I won't keep you, Jack.'

Mack smiled. 'Always a pleasure, Miz Drummond. See you tomorrow.'

Atlanta, Tuesday, January 30, 8:00 A.M.

Daniel joined Chase and Ed at the team table, fighting a yawn. 'Our ID's confirmed. Felicity said Janet's dental records match. It's amazing how fast things get done for a congressman,' he added dryly. 'The dentist met me here with the x-rays at five a.m.'

'Good work,' Chase said. 'What about the boyfriend? The jazz singer?'

'Lamar has an alibi, confirmed by ten witnesses and the jazz club's security tapes.'

'He was performing when Janet was killed?' Ed asked.

'In front of a full house. The boyfriend's really torn up. He sat and sobbed when I told him she was dead. Said he'd heard about the murder but had no idea it was Janet.'

Ed frowned. 'What did he think when she didn't show up for their weekend date?'

'He got a voicemail from her. He said she told him her father had some state function and he expected her to be there. Call came in Thursday at eight p.m.'

'So she was still alive at eight p.m. and probably dead around midnight,' Chase said. 'She spent the day at Fun-N-Sun and left when?'

'I don't know yet. Lamar said she'd taken a group of kids from Lee Middle School.'

'She was a teacher?' Chase asked.

'No, a volunteer. Seems Janet was ordered to do community service after a little diva-brawl with another cellist in the orchestra last year.'

Chase snorted a surprised laugh. 'Cellists brawling? What, did they cross bows?'

Daniel rolled his eyes at the lame joke. 'I haven't had enough sleep for that to be funny. The other cellist accused Janet of damaging her cello so that Janet could get the first chair. The two women had an out-and-out catfight, pulling hair and scratching each other. The other cellist charged Janet with assault and property damage. Apparently they caught Janet on tape messing with the cello, so she pleaded out. Her brother Michael said the volunteer work had made an impact. This group of kids was important to her.'

'They went to an amusement park on a school day?' Ed asked skeptically.

'Lamar said it was her reward to kids with straight As and the principal approved it.'

'It's a four-hour drive from the amusement park back to Atlanta,' Chase said. 'If she called Lamar at eight under duress, her killer had her by then. We need to find out what time she and the kids left the park. We could have a nice, tight window of opportunity.'

'I called the school, but nobody was there yet. I'll head out there when we're done.'

'Hopefully you'll get more than we got at her apartment,' Ed said glumly. 'We took prints, checked her voicemail and computer. So far, nothing pops.'

'We're assuming she called Lamar under duress,' Chase said. 'What if she was two-timing him? What if she was meeting some other guy for the weekend?'

'I've got a request for her LUDs,' Daniel said. 'I'll see if she called anyone else. But speaking of LUDs, we got the warrant for Jim Woolf's. I should have them soon.'

'Woolf was there last night, at the Bowies' house,' Ed mused. 'How did he know?'

'He said he followed the line of cars up the hill,' Daniel said, and Ed sat up straighter.

'Speaking of cars, Janet Bowie drives a BMW Z-4 and it's not in the parking garage under her apartment or at the Bowies' house in Dutton.'

'She didn't get those kids down to Fun-N-Sun in a Z,' Chase said. 'It's a two-seater.'

'I'll ask the principal. Maybe a parent drove. None of the kids would be old enough.'

'Chase?' Leigh opened the door. 'You've got a call from Sheriff Thomas in Volusia.'

'Tell him I'll call him back.'

She frowned. 'He said it was urgent. Danny, here's your fax – it's Woolf's LUDs.'

Daniel scanned the LUDs as Chase took his phone call. 'Jim Woolf got a call at six Sunday morning on his home line.' He flipped pages. 'He got a call two minutes earlier from the same number on his office phone. And . . . he got another call from that same number . . . Oh, hell.' He looked up with a frown. 'This morning at six.'

'Fuck,' Ed muttered.

'Fuck is right,' Chase said, hanging up the phone.

Daniel sighed. 'Where?'

'Tylersville. One girl, brown blanket, with a key tied to her toe.'

'You were right, Ed,' Daniel murmured, wondering if this could be Bailey. The possibility of breaking the news to Alex made him sick, but the reality of their situation made him sicker. 'Gentlemen, we've got ourselves a serial killer.'

Tuesday, January 30, 8:00 A.M.

She heard the scraping again. Bailey blinked, the pain in her head nearly unbearable. He'd been brutal last night when he'd taken her away, but she'd held on. She hadn't told him anything, but at this point she wasn't sure it would matter if she did. He was enjoying the torture. He laughed at her pain. He was an animal. A monster.

She tried to focus on the scraping. It was rhythmic, like the tick of a clock. Time was passing. How long had she been here? Who had Hope? *Please, I don't care if he kills me now, just let my baby be all right.*

She closed her eyes and the scraping faded. Everything faded.

Volusia, Georgia, Tuesday, January 30, 9:30 A.M.

'Who found her?' Daniel asked Sheriff Thomas.

Thomas's jaw tightened. 'Brothers, fourteen and sixteen. The sixteen-year-old called it in on his cell phone. All the kids cut through here on their way to school.'

'Then he wanted her to be found again.' Daniel looked around the heavily treed area. 'On the last scene we had a reporter hiding up a tree taking pictures. Can you have your deputies walk through the trees and check?'

'We've been here since the kid called it in. No reporters could have gotten through.'

'If he's the same guy, he was here before the kids found her.'

Thomas's eyes narrowed. 'This sicko is *feeding* him?'

'We think so,' Daniel said, and Thomas's mouth twisted in distaste.

'I'll go with them, make sure they don't disturb anything you guys might need later.'

Daniel watched Thomas motion a couple of his deputies to the treeline, then turned to Felicity Berg as she climbed from the ditch.

'Same, Daniel,' she said, peeling off her gloves. 'Time of death was between nine and eleven last night. She was put here some time before four this morning.'

'The dew,' Daniel said. 'The blanket was wet. Sexual assault?'

'Yes. And her face was broken the same way as Janet Bowie's. Same bruising around her mouth. I think I'll find it's postmortem when I get her into exam. Oh, and the key? It was tied on super-tight. If she'd been alive it would have cut off all circulation to her toe. He wanted you to find that key.'

'Did she have track marks on her arms, Felicity?'

'No. Nor a lamb tattoo on her ankle. Tell Miss Fallon this isn't her stepsister, either.'

Daniel breathed out a sigh of relief. 'Thank you.'

Felicity drew herself straighter as the techs brought the body over the edge. 'I'll take her in now and see if we can't find out who she is.'

As the ME vehicles drove away, Daniel heard a shout and turned in time to see Sheriff Thomas and one of his deputies pull Jim Woolf out of a tree, none too gently.

'Woolf,' Daniel called when Thomas had dragged him closer. 'What the hell do you think you're doing?'

'My job,' Woolf snapped.

The deputy held up Woolf's camera. 'He was snappin' away.'

Woolf glared. 'I was outside the crime scene and on public land. You can't take my camera or my pictures without a court order. I gave you the other pictures to be nice.'

'You gave me the other pictures because you'd already used them,' Daniel corrected. 'Jim, think about it from my point of view. You get a phone call at six a.m. on Sunday and then again at six a.m. today from the same caller. Both days you show up at a homicide scene before we do. I might think you had something to do with this.'

'I didn't,' Woolf gritted.

'Then prove your good intentions. Download that memory card onto one of our computers. You walk away with your pictures and I'm reasonably pacified.'

Woolf shook his head, angry. 'Whatever. Let's get this done so I can get to work.'

'Took the words right outta my mouth,' Daniel said mildly. 'Let me get my laptop.'

Dutton, Tuesday, January 30, 10:00 A.M.

Meredith closed the front door behind her, shivering in her running clothes. 'It's got to be twenty degrees colder this morning than yesterday.'

Alex held up her hand, her eyes fixed to the TV. The sound was muted and she'd moved Hope's chair so that the child couldn't see the screen. 'Sshh.'

'What's happened?' Meredith asked urgently.

Alex worked very hard to keep the fear from her voice. 'Breaking news.'

Meredith swallowed. 'Another?'

'Yeah. No details yet, and no pictures.'

'Vartanian would have called you already,' Meredith said softly.

As if cued, Alex's cell phone rang and her heart dropped to her gut as she checked the caller ID. 'It's him. Daniel?' she asked, unable to control the tremble in her voice.

'It's not Bailey,' he said without preamble.

Relief shuddered through her. 'Thank you.'

'It's okay. I take it you'd heard already.'

'The news didn't give any real information. Just that there's another.'

'That's about all I know, too.'

'Just like . . . ?'

'Just like,' he confirmed quietly. Alex could hear the slam of a car door and his engine starting. 'I don't want you going out alone. Please.'

A shiver shook her, unpleasant and unwelcome. 'I have places to go today, things to do. People to talk to. I won't get another chance until Meredith can come back.'

He made an impatient noise. 'Fine. Just stay in public and don't park your car anywhere secluded. Better yet, let a valet do your parking and don't go to Bailey's house by yourself. And . . . call me a few times so I know you're okay. Okay?'

'Okay,' she murmured, then cleared her throat when Meredith gave her a knowing look. 'Will Loomis search Bailey's house now that she's been declared missing?'

'I'm headed into Dutton to see Frank Loomis right now. I'll check for you.'

'Thank you. And, Daniel, if you can't make it tonight, I'll understand.'

'I'll do my best. Gotta make some more calls. Bye.'

And he was gone. Carefully Alex closed her phone. 'Bye,' she murmured.

Meredith sat down next to Hope, then tilted her head, looking from Alex's picture to Hope's. 'You all have similar technique. You both stay inside the lines.'

Alex rolled her eyes. 'Yes, I am a control freak.'

'Yes, but you color a pretty picture.' Meredith

hugged the little girl's shoulders. 'Your aunt Alex needs to have fun. Make sure you guys play while I'm gone.'

Hope's chin jerked up and her gray eyes widened in panic.

Meredith just smoothed her thumb over Hope's cheek. 'I'll be back. I promise.'

Hope's lower lip trembled, breaking Alex's heart. 'I won't leave you alone, honey,' she murmured. 'While Meredith is gone, I'm sticking to you like glue. *I promise.*'

Hope swallowed, then dropped her eyes back to her coloring.

Alex leaned back in her chair. 'Well.'

Meredith laid her cheek on Hope's curls. 'You're safe, Hope.' She met Alex's eyes. 'Keep telling her that. She needs to hear it. She needs to believe it.'

Me, too. But Alex nodded firmly. 'I will. Now, I've got lots of stuff to do today. My first stop is the county courthouse. I've got to apply for a license to carry the . . . thing.'

'How long does that take to get?'

'The website said a few weeks.'

'And until then?' Meredith asked meaningfully.

Alex looked at Hope's coloring book. *All that red*. 'I can keep it in my trunk legally.'

Meredith sucked in her cheeks. 'You know a half-truth's the same as a lie.'

Alex lifted her chin. 'You gonna call a cop?'

Meredith rolled her eyes. 'You know I'm not. But you will, because you promised Vartanian you would. And you'll call me right after you call him.'

'Every few hours.' She pushed back from the table and headed to the bedroom.

'I have to leave here at five to make my flight,' Meredith called behind her.

'I'll be back by then.' She had only seven and a half hours to apply for a concealed-weapons permit and then to talk to anybody who knew Bailey's habits, her friends. Her enemies. It would have to be enough.

Tuesday, January 30, 11:00 A.M.

'Hello.'

It was just a dream. *Wasn't it?*

'Hello.'

Bailey lifted her head a fraction of an inch, reeling when the room twisted around her. It wasn't a dream. It was a whisper and it came from the other side of the wall. She forced herself to her hands and knees, gagging when the nausea hit her like a brick. But nothing came up, because she'd been given nothing to eat. Or drink.

How long? How long had she been here?

'Hello.' The whisper came through the wall again.

It was real. Bailey crawled to the wall and collapsed on her face, watching as the floor moved, just a little. A teaspoonful. Gritting her teeth, she brushed at the dirt.

And touched something solid. A finger. She sucked in a breath as the finger wiggled and pulled back through the hole, taking some of the dirt from her side with it.

'Hello,' she whispered back. The finger reappeared and she touched it, a sob heaving up from her chest.

'Don't cry,' he whispered. 'He'll hear you. Who are you?'

'Bailey.'

'Bailey Crighton?'

Bailey stopped breathing. 'You know me?'

'I'm Reverend Beardsley.'

Wade's letter. The letter that had contained the key *he'd* demanded every time he took her from this cell. Every time he . . . 'Why are you here?'

'Same reason you are, I'd guess.'

'But I never told. I never told him anything. I swear it.' Her voice shook.

'Sshh. Good for you, Bailey. You're stronger than he thinks. So am I.'

'How did he know about you?'

'I don't know. I visited your house . . . yesterday morning. Your stepsister was there.'

'Alex?' The sob rose again and she pushed it back. 'She came? She really came?'

'She's looking for you, Bailey. She has Hope. She's safe.'

'My baby?' The tears did come now, quiet but

steady. 'You didn't tell her, did you?' She heard the blame in her own voice, but couldn't stop it.

He was quiet for a long moment. 'No, I didn't. I couldn't. I'm sorry.'

She should say *I understand*. But she wouldn't lie to a reverend. 'Did you tell *him*?'

'No.' She heard the pain behind the single word.

She hesitated. 'What has he done to you?'

She heard him draw a deep breath. 'Nothing I can't take. And you?'

She closed her eyes. 'The same. But I don't know how much longer I can take it.'

'Be strong, Bailey. For Hope.'

Hope needs me. The mantra would have to keep her going a little longer. 'Can we get out of here?'

'If I think of a way, I'll let you know.' Then his finger disappeared and she heard dirt trickling back into the hole as he covered it up from his side.

She did the same, then crawled back to where she'd lain before. *Alex has Hope. My baby is safe*. That's all that really mattered. Everything else . . . *Everything else I brought on my own head*.

Chapter Eight

Dutton, Tuesday, January 30, 11:15 A.M.

Wanda Pettijohn looked at Daniel over her half-glasses. 'Frank's not here.'

'Is he out on call, or sick?'

Deputy Randy Mansfield came out of Frank's office. 'Just not here, Danny.' Mansfield's voice was even, but the message was clear – *it's none of your business, so don't ask*. Randy slid a thin folder across the counter. 'He asked me to give you this.'

Daniel scanned the few papers inside. 'This is the Alicia Tremaine file. I expected it to be thicker. Where are the crime scene photos, the interviews, victim photos?'

Randy lifted a shoulder. 'That's all Frank gave me.'

Daniel looked up, eyes narrowed. 'There had to have been more than this.'

Randy's smile dimmed. 'If it's not there, it didn't exist.'

'No one took a Polaroid of the scene or made a sketch? Where was she found?'

Jaw cocked, Randy pulled the folder around and ran his finger down the page that was the initial police report. 'On Five Mile Road.' He looked up. 'In a ditch.'

Daniel bit his tongue. 'Where on Five Mile Road? What was the nearest intersecting road? Who were the first responders? Where's the copy of the ME's report?'

'It was thirteen years ago,' Randy said. 'Things were done differently then.'

Wanda came to the counter. 'I was here then, Daniel. I can tell you what happened.'

Daniel felt a migraine coming on. 'Okay. Fine. What happened, Wanda?'

'It was the first Saturday in April. The Tremaine girl wasn't in her bed when her mother came to wake her up. She hadn't been there all night. She was a fast girl, that Alicia. Her mother started calling all around to her friends, but nobody'd seen her.'

'Who discovered the body?'

'The Porter boys. Davy and John. They were out riding their dirt bikes.'

He jotted it in his notebook. 'Davy and John were the middle kids of six, as I recall.'

Wanda gave a nod of respect. 'You recall correctly. Davy was about eleven and John was thirteen. There are two brothers younger and two more older.'

Davy and John would be twenty-four and twenty-six now. 'So what did they do?'

'After he threw up, John rode his bike up to the Monroe farm. Di Monroe called 911.'

'Who was the first policeman on the scene?'

'Nolan Quinn. He's passed now,' Wanda added soberly.

'He was never the same after finding Alicia,' Randy said quietly, and Daniel made himself remember that this wasn't just a file for them. It was perhaps the worst crime Dutton had seen up until this weekend. 'I joined the force out of school the next year and Nolan was never the same.'

'I can't imagine anyone could discover something like that and be unaffected,' Daniel murmured, thinking of the Porter boys. 'Who did the autopsy, Wanda?'

'Doc Fabares.'

'Who's also since passed,' Randy said and shrugged. 'That whole generation is mostly gone. Or sittin' on the barbershop bench.'

'But Doc Fabares would have kept records,' Daniel said.

'Somewhere,' Randy said, as if *somewhere* wasn't anywhere they'd be likely to find.

'What was found on the body?' Daniel asked.

Wanda frowned. 'What do you mean? She was naked, wrapped in a blanket.'

'No rings or jewelry?' *Or keys?* But the keys Daniel would keep to himself.

'None,' Wanda said. 'The drifter had robbed her.'

Daniel found the arrest report. 'Gary Fulmore.' A mug shot was stapled to the report. Fulmore's eyes were wild and his face was haggard. 'He looks stoned.'

'He was stoned,' Randy said. 'That much I remember. He was high on PCP when they found him. Took three men to hold him down so Frank could get the cuffs on him.'

'So Frank arrested him?'

Randy nodded. 'Fulmore had wrecked Jacko's autobody shop, breaking glass and waving a tire iron. They arrested him, then found Alicia's ring in his pocket.'

'That's all? No semen or other physical evidence?'

'No, I don't remember them actually finding any semen in her. That would be in Fabares's records, most likely. But the way her face was beaten in . . . only a person hopped up on PCP could've done that kind of damage. And he had the tire iron.'

'He was found in an autobody shop. Of course he had a tire iron.'

'I'm just telling you what I remember,' Randy said, annoyed. 'You want it or not?'

'I'm sorry. Please go on.'

'The tire iron had Alicia's blood on it and they found her blood splattered on the cuffs of his pants.'

'Pretty solid evidence,' Daniel said.

Randy's mouth twisted in a fuck-you smile. 'Glad you approve, Agent Vartanian.'

Daniel closed the folder. There was nothing more in it. 'Who took his statement?'

'Frank did,' Wanda said. 'Fulmore denied

everything, of course. But he also claimed to be some rock singer, as I recall.'

'He said he was Jimi Hendrix.' Randy shook his head. 'He said a lot of things.'

'Randy's daddy prosecuted him,' Wanda said proudly, then her mouth drooped. 'But he's passed, too. Heart failure, twelve years ago now. He was only forty-five.'

Daniel had read that Mansfield's father had prosecuted in one of the articles Luke had downloaded, but he didn't know the man had died. Not being able to interview any of the original players was damned inconvenient. 'I'm sorry to hear about your father, Randy,' he said, because it was expected.

'I'm sorry to hear about yours,' Randy replied in a tone that said he really wasn't.

Daniel let it go. 'Judge Borenson tried Fulmore's case. Is he still alive?'

'Yes,' Wanda said. 'He retired and has a place up in the mountains.'

'He's an old hermit,' Randy said. 'I don't even think he has a phone.'

'He has one,' Wanda said. 'He just never answers it.'

'Do you have his number?' Daniel asked and Wanda flipped through her Rolodex.

She wrote it down and gave it to him. 'Good luck. He's a hard man to track down.'

'What happened to the blanket Alicia was found in?'

Wanda grimaced. 'We got flooded during Dennis

and lost everything below the four-foot waterline. That file was stored higher up, or it would've been gone, too.'

Daniel sighed. Hurricane Dennis had caused massive flooding in Atlanta and the surrounding counties a few years before. 'Damn,' he murmured, then winced when Wanda glared. 'Sorry,' he muttered.

Her glare became a worried frown. 'The man who killed Janet. He's killed another.'

'Last night. He seems to be copying the details from this old murder pretty closely.'

'Except for the key,' Wanda said, and it took all of Daniel's control not to blink.

'Excuse me?'

'The key,' Wanda repeated. 'The one that was found on the new victim's toe.'

'Pics are on the Internet,' Randy added. 'The key tied to her toe was pretty clear.'

Daniel shoved his temper back down. 'Thanks. I hadn't seen the news reports yet.'

Randy's expression slid from sober to just shy of smug. 'I'd say you have a leak.'

Or a damn dog named Woolf. 'Thanks for your time.' He turned to go, then remembered his promise to Alex. 'Oh, one more thing. Bailey Crighton.'

Wanda's lips thinned. Randy rolled his eyes dramatically. 'Danny . . .'

'Her stepsister is worried,' Daniel said, making his tone apologetic. 'Please.'

'Look, Alex didn't really know Bailey.' Randy shook his head. 'Bailey Crighton was a hooker, plain and simple.' He looked over at Wanda. 'Sorry.'

'It's the truth,' Wanda said, dark color flooding her cheeks. 'Bailey was white trash. She's not *missin'*. She's just *gone*, run off like the druggie tramp she's always been.'

Daniel blinked at the venom in Wanda's tone. 'Wanda.'

Wanda wagged her finger at Daniel. 'And you'd best be watching yourself with the stepsister. She may look all sweet in the moonlight, but she was trouble, too.'

Randy put his hand on Wanda's shoulder and squeezed. 'It's okay, sweetheart,' he murmured to the old woman, then turned to Daniel, his eyes telegraphing *back down*. 'Wanda's son had a . . . relationship with Bailey a few years back.'

Wanda's eyes blazed. 'You make it sound like my Zane intended to take up with that whore.' She shook with fury. 'She seduced him and nearly broke up his marriage.'

Daniel searched his memory. Zane Pettijohn was his age and had played ball at the public school. He'd had a penchant for curvy girls and hard liquor then. 'But all's well?'

Wanda was still trembling from rage. 'Yes, with no thanks to that tramp.'

'I see.' Daniel let a few beats pass and Wanda sat

back down in her chair, her scrawny arms crossed over her scrawnier bosom. 'All that notwithstanding, what's been done about Bailey? I mean, have you searched her house? Where's her car?'

'Her house is a sty,' Randy said with contempt. 'Garbage everywhere. Needles . . . dammit, Danny, you should have seen that little girl we took out of the closet. She was terrified. If Bailey's gone, she left on her own two feet or one of her johns got her.'

Daniel widened his eyes. 'She was still hooking?'

'Yeah. If you run her record, you'll find she's got a sheet as long as your arm.'

Daniel had, actually, and found Bailey's last arrest was five years ago. She'd been busted for solicitation and possession several times before that. But she'd been clean for five years and nothing Randy had said about Bailey's house matched what he'd heard from Sister Anne the night before. Either Bailey had gotten really good at not getting caught or something wasn't right. Daniel was leaning toward the second one.

'I'll run her record when I get back to the office. Thanks. Y'all have been a big help.'

He was in his car when it hit him. *You'd best be watching yourself with the stepsister. She may look sweet in the moonlight* . . . He'd kissed Alex last night, on her front porch, in the moonlight. Someone had been watching them. The bungalow was right off Main Street, so it might have been a goggle-eyed biddy and nothing more. Still, he was uneasy and Daniel was a man who listened to his instincts.

Which was why he'd kissed Alex Fallon last night, in the moonlight. His skin warmed at the memory. Which was why he planned to do so again, very soon. But his unease persisted, shifting to worry. Someone had been watching them. He dialed her number and got her cool voice as the call went to voicemail.

'It's Daniel. Call me as soon as you can.' He started to pocket his phone and then frowned. *Woolf*. He called Ed. 'Have you seen the news?'

'Yeah,' Ed said glumly. 'Chase is on the phone with the powers that be, explaining how Woolf managed it.'

'So how did he?'

'BlackBerry. Snapped the picture and winged it off onto the Internet.'

'Dammit. I didn't list his BlackBerry in the warrant. I have to call Chloe and re-up.'

'I already did, only the BlackBerry's not in his name. It's in his wife's.'

'Marianne,' Daniel said with a sigh. 'Can Chloe turn it around fast?'

'She thought so. Hey, you get any of the old evidence from the Tremaine case?'

'No,' Daniel said, disgusted. 'Flooding took out their evidence room and the file is pathetic. The only thing I can tell you is that there was no key. That's a new MO.'

'The two keys match,' Ed said. 'Same exact cut, but

that's not surprising. Did you talk to the principal of that middle school?'

'Yeah, on my way from the crime scene to the police station. She said Janet rented a minivan to take the kids to Fun-N-Sun. I called the parents and all of them say Janet dropped off the kids at seven-fifteen. Leigh's running down the car rental place from Janet's credit cards. If anybody asks, I'm headed over to the morgue. I'll call you later.'

Atlanta, Tuesday, January 30, 12:55 P.M.

Alex gave the photo of a smiling Bailey one last look before she slid it into her satchel, which sagged from the weight of her gun. Meredith had frowned when Alex had taken the gun from its lockbox, but Alex was taking no chances. Hefting the strap of her satchel higher on her shoulder, she looked up into the face of Bailey's boss.

'Thank you, Desmond. For everything.'

'I just feel so helpless. Bailey's been with us for three years now and she's become more like part of our family. We just want to *do* something.'

Alex toyed with the yellow ribbon someone had tied across Bailey's station in the very upscale Atlanta salon. 'You've done a lot.' She pointed to the flyer they'd posted. She'd seen dozens like it as she'd walked through Atlanta's Underground shopping mall. It was a picture of Bailey, along with an offer of a reward for information leading to her whereabouts. 'I wish the people in her hometown were as generous.'

Desmond's jaw hardened. 'They would never let her live down her mistakes. We begged her to leave, to move here, but she wouldn't.'

'She commuted every day?' It was an hour each way.

'Except on Saturday nights.' He pointed to an empty station. 'Sissy and Bailey were best friends. On Saturdays, Sissy's daughter babysat Hope while Bailey worked, then they'd stay over in Sissy's place. Bailey volunteered at one of the downtown shelters every Sunday morning. It was like her religion.'

'I wish I'd talked to you yesterday afternoon. It took me hours to find that shelter.'

Desmond's eyes widened. 'You've been there, then?'

'Last night. They seem to love Bailey there.'

'Everybody loves Bailey.' His eyes narrowed. 'Except that *town*. If you ask me, somebody needs to check out the slime that live there.'

Alex could see his point. 'Can I talk to Sissy?'

'She's off today, but I'll get her number for you. Give me your parking voucher. I'll validate it while I'm at it.'

Alex dug the voucher from her purse, pulling her cell phone out with it. The light was blinking. 'That's weird. I've got a message, but I didn't hear it ring.'

'Sometimes reception is wonderful down here and sometimes it's a dead zone.' Immediately he winced. 'I didn't mean to say that. I'm sorry.'

'It's all right. We have to believe we'll find her.' Desmond walked away, his head bowed low, and Alex checked her call log. Daniel had called four times. Her pulse raced.

He was probably just calling to check on me. But what if he'd made a mistake? What if the woman he'd found that morning was Bailey? She found Desmond at the front counter, took her voucher, and shook his hand. 'I have to go. Thank you,' she called over her shoulder as she ran up the escalator to street level and the parking valet.

Atlanta, Tuesday, January 30, 1:00 P.M.

'A single hair, long and brown.' Felicity Berg held up a small plastic bag in which the hair was curled like a lariat. 'He meant for you to find it.'

Daniel crouched to study the newest victim's toe. 'He wrapped the hair around the big toe of her left foot, then wrapped the string for the key over it.' He stood up, blinking at the headache that had spiraled in intensity. 'So it's important. Male or female hair?'

'I'd say there's a good chance it's female. And he was nice enough to give us a hair with a full follicle, so I should have no trouble getting DNA.'

'Can I see it?' He held it up to the light. 'It's hard to tell color from just one hair.'

'Ed can run a color match and give you a hair swatch.'

'Other than that, what else can you tell me about this woman?'

'Early twenties. Recent manicure. Cotton fibers in the lining of her cheeks and evidence of sexual assault. We're running the blood test for Rohypnol. I put a rush on it. Come look at this.' She angled the overhead light so that a spotlight shone on the woman's throat. 'Look at the circular bruising on her throat. It's very faint, but there.'

He took the magnifying glass she offered and looked where she pointed. 'Pearls?'

'Big ones. He didn't strangle her with them or the bruises would have been readily apparent. I'm thinking he may have grabbed them at some point, maybe to put mild pressure on her trachea. And look here. See that little nick?'

'He held a knife to her throat.'

Felicity nodded. 'One last thing. She was wearing Forevermore. It's a perfume,' she added when Daniel frowned. 'Four hundred an ounce.'

Daniel's eyes widened. 'And you know that how?'

'I know the scent because my mother wears it. I know the price because I checked when I was looking to buy her birthday present.'

'Did you give your mother the perfume?'

'No. That was way out of my price range.' Her eyes

crinkled and Daniel knew she was smiling under the mask. 'I gave her a wafflemaker instead.'

Daniel smiled back. 'A far more practical choice.' He gave her back the magnifying glass and straightened, sobering as he looked down into the face of their second victim. 'Pearls and perfume. This woman is wealthy or gets gifts from someone who is.' His cell phone buzzed and the caller ID had his pulse going a little faster.

Alex handed her voucher to the valet as Daniel's cell phone rang in her ear.

'Vartanian.'

'Daniel, it's Alex.'

'Excuse me,' she heard him say. 'I need to take this.' A few moments later he was back and mad. 'Where have you *been*?' he demanded. 'I called three times.'

'Four, actually,' Alex said. 'I've been with the owner of the salon where Bailey works. They've posted flyers all over the Underground offering a reward for information.'

'That's nice,' he said more gently. 'I'm sorry. I got worried.'

'Why? What's happened?'

'Nothing, really.' He dropped his voice. 'Just that we were . . . watched. Last night.'

'What?' Alex frowned and stepped off the curb. 'That's—'

But no more words came. Just the squeal of tires and

the shout of a stranger. Then screams and her own grunt of pain as a body slammed into her from behind, knocking her forward onto the sidewalk. Her palms and knees burned as she skidded to a stop.

Time seemed to stand still as she lifted her head, still on her hands and knees. There was a queer bubble of muted sound as a man's face filled her field of vision. His lips were moving and she squinted, trying to hear him. People were grabbing at her arms, helping her up. One man handed her the satchel, another woman her purse.

Dazed, Alex blinked and turned slowly to the street where the valet was bolting out of her rental car, his face pale and shocked. 'What happened?' Alex asked, her voice thin and spindly. Her knees went wobbly. 'I need to sit down.'

The hands holding her arms led her to a giant cement planter and she gingerly lowered herself to its edge. A new face appeared in front of her, this one calm. And wearing a police officer's hat. 'Are you all right? Do we need to call an ambulance?'

'No.' Alex shook her head and winced. 'I'm just banged up.'

'I don't know.' The first face she'd seen appeared over the cop's, as if their heads were stacked. 'She took a pretty bad fall.'

'I'm a nurse,' Alex said firmly. 'I don't need an ambulance.' She looked at her scraped palms and winced. 'Just some basic first aid.'

'What happened?' the cop demanded.

'She was stepping into the street to get her car when this other car came zooming around the corner like a bat outta hell,' the first man said. 'I pushed her out of the way. I hope I didn't hurt you too bad, ma'am,' he added.

Alex smiled at him, light-headed. 'No, I'm fine. You saved my life. Thank you.'

You saved my life. Reality hit and with it a wave of nausea. Someone had tried to kill her. Daniel. She'd been talking to Daniel. He said they'd been watched last night. *Somebody just tried to kill me.*

She gulped a lungful of air, willing her stomach to settle. 'Where's my cell phone?'

'*Alex?*' Daniel shouted her name into the phone but there was nothing but dead air. He turned to find Felicity watching him, her eyes unreadable behind her goggles.

'What happened?' she asked.

'She was talking and then I heard squealing tires and screams. Then nothing. I need to use your phone.' A minute later he was talking to the Atlanta PD dispatch. 'She was outside the Underground,' he said, willing his voice to stay steady. 'Her name is Alex Fallon. She's five-six, slim, brown hair.'

'We'll check it out right away, Agent Vartanian.'

'Thanks.' Daniel turned back to Felicity, who still watched him.

'Sit down, Daniel,' she said calmly. 'You're pale.'

He obeyed. He made himself breathe. Made himself think. Then his cell phone buzzed in his hand. Alex's number. He answered, heart in his throat. 'Vartanian.'

'Daniel, it's Alex.'

It was her cool voice. She was scared. 'What happened?'

'I'm okay. Daniel, somebody just tried to run me over.'

The heart in his throat began to race. 'Are you hurt?'

'Just scraped up. There's a policeman here. He wants to talk to you. Hold on.'

'This is Officer Jones, APD. Who is this?'

'Special Agent Vartanian, GBI. Is she hurt?'

'Not badly. She's a little disoriented and banged up a bit. She says she's a nurse and doesn't need the ER. Is she part of an ongoing investigation?'

'She is now.' Too late Daniel remembered Alex's satchel. He'd bet good money she had her gun with her. If she set one foot inside a police station, she'd be busted for carrying a concealed. 'But she's not a suspect, so there's no need to transport her. Are you outside the Underground?'

'By the valet station. Are you coming or sending someone for her?'

The thought of sending anyone else hadn't entered his mind. 'I'm coming myself. Will you wait with her until I get there?'

'Yes. My partner ran after the car that tried to hit her,

but he lost them. We'll take statements from the crowd. Once we get a description of the car, we'll put out an APB.'

'Thanks.' Daniel flipped his phone shut. 'Felicity, I have to go.' He handed her the bag containing the hair the killer had left for them to find. 'Can you have someone take this out to Ed? Ask him to run a color check.'

Felicity nodded, her eyes still unreadable, and Daniel got the uncomfortable feeling she was working very hard to keep them that way. 'Sure. I'll call you when I have more.'

Tuesday, January 30, 1:15 P.M.

'You know, Bailey, you're becoming a real pain in my ass.'

Blearily Bailey looked up through the haze of pain and fear. He was standing over her, breathing hard. He'd broken a few of her ribs this time, and she wasn't sure how many more kicks she could take before she lost consciousness. Again. 'Too bad.' She'd meant for it to come out sarcastic and strong, but it was a pathetic little croak.

'Are you going to talk into the nice little machine or not?'

She glanced over at the tape recorder with contempt. 'Not.'

He smiled then, his cobra smile. It had terrified her

at first. Now she was beyond terror. What more could he do? *Except kill me.* At least then the pain would stop.

'Well then, Bailey, darlin', you've left me no choice. You won't tell me what I want to know and you won't say what I want you to say. I'm going to have to go with Plan B.'

This is it. He'll kill me now.

'Oh, I'm not going to kill you,' he said, amusement in his voice. 'But you'll wish I had.' He turned around to pull something from a drawer and when he turned back . . .

'No.' Bailey's heart froze. 'No, please not that. Not that.'

He just smiled. 'Then talk into the tape recorder or . . .' He tapped the end of the syringe and pushed the stopper just enough to force a few drops of liquid from the needle. 'It's the good stuff, Bailey. You remember the good stuff.'

A sob tore from her parched throat. 'Please, no.'

He sighed dramatically. 'Plan B it is. Once a junkie, always a junkie.'

She struggled, but her attempts were as pathetic as her voice. He held her down easily, shoving one knee into her back and grabbing her arm. She tried to pull away, but even healthy she would have been no match for his strength.

Quickly he tied the rubber strap around her arm and pulled with the quick expertise of someone who'd had years of practice. He ran his thumb along the inside of her forearm. 'Do you have good veins, Bailey?' he taunted. 'This one will do nicely.'

There was a quick prick, the slide of the plunger, then . . . She was floating. Soaring. 'Damn you,' she croaked. 'Damn you to hell.'

'That's what they all say. A few more hits and you'll be begging to do anything I ask.'

Atlanta, Tuesday, January 30, 1:30 P.M.

Alex winced as Desmond swabbed her palm with disinfectant. She still sat on the edge of the planter and he knelt on the pavement beside her. Word traveled fast in the Underground Mall, and Desmond had come running. 'That smarts.'

He looked up, his eyes unsmiling. 'You should go to the hospital.'

She patted his shoulder with her fingertips, the only part of her hands that didn't burn like fire. 'I'm fine, truly. Just a poor patient.'

'First Bailey, now this,' Desmond muttered. He swabbed the other palm and again she winced, purposing to be a little more sympathetic the next time she did the same for a patient in the ER. It did really smart. *But it could have been so much worse.*

Desmond pulled an Ace bandage from his drugstore bag. 'Hold your hands out, palm up.' He applied the gauze, then wrapped each hand with gentle care.

'You should be a nurse, Desmond.'

He gave her another unsmiling look. 'This is a nightmare.' He rose from his knees to sit next to her. 'You could have been dead like Bailey.'

'She's not dead,' Alex said, just as quietly. 'I won't believe it.' He said no more, just sat quietly beside her until Daniel's car pulled up to the curb.

He's here. He came.

Daniel approached her as he had the night before, his face almost stern, his eyes piercing, his stride full of purpose. She stood, wanting to meet him on her own two feet, although the very sight of him made her almost dizzy with relief.

He checked her out from head to toe, his gaze lingering on her bandaged hands. Then he gently pulled her to him and threaded his hand through her hair, holding her head against his chest where his heart thundered hard and fast. He rested his cheek on the top of her head and let out a single shuddering breath, as if he'd held it all in.

'I'm all right,' she said and held up her hands, attempting a smile. 'All taken care of.'

'Her knees are scraped up, too,' Desmond said from behind her.

Daniel moved his stare to Desmond's face. 'You are?'

'Desmond Warriner. Bailey Crighton's boss.'

'He bandaged me up,' Alex said.

'Thank you,' Daniel said, his voice gone husky.

'Are you looking for Bailey?' Desmond asked tightly. 'Please say someone is.'

'I am.' Daniel took her purse and satchel in one hand and slid the other to her waist, then turned her toward his car, against which a tall black-haired man now leaned, regarding her thoughtfully. 'That's my friend, Luke. He's going to drive your car and you're going to come with me.' Luke gave her a courteous nod.

Alex gave Desmond a quick hug. 'Thanks again.'

'Take care of yourself,' Desmond said fiercely, then pulled a card from his pocket. 'Sissy's phone number. Bailey's friend,' he added. 'You ran off before I could give it to you. I was trying to catch you when I heard . . . Just call me when you hear anything.'

'I will.' She looked up at Daniel, who still looked very stern. 'I'm ready to go.' She let him put her in his car, but stopped him when he started to buckle her in. 'I can do that. Honestly, Daniel, I'm not hurt that badly.'

He dropped his head, staring at her hands. When he looked up his eyes were no longer stern, but stark. 'When you called I was in the morgue with the second victim.'

Her heart clenched. 'I'm sorry. You must have been scared.'

One side of his mouth lifted wryly. 'That's putting it mildly.' He put her satchel and purse at her feet. 'Just stay here and try to rest. I'll be back.'

Daniel stepped back from the car. His hands were

shaking, so he shoved them into his pockets and turned away from her before he did something that might embarrass them both. Luke was coming toward him, a set of keys in his hand.

'I got her keys,' Luke said. 'You need me to stick around?'

'No. Park her car in the visitors' lot and leave the keys on my desk. Thanks, Luke.'

'Relax. She's okay.' He studied Alex, who sat with her head back and her eyes closed. 'She does look like Alicia. No wonder she gave you a jolt.' Luke lifted his brows. 'It appears she's continuing to give you jolts of a different nature. Mama will be happy to hear this, except that now she'll turn all her attention back on me.'

Daniel smiled, as Luke had intended. 'No less than you deserve. Where's Jones?'

'He's the one talking to the valet. His partner is Harvey. He's over there talking to the man with the blue shirt, who, from what I overheard, was the one who pushed Alex out of the way. He might have seen the driver's face. I'm going now. See you later.'

From Officers Harvey and Jones, Daniel learned the car had been a late model, dark sedan, probably a Ford Taurus, with South Carolina plates. The driver had been young, African-American, thin, with a beard. He'd come from around the corner where he'd been waiting for an hour, according to witnesses who remembered seeing the vehicle. From that vantage point the driver could have easily seen Alex exit the Underground.

That last piece of information made Daniel the angriest. The scum had waited for her, then pounced. Had it not been for a stranger with quick reflexes, Alex might be dead. Daniel thought of the two victims, of the missing Bailey. Alex would not be next. That he promised himself. He would take care of her.

Why? she'd asked last night. Last night he had no answer. He had one now. *Because she's mine.* It was a primal response and probably exceedingly premature, but . . . it didn't matter. *For now, she's mine. Later . . . we'll see how it goes.*

He thanked the officers and the man who'd pushed her out of the way, then drove five blocks before pulling to the curb, leaning over, and kissing her with all the emotion that he'd kept in check. When he lifted his head, she sighed.

'You do that well,' she murmured.

'So do you.' And he kissed her again, longer and deeper. When he pulled away, she rolled her head to look at him, want and fear warring in her eyes.

'What do you want from me, Daniel?'

Everything, he wanted to say, but because she'd suspected his motives the night before, he didn't. Instead he ran his thumb over her lips, felt her tremble. 'I don't know. But it won't be anything you're not willing and . . . anxious to give.'

Her smile was sad. 'I see,' was all she said.

'I'm going to take you back to my office. I've got a press conference at two-thirty, but after that I can break away and drive you back to the bungalow.'

'I hate for you to have to do that.'

'Be quiet, Alex.' He said it mildly to take away some of the sting of his words. 'I'm not sure how you connect to all this, but every instinct I have is screaming that you are.'

She flinched, a minute motion. 'What?' he asked. 'Alex?'

She sighed. 'When I dream, I hear screams. When I get tense, like back there, I also hear them.' She glanced at him warily. 'Now you think I'm crazy.'

'Hush. You're not crazy. Besides, at least some of the screams back there were real. I heard them, too, right before I lost your call.'

'Thanks.' Her smile was self-deprecating. 'I really needed to hear that.'

Last night she'd been dreaming, she'd said. *Then you were there*. 'When you hear the screams, what do you do?'

She lifted a shoulder, looking away. 'I concentrate and make them stop.'

He remembered what she'd said to the girl in the shelter. 'Push them in the closet?'

'Yes.' It was an embarrassed admission.

He cupped her face and brushed his thumb across her flushed cheek.

'It must take a lot of mental energy to do that. I'd be exhausted.'

'You have no idea.' Her voice grew cool. 'We should go now. You have a job and I have too much to do to be sitting here feeling sorry for myself.' She lifted her chin, away from his hand. 'Please.'

She was terrified. She had a right to be. Someone had tried to kill her. The knowledge left his gut tied in a knot. She wasn't driving around on her own, not while he had breath. But he'd argue the point later. Now she looked fragile, even as her chin jutted out like that of a prizefighter looking for a fight.

Saying no more, Daniel put his car back into gear and drove.

Chapter Nine

Atlanta, Tuesday, January 30, 2:15 P.M.

He'd locked her satchel in the trunk of his car and taken her keys. Alex shifted in the chair in the GBI waiting room, trying not to be annoyed at Daniel's heavy-handed attempts to protect her, but conscious of the minutes ticking away.

Meredith was leaving in a few hours and Alex still hadn't visited Hope's preschool or Bailey's friend Sissy. Tomorrow she'd have no opportunity to search for Bailey. Not that she was getting anywhere. All she'd found was that Atlanta people loved Bailey. Dutton people hated her. And the last person to see her was Hope, who wasn't talking.

The last place Bailey was seen was the old house. *You have to go in there, Alex,* she told herself. *No matter what it takes. You've been foolish not to go before now.*

Still, someone had tried to kill her today and Daniel's warnings not to go to the Crighton place alone would not go unheeded. *I'm a neurotic coward, but I'm not stupid.*

But she was late. 'Excuse me,' she called to Leigh, their office clerk. 'Do you know how much longer Agent Vartanian will be? He has the keys to my rental car.'

'I don't know. He had three people waiting for him when he got back and we have a press conference scheduled in a few minutes. Can I get you some water or something?'

Alex's stomach growled at the woman's mention of food and she remembered she'd had nothing since that morning. 'Actually I'm starving. Is there a cafeteria nearby?'

'It's closed now. Lunch was over an hour ago. But I have some cheese crackers and a few bottles of water in my desk. It's not much, but it's better than nothing.'

Alex nearly said no, but the growling in her stomach overruled her. 'Thank you.'

Leigh slid the water and crackers over the counter with a smile. 'Now, don't you go telling people we only gave you bread and water, okay?'

Alex smiled back. 'I promise.'

The door behind her opened and a tall, lean man wearing wireframe glasses headed straight back to the offices without stopping. 'Is Daniel back?'

'Yeah, but . . . Ed, wait.' Leigh stopped him. 'He's in with Chase and' – she looked over her shoulder at Alex – 'a few other people. You should wait.'

'This can't wait. I . . .' His words trailed. 'You're Alex Fallon,' he said, his voice odd.

Feeling like the newest addition to the zoo, Alex nodded. 'Yes.'

'I'm Ed Randall. I'm with the Crime Scene Unit.' He reached over the counter to shake her hand, then noticed her bandages. 'Looks like you had an accident.'

'Miss Fallon was nearly hit by a car this afternoon,' Leigh said softly, and Ed Randall's expression abruptly changed.

'My God.' His jaw tightened. 'But you're uninjured, besides your hands, that is?'

'Yes. A fast-thinking stranger pushed me out of the way.'

Leigh twisted the top off the water bottle for Alex. 'Ed, they have to be done soon. They have a press conference in less than twenty minutes. I'd really wait if I were you.'

Alex took her crackers and water back to her chair and left the two to whisper. She hadn't recognized the man who was waiting when they came in. He was pacing when they arrived and had nearly launched himself at Daniel, demanding 'answers.'

A door opened behind the counter and Daniel and his boss emerged with the pacing man and two others. The pacing man was ashen. His news had not been good then.

'I'm sorry, sir,' Daniel said. 'We'll call you the

moment we know anything new. I know it doesn't help right now, but we're doing everything we can.'

'Thank you. When can I have . . .' His voice broke and for the first time that day tears welled in Alex's eyes. She pursed her lips and fought the sudden wave of compassion.

'We'll have her body released as soon as we possibly can,' Daniel's boss said gently. 'We're so sorry for your loss, Mr Barnes.'

Mr Barnes was walking to the door when he stopped cold and stared at her and what little color remained in his face drained away. 'You.' It was barely a murmur.

Alex looked at Daniel from the corner of her eye. She had no idea of what to say.

'Mr Barnes.' Daniel stepped forward. 'What is it?'

'Her picture was on the news yesterday. My Claudia saw it.'

Alicia. The news had quickly picked up on the Arcadia story, and its link to Alicia's murder. *This man had seen Alicia's picture,* not mine. Alex stood on wobbly knees and opened her mouth but still had no idea of what to say.

'What did your wife say about the picture?' Daniel's boss asked.

'She knew the girl . . . remembered the case. Claudia was just a little girl, but she remembered. It upset her. She almost stayed home last night, but she had to go to that damn party. I should have gone with her. I should have been with her.' Barnes glared at Alex, horrified disbelief in his eyes. 'You're supposed to be dead. Who are you?'

Alex lifted her chin. 'The picture you saw was my sister, Alicia.' Her lips were trembling and she firmed them. 'Your wife knew my sister? Was she from Dutton?'

The man nodded. 'Yes. Her maiden name was Silva.'

Alex brought a bandaged hand to her mouth. 'Claudia Silva?'

'You knew her, Alex?' Daniel asked gently.

'I babysat Claudia and her little sister.' She closed her eyes and focused on quieting the screams that tore through her mind. *I'm losing my mind*. She opened her eyes and pushed past the noise, focusing on the man and his grief. 'I'm so very sorry.'

Roughly he nodded, then turned to Daniel's boss. 'I want every man you can spare on this case, Wharton. I know people . . .'

'Rafe,' one of the other men murmured. 'Let them do their jobs.' They ushered Barnes from the room, leaving a hush behind them.

Alex met Daniel's eyes. 'Two women from Dutton are dead and Bailey's still missing,' she said harshly. 'What the hell is happening here?'

'I don't know,' Daniel said, his face stern. 'But we're sure as hell going to find out.'

Ed Randall cleared his throat. 'Daniel, we need to talk. *Now*.'

Daniel nodded. 'Okay. Just a little longer, Alex, and I can take you home.'

The men went to the back offices, leaving Alex and Leigh alone in the front. Alex lowered herself into her chair. 'I feel . . . responsible somehow.'

'Involved,' Leigh corrected. 'Not responsible. You're a victim in this, too, Miss Fallon. You may want to consider requesting protection.'

Alex thought of Hope. 'I will.' Then she thought of Meredith. She hadn't called her cousin in some time. When she found out about the near miss, Alex imagined some level of hell would break loose. 'I need to make a call. I'll be out in the hall.'

Ed leaned against the corner of Daniel's desk. 'We may have tracked the blankets.'

Daniel rummaged in his desk drawer for a bottle of aspirin. 'And?'

'They were bought at a sporting goods store three blocks away.'

'Right under our noses,' Daniel said. 'Intentional?'

'We can't discount it,' Chase said. 'Did they have security tapes?'

Ed nodded. 'Yep. Purchase was made by a kid, maybe eighteen. White, five-ten, one-fifty. Looked right up into the camera, so we got his face. Kid paid cash. The store clerk remembered, because it was a lot of cash.'

Daniel dry-swallowed two aspirin. 'Of course he

paid cash.' He tossed the bottle back into the drawer. 'I'm afraid to ask. How many blankets did he buy, Ed?'

'Ten.'

Chase hissed. *'Ten?'*

Bile rose in Daniel's throat. 'We need to get his photo posted to all units.'

'Already done,' Ed said. 'But the kid didn't look like he had anything to hide. I bet he's a stooge, probably hired to buy the blankets. It's not illegal to buy blankets.'

'He can still tell us who hired him,' Chase said tightly. 'Is that it? We've got a press conference in five.'

'No. There's more.' Ed put the small plastic bag containing the single hair on Daniel's desk. 'This is the hair you got off of this morning's vic.'

'Claudia Barnes,' Chase said.

'It's not hers.'

'We knew that,' Daniel said. 'Claudia was a blonde. This hair is brown.'

'I ran it through the colorimeter.' From a paper bag, Ed took a fake ponytail, looped in a teardrop shape. 'I pulled the closest match from our hair samples.'

Daniel picked up the sample with a frown, immediately seeing the significance. It was caramel colored. Just like Alex's. 'Fuck.'

'I swear to God, Danny, I took one look at Alex Fallon out there and did a double-take. He's left a hair, if not her color, then damn close.'

Daniel passed the sample to Chase, keeping his fury

tamped down. 'This guy's playing with us.' And with Alex.

Chase held the single hair up to the light. 'Is it possible this is a fake hair, like from your ponytail sample? I've seen them in the drugstore where they sell hair color.'

'No, it's definitely real and definitely human,' Ed said. 'And it's old.'

Dread settled in the pit of Daniel's stomach. 'How old?'

'One of the guys in the lab is a hair expert. He thinks at least five years. Maybe ten.'

'Or thirteen?' Daniel asked and Ed shrugged.

'Maybe. I can test it, but once I run the test there won't be a lot left for DNA.'

'Run the DNA first,' Chase said grimly. 'Daniel, get Alex to give us some hair. I want them tested side by side.'

'I'll have to tell her why.'

'No, you don't. Tell her anything you want, just don't tell her why. Not yet at least.'

Daniel frowned. 'She's not a suspect, Chase.'

'No, but she's involved. If it's a match, then tell her. If not, why upset her?'

That at least made sense. 'All right.'

Chase straightened the knot of his tie. 'Now, it's showtime. I'll field the questions.'

'Wait a minute,' Daniel protested. 'I'm lead. I can field my own damn questions.'

'I know, but remember what I said about hearing "Vartanian" and "Dutton" in the same sentence. The brass wants me to face the press. Nothing else changes.'

'Fine,' Daniel muttered, then stopped when he got to Leigh's desk. Alex was gone. 'Where is she?' He shoved his hand into his pocket. He still had her car keys. She could have taken a cab, but surely she wasn't that stupid. If—

'Relax, Danny,' Leigh said. 'She's in the hall making a phone call.'

Daniel felt a spike of tension in his neck ebb. 'Thanks.'

'Daniel.' Chase was holding open the door. *'Let's go.'*

Daniel could see her at the end of the hall as he, Chase, and Ed walked the other way. She was on her cell phone, bowed over, hugging herself with one arm. Her shoulders were shaking and with a jolt he realized she was crying.

He stopped, the pressure on his chest making it hard to breathe. After all she'd been through in the last two days, he hadn't seen her cry. Not once.

'Daniel.' Chase grasped his shoulder and yanked. 'We're late. Let's go. I need you focused. You can talk to her later. She can't go anywhere, you took her keys.'

Ed shot him a look of surprised sympathy and Daniel realized everything he felt must be showing on his face. He carefully drew a blank expression and left Alex crying in the hall.

He'd do his job. He'd track down this killer who taunted them with keys and clues. He had to make sure no other women were found in ditches. He had to keep Alex safe.

Atlanta, Tuesday, January 30, 2:30 P.M.

'I'm so sorry, Miss Fallon,' Nancy Barker said. The county social worker sounded almost as devastated as Alex felt. 'I don't know what else to tell you at this point.'

'Are you sure?' Alex insisted. She wiped her face with the back of her bandaged hand. She hated the weakness of tears. They never helped. But she'd gone for days expecting to hear Bailey was dead. She hadn't expected . . . this. Not this. And on top of the events of the day . . . Alex supposed everyone had a limit and she'd reached hers.

'I know this is hard, but Bailey was an addict. Heroin addicts have a much higher recidivism rate. You're a nurse. I'm not telling you anything you don't know.'

'I know. I also know everyone in Bailey's recent life has sworn she'd gone clean.'

'Maybe she was under stress and just couldn't take it anymore. Addicts go back to the life for all kinds of reasons. All I know is that she called the office and left a message for, quote, "whoever has my baby, Hope Crighton." The social worker who took the call knew

Hope was one of my cases and forwarded the message to me.'

'So nobody physically talked to Bailey.' The initial shock was wearing off and Alex's mind was working again. 'When did she leave the message?'

'Today, about an hour ago.'

An hour ago. Alex looked at her bandaged hands. No coincidences, Daniel had said. 'Can you forward that message to my phone?'

'I don't know. We have an internal phone system. Why?'

Alex heard the mild disapproval in the social worker's voice. 'Miss Barker, I'm not trying to be difficult or in denial, but two women from Bailey's hometown are dead. You can't blame me for being suspicious of a phone call allegedly from Bailey that says she's really run off and left Hope to the system.'

'*Two* women?' Barker said. 'I read about the first woman, the congressman's daughter being from Dutton, but now there's another?'

Alex bit her lip. 'That's not public knowledge yet.' Although Daniel was off at his press conference by now, so it would be soon. 'You can understand my apprehension.'

'I suppose so,' Barker said thoughtfully. 'Well, I don't know how to forward a message outside our phone system, but I can have it recorded for you.'

'That would be wonderful. Can I pick up the tape today?'

'It might be tomorrow. Bureaucracy, you know.'

She sounded doubtful, so Alex pushed harder. 'Miss Barker, right before that call came into your office, someone tried to run me down in the street. If someone hadn't pushed me out of the way, I could be dead right now.'

'Oh my God.'

'Now you understand.'

'Oh my God,' Barker repeated, stunned. 'Hope could be in danger.'

The thought of anyone touching Hope left Alex cold. Still she kept her voice confident. 'I'm requesting police protection. If I have to, I'll move Hope out of town.'

'Who's with Hope right now?'

'My cousin.' Meredith had been exceedingly upset by the news of the near miss that afternoon. Alex had been on the phone with Meredith when the call from Barker had beeped through. 'She's a child psychologist from Cincinnati. Hope's in good hands.'

'Fine, then. I'll call you once I've recorded this message.'

Alex called Meredith back, bracing herself for a tirade. She was not disappointed.

'You're coming home with me,' Meredith stated, bypassing any greeting.

'No, I'm not. Mer, that call was from the social worker. Somebody claiming to be Bailey called saying she'd just come off a high and wanted to be sure someone had Hope, that they should keep her, that she was never coming back.'

'Maybe it *was* Bailey, Alex.'

'The call was placed an hour ago, right about when that car tried to mow me down. Somebody wants me to stop looking for Bailey.'

Meredith was quiet for a few beats, then she sighed. 'Did you tell Vartanian?'

'Not yet. He's at a press conference. I'm going to request protection, but I don't know if they'll give it to me. Maybe you should take Hope to Ohio with you.'

'No, not yet. We may have something. I was afraid to turn the TV on today because they keep talking about the murders. So I plugged the organ in and played "Twinkle, Twinkle Little Star." One-fingered, nothing fancy. Just to keep myself sane.'

'And then?'

'And then Hope got this strange look on her face. It was creepy, Alex.'

'Where is Hope now?'

'Playing the damn organ like she has been for the last two hours. I'm on the front porch. I had to have a break or I was going to scream. She picked out this tune. Six notes. She keeps playing it again and again. I'm half expecting her to start building mountains out of mashed potatoes any minute.'

'What's the tune?' Alex listened with a frown as Meredith hummed it. 'I've never heard it before. Have you?'

'No, but if the organ is anything like the coloring, we'll be hearing it for a long time.'

Alex thought for a minute. 'Do me a favor. Call her preschool and ask if they've heard it. Maybe it's a song they sing in school.'

'Good idea. Did the preschool mention Hope's being autistic?'

'I haven't talked to them yet. They were on my list for this afternoon.'

'I'll ask when I call. If these repetitive behaviors are endemic to Hope versus being trauma-induced, then I'm going about things the wrong way. When will you be back?'

'Whenever Daniel comes back. He's got my car keys.'

Meredith snorted a chuckle. 'I suppose that's one way to get you to listen.'

'I listen,' Alex protested.

'Then you do whatever the hell you want to do.' She sighed. 'I can't go back.'

'What do you mean? Are you staying?'

'For a few more days. If I leave and something happens, I'd never forgive myself.'

'I can take care of myself, Meredith,' Alex said, torn between gratitude and annoyance. 'I've been taking care of myself for years.'

'No you haven't,' Meredith said quietly. 'You've been taking care of everyone else for years. You don't take care of Alex. Come back soon. I need a break from this tune.'

Tuesday, January 30, 2:30 P.M.

The Jag rolled up beside him and the window slid down, revealing a very angry man. 'What the fuck happened?'

He'd known he was in trouble when he'd gotten a call to meet in the middle of the day. It was a remote location and neither of them would leave their vehicles, but the sheer risk of being seen together . . .

'You said to make her stop asking about Bailey. My guy said she went straight to the county courthouse today. I'd told him if she got too close to make her stop.'

'And you left it up to "your guy" to decide when and how to do that?'

'He definitely overplayed his hand. You're right.'

'Goddamn straight, I'm right. Do you even know why she was in the courthouse?'

'No. My guy couldn't follow her in. He . . . would have been recognized.'

Dark eyes rolled. 'Oh, for God's sake. You hired some ape with a fucking wanted poster hanging in the county courthouse? God, this town is filled with fuck-ups. I told you I would deal with Bailey.'

He jutted out his chin, unwilling to be lumped with the town fuck-ups. 'You've had her for almost a week. You said you'd have the goddamn key in two days. If you'd delivered *your* end, the stepsister never would have started all this poking around, because I would have delivered *my* end and Bailey Crighton would have already been found in a dumpster somewhere outside Savannah by now.'

His dark eyes flashed dangerously. 'What you've done could blow up in somebody's face and it sure as hell won't be mine. Hell. If you'd planned to hire a felon, why not hire one with a little more finesse? A hit-and-run in downtown in the middle of the goddamn day? Your guy is beyond stupid. He's a liability now. Get rid of him.'

'How?'

'I don't care. Just do it. And don't fuck it up. Then find out *why* Alex Fallon was at the courthouse today. All we need is her digging up trial transcripts.'

'She won't find anything in the trial transcripts.'

'Yeah, and she was supposed to believe her stepsister was some strung-out junkie who skipped town, but she didn't buy that, did she? I don't trust what she'll find.'

Because he also wasn't sure what Alex Fallon would find, he turned his attention to the bigger failure. 'So how *will* you handle Bailey Crighton?'

The man's cobra smile raised the hair on his neck. 'Bailey's gone back on the juice.'

That actually surprised him. Bailey had been sober for five years. 'Voluntarily?'

His sinister smile widened. 'Now what fun would there have been in that? By tomorrow she'll be begging for her next fix, just like old times. She'll tell me what I want to know. But Bailey and her stepsister aren't why I called you. I want to know what the fuck's going on with these dead women?'

He blinked. 'I thought . . .'

'You thought it was me? Shit. You're a bigger idiot than I thought.'

His cheeks flushed hot. 'Well, it's not me or any of the others.'

'And you're sure of this because . . . ?'

'Bluto doesn't have the balls to kill anybody and Igor's just a whiny little bastard. He's frothing at the mouth, calling Bluto, meeting him in the park at all hours in plain view of half the town. That boy's gonna blow the whole damn thing out of the water.'

'You should have told me before now.' It was said softly, maliciously.

His stomach wrenched when he realized exactly what he'd done. 'Wait a minute.'

His dark eyes became amused. 'You're in too deep, Sweetpea. You can't back out.'

It was true. He was in way too deep. He licked his lips. 'Don't call me that.'

'The nicknames were your idea. It's not my fault you don't like yours.' The mocking smile disappeared. 'You fool. You're worried about a *nickname* when you don't know who's doing these women? You think Igor can blow us out of the water? You think Alex Fallon's questions are a threat? Those are *nothing* compared to what these killings can do to us. The press has picked up on the connection. The Tremaine girl's picture was all over the news last night. *What do you know?*'

His mouth went dry. 'I thought it was some copycat at first. Maybe some wacko who read about it after all the news about what happened to Simon up north.'

'I don't care what you thought. I asked what you *know*.'

'Claudia Silva was the second victim. She was found with a key tied around her toe.'

He stiffened. A match flared and cigarette smoke billowed from the Jag. 'Has Daniel found Simon's key yet?'

Simon's key. The carrot with which Simon Vartanian taunted them all, even from his grave. His real grave this time. At least Daniel had gotten that right. 'If he has, he hasn't said anything.'

'He's not going to tell you. Has he been back to his house?'

'Not since before the funeral.'

'And you've searched the house?'

'I've been through the old Vartanian place ten times.'

'Make it eleven.'

'He can get into the box without the key, you know.'

'Yeah, but he may not know about the box. The minute he finds a key, he'll start looking for the box. If he hasn't already. This asshole who's killing the women knows about the key. He wants the cops to know about the key. So make sure Daniel doesn't find Simon's key.'

'He hasn't been to the bank. I know that. But he is seeing the Fallon woman. Half the town saw him shoving his tongue down her throat on her front porch last night.'

Again the cobra smile. 'You can work with that. After you take care of Igor.'

His blood went cold. 'I'm not killing Rhett Porter.' He used Igor's real name, hoping it would shock some reason back into the conversation. But he'd wasted his breath because the cobra smile just widened.

'Sure you will, Sweetpea.' The window rolled up and the Jag drove away.

And he sat there staring straight ahead, knowing he would, just like he had the last time he'd been told to kill. Because he was in way too deep. He had to kill Rhett Porter. He commanded his churning stomach to settle. After all, what was one more?

Atlanta, Tuesday, January 30, 3:25 P.M.

'And so the social worker is recording it for me,' Alex finished. Sitting in the chair in front of Daniel's desk she glanced from Daniel to Chase Wharton, whose body language was tense, but whose face was carefully blank. From the corner of her eye she looked at Ed Randall, who regarded her with a scrutiny that made her feel as if she was on display.

Chase turned to Daniel. 'Call Papadopoulos. Make sure that recording is made correctly so we can separate out any background noise.'

'Who is Papadopoulos?' Alex asked, twisting her fingers together. That they hadn't even suggested that Bailey had really made the call made her nervous.

'Luke,' Daniel said. 'You met him earlier. He's the one who drove your car back.'

'Speaking of which,' Alex said, nearly flinching at the warning look Daniel blasted her way, 'I need my keys back, Daniel. I can't stay here all day. I need to talk to Hope's preschool. She's doing other weird things we don't understand. And at some point I need to go through Bailey's house. If Loomis's office won't do it, then I have to.'

Chase turned to Ed. 'Get a team out to Bailey Crighton's house. Go through everything. Alex, you're welcome to join him if you like.'

Alex's hands stilled in her lap as the breath backed up in her lungs and the screeching began. It was louder now. It was just the stress of the afternoon. *Quiet*. *Quiet*. She closed her eyes and concentrated. *Grow up, Alex. It's just a damn house*. She looked up at Chase Wharton, resolute. 'Thank you. I will.'

'I'll get that team together,' Ed said. 'Do you want to ride with me, Miss Fallon?'

She met Daniel's stern glare. He was scared again,

she thought. 'I'd actually like to drive my own car, but I'd feel safer if I drove in front of you on the way out to Dutton. I think that would address Agent Vartanian's concerns as well, wouldn't it?'

She saw Ed's lips twitch and decided she liked the man, even if he did stare at her strangely. 'I'll call you when I'm ready to go,' he said and closed the door behind him.

'Daniel's told me about the child. What weird new thing is she doing?' Chase asked.

'She's playing a tune on the old organ in the bungalow I'm renting. Same six notes over and over. Neither of us knows the tune.'

'Maybe Sister Anne knows it,' Daniel said thoughtfully. 'We can ask her tonight when we take Hope back up to the shelter.'

Alex's eyes widened. 'I assumed you'd be too busy.'

He gave her a look of tolerant annoyance. 'I may not be able to get down to your place for dinner, but we need to take Hope to see Sister Anne. If Hope saw something, we need to know. Bailey is connected to all this. She might even be an eyewitness.'

'I agree,' Chase said. 'Miss Fallon, we're arranging for police protection for you and your niece. It won't be twenty-four-hour because we simply don't have the resources, but we'll have drive-bys. You'll also have a list of all our cell phone numbers in case of an emergency. Do not hesitate to call us if you think you're in danger.'

'I won't. Thank you.' She stood up and held out her hand. 'My keys?'

Jaw cocked, Daniel pulled her keys from his pocket. 'Call me. And stay with Ed.'

'I'm not stupid, Daniel. I'll be careful.' She turned at his office door. 'My satchel?'

His blue eyes narrowed. 'Don't push your luck, Alex.'

'But you'll bring it later?'

'Yeah, sure. Later.' He almost growled it.

'And Riley?'

One side of his mouth lifted. 'And Riley.'

She smiled at him. 'Thank you.'

'I'll walk you out. This way.' He pulled her into a dark little hallway, tipped up her chin, and searched her face. 'You were crying earlier. Are you really okay?'

Alex's cheeks heated and she had to fight the urge to tug away from his probing gaze. 'I had a bad couple of moments when I was talking to the social worker. You know, when the adrenaline crashed and I wasn't thinking clearly. But I'm okay. Really.'

He brushed his thumb over her lower lip. Then his mouth was covering hers. A natural calm settled over her, despite the sudden pounding of her heart.

He lifted his head just far enough to let her catch her breath. 'Are we on a camera somewhere?' she asked and felt him smile against her mouth.

'Probably. So let's give them something to talk about.' And she forgot about the camera and even about breathing when he kissed her harder and hotter than anyone had before. Abruptly he pulled back, swallowing hard. 'You should probably go now.'

She nodded unsteadily. 'I probably should. I'll see you later.' She turned to leave and flinched. 'Ouch.' She rubbed her scalp and glared at his sleeve. 'That hurt.'

He pulled a few strands of her hair from his button and kissed the top of her head. 'The woman nearly gets flattened by a car and she complains about a little pulled hair.'

She chuckled. 'I'll see you tonight. Call if you do get busy.'

Chase was still in his office when he got back. Daniel slumped in his chair, aware of Chase's openly curious appraisal. 'Go ahead and tell me,' he said.

'Go ahead and tell you what?' Chase's tone held mild amusement.

'I'm in too deep, I'm too emotionally invested, I'm moving too fast . . . take your pick.'

'How fast you move in your personal life is your business, Daniel. But I'm told that when it hits you, there's not a lot you can do about it. So are you in too deep?'

'I have no idea. Right now I just want to keep her alive.' Feeling lower than dirt, Daniel laid the hairs from Alex's head next to the hair swatch. 'Damn. They're close.'

Chase sat in one of Daniel's chairs. 'What did you tell her?'

Daniel scowled at him. 'I didn't.'

Chase's eyes widened. 'You just yanked it?'

'Not exactly. I used a little more finesse than that.' And if she found out, she'd be more hurt than just a stinging scalp. But he'd cross that bridge when he got there.

Chase's shrug was restless. 'You'll find a way to tell her the truth when you have to. For now, like you said, let's focus on keeping her alive by finding the guy who's killed two women and copied a thirteen-year-old crime scene. I want to know why he's doing this now. Is it just the publicity Dutton's gotten in the last week?'

I'll see you in hell, Simon. Daniel bit his lower lip and knew he had to speak the truth. 'It has something to do with Simon.'

Chase narrowed his eyes. 'I don't think I want to hear this, do I?'

'No. But it might make a difference.' He told Chase about the letters Bailey's brother had written and the visit from the army chaplain. *I'll see you in hell, Simon.*

Chase frowned. 'How long have you known about this, Daniel?'

Ten years. No, not true. Those pictures might have nothing to do with any of the murders, thirteen years ago or this week. *You're lying to yourself.* 'Since last night,' he said. 'How Simon and Wade connect to these two murders, I don't know.'

Tell him. But as soon as he did, he'd be off the case. He didn't want to take the risk, so he told the only truth he absolutely knew. 'I do know that Simon did not kill Janet or Claudia. Nor did he abduct Bailey or try to kill Alex.'

Chase blew out a breath. 'Hell. I'm gonna give you some rope. Don't hang yourself.'

Relief was a palpable thing. 'I'm going to the Barneses' condo. Their parking attendant told Mr Barnes he saw Claudia's Mercedes leave the garage last night, but she never came back. Maybe he ambushed her in the parking garage.'

'What about Janet Bowie's car?'

'No hits on the APB. Leigh checked Janet's credit card and found the company that rented her the minivan she drove to Fun-N-Sun on Thursday. She never brought it back. She dropped the kids at the school at seven-fifteen and called her boyfriend at eight-oh-six.'

'So there's only a fifty-minute window of opportunity for the killer to abduct her. Where was she when he abducted her?'

Daniel sifted through the faxes Leigh had left on his desk while they'd been at the press conference. 'Here's something from the cell phone company. I had them triangulate the call Janet made to Lamar. She called him from a parking lot about a mile from the rental car place, which is about a thirty-minute drive from the school.'

'That leaves twenty minutes for him to grab her. So where and how? And where is the minivan? Did he dump it? Hide it?'

'And where is Janet's car?' Daniel mused. 'Did she leave it at the rental place when she picked up the van? Was the van delivered somewhere else? I'll call and find out.'

Chase stood up and stretched. 'I need some coffee. You want some?'

'Yeah, thanks. I'm running on only about an hour's sleep.' Daniel looked up the number for the rental place, talked to the manager, and was hanging up when Chase came back with coffee and bags of cookies from the vending machine.

'Oatmeal or chocolate chip?' he asked.

'Chocolate.' Daniel caught the bag and tore it open with a grimace. 'I have Luke's mama's leftovers in my fridge but I keep forgetting to bring them in.'

'We could steal Luke's lunch.'

'He already ate it. Okay. Janet left her Z-4 in front of the rental place early Thursday and when they came in on Friday morning it was gone. They've got a security camera on the parking lot. I'll stop by and get the tapes for Thursday night into Friday morning.'

'Check out the area the wireless company pinpointed, too. Maybe we'll get lucky and find there was a security camera wherever he grabbed her.'

'I will.' He munched the cookie, thinking. 'Janet calls her boyfriend, most likely under duress. Today Bailey calls to say she's skipped town and abandoned her child.'

'Can Alex identify Bailey's voice once we get that message from Social Services?'

'She hasn't talked to Bailey in five years, so I doubt it. I'll check with the salon where Bailey worked. They're most familiar with her voice.'

'It's not looking good for Bailey,' Chase said. 'She's been gone five days now.'

'I know. But she's the connection. Hopefully Ed will find something at her house. I called the army chaplain who visited yesterday, but I haven't heard back from him.'

'You're not gonna get anything out of the chaplain and you know it. Focus on getting something out of the little girl. Get her in to see Mary McCrady. If this kid has seen something, the sooner we pry it out of her the better.'

Daniel winced. Mary was their department psychologist. 'It's not like the kid's a splinter or something, Chase.'

Chase rolled his eyes. 'You know what I mean. Sensitize it up for Fallon, but I want the kid in Mary's office tomorrow morning.' He went to the door, then turned, troubled. 'When I heard what happened up in Philly, I thought whatever demons have been driving you ever since I've known you were finally dead. But they're not, are they?'

Slowly Daniel shook his head. 'No.'

'Have I given you enough rope to at least hog-tie 'em?'

Daniel chuckled in spite of himself. 'Either that, or I'll hang myself trying.'

Chase didn't smile. 'I won't let you hang yourself. I don't know what you think you have to prove, but you're a good agent and I won't let you sacrifice your career.' Then he was gone, leaving Daniel with a pile of paper and a few strands of Alex Fallon's hair.

Get busy, Vartanian. The demons have a head start.

Chapter Ten

Tuesday, January 30, 3:45 P.M.

'Bailey.' Beardsley's voice was muffled. 'Bailey, are you there?'

Bailey opened one eye, then closed it again when the room spun wildly. 'I'm here.'

'Are you all right?'

A sob tore free. 'No.'

'What did he do to you?'

'Injection,' she said, trying not to let her teeth chatter. She was shaking so hard she thought her bones would pop out of her skin. 'Smack.'

There was silence, then a muted 'Dear God.'

He knew then, she thought. 'I worked so hard to kick it . . . the first time.'

'I know. Wade told me. You'll get out of here and you'll kick it again.'

No, Bailey thought. *I'm too tired to go through that again.*

'Bailey?' Beardsley's whisper was urgent. 'You still

with me? I need to keep your mind clear. I may have a way out of here. Do you understand?'

'Yes.' But she knew it was useless. *I'll never leave.* Five years she'd fought the demons every day. *Feed me, feed me. Just a taste to get you going*. But she'd resisted. For Hope. For herself. And with one push of a syringe, *he'd* destroyed it all.

Tuesday, January 30, 3:45 P.M.

The phone on his desk was ringing. He ignored it, staring at the newest letter. *Of course I'm the one he calls.* This was worse than he'd ever thought possible.

The phone on his desk stilled and his cell phone immediately began to trill. Furious, he grabbed it. 'What,' he snarled. 'What the hell do you want?'

'I got another one.' He was breathless, terrified.

'I know.'

'They want a hundred grand. I don't have that much. You have to loan it to me.'

The photocopied page had come with instructions on how to deposit the funds. It was crunched by his own hands, his knee-jerk reaction at what seemed like an innocent page of pictures, but in reality was obscene. 'What else did you get?'

'A page with yearbook pictures. Janet's and Claudia's. Did you get one?'

'Yeah.' A page of photos cut from their yearbook and

pasted in alphabetical order. Ten girls in all. With Xs through Janet's and Claudia's faces. 'Kate's picture's there,' he said hoarsely. *My baby sister*.

'I know. What am I going to do?'

What am I *going to do*. That phrase summed up Rhett Porter. For God's sake, *Kate's picture* was on that page and Rhett was only worried about himself. Selfish, whiny little prick. 'Did you get anything else?' he asked.

'No. Why?' Panic hitched Rhett's voice up a half octave. 'What else did you get?'

As if Kate's picture weren't enough. 'Nothing.' But he couldn't keep the contempt from his voice.

'Dammit, tell me.' Rhett was sobbing now.

'Don't call me anymore.' He flipped his phone shut. Immediately it began to trill again. He turned it off, then threw it as hard as he could against the wall.

He pulled an old ashtray from his desk drawer. Nobody was allowed to smoke in his office anymore, but the ashtray had been a Father's Day present from his son, made clumsily by five-year-old hands. It was a treasure he'd never throw away. His family was everything. They must be protected, at all costs. They could never know.

You're a coward. You have to say something. You have to warn these women.

But he wouldn't. Because if he warned them, he'd have to tell how he knew and he wasn't willing to do that. He flicked his lighter and touched the flame to the corner of the photocopy. It burned slowly, curling on itself until he could no longer see the picture of his own sister, circled for emphasis. Kate had graduated the same year as Janet Bowie and Claudia Silva Barnes. The threat was clear. Pay up or Kate would be next.

The last picture to burn was the eleventh, the one only his paper apparently had. He stared as Rhett Porter's face melted, then burned to ash.

Rhett. You dumb fuck. You're a dead man because you couldn't keep your damn mouth shut. When the photocopy was fully burned, he dumped the ashes in the coffee he'd left untouched from the morning. He stood up, smoothed his tie.

I, on the other hand, can be taught. He carefully folded the instructions for the required bank deposit and slipped them into his wallet. He knew a guy who could do a bank transfer and keep his mouth shut. He wiped the dust from the ashtray with a tissue, then carefully placed the ashtray back in his drawer. He had to get to the bank.

Dutton, Tuesday, January 30, 5:45 P.M.

Oh, God. *Alex*. Daniel's heart started to race as he pulled into the street to Bailey Crighton's house. An ambulance was parked on the curb, its lights flashing.

He ran to the ambulance. Alex sat inside in the back, her head between her knees.

He forced his voice to be calm even though his heart was stuck in his throat. 'Hey.'

She looked up, pale. 'It's just a house,' she hissed. 'Why can't I get over this?'

'What happened?'

The paramedic appeared from the other side of the rig. 'She had a garden-variety panic attack,' he said, condescension in his tone. Alex's chin shot up and she glared. But she said nothing and the paramedic made no apology.

Daniel put his arm around her. 'What exactly happened, honey?' he murmured, glancing at the paramedic's badge. P. Bledsoe. He vaguely recalled the family.

Alex leaned against him. 'I tried to go in. I got to the front porch and I got sick.'

Bledsoe shrugged. 'We checked her out. She had a slightly elevated BP, but nothing out of range. Maybe she just needs some tranquilizers.' He said it with sarcasm and it wasn't until Alex stiffened that Daniel understood what the man had meant.

Sonofabitch. Daniel stood, fury hazing the edges of his vision. *'Excuse me?'*

Alex grabbed his jacket between her fingertips. 'Daniel, please.'

But there was shame in her voice and his temper blew. 'No. That was inexcusable.'

Bledsoe blinked innocently. 'I was just suggesting that Miss Tremaine calm down.'

Daniel's eyes narrowed. 'Like hell you were. Plan on filling out about fifty forms, buddy, because your supervisor's going to hear about this.'

The color rose in Bledsoe's cheeks. 'I really didn't mean any harm.'

'Tell it to your supervisor.' Daniel lifted Alex's chin. 'Can you walk?'

She looked away. 'Yeah.'

'Then let's go. You can sit in my car.' She was quiet until they got to his car. He opened the front passenger door, but she pulled back when he tried to guide her in.

'You shouldn't have said anything. I don't need to make more enemies in this town.'

'Nobody should talk to you like that, Alex.'

Her mouth twisted. 'Don't you think I know that? Don't you think it's humiliating enough that I can't even walk into that place?' Her voice became cool. 'But what he intimated is true. I did swallow a bottleful of tranquilizers and nearly offed myself.'

'That's not the point.'

'Of course it's not the point. The point is that I need the people in this town until I find out what happened to Bailey. Long term, I don't care. It's not like I plan to live here.'

Daniel blinked, for the first time considering that at some point she'd return to the life she'd dropped so abruptly. 'I'm sorry. I didn't think about it that way.'

Her shoulders sagged, the cool façade vanishing.

'And I'm sorry. You were trying to help. Let's just forget it.' She bent to get into his car and her face relaxed. 'Riley.'

Riley sat behind the wheel, alert and sniffing. 'He likes the car,' Daniel said.

'I can see that. Hey, Riley.' Scratching Riley's ears, she looked through the driver's window to Bailey's house. 'A grown woman shouldn't be afraid of a house.'

'You want to try again?' Daniel asked.

'Yes.' She backed out of the car and Riley stepped over the gearshift, following her to the passenger seat. Her expression was severe. 'Don't let me run. Make me go in.'

'Ed won't like it if you throw up on his crime scene,' he said mildly, taking her arm and slamming the car door in Riley's face.

She huffed a chuckle. 'If I turn green, run.' But the chuckle disappeared as they neared the house. Her step slowed and her body trembled. This was a real physical reaction, Daniel realized.

'PTSD,' he murmured. Post-traumatic stress disorder. She had all the signs.

'I figured that out on my own,' she muttered. 'Don't let me run. Promise me.'

'I promise. I'll be right behind you.' He lightly pushed her up the front porch stairs.

'I got this far before.' She said it between her teeth. Her face had grown very pale.

'I wasn't with you before,' he said. She leaned back at the open front door and Daniel gently but firmly propelled her forward. She stumbled, but he caught her, keeping her upright. Her body was shaking now and he could hear her muttering to herself.

'Quiet, quiet.'

'The screams?' he asked and she nodded. He looked over her shoulder. Her arms were crossed tight over her chest, her face was clenched, her eyes closed tight. Her lips moved in a silent mantra of 'Quiet, quiet.' Daniel slipped his arms around her waist and held her to him. 'You're doing great. You're in the living room, Alex.'

She only nodded, her eyes still clenched shut. 'Tell me what's here.'

Daniel puffed out a breath. 'Well, it's a mess. There's garbage on the floor.'

'I can smell it.'

'And there's an old mattress on the floor, too. No sheet. The mattress is stained.'

'With blood?' she asked through her teeth.

'No, probably sweat.' She was still trembling, but not as violently. He tucked her under his chin. She fit perfectly. 'There's an old picture hanging on the wall, crooked. It's one of those beach scenes with the sand dunes. It's discolored and old.'

She was relaxing into him a little more each minute. 'That was never here before.' She opened her eyes and drew a sharp breath. 'The walls are painted.' There was relief in her voice and Daniel thought about how this house must appear in her dreams.

She'd found her mother dead in this room. He'd discovered gun-to-the-head suicides over the course of his career. At least one of the walls would have been covered in blood, brains, and bits of bone. What a horrific memory to have carried all these years.

'The carpet is blue,' he said.

'It was brown before.' She turned her head, taking it all in. 'It's all different.'

'It's been thirteen years, Alex. It's to be expected that they'd clean up. Paint. Nobody would leave the house the way you remembered it.'

Her laugh was self-deprecating. 'I know. I should have known, anyway.'

'Sshh.' He kissed the top of her head. 'You're doing great.'

She nodded, her swallow audible. 'Thank you. Wow, the cops were right. This place is a sty.' She nudged the mattress with her toe. 'Bailey, what were you thinking?'

'You want to come with me to look for Ed?'

She nodded quickly. 'Yes,' she blurted. 'Don't—'

Don't leave me alone. 'I won't leave you, Alex. You ever see those old vaudeville acts? We'll just walk like them.'

She chuckled, but it was a pained sound. 'This is ridiculous, Daniel.'

He started walking, keeping her close. 'Ed?' he called.

The back door slammed and Ed came in through the kitchen. His serious expression became one of surprise when he saw Alex. 'Did the EMTs say she was okay?'

'You called them?' Daniel asked.

'Yeah. She was white as a sheet and her pulse was through the moon.'

'Thank you, Agent Randall,' she said, and Daniel could hear the embarrassment in her voice. 'I'm okay now.'

'I'm glad.' He looked at Daniel, gentle amusement in his eyes. 'I offered to hold on to her, but she turned me down flat.'

Daniel gave him a don't-even-think-about-it look and Ed bit back his smile, then sobered, his hands on his hips as he looked around the room. 'This is staged,' Ed declared, and beneath Daniel's chin, Alex's head shot up.

'What?' she demanded.

'Yes, ma'am. Somebody wanted this place to look like a mess. This carpet is dirty, but the dirt's not ground in. The base of the carpet fibers are clean – somebody's vacuumed recently and often. The dust on everything? We've taken samples and will run all the tests back at the lab, but I'm betting it's all the same composition. Looks like a mix of ash and dirt. The toilets are so clean you can drink out of them.' His lips curved. 'Not that I'm recommending it, mind you.'

'The social worker said Hope was found in a closet.' She pointed. 'Right there.'

'We'll check it out.'

Daniel knew Ed well enough to know there was more. 'What did you find?'

Alex went rigid against him. 'Tell me. Please.'

'Outside in the woods in back of the house, there was a struggle. We found blood.'

'How much blood?' Alex asked, very quietly.

'A lot. Someone had covered the area with leaves, but the wind last night blew them around. We're finding a lot of leaves with blood smears. I'm sorry.'

Unsteadily she nodded. She was trembling again. 'I understand.'

Daniel tightened his hold on her. 'Did you find blood here in the house, Ed?'

'Not yet, but we've really just started. Why?'

'Because Hope is coloring with red crayons,' Alex answered for him. 'If she was hiding in the closet the whole time, she wouldn't have seen the blood.'

'So she was either looking through a window or she was out there,' Daniel finished.

'We'll check it out,' Ed promised.

Daniel tugged on Alex. 'Come on, Alex. Let's go outside. You've seen enough.'

Her chin went up. 'Not yet. Can I go upstairs, Agent Randall?'

'If you don't touch anything.'

But she didn't move. Daniel leaned down to

murmur in her ear, 'You want to walk vaudeville or ride over my shoulder, caveman style?'

She closed her eyes and her hands clenched around the bandages. 'I have to do this, Daniel.' But her voice shook. She was past cool, past scared.

Daniel didn't necessarily agree that this was a good idea. He could already see the change in her face. She was pale, her forehead clammy. Still, he gave her a squeeze of encouragement. 'If you think so, then I'll go with you.'

She got to the stairs and stopped. She was shaking head to toe, her breath shallow and rapid. She grabbed the banister, her fingers digging in like claws. 'Just a damn house,' she muttered and pulled herself up two of the stairs before stopping again.

Daniel turned her face so that she looked at him. Her eyes were glassy and terrified.

'I can't,' she whispered.

'Then don't,' he whispered back.

'I have to.'

'Why?'

'I don't know. But I have to.' She closed her eyes, wincing with pain. 'It's really loud,' she said, sounding more like a child.

'What do they say?' he asked and her eyes flew open.

'What?'

'What do they say when they scream?'

' "No." And she says, "I hate you, I hate you. I wish

you were dead." ' Tears rolled down her ashen cheeks.

Daniel smoothed away her tears with his thumb. 'Who says that?'

She was sobbing now, silently. 'My mom. It's my mom.'

Daniel turned her into his arms and she clutched the lapels of his suit as her whole body shook with the force of her silent weeping. He backed down the few stairs she'd climbed, taking her with him.

When they got outside, the ambulance was packing up to leave. Bledsoe took one look at Alex, bowed over and stumbling, and started toward them. Daniel leveled the man his coldest look and Bledsoe stopped in his tracks.

'What happened?' Bledsoe asked.

'This is not a garden-variety panic attack,' Daniel bit out. 'Get out of the damn way.'

Bledsoe started walking backward. 'I'm sorry. I didn't think . . .'

'Damn straight you didn't think. I said *move*.'

Bledsoe had backed his way to the curb, looking distressed. 'Is she all right?'

She was still weeping in his arms, and it broke Daniel's heart. 'No, but she will be.'

Dutton, Tuesday, January 30, 6:45 P.M.

A willowy redhead was sitting on Alex's front porch steps, her head in her hands. The front door stood open and as soon as he got out of the car Daniel could hear the six notes Alex had told him about. Again and again and again.

The redhead lifted her head and Daniel saw a frustrated woman at the edge of control. Then she saw Alex and stood, her eyes focused. 'My God. What happened?'

'She's okay,' Daniel said. He went around the car and helped Alex to her feet. 'Come on, Riley.' The hound took a lazy leap to the street.

Alex winced at the music. 'She's still playing?'

The redhead nodded. 'Yes.'

'Why not just unplug the organ?' Daniel asked, and the woman gave him a look so filled with ire that he almost stepped back. 'Sorry.'

'I *tried* to unplug the organ,' she said through gritted teeth. 'She started to scream. Loudly.' She glared at Alex in helpless frustration. 'Somebody called the cops on me.'

'You're kidding,' Alex said. 'Who came?'

'Some deputy named Cowell. He said he'd have to call Social Services if we couldn't get her to stop screaming, that the neighbors were complaining. I plugged the organ back in until we could decide what to do next. Alex, we may need to sedate her.'

Alex's shoulders sagged. 'Hell. Daniel, my cousin, Dr Meredith Fallon. Meredith, Agent Daniel Vartanian.' She looked down at her feet. 'And Riley.'

Meredith nodded. 'I figured that out. Come in, Alex. You look like hell. Please excuse my rudeness, Agent Vartanian. My nerves are running thin.'

The music was already starting to grate on him after only a few minutes. He couldn't imagine listening to it for hours. He followed them into the bungalow where a little girl with golden curls sat in front of the organ playing the same six notes with one finger. She didn't act like she even knew they were there.

Alex's jaw tightened. 'This has gone on long enough. We need Hope to talk to us.' Alex walked to the wall and unplugged the organ. Immediately the music ceased and Hope's head shot up. Her mouth opened and her chest expanded as she dragged in a deep breath, but before she could make a sound, Alex was in her face. 'Don't. Don't scream.' She put her hands on the little girl's shoulders. 'Look at me, Hope. Now.'

Startled, Hope lifted her face to Alex's. Beside him, Meredith huffed a frustrated sigh. '*"Don't scream,"*' she muttered sarcastically. 'Wish to hell I'd thought of that.'

'Sshh,' Daniel cautioned.

'I just came from your house, Hope,' Alex said. 'Baby, I know what you saw. I know somebody hurt your mommy.'

Meredith stared at Daniel. 'She went to the house?' she mouthed, and he nodded.

Hope was staring up at Alex, a tortured look on her little face, but instead of screaming, silent tears began to roll down her cheeks.

'You're scared,' Alex said. 'And so am I. But, Hope, your mommy loves you. You know she does. She never would have left you on purpose.'

Daniel wondered who Alex was trying to convince, herself or Hope. *I hate you. I wish you were dead.* Whether or not her mother had actually said the words, they were real in Alex's mind. It was a terrible burden to live with. This he knew.

Tears still streaming down her cheeks, Hope began to rock on the organ bench. Sliding on the bench next to her, Alex pulled Hope into her arms and rocked with her. 'Sshh. I'm here. Meredith's here. We won't leave you. You're safe now.'

Riley padded over to where Alex rocked Hope and poked her thigh with his nose.

Alex took Hope's clenched fist and, spreading the little fingers wide, put Hope's hand on Riley's head. Riley gave one of his giant sighs and laid his nose on Hope's knee. Hope began to pet Riley's head.

Beside him Meredith Fallon drew a shaky breath. 'I hope she doesn't pet your dog like she colored or played that organ. Riley will be bald by bedtime.'

'We'll put Rogaine in his dog chow,' Daniel said.

Meredith snorted a laugh that sounded more like a sob. 'She went into the house.'

Daniel sighed. 'Yes.'

'And you went with her.'

'Yes.'

'Thank you.' She cleared her throat. 'Alex, I'm hungry and I have to get out of this house. When I was running this morning I passed a pizza place next to the post office.'

'Presto Pizza?' Daniel asked, surprised.

'You know it?' Meredith asked and he nodded.

'I lived on their pepperoni slices when I was a kid. I didn't know it was still there.'

'Then that's where we're going. Alex, put on some makeup. We're eating out.'

Alex lifted her face, frowning. 'I don't think so. We're going to see Sister Anne.'

'We'll do that after we eat. Hope needs to get out, too. I've been treating her with kid gloves, observing her. You made a breakthrough. I don't want her sliding backward.'

'We still need to eat, Alex,' Daniel said, earning him an appreciative glance from Meredith. 'It won't take long, then we can go to the shelter. Besides, who knows who'll show up while we're eating? The guy that tried to run you down had been watching you. If he wasn't the same person who took Bailey, he may know who did.'

She nodded. 'You're right. And it's not only Bailey.

There are the other women, too. I'm sorry, Daniel. I'm being selfish. I guess I'm not thinking too straight right now.'

'It's okay. You've had kind of a busy day.' And because she looked like she needed it, he went to her and pulled her into his arms. She rested her cheek against his chest and he realized he'd needed this, too. 'Go on, change your clothes.' He looked down at Hope, who was still stroking Riley's head. Riley gave him a soulful look and Daniel chuckled. 'Hurry, before poor Riley needs a toupee.'

Tuesday, January 30, 7:00 P.M.

He gripped the steering wheel, glancing up at his rearview mirror. He licked his lips nervously. It was still there. The car had been tailing him since he'd hit US-19.

Rhett Porter had no idea where he was going. All he knew was that he had to get away. *Get away*. He was a marked man. He'd known it as soon as he'd heard his friend say 'Nothing' with such contempt. *His friend*. Ha. One hell of a friend, dropping him like a hot potato as soon as things got rough.

He'd get away. He knew things. Things any upstanding district attorney would want to know. Would pay to know. He'd take his payment in the form of witness protection.

He'd move to the middle of nowhere, lose his drawl. Disappear.

He heard the rev of the engine behind him a moment before he felt the jolt. The steering wheel wrenched from his hands as the tires slipped off the edge of the road. He fought for control, but it was too late. He saw the road drop away. Saw the rush of trees past his windows. Heard the crunch of metal against wood.

Felt the crushing blow to his skull, the piercing pain in his chest, the dizziness as his car began to roll. He smelled the iron odor of blood. His own blood. *I'm bleeding*.

When the world stopped moving, he looked up, dazed. He was hanging upside down, still strapped to his seat. He heard footsteps, saw knees as someone crouched to look into the wreckage that had been his car. His hope died when eyes he knew and had once trusted stared at him through the splintered glass of his windshield.

Still he tried. 'Help me,' he moaned.

The eyes rolled. 'You would have to wear a seat belt. You can't even die right.'

The eyes disappeared. The footsteps retreated, then returned.

'Help me. Please.'

'You're a fuck-up, Porter.' He pushed the broken glass aside with his elbow, reached in, and took the keys from his ignition. A moment later, the keys were returned. One key, Rhett knew, would be missing. He almost smiled, wishing he could be there to see their stunned reactions when they saw what it unlocked.

Then he smelled gasoline, then the acrid smell of burning tinder and he knew.

I'm going to die. He closed his eyes, cursing the men he'd protected for so long. Thirteen years he'd kept the secret. Now . . . *I'll see you all in hell.*

He stood on the road, fists on his hips, watching the fire licking around the car below. He could feel the heat from where he stood. Someone would come soon. He put the gas can in his trunk and drove away. *Bye, Igor. You stupid sonofabitch.*

He swallowed as he drove. They had numbered seven once. Now they were three.

He'd been responsible for the elimination of two of them. DJ's body had never been found. He remembered the sulfur smell of the swamp, the splash as he'd chucked DJ's body over the side of his boat. He imagined a gator had feasted that night.

DJ had been a liability. The gambling, the liquor, the women. Lots of women. They hadn't nicknamed Jared O'Brien 'Don Juan' for nothing. Jared had gone off on rants when he got drunk. It had been only a matter of time before he exposed them all. It had been Jared or the rest of them. The choice hadn't been that difficult.

Somehow killing Igor had been a lot harder. When the fire was done with Rhett Porter, there wouldn't be much of his body left either. So it all amounted to the same difference, except that somewhere a gator was going to bed with an empty stomach.

He thought of the other two that were now gone. Daniel Vartanian had taken down Ahab. Of course they'd never called Simon that to his face. Simon had been a scary SOB, his peg leg just one of many untouchable subjects. He remembered the day they'd buried Simon the first time. The relief they'd all felt, but no one had voiced.

And the other? It had only been a matter of time. He was frankly shocked Po'boy had lived as long as he had, dodging bullets in every godforsaken war zone on the planet. Finally it had been an Iraqi insurgent that had taken Wade out. He'd first felt relief at the news that Dutton's war hero was coming home in a box. For years Wade Crighton had been an unsnipped thread, the only one of them to leave the town, the only one of them out of the sight and control of the others.

Well, except for Simon, he thought. They'd thought they'd been safe with him dead all those years. He supposed they should thank Daniel Vartanian for killing the scary SOB once and for all, but the thought of thanking Daniel Vartanian for anything made him sick. Simon had been scary, but Daniel was smug and that made him angry.

Now both Simon and Wade were gone, as were Rhett and Jared.

Now they numbered only three. Both Simon and Wade had died beyond his reach, leaving the whereabouts of their keys in question. A week ago he would have thought finding their keys would solve all of his problems. But now the keys were the least of his problems.

Janet and Claudia, both dead, found just like Alicia Tremaine. *And I didn't kill them*. Neither had his boss. *I was an idiot to ever think that he would*. Harvard was sick and twisted, but not stupid.

They'd all been stupid kids, but now they were men. Leaders of the community. They'd managed this uneasy truce among themselves for years, no one wanting to lose the lives they'd built for themselves. The respectability they'd earned.

Somebody else had killed Janet and Claudia, someone who'd mimicked Alicia Tremaine's death down to the smallest detail. It might have been a copycat.

Except that somebody knew about the keys. Somebody was taunting them. He thought of Rhett Porter. Somebody wanted them to panic. Rhett had panicked and now he was dead.

Now they were three. If no one else panicked, there was no way anyone else would find out, no way they could be linked to Alicia Tremaine.

Because they hadn't killed her. They'd raped Alicia Tremaine, but they hadn't killed her nor had they dumped her blanket-wrapped body in a ditch. The man that had killed Alicia Tremaine had been rotting behind bars for thirteen years. No one could pin anything on them now, as long as they stayed calm. They just needed to stay calm.

Stay calm. And think. He needed to find out who was killing these women before Vartanian did. If Vartanian got to this bastard first . . . Whoever had killed Janet and Claudia knew about the club. The bastard would tell. And everything they'd built for themselves would be taken away. Destroyed.

I need to find out what the hell Daniel Vartanian knows. Why had Vartanian, of all people, been assigned to this case? Did Vartanian know? Did he know about Simon . . . *and us?* Had Vartanian found Simon's key?

He gritted his teeth and tapped his brakes. The car in front of him was crawling, in no hurry at all. He flashed his headlights and immediately the car changed lanes, allowing him to pass. *Better.*

He focused on the open road ahead. It helped him to clear his mind, to think. If Vartanian suspected anything, he wasn't saying, but Daniel had always been the closemouthed kind. Scary in his own way with those eyes of his.

And Vartanian had taken up with Alex Fallon, a major problem in her own right. Even if they found out who'd killed Janet and Claudia, the damage had been done. Everyone was talking about Alicia Tremaine, how she'd died. And now, having Alex Fallon walking around town, looking so much like Alicia, it was just fanning the flames.

Alex Fallon was walking around town because Bailey was still missing. He no longer had control over what happened to Bailey Crighton, but he did have control over what happened to Alex Fallon. His guy had fucked up big-time this afternoon. The man was only supposed to watch Fallon, report back, stop her from talking to the wrong people. He'd never intended him to run her down in the street. There were other, more discreet ways of making people go away.

This he knew. He'd get rid of Alex Fallon, discreetly. Then he'd find out who was taunting them with dead women and keys. Before Vartanian got to the bastard first.

Because if Daniel found out what had really happened, nothing else would matter. They'd go to prison. *I'll die first*. He pressed the accelerator to the floor, speeding back to town. He had no intention of going to prison or dying first. He had work to do.

Mack lowered his camera, a grim smile on his face. He'd known they'd turn on each other. He hadn't expected it so quickly. But any time any of the four had taken a drive out of town in the last month, Mack had followed. Usually he was rewarded with wonderful new secrets he knew none of the men would want revealed, and of course tonight had been no exception.

Now the four were three and Mack was one step

closer to the culmination of his dream. He clicked through the photos he'd just taken. His plan for the remaining three was solid, but these photos would make for a handy Plan B should his base plan fall apart. Always have a contingency, a back door, an escape hatch. A Plan B. Just another one of those prison lessons he'd learned well.

Speaking of lessons, he had another to deliver. In a few hours, he'd be the proud owner of one more girl and a very nice 'Vette.

Chapter Eleven

Dutton, Tuesday, January 30, 7:30 P.M.

'Well.' Meredith sipped at her drink, looking out of the corners of both eyes like a spy. 'Nothing like being a little conspicuous.'

Alex gave her a rueful look across the table at Presto's Pizza Parlor. 'I tried to warn you this would happen. People have been staring at me all week.' She looked up at Daniel, who'd made a big show of draping his arm around her shoulders as soon as they'd been seated in the booth. 'And you're not helping.'

He shrugged. 'They already know I kissed you last night.'

'And that he went into Bailey's house with you,' Meredith added.

Alex winced. 'How? That just happened a few hours ago.'

'Heard it at the jukebox. You fainted and Daniel carried you out in his arms.'

'I did not faint. And I walked out of that house on my own two feet.' She pursed her lips. 'I swear to God. These people should just get lives.'

'They did,' Daniel murmured. 'Ours. It's not often two prodigal children return home at the same time.'

'And start fornicatin'.' Meredith lifted her hand. 'Their word, not mine. I swear.'

Alex narrowed her eyes. 'Whose?'

Daniel pulled her closer. 'It doesn't matter,' he said. 'We're here and we're fodder for public consumption until something more interesting happens.'

Meredith looked at the cartoon Hope had colored on the placemat. 'Very nice, Hope.'

Alex sighed. 'And very red,' she said, so quietly only Daniel could hear. He squeezed her shoulder in silent reply. She looked up at him. 'Did Agent Randall find anything that helps you on the other two women?' she whispered. He pressed his forefinger to her lips and shook his head.

'Not here,' he whispered. He looked around, taking in the faces watching them. His eyes became hard and circumspect and she knew he was wondering if the person responsible for two deaths and Bailey's disappearance was there, watching them.

Watching me, she thought, quelling the sick feeling in the pit of her stomach. She stared at her scraped palms. She'd removed the bulky bandages, but she had only to glance at her hands and the shock of the afternoon returned. The screeching tires, the screams – both those of the bystanders and the ones in her head.

Someone had tried to kill her. It still hadn't completely sunk in.

Someone had killed two women. That hadn't completely sunk in either.

Someone had taken Bailey. Although she'd known it, knowing blood had been spilled made it more real. She thought about the house. Now that she was no longer there, she could consider the event with a bit more objectivity.

'Nobody ever asked me before,' she murmured, then realized she'd said it aloud.

Daniel pulled back to look at her face. 'Asked you what?'

She met his eyes. 'What they screamed.'

His blue eyes narrowed slightly. 'Really? That surprises me. So . . . did you know what they said before, or did you just remember today?'

I hate you. I wish you were dead. She looked away. 'I knew before, but standing there . . . it was so clear. I could hear her voice again. Like it was yesterday.'

His hand moved under her hair to cup the back of her head, his thumb finding the exact place in her neck that throbbed. 'Who says "No"?'

She swallowed hard. 'That would be me. I think. I'm not sure.' His thumb continued to work its magic on her neck and a little of the tension ebbed from her shoulders. She dropped her chin to her chest and . . . absorbed. 'You do that well, too.'

His chuckle warmed her. 'Good to know.' Too soon he stopped, withdrawing his hand. 'Pizza's here.'

The pan slid across the table and Alex looked up into the face of the waitress, a woman with a harsh face and red lipstick. She looked familiar, but Alex couldn't place her face. She wore too much makeup and her eyes were hard. She was somewhere between twenty-five and thirty-five. Her name tag said 'Sheila' and her eyes were glued to Daniel's face, but not in an alluring way. She seemed to be weighing her words.

'You're Daniel Vartanian,' Sheila finally said flatly.

He was searching her face. 'I am,' he said. 'But I don't remember you. I'm sorry.'

Her red lips thinned. 'No, you wouldn't remember me. We ran in slightly different circles. My father worked at the mill.'

Alex's shoulders stiffened. The paper mill employed half the town at one time or another. Bailey's father had worked there. That's where Craig Crighton had been that night. The night her mother needed him. *The night I needed my mother*. She closed her eyes. *Quiet. Be quiet*. Daniel's thumb returned to her neck, applying pressure, and once again the tension began to ebb, making room for other memories to surface.

'You're Sheila Cunningham,' Alex said. 'We sat next to each other in biology.' *The year I didn't finish. The year Alicia died*.

Sheila nodded. 'I didn't think you'd remember me.'

Alex frowned. 'There's a lot I don't remember.'

Sheila nodded again. 'There's a lot of that going around.'

'What can we do for you, Sheila?' Daniel asked.

Sheila's jaw tightened. 'You were out at Bailey's house today.'

Meredith looked up, alert and listening. The people in the booth behind them had turned, obviously listening as well. Sheila didn't seem to notice. Her eyes had narrowed and a vein throbbed in her neck.

'People in this town would have you believe Bailey was a tramp. That she was trashy. But it's not true.' Sheila aimed a look at Hope. 'She was a good mother.'

'You say "was,"' Daniel said quietly. 'Do you know what happened to her?'

'No. If I did, I'd tell you. But I know she didn't walk away from that kid.' She sucked in her cheeks, visibly fighting to hold whatever she really wanted to say in check. 'Everyone's all upset that those rich girls are dead. Nobody cared about the regular girls. Nobody cares about Bailey.' She looked at Alex. 'Except you.'

'Sheila.' The barked order came from the window to the kitchen. 'Get back here.'

Sheila shook her head, a mocking smile on her lips. 'Oops. Gotta go. Said too much. Wouldn't want to rock the boat or upset the powers that be.'

'Why?' Daniel asked. 'What would happen if you rocked the boat?'

Her red lips twisted in a sneer. 'Ask Bailey. Oh, wait. You can't.' She spun on her heel and went back to the kitchen, smacking the swinging door with the flat of her hand.

Alex leaned back against the bench seat. 'Well.'

Daniel was watching the door to the kitchen, which was still swinging. 'Well, indeed.' He turned his attention to the pizza, pulling it onto their plates, but there was a troubled frown on his face. 'Eat up.'

Meredith pushed a plate under Hope's downturned face, but the little girl only stared at the food. 'Come on, Hope,' she cajoled. 'Eat.'

'Has she eaten at all?' Daniel said.

'Eventually she eats if I leave it in front of her long enough,' Meredith answered, 'but we've only eaten sandwiches. This is our first real meal since I got here.'

'I'm sorry,' Alex said. 'I haven't been a very good hostess.'

'I wasn't going to say anything.' Meredith bit into the pizza and closed her eye in appreciation. 'It's good, Daniel. You were right.'

Daniel took a bite and nodded. 'I guess for some things you can go back.' Then he sighed when the door to the outside opened. 'Wonderful.'

A big man in an expensive suit crossed the restaurant, scowling. 'The mayor,' Alex murmured to Meredith. 'Garth Davis.'

'I know,' Meredith murmured back. 'I saw his picture in the paper this morning.'

'Daniel.' The mayor stopped at their table. 'You promised to call.'

'When I had something to tell you. I don't have anything to tell you yet.'

The mayor put both hands on the table and leaned forward, getting in Daniel's face. 'You said to give you a day. You said you were working on it. And here you sit.'

'And here I sit,' Daniel said mildly. 'Get out of my face, Garth.'

The mayor didn't budge. 'I want an update.' He was speaking loudly, for his audience, Alex thought. His constituency. Politicians.

Daniel leaned in closer. 'Get out of my face, Garth,' he murmured, leveling the mayor a look so cold even Alex flinched. 'Now.' The mayor slowly straightened and Daniel drew a breath. 'Thank you, Mayor Davis. I can appreciate your wanting to have the most recent information. You need to appreciate that even if I had anything to tell you, this isn't the place for me to share it. I did call your office this afternoon with an update. The phone rang, but no one answered.'

Davis narrowed his eyes. 'I was out at Congressman Bowie's this afternoon. I didn't get the message. I'm sorry, Daniel.' But his eyes said he was anything but. 'I'll be sure to talk to my aide and find out why he didn't answer your call.'

'Do that. If you'd still like an update, I'm glad to talk when I'm not in a public place.'

The mayor's cheeks flushed. 'Of course. This has been a terrible day, finding out about Janet and Claudia.'

'And Bailey Crighton,' Alex said coldly.

Mayor Davis had the good grace to look embarrassed. 'And Bailey. Of course. Daniel, I'll be in my office most of the evening. Call me if you would.'

'That's enough to spoil your appetite,' Alex said when he was gone.

'Alex.' Meredith's voice was strained and Alex immediately saw why.

Hope had pushed the cheese off the pizza and had smeared sauce all over her own hands and all over her face. She looked like she was covered in blood. And she was rocking in a way that made Alex's blood run cold.

Daniel was quick to react. He stood up, wiping the sauce from Hope's face and hands with a napkin. 'Hope, honey,' he said, injecting a humor into his voice that Alex knew he didn't feel. 'Look at this mess. And on your pretty new dress, too.'

The couple in the next booth turned around and Alex recognized Toby Granville and his wife. 'Can I help?' Toby asked, frowning his concern.

'No, thanks,' Daniel said easily. 'We're just going to take her home and get her cleaned up. You know how kids are.' He pulled his wallet from his pocket and Sheila came from the kitchen, a wet towel in her hands.

She'd obviously been watching. As had everyone else in the place.

Daniel handed her a folded-up bill and Alex could see the white edge of his business card poking above the green ink. 'Keep the change.' He pulled Alex from the booth and she winced, her knees stiff. But she made her legs move, following Meredith to the door. Daniel scooped Hope up into his arms. 'Let's go, pretty girl. Let's get you home.'

Alex gave Sheila a last look, then followed Daniel to his car.

In less than five minutes they were back at the bungalow. Meredith ran ahead of them, and when Alex limped across the threshold, Meredith had the Princess Fiona hairstyling head on the table. Meredith took Hope from Daniel's arms and put her in front of the styling head, then crouched to look into Hope's face.

'Show us what happened to your mother, Hope,' Meredith said urgently. She grabbed the can of red Play-Doh and shook it out into her palm. 'Show us.'

Hope smeared a glob on the Fiona head. She repeated it, until red Play-Doh covered Fiona's face and hair. When finished she stared at Meredith helplessly.

Alex felt the breath seep from her lungs. 'She saw it all.'

'Which means she may have seen who did it,' Daniel said, his voice tight. 'We'll go to the shelter tomorrow, Alex. I want to get Hope in with a forensic artist tonight. Meredith, my boss wanted me to take Hope into our department psychologist tomorrow morning, but I think that needs to be tonight, too.'

Alex bristled. 'Meredith is a fine child psychologist. And Hope trusts her.'

But Meredith was nodding. 'I've gotten too close, Alex. Call your consult, Daniel. I'll help in whatever way I can.'

Atlanta, Tuesday, January 30, 9:00 P.M.

There were a dozen pretty girls at the bar already, but Mack knew exactly which one he'd be taking home. He'd known for five long years, ever since the night she and her two friends had pulled their cute little trick and taken his life away. They'd thought themselves so clever, so smart. Now Claudia and Janet were so dead. And Gemma would soon follow. A fine buzz of anticipation singed his skin as he approached her. However she responded, her evening would end the same.

Done, dead, and wrapped in a brown wool blanket. Just one more tool to terrify the pillars of Dutton. He leaned against the bar, ignoring the protest of the woman behind him as he crowded her off her stool. He had eyes only for his prize.

Gemma Martin. She'd been his first fuck. He'd be her last. They'd been sixteen and her price had been an hour behind the wheel of his 'Vette. She'd been drunk and put a dent in his left fender that night. She was well on her way to being drunk tonight, and the dent he left would be in her. Mack planned to enjoy his revenge very much.

'Excuse me,' he said over the blare of the band.

She turned her head, sweeping her eyes from his head to his feet in blatant assessment, her eyes sharpening with interest. Five years ago she'd laughed at him. Tonight, she was interested and completely unaware of who he was.

She tilted her head. 'Yes?'

'I couldn't help but notice that gorgeous red Corvette you drove in. I'm thinking of buying one. What do you think of yours?'

Her smile was feline and Mack knew he wouldn't be needing the little bottle of Rohypnol in his pocket to lure her away. She'd come because she wanted to. It would make her end that much more delicious. 'It's the perfect car. Hot, fast, and dangerous.'

'Sounds like exactly what I'm looking for.'

Atlanta, Tuesday, January 30, 9:00 P.M.

'Please call me if you hear anything,' Daniel said into the phone, then hung up just as Chase came into his office, looking as tired as Daniel felt. Chase had just come from a meeting with the brass and from the look in his eyes, it had not ended well.

'Who was that?' Chase asked.

'Fort Benning. I'd left a bunch of messages for that army chaplain.'

'The one who came to see Bailey yesterday morning and ended up talking to Alex.'

'Yeah. He'd flown into Benning for his R&R. He was headed south of Albany, to his parents' house, but he never showed up. Even with his stop in Dutton, he should have been in Albany by suppertime, easily. They're declaring him missing.'

'Hell, Daniel. Tell me some good news.'

'I think I know where Janet was grabbed. I canvassed the area where the phone call to her boyfriend originated and found a guy behind the counter at a sub shop that remembers her, down to the meatball sub she ordered. They have her on their security tape making the order. Felicity didn't find the sub in Janet's stomach contents, so she never ate her dinner. I'm thinking he broke into her minivan and overpowered her when she came out.'

'Did we get the van on camera?'

'Nope. No cameras in the parking lot, only inside. And none of the surrounding businesses have cams either. I checked.'

Chase glared. 'Then at least tell me the artist's making some headway with the kid.'

'The artist isn't available until tomorrow morning,' Daniel said, holding up a weary hand when Chase started to explode. 'Don't fight with me about it.

Both artists are with victims. We're next in the queue.'

'Then who's got the kid now?' Chase demanded.

'Chase.' Mary McCrady came into Daniel's office, giving Chase an admonishing look. 'The *kid's* name is Hope.'

Daniel had always liked Mary McCrady. She was slightly older than he was, slightly younger than Chase. She had a no-nonsense attitude about the world and never allowed anyone to intimidate her – or any of the patients she took under her wing.

Chase rolled his eyes. 'I'm tired, Mary. For the last hour I've had my guts sliced and diced by my boss and *his* boss. Tell me you've made progress with *Hope*.'

Mary lifted a shoulder. 'You're a big boy, Chase. You can take a little slicing and dicing. Hope's a traumatized child. She can't.'

Chase started to rant, but Daniel cut him off. 'What have you been able to learn, Mary?' Daniel asked calmly, and Mary sat down in one of his chairs.

'Not much. Dr Fallon did exactly what I would have. She's used play therapy and made Hope feel safe. I can't pull anything out of Hope that she's not ready to let go.'

'So you have nothing.' Chase banged his head against the wall. 'Wonderful.'

Mary threw an annoyed glance over her shoulder. 'I didn't say we have nothing. I said we have not much.' She pulled a piece of paper from her folder. 'She drew this.'

Daniel studied the page. It was the crude drawing style of a child, one figure prone, the head scribbled over with red. The other figure, male and standing upright, nearly filled the page. 'It's more than we've gotten before. Since she was found in that closet on Friday she's only colored predrawn pictures in coloring books.'

Mary got up and went around to his side of the desk. 'As close as we can figure, this is Bailey.' She pointed to the prone figure.

'Yeah, that I got. The red was the giveaway.' He looked up at her from the corner of his eye. 'Meredith Fallon told you about the pizza sauce and the Play-Doh, right?'

'Yes.' Mary frowned. 'I hated to push this baby this far, but we need to find out exactly what she saw.' She pointed to the figure standing up. 'Bailey's attacker.'

'Well, yeah, I got that, too. He's huge, three times bigger than Bailey.'

'It's not the man's actual size,' Mary said.

'It's his threat, his power,' Chase said from the door and looked a bit sheepish when Mary looked up, surprised. 'I'm not a monster, Mary. I know this kid's been through hell. But the sooner she gets it out, the sooner you can start . . . fixing her.'

Mary sighed with affectionate exasperation. 'We'll treat her, Chase. Not fix her.' She looked back down at the picture. 'He's wearing a cap.'

'A baseball cap?' Daniel asked.

'Hard to say. Kids her age only have a limited number of graphic images they can draw. All hats mostly look the same. All figures look the same. But look at his hand.'

Daniel rubbed his eyes and brought the picture close. 'A stick. Dripping with blood.'

'Did Ed's team find any bloody sticks?' she asked.

'They're still processing the scene,' Daniel said. 'They've set up lights in the woods, looking for the place where Hope might have hidden. Why's the stick so small?'

'Because she's repressing it,' Chase said. 'It terrifies her, so she makes it as small as she can in her mind.'

Mary nodded. 'Pretty much. I thought you'd want to see this. We broke for the night. After we got this, I was afraid to push her anymore. We can continue tomorrow. Get some rest, Daniel.' One side of her mouth lifted. 'Doctor's orders.'

'I'll try. Good night, Mary.' When she'd gone, Daniel looked at Hope's drawing, feeling guilty and torn. 'Part of me wants all three of them in a safe house, Alex, Hope, and Meredith. But so far Hope and Alex are our only link to whoever's orchestrating this. If we hide them away . . .'

Chase nodded. 'I know. I increased the police presence. Twenty-four-seven. That's part of what was on the agenda in this last meeting.'

'That should settle Alex's mind. And mine. Thank you, Chase.'

'Mary's right. Get some sleep, Daniel. I'll see you in the morning.'

'I'll have Ed meet us at eight,' Daniel said, mentally calculating how long the commute would be from Dutton to the GBI building with morning traffic. Because even with the police presence outside, Daniel wasn't taking any chances. There was a sofa in the bungalow's living room. He'd be sleeping there tonight.

Tuesday, January 30, 9:00 P.M.

His cell phone rang. The one that wasn't registered in his name. He didn't have to look at the caller ID. *He* was the only one who ever called this number.

'Yeah.' He sounded tired to his own ears. Because he was. Body and . . . soul. If he still had a soul. He remembered the look in Rhett Porter's eyes. *Help me.*

'Is it done?' His voice was cold and would suffer no weakness.

So he straightened his spine. 'Yeah. Rhett went up in a blaze of glory.'

He grunted. 'Shoulda fed him to the gators like you did DJ.'

'Yeah, well, I didn't. I didn't have time to get down to the swamp and back. Look, I'm tired. I'm going home and—'

'No, you're not.'

He wanted to sigh, but he sucked it in. 'And why not?'

'Because you're not finished.'

'I'll take care of Fallon. I've already got plans in motion. Discreet plans.'

'Good, but now there's more. Vartanian went out to dinner tonight with Alex Fallon and Bailey's kid.'

'The kid's talking?'

'No.' There was an angry pause. 'But she covered her face in pizza sauce. Like she was covered in blood.'

He froze, his mind wildly searching for an explanation. 'That's impossible. She was in the closet. She didn't see anything.'

'Then maybe she's psychic.' The words were biting and harsh. 'But Bailey's kid saw something, Sweetpea.'

His gut twisted. 'No.' *She's just a child*. He'd never . . . 'She's only a little girl.'

'If she saw you, you're fucked.'

'She didn't see me.' Desperation clawed at his throat. 'I was outside.'

'Then you went inside.'

'But all she would have seen is me trashing the place. I grabbed Bailey outside.'

'And I'm telling you a restaurant full of people saw that kid cover her face in sauce.'

'Kids do that. Nobody'll think anything of it.'

'On its own, perhaps not.'

'What else?' he asked dully.

'Sheila Cunningham.'

He closed his eyes. 'What did she say?'

'Mostly that Bailey wasn't the trashy slut everyone's made her out to be. And that while everyone is upset about the rich girls being dead, that nobody cared about the regular girls, that nobody cares about Bailey.'

'That's all?' He felt marginally better. 'So she didn't say anything.'

'Weren't you listening to me?'

'Yes, I was,' he said, defensive now. 'What are you talking about?'

There was total silence on the other end, and in the quiet, the words clicked.

'Oh, hell.'

'Yeah. And you can bet good old Danny boy heard it, too. *He's* no idiot.'

He absorbed the barb. 'So did he talk any more with Sheila?'

'Not yet. He whisked Bailey's kid out of there so fast it made everybody's head spin. But he did give Sheila his card.'

Fuck. 'Were you there?'

'Yes. I saw it all. And people are talking all over town.'

'Has Vartanian gone back to talk to Sheila again?'

'Not yet. They took the kid back to the place the Fallon woman is renting, then fifteen minutes later all four of them piled in Vartanian's car and headed out of town.'

'Wait. I thought you said there were three.'

'You don't know what's going on in your own town, do you? The Tremaine woman's brought her cousin in to help her take care of the kid. The woman's a kid shrink.'

What little hope he had of being able to control what happened next fizzled and died. 'You want them all gone?'

'Discreetly. If Vartanian knows they're dead, he won't stop till he finds out who did it. So make it look like they all just went home.'

'He'll find out sooner or later.'

'And by then I will have dealt with him. Take care of Sheila first, then the other three. Call me when you're done.'

Tuesday, January 30, 11:30 P.M.

Mack looked up from the 'Vette's engine to where Gemma Martin lay on his makeshift garage floor, wide-eyed, hog-tied, and terrified. 'You've kept the engine well maintained,' he said with approval. 'This one I believe I'll keep.' He had buyers already lined up for the Z and the Mercedes. It was one of the few perks of being inside. You met all kinds of helpful people.

'Who are you?' she said hoarsely and Mack laughed.

'You know who I am.'

She shook her head. 'Please. If it's money you want . . .'

'Oh, I want money and I've got a good bit of yours.' He held up the cash he'd found in her purse. 'Once I carried around a wad like this. But times change and tables turn.' Feeling a bit like one of the old *Mission: Impossible* agents, he peeled off the thin latex with which he'd covered his cheeks. Along with makeup, it had allowed him to hide his one identifying feature.

Gemma's eyes widened even more. 'No. You're in prison.'

He chuckled. 'Obviously not anymore, but logic was never your strong suit.'

'You killed Claudia and Janet.'

'And didn't they deserve it?' he said mildly. He sat down on the floor next to her. 'And don't you?'

'We were kids.'

'You were bitches. Tonight you'll be a dead bitch.' He pulled his switchblade from his pocket and began cutting away her clothes. 'You three thought you were so clever.'

'We didn't mean any harm,' she cried.

'What did you think would happen, Gemma?' he said, still mildly. 'I asked you to the prom, you agreed. But you didn't want to go. I was no longer of your class.'

'*I'm sorry*.' She was crying now, huge terrified tears.

'Well, it's too late for that now, even if I were so inclined to accept. Which I'm not. Do you remember that night, Gemma? Because I do. I remember picking you up in my sister-in-law's old car because it was all we had left to drive. I expected you to offer your own car. I should have been suspicious when you didn't. I remember meeting your friends. Then I don't remember anything else until I woke up hours later, naked at a rest stop a hundred miles away. My car was gone and so were you and your friends.'

'We didn't mean anything,' she said, choking on her sobs.

'Yes, you did. You meant for me to be humiliated and I was. I remember what happened after that. I remember waiting in the bushes until a man about my size stopped to use the john. I stole his car so that I could get home. He came back while I was still hot-wiring his engine. He and I fought and I was so angry at you that I beat him unconscious. I hadn't made it five miles before the cops pulled me over. Assault, battery, grand theft. I did four years because nobody in Dutton would help me. Nobody would help my mother raise the bail. Nobody helped me get a decent lawyer.

'You didn't mean anything,' he finished coldly. 'But you took everything. Now, I get to take your everything.'

'Please,' she sobbed. 'Please don't kill me.'

He laughed. 'When the pain gets so bad, you scream that for me, sugar.'

Dutton, Tuesday, January 30, 11:30 P.M.

Daniel pulled into the bungalow's driveway. The car had been silent since they'd left Atlanta. In the back Meredith and Hope slept soundly. Beside him, Alex had been awake and deep in troubled thought. Several times he'd almost asked what was wrong, but the question was ludicrous. What wasn't wrong? Alex's life had fallen apart once. It was doing so again. *And I'm about to make it a million times worse for her.*

Because the silence had given him time to finally think, to start pulling pieces together, and a single phrase wouldn't leave him alone. It had been pushed to the back of his mind with the appearance of Garth Davis and Hope's breakthrough. The phrase had come from Shelia at the pizza parlor, bitterly delivered through her red lips.

Nobody cared about the regular girls. Cared. Sheila the waitress had used the present tense when talking about 'the rich girls' and Bailey. *Everybody's upset about the rich girls. Nobody cares about Bailey.*

But nobody *cared* about the regular girls. He was starting to understand. When he'd first looked at Sheila's face, he'd seen something he'd recognized. First he thought he'd known her from school. But that's not where he'd seen her before.

He killed the engine and the silence became complete, except for the rhythmic breathing from the backseat. Alex's gaze moved to the unmarked police car parked on her curb, her profile silvered from the pale light of the moon. Delicate, was the way he had described her in his mind yesterday morning. She looked fragile now. But he knew she was neither. Alex Fallon might be stronger than any of them. He hoped she was strong enough to endure what he knew he could keep secret no longer.

He'd wait until Meredith and Hope slept. Then he'd tell her and accept whatever her reaction would be. Whatever penance he'd have to do. But she had a right to know.

'Your boss moved quickly,' she murmured, referring to the unmarked car.

'It's either this or a safe house. Do you want a safe house, Alex?'

She looked to the backseat. 'For them, maybe, but not for me. If I hide, I can't look for Bailey, and I think I'm getting close.' She dropped her eyes to her palms. 'Or, at least, somebody doesn't want me looking. Which, unless I've watched too much television, means I'm making somebody nervous.'

She was speaking in her cool voice. She was afraid. But he couldn't lie to her. 'I think that's a fair assumption. Alex . . .' He let out a quiet breath. 'Let's go inside. There are things you need to know.'

'Like what?'

'Let's go inside.'

She grabbed his arm, then flinched and pulled her scraped palm away. 'Tell me.'

Her eyes had widened and in them he saw her fear. He shouldn't have said anything until they were inside and alone. But he had, so he'd tell her what he could now, just to get her in the house. 'Beardsley is missing.'

Her mouth fell open. 'I just saw him yesterday.' Pained understanding filled her eyes. 'Somebody's been watching me since then.'

'I think that's a fair assumption, too.'

She pursed her lips. 'You need to know something, too. While Dr McCrady was in with Hope, I called Bailey's best friend from the salon. Her name is Sissy. I'd been trying to call off and on all day, but I never got through. I just got her answering machine. So I used one of the phones there at your office. She picked up right away.'

'You think she was avoiding your phone number?'

'I know she was. When I told her who I was, she got defensive. I asked her if I could come talk to her about Bailey and she said she didn't really know Bailey all that well. That I should talk to one of the other girls at the salon.'

'But the owner said she was Bailey's best friend?'

'He said Bailey stayed over at her house every Saturday night. And the social worker said Sissy was the one to come to Bailey's house on Friday.'

'Somebody got to her then,' Daniel said.

'Sissy has a daughter, old enough to babysit Hope when Bailey worked on Saturdays.' Alex bit her lower lip. 'If somebody threatened Sissy, and Beardsley's missing, maybe Sister Anne and Desmond are in danger, too.'

Daniel reached over and pressed his thumb to her lip, smoothing away the marks her teeth had left behind. 'I'll have a unit go by the shelter and Desmond's house.' He pulled his hand away. He'd wanted to hold her all day. The quiet had just intensified his need. 'Let's get Hope into bed. It's late.'

Alex had the back door open and was reaching for Hope, but Daniel gently nudged her aside. 'You unlock the front door. I'll carry her in.' He shook Meredith's shoulder and she jerked awake, blinking. He unlocked the child seat and lifted Hope into his arms. She cuddled against his shoulder, too exhausted to be afraid.

He followed Alex into the bungalow, conscious of the agents Chase had assigned to watch. He'd known and trusted Hatton and Koenig for years. He gave them a nod as he passed. He'd come back out and talk to them in a few minutes.

Riley sat up when they came in, immediately padding over to follow them.

Alex led him to the bedroom on the left. Gently he laid Hope on the bed and slipped off her shoes. 'Do you want to change her into her pajamas?' he whispered.

She shook her head. 'It won't hurt her to sleep in her clothes,' she whispered back.

Daniel pulled the blanket to cover Hope, then

brushed a golden curl from her face, flushed with sleep. He swallowed. The pizza sauce had stained her skin and hair. It still looked like blood. Carefully, he brushed the curl back, hiding the stain.

He already had too many disturbing images in his mind. He didn't need to add a bloody four-year-old to the mix.

'I sleep in here, too,' Alex whispered, standing by the other side of the bed. Daniel looked at the crisp white sheets, then back at Alex, who was giving him a pointed stare.

Daniel frowned. 'You're going to sleep *now*?' he asked.

'I guess not. Come on.' She turned at the door and her brows lifted. 'Oh, look.'

Riley had climbed up onto a suitcase and was struggling to pull himself onto the chair that sat next to Hope's side of the bed. 'Riley,' Daniel whispered. 'Get down.'

But Alex gave Riley the needed boost to the chair. From there the hound scrabbled to the bed, padded to Hope's side, and flopped on his stomach with one of his big sighs.

'Riley, get out of that bed,' Daniel whispered, but Alex shook her head.

'Leave him. If she wakes up with bad dreams, at least she won't be alone.'

Dutton, Tuesday, January 30, 11:30 P.M.

He tugged at his tie and settled into the seat, but a big man could only get so comfortable keeping watch from his car. His sister Kate was home from work now, her sensible Volvo parked safely in her garage. He could see her moving around inside her house, window to window, feeding her cat, hanging up her coat.

He planned to sit in front of her house every single night until this was over. He'd followed her from town, careful to stay far enough back so that she didn't see him. If she did see him, he'd admit to being worried about her safety. But there was no way he could tell her she was a target. If he did, she'd want to know how he knew.

She couldn't know. No one could know. And no one *would* know if he just kept his head down and his mouth shut. Both women had been killed between 8:00 p.m. and 2:00 a.m. Both women had been taken from their cars, so he'd just stick to Kate like glue while she drove home from work and watch over her during the night. During the day she was safe enough, he thought, surrounded by people at her job.

Thoughts of the yearbook photos intruded into his mind. Ten pictures, the two already X-ed out. He'd been trying to push them away all night. It was a clear warning. Seven other women besides Kate had been on that paper. Seven other women were targets. He could have turned that photocopy over to Vartanian, could have saved those other seven. But he thought of his sister Kate. His wife. His children. And knew given the opportunity, he'd burn the paper again. They could never know.

If he'd given the paper to Vartanian, Daniel would have wondered why he'd been the recipient of the warning. Even if he'd sent it anonymously, Daniel would have seen the circle around Kate's picture and wondered why his sister had been singled out.

You could have cut Kate's picture away and sent the rest. You could have protected those other seven women. You should have protected them.

And chance that Vartanian's GBI lab would find his fingerprints on the rest of the paper after he'd cut it apart? No, it was too big a chance. Besides, Vartanian would have started to dig, and God only knew what he'd unearth.

If one of those other seven women dies, their blood will be on your hands.

Then so be it. He had his own family to protect. If the families of the other women who'd gone to school with Janet and Claudia were smart, they'd be protecting their women, too. *But they don't know what you know.*

He'd done things in his life. Horrible, deviant things. But he'd never had anyone's blood on his hands before. *Yes, you have.* Alicia Tremaine. Alicia's face whipped into his mind, and the memory of that night thirteen years ago.

But we didn't kill her. But they had raped her. All of them had. All except Simon. He'd just taken the pictures. Simon had always been a sick bastard that way.

And you weren't? You raped that girl, and how many others?

He closed his eyes. He'd raped Alicia Tremaine and fourteen others. They all had. Except for Simon. He'd just taken the pictures.

And where were the pictures?

The thought had haunted him for thirteen years. The pictures had been locked away, insurance that none of them would tell what they'd all done. Damn stupid kids that they'd been. Nothing he could ever do would erase what they'd done. *What I did*.

Every hideous thing he'd done. Recorded in those pictures. When Simon had died the first time they'd all been relieved and terrified at the same time that the pictures would surface, but they never had and the years had passed. Uneasily.

They'd never spoken of the pictures again, or the club, or the things they'd done. Not until DJ became a drunk. And disappeared.

Just like Rhett had disappeared tonight. He knew Rhett was dead. Rhett had been ready to talk and he'd been disposed of. Just like DJ.

I, on the other hand, am smart enough to keep my mouth shut and my head down until this is all over. Back then, the pictures had ensured their silence. If one went down, they'd all go down. But now, all these years later . . . They were no longer stupid kids. They were grown men with respectable jobs. And families to protect.

But now, all these years later . . . somebody was killing their women. Women who thirteen years ago had been innocent little girls. *The girls you raped were innocent girls, too. Innocent. Innocent. Innocent.*

'I know.' He spat the words aloud, then whispered, 'God, don't you think I know?'

Now, all these years later, somebody else knew. They knew about the key, so they knew about the club and they must know about Simon's pictures, too. It wasn't one of them, not one of the four that remained. No, not four. He thought about Rhett Porter. Rhett was dead. *The three that remained.* None of them would do this.

That this whole nightmare began one week after Simon Vartanian's real death could not be a coincidence. Could Daniel have found Simon's pictures?

No. Not a chance. If Daniel Vartanian had the pictures, he'd be investigating.

He is *investigating, you idiot.*

No, he's investigating the murders of Janet and Claudia.

So Daniel didn't know. That meant somebody else did. Somebody who wanted money. Somebody who'd killed two women to show them he meant business. Somebody who'd threatened to kill more if they didn't listen.

So he'd listened. He'd followed the instructions that

had come with the photocopy of the yearbook photos. He'd had a hundred thousand dollars transferred to an offshore account. There would be another demand for more money, he thought. And he'd continue to pay whatever he needed to ensure his secret stayed exactly that. *Secret*.

Chapter Twelve

Dutton, Tuesday, January 30, 11:55 P.M.

Meredith's head was in the refrigerator when Alex closed the bedroom door on Hope and Riley. 'I am so hungry,' Meredith complained. 'I only ate two bites of that pizza.'

'I don't think any of us got any more than that,' Daniel said, rubbing the flat of his hand against his equally flat stomach. 'Thanks for reminding me,' he added wryly.

Alex looked away from Daniel Vartanian's very lean torso, startled at the sudden desire that had warmed her inside out. After everything that had happened, she did not need to be thinking about rubbing Daniel's flat stomach. Or anyplace else.

Meredith put a jar of mayonnaise and some shaved ham on the counter that separated the kitchen from the living room. She met Alex's eyes, her lips twitching into a knowing smirk. Alex glared at her, daring her to say a word.

Meredith cleared her throat. 'Daniel, can I make you a sandwich?'

Daniel nodded. 'Please.' He leaned against the counter, both forearms flat on the granite and his shoulders sagged. When he sighed, Meredith snickered.

'You look like your dog when you do that,' she said, heaping ham on slices of bread.

Daniel chuckled wearily. 'They say people resemble their dogs. I hope that's the only way I resemble Riley. He's an ugly mug.'

'Oh, I don't know about that. I think he's cute,' Meredith said, and gave Alex another smirk as she pushed Daniel's plate across the countertop. 'Don't you, Alex?'

Alex rolled her eyes, too tired to be amused. 'Just eat, Mer.' She walked to the window and pulled the curtains back to look at the unmarked car on her curb. 'Should we take them coffee or something?'

'They'd appreciate it, I'm sure,' Daniel said. 'If you'll make it, I'll take it out to them. I don't want you all going outside unless you absolutely have to.'

Meredith took her plate to the table. She pushed the Play-Doh-covered Princess Fiona aside and sat down with a sigh of her own. 'Are we under house arrest, Daniel?'

'You know you're not. But we'd be remiss if we didn't make sure you were safe.'

Alex busied herself making the officers' coffee. 'It's either that or a safe house.'

Meredith frowned. 'I think you and Hope should go.'

Alex glanced up from scooping the coffee. 'I was thinking you and Hope should go.'

'Of course you were,' Meredith said. 'Dammit, Alex, you've got the thickest skull. Nobody's tried to kill *me*. You're the one in the crosshairs.'

'So far,' Alex said. 'The reverend is missing, Mer. And I think somebody's threatened Bailey's friend. You're *my* friend. Don't think they haven't noticed you.'

Meredith opened her mouth, then closed it, pursing her lips. 'Shit.'

'Eloquently put,' Daniel said. 'Think on it tonight. You can decide on the safe house tomorrow if you want. The car outside isn't going anywhere for at least a day.' He rubbed his forehead. 'Do you ladies have any aspirin?'

Alex reached across the counter and lifted his chin. She could see the ache in his eyes. 'Where does it hurt?'

'My head,' he said petulantly.

She smiled. 'Lean forward.' Eyes narrowed suspiciously, he did. 'And close your eyes,' she murmured, and after a last glance, he complied. She pressed her fingertips to his temples until his eyes blinked open.

'That's better,' he said, surprised.

'Good. I took some classes in acupressure hoping it would work on me, but I've never been able to make my own headaches go away.'

He walked around the counter and slid his hand up under her hair. 'Still hurts here?'

She nodded and let her head drop forward while his thumb unerringly found the right place on her neck. A shiver ran down her spine. 'Yeah, right there.' But the words came out husky and suddenly there wasn't quite enough air.

The room grew quiet as his hands moved to her shoulders, kneading through the thick tweed of her jacket. All Alex could hear was the dripping of the coffeepot and the sound of her own pulse thrumming in her head.

Meredith cleared her throat. 'I think I'll go to sleep now,' she said.

Meredith's door closed, leaving them alone. Another shiver shook Alex as he slipped her jacket from her shoulders, but the warmth of his hands chased the chill away.

'Umm.' It was a throaty little moan as she leaned on her forearms as he had done.

'Don't go to sleep,' he murmured, and she let out a breath.

'No chance of that.'

He turned her so that she looked up at him. His eyes seemed bluer, more intense, and set off little tingles through her body. The pulse that thrummed in her head now beat a steady rhythm between her legs, making her want to press against him.

Then the thumb that had worked its magic on her neck lightly brushed her lip and she wondered what it would feel like . . . elsewhere. And she wondered how a woman went about asking for such a thing.

Then she stopped thinking when his lips covered hers. Her arms wound around his neck and she gave herself up to the riot of sensation she hadn't felt since . . . since the last time he'd kissed her. His mouth was soft and hard all at once and his hands . . . They pressed hard into her back, then slid down and around until they bracketed her ribs. Until his thumbs rested beneath her breasts and his fingers dug into her sides.

Touch me. Please. But the words didn't come and when he looked into her eyes she hoped he'd understand. His thumbs swept up, over her nipples, and her eyes slid shut. 'Yes,' she heard herself whisper. 'Right there.'

'What do you want, Alex?' he asked, his voice a low rumble.

He asked the question even as he toyed with her breasts, caressing, teasing, until her knees went weak. 'I . . .'

'I want you,' he murmured against her mouth. 'I'm giving you fair warning. If this isn't what you want . . .'

She was trembling. 'I . . .'

She felt him smile against her lips. 'Then just nod,' he whispered, so she did, then sucked in a breath when he pushed her against the cabinet, rocking against her.

'Oh, yes. Right there,' she said, then stopped talking when he took her mouth in the hardest, hottest kiss yet. His hands slid to her hips, lifting her higher, fitting her better . . .

Then the pounding at the front door shattered it all. 'Vartanian!'

Daniel lurched back, rubbing one hand over his face, his eyes instantly focused. His right hand went to the gun he had holstered at his hip. 'Stay here,' he ordered, then opened the door so that she was shielded from view. 'What's wrong?' he asked.

'Radio call for all local units,' said a male voice, and Alex moved until she could see around the door. It was one of the officers from the car outside. 'Shots fired at 256 Main Street. A pizza parlor. There's an officer down and two other victims. One of the victims is the waitress who was closing the place.'

'Sheila,' Alex said, her heart sinking.

Daniel's jaw clenched. 'I'll go, you come in. Koenig's still in the car?'

'Yeah.' The officer walked in and gave Alex a nod. 'Ma'am. I'm Agent Hatton.'

'You can trust Agent Hatton, Alex,' Daniel said. 'I've got to go.'

Dutton, Wednesday, January 31, 12:15 A.M.

Holy hell. The silence was surreal as Daniel edged through the door of Presto's Pizza where he'd brought Alex and Hope just hours before. He gripped his Sig, every sense on alert, but immediately saw he was too late.

Draped over the counter by the open cash register was a black man. His arms lay limply over the edge, both hands open, and on the floor lay a .38. Blood had pooled on the counter and was dripping down the side and Daniel couldn't help but think of Hope's little face, covered in pizza sauce.

Swallowing his shudder, he saw Sheila sitting on the floor in the corner by the jukebox. Her legs were spread wide, her eyes wide and lifeless, her red lipstick garishly bright against her waxy face. She still held a gun clasped in both hands, limp now in her lap. Her uniform was shiny as blood still oozed from the holes in her abdomen and chest. The wall behind her was covered in blood. A .38 left one hell of an exit wound.

From the corner of his eye Daniel detected a movement and lifted his Sig, ready to fire. 'Police. Stand, with your hands where I can see them.' A man rose from behind an overturned table and Daniel lowered his weapon in stunned recognition. 'Randy?'

Deputy Randy Mansfield nodded, mutely. His white uniform shirt was covered in blood and he took a staggering step forward. Daniel rushed to catch him and lowered him into a chair, then sucked in a breath.

'Fuck,' he whispered. Behind the table, a young officer wearing a Dutton sheriff's department uniform lay flat on his back, one arm outstretched, his finger still curled around the trigger of his service revolver. His white uniform shirt had a six-inch stain across the abdomen and blood ran in a little stream from his back.

'They're all dead,' Randy murmured, in shock. 'All dead.'

'Are you hit?' Daniel demanded.

Randy shook his head. 'We both fired. Me and Deputy Cowell. Cowell got hit. He's dead.'

'Randy, listen to me. Are you hit?'

Again Randy shook his head. 'No. The blood's his.'

'How many gunmen?'

The color was slowly returning to Randy's face. 'One.'

Daniel pressed his fingers to the young officer's throat. No pulse. Holding his gun at his side he slipped inside the kitchen through the swinging doors.

'Police!' he announced loudly, but there was no reply. No sound at all. He checked inside the walk-in freezer and found it empty as well. He opened the door to the alley behind the restaurant, where a dark Ford Taurus was parked, its motor still running. If the shooter had had any company, that person had long since fled.

He holstered his weapon and returned to where Sheila sat slumped in the corner, looking like a discarded Raggedy Ann doll. He saw something white peeking out of her pocket. Pulling on a pair of the latex gloves he always kept in his pocket, he crouched beside her, knowing what he'd find.

The something white was the edge of a business card. His own.

Daniel swallowed back the bile as he studied her face. Had he seen her this way first, he would have recognized her immediately, he thought bitterly. With her dead eyes and lax facial muscles, the resemblance to one of the women in Simon's pictures was much clearer.

'What the hell do you think you're doing?'

The voice shook him and Daniel slowly rose to find Frank Loomis standing in the middle of the restaurant, twin flags of color standing out on his pale face.

'She was my witness,' Daniel said

'Well, this is my town. My jurisdiction. My crime scene. You're not invited, Daniel.'

'You're a fool, Frank.' Daniel looked at Sheila and knew what he had to do. 'I've been one, too. But I'm not anymore.' He walked from the pizza parlor, past the small crowd of shocked townspeople that had gathered. When he was alone, he called Luke.

'Papadopoulos.' He could hear the TV in the background.

'Luke, it's Daniel. I need your help.'

In the background the TV was abruptly silenced. 'Name it.'

'I'm in Dutton. I need those pictures.'

Luke was silent a moment. 'What happened?'

'I think I've identified another one.'

'Alive?'

'Until twenty minutes ago, yes. Now, no.'

'God.' Luke blew out a breath. 'What's the combo to your safe?'

'Your mama's birthday.'

'I'll be there as soon as I can.'

'Thanks. Bring them to 1448 Main. It's a little one-story bungalow next to a park.'

Daniel hung up, and before he could change his mind, he called Chase. 'I need you in Dutton. Please come.'

Dutton, Wednesday, January 31, 12:55 A.M.

'Are you sure I can't get you anything, Agent Hatton?'

'I'm fine, ma'am.'

'Well, I'm not,' Alex muttered, pacing the length of the small living room and back.

'Alex, sit down,' Meredith said calmly. 'You're not helping anything.'

'I'm not hurting anything either.' She started to walk toward the window, then caught Agent Hatton's warning glance. 'Sorry.'

'Your cousin is right, Miss Fallon. You should try to relax.'

'She's running on no sleep and no food,' Meredith told the agent.

Hatton shook his head. 'And you're a nurse. You oughta know better than that.'

Alex glared at them both and sat down hard on the sofa. Then popped up a second later when there was a knock at the door.

'It's Vartanian,' Daniel called, and Hatton opened the door.

'Well?'

'Three dead,' Daniel said. 'One of them my witness. Hatton, I need to talk to Miss Fallon,' he said, and Agent Hatton touched his temple in a mock salute.

'Ladies,' he said. 'I'll be outside,' he said to Daniel.

'Should I go?' Meredith asked and Daniel shook his head. Then he closed the door and stared at it for a long, long time, and with every moment Alex felt her panic climb.

Finally she could stand his silence no longer. 'What did you need to tell me?'

He turned. 'It's not good.'

'For who?' she asked.

'Any of us,' he said cryptically, then walked to the counter where he'd kissed her, and leaned against it, head bowed. 'When I first saw you I was shocked,' he said.

Alex nodded. 'You'd just seen Alicia's picture in the old article.'

'I'd seen her face before that. You read the articles about my brother Simon.'

'Some of them.' Alex lowered herself to the sofa. ' "I'll see you in hell, Simon," ' she murmured. 'You knew what it meant when I first told you.'

'No. Not until tonight. Did you read the article that talked about how my parents went to Philadelphia looking for a blackmailer?'

Alex shook her head but Meredith said, 'I read that one.' She shrugged. 'I couldn't color all the time. I was going crazy. The article said a woman was blackmailing Daniel's parents. When they went to Philadelphia to confront her, they learned Simon had been alive all that time and he killed them.'

'You didn't get the latest, greatest,' Daniel said sardonically. 'My father had known Simon was alive all along. He'd thrown him out of the house when Simon turned eighteen. He had . . . insurance to make sure he stayed gone. Then he told everyone Simon was dead so my mother wouldn't keep looking. He faked Simon's death, burial . . . everything. I believed he was dead. We all did.'

'You must have been shocked to find he was alive,' Meredith said quietly.

'That's putting it mildly. Simon was always bad. When he was eighteen my father found something that was the straw that broke the camel's back. It was because of this he banished Simon and it was this that he used as insurance that he would stay dead.'

'What was it, Daniel?' Alex demanded. 'Just tell me.'

A muscle in his jaw spasmed. 'Pictures of women, girls. Teenagers. Being raped.'

She heard the quick intake of Meredith's breath, but for Alex there was no air.

'Alicia was one of them?' Meredith asked.

'Yes.'

Meredith moistened her lips. 'How did that blackmailer get these pictures?'

'She didn't. My mother had them, and when she realized Simon had been alive all that time, she left them for me in the event she didn't . . . survive. The blackmailer knew Simon when they were kids. She saw him in Philly and knew he should be dead.'

'So,' Meredith said, 'she blackmailed your father on the faked death and burial.'

'Essentially, yes. Two weeks ago, I found the pictures my mother had left for me. That was the day I learned my folks were dead. A few days later, Simon was dead, too.'

'So what did you do then?' Meredith asked. 'With the pictures, I mean.'

'I gave them to the detectives in Philadelphia,' Daniel said. 'The day I got them. At the time I still thought they were the reason for the blackmail.'

'So they're up there?' Alex asked. 'Pictures of *Alicia* are up there . . . with *strangers?*' She heard the thread of hysteria in her voice and fought it back.

'Copies, yes. But I kept the originals. I vowed I'd

find the women. I didn't know who they were or what part Simon played in it all. I didn't know where to start. And then my first day back we found the woman in Arcadia.'

Meredith drew a breath, understanding. 'The blanket and the ditch. It was the same.'

'One of the Arcadia men remembered Alicia's murder. When I saw her picture in an old newspaper article, I knew she was one of the girls in Simon's pictures. I was going to track down Alicia's family the next day.' He looked at Alex. 'And then you walked in.'

Alex stared at him, stunned. 'Simon raped Alicia? But they caught the man who killed her. Gary Fulmore. He was a drifter. On drugs.'

Daniel hung his head wearily. 'There were fifteen girls in those pictures. Only one of them had died, that I knew of anyway. Alicia. Until tonight.'

'Oh, God,' Meredith murmured. 'Sheila.'

Daniel lifted his head, his eyes bleak. 'I think so.'

Alex stood, vicious rage bubbling up from deep inside her. 'You *knew*. You *bastard*. You *knew* and you didn't tell me.'

'Alex,' Meredith cautioned.

Daniel's face became stern. 'I didn't want to hurt you.'

Alex shook her head. 'You didn't want to *hurt* me?' she repeated, stunned. 'You knew that your brother raped my sister and *you didn't want to hurt me*?'

'Your stepbrother may have been involved,' Daniel said quietly.

Alex stopped cold. 'Oh my God. His letter.'

Daniel nodded and said nothing.

'And the letter he sent to Bailey,' she added. Dazed, she sat down. 'My God. And the reverend.' Her eyes flew to his. 'Wade confessed to Beardsley.'

'And now he's missing,' Daniel said.

'Wait.' Meredith stood up, shaking her head. 'If Simon and Wade raped these girls, and both of them are dead, then who's behind all this? Who took Bailey? And who killed all those women?'

'I don't know. But I don't think Simon did the raping.'

Alex's temper blew again. 'Of all the—'

Daniel held up his hand, wearily. 'Alex, please. Simon was an amputee. None of the men in the pictures were missing a leg. I think Simon may have taken the pictures. It would have been just like him to do.'

'Wait,' Meredith said again. '*Men?* Like more than one man in the pictures?'

'Maybe five, maybe more. It's hard to say.'

'So others were involved,' Alex said.

'And they don't want anyone to know.' Meredith sighed. 'Fifteen girls. That's a hell of a secret to need to keep.'

Alex closed her eyes to keep the room from spinning. 'Where are these pictures?'

'They were in my safe, at my house. Luke's bringing them here, as we speak.'

She heard him push away from the counter and walk across the room. He sat next to her, but didn't touch her. 'I also called my boss. I need to tell him.'

She opened her eyes. He was sitting on the edge of the sofa cushion, back bowed, head down. 'Will you be in trouble for not telling him before?'

'Probably. But I didn't know what do.' He rolled his head to look at her and she saw the pain in his eyes. 'If he allows it, I want you to look at the other pictures. You recognized Sheila tonight. Maybe you know some of the other girls.'

She trailed her fingertips down his back lightly. The pain in his eyes had banked her temper. 'And maybe we know some of the other men.'

He swallowed. 'That, too.'

'You both lived here.' Meredith said. 'Why should Alex recognize faces you don't?'

'I was five years older,' Daniel said. 'When it all happened, I was away at college.'

'And he was rich,' Alex added. 'The rich kids all went to the private school. Alicia and Sheila and Bailey and I, we all went to the public school. There was a very rigid line between the two worlds.'

'But Simon and Wade were friends.'

'Or at least accomplices,' Daniel said. 'Simon was expelled from private school. He graduated from the public school. We need to get our hands on some yearbooks.'

'How do Janet and Claudia fit?' Alex asked. 'They were only nine when Alicia died.'

'I don't know,' Daniel said. He leaned back against the sofa and closed his eyes. 'I do know that Sheila had something to tell me. My business card was in her pocket.'

'Who killed her?' Meredith asked.

'Some guy robbing the cash register.' Daniel shrugged. 'Or that's what we're supposed to think.' Abruptly he lurched to his feet, stunned realization on his face. 'I can't believe I missed that.' He opened the door. 'Hatton! Can you come here?' He turned to Alex. 'I'm going to meet Luke and Chase at the restaurant. Stay here.'

Dutton, Wednesday, January 31, 1:35 A.M.

Daniel walked back into Presto's Pizza, where Corey Presto was standing just inside the door, shell-shocked. He'd been crying, his face tear-streaked but now dry.

Dr Toby Granville was examining the body draped over the counter and one of Frank's deputies was taking pictures with a digital camera. Frank was crouched next to where the young officer had died, staring at the floor. They must have taken the young man to the morgue first. Sheila still sat in the corner, in her grotesque doll-like pose.

Daniel didn't see Randy Mansfield and assumed he'd been either taken to the hospital or released. 'Frank,' Daniel said.

Frank looked up, and for a moment desperation flashed in his eyes. Then the moment was gone and his old friend's eyes were flat. 'Why are you back, Daniel?'

'I'm taking over this scene. Toby, if you wouldn't mind, please step away from that body. I'll be calling in the state ME and crime lab.'

Toby Granville's gaze swung to Frank, who'd stood slowly, his fists on his hips. 'No, you're not,' Frank said.

'That car out back was involved in a hit-and-run with a witness under my protection, just this afternoon. Now it's here and another witness is dead. This restaurant is now a GBI crime scene. Please, Frank. Move, or I'll move you.'

Frank's mouth had fallen open and he jerked to stare at the man hanging across the counter. 'Hit-and-run?' he asked unsteadily. 'Where? Who?'

'In Atlanta, outside the Underground,' Daniel answered. 'Alex Fallon.' He looked at the doctor. 'I'm sorry, Toby. I need to process this internally. No offense.'

Granville backed away, gloved hands out. 'None taken.'

'Wait,' Corey Presto was shaking his head as if to clear it. 'You're sayin' this wasn't a robbery? That that man meant to kill Sheila?'

'I'm just saying that car was involved in an attempted vehicular homicide earlier today.' Daniel turned his gaze to Frank, who looked broken. 'And Sheila is dead.'

'What was she a witness to?' Frank asked quietly, and Daniel glimpsed the man he'd known so well. That he thought he'd known, anyway.

'That information's need-to-know. I'm sorry, Frank.'

Frank dropped his gaze to the bloodstained floor. 'Sam was only twenty-one.'

'I'm sorry, Frank,' Daniel said again. 'You can stay while we process the scene if you like.' He turned to Presto. 'Mr Presto, we need to know if any cash is missing.'

Presto wiped his mouth with the back of his hand. 'I'd already made the deposit.'

'You were here tonight,' Daniel said, 'when I was here with Alex Fallon.'

'Yeah, I was here.' He lifted his chin. 'So?'

'Sheila was talking to me. You called her back to the kitchen, and not kindly.'

'I had orders pilin' up. I don't pay her to gab.'

'She said that she'd said too much, that she wouldn't want to upset the powers that be. Who do you think she was talking about?'

'I don't know.' But the man was lying and they both knew it.

'How long had she worked for you?'

'Four years. Since she got out of rehab. I gave her a chance.'

'Why? Why did you give her a chance?'

Presto's cheeks flamed. 'Because I felt sorry for her.'

Daniel softened his expression. 'Why?'

Presto swallowed hard. 'She'd had a hard time. I felt sorry for her, that's all.' But when he looked at Sheila's lifeless body his throat convulsed and a unique pain filled his eyes, along with new tears, and Daniel understood.

'You loved her,' he said gently.

Presto's chest heaved once and he dropped his chin, his fists clenched at his sides. No further answer was required.

'Daniel.' Toby Granville had come up behind him, sympathy on his face. 'Let him go. He can answer your questions tomorrow.' Toby put his arm around Presto's shoulders and led him from the restaurant. Ed Randall passed them on his way in.

Ed took one look at the restaurant and whistled softly. 'My God.'

'One of the bodies has already been moved,' Daniel said. 'I can give you a detailed description of the scene when I came in. Deputy?'

The young officer who'd been taking pictures looked startled. 'Y-yes?'

'If you could give us your camera, I can make a copy of the files and return it to you.'

The deputy looked at Frank, who nodded. 'That's fine. You're dismissed, Alvin.'

The deputy looked infinitely relieved and made a quick exit.

'I'd just finished securing the scene at Bailey Crighton's when I got your call,' Ed said. 'I wasn't more than twenty minutes out of Dutton when I turned around. I'm guessing the ME guys'll be here in twenty. Until then, tell me what you saw.'

Luke arrived as Malcolm and his partner Trey were pushing the gunman out on a gurney zipped up in a body bag. Sheila was lying on a second gurney, the body bag zipped only to the middle of her chest. Luke walked straight to Sheila's body and stood for a moment studying her face, his expression hard.

'You're right,' he murmured. 'I'd hoped you were wrong.'

'Where are they?' Daniel asked quietly.

'Locked in my trunk. My mother's birthday is June first, by the way, not the fourth.'

'Don't tell her, okay?'

'Your secret's safe with me,' he said, but didn't smile. 'You sure about doing this?'

Daniel looked at Sheila's waxen face and knew he'd never been more sure of anything. 'Yeah. If I'd said something a week ago, she might still be alive.'

'You don't know that.'

'And I never will. Neither will she.'

Luke sighed. 'I'll go get the envelope.'

Daniel stood to one side when Malcolm and Trey came back for the other gurney. Chase came in as they were zipping Sheila up. His boss stood in the middle of the restaurant looking around before bringing his gaze squarely to Daniel's.

'In my car,' he said.

'Okay.' Daniel passed Luke and Luke slipped the envelope under his arm.

'I'll wait,' Luke said and Daniel only nodded.

Feeling like a dead man walking, Daniel got into Chase's car and pulled the door closed. Chase got behind the wheel.

'What's in the envelope, Daniel?'

Daniel cleared his throat. 'My demons.'

'I kind of figured that.'

He watched Malcolm and Trey lift the gurney into the rig and slam the back doors shut. *Sheila's blood is on my hands*. No more secrets. No more lies. 'It ends here.'

'What ends here, Daniel?'

'Hopefully not my career. Although if it comes to that, I won't fight you.'

'Why not let me be the judge?'

An appropriate starting place, Daniel thought. 'My father was a judge,' he said.

'Yes, I know. Daniel, spit it out. We'll deal with whatever we need to deal with.'

'I am spitting it out. It all started with my father, the judge.' And Daniel told him the entire story, including the details he had not shared with Alex earlier – the part when he'd first laid eyes on the pictures eleven years before, but his father had burned them to keep him from revealing the secret to the police. When he finished, Chase was staring straight ahead, elbows on his steering wheel, his chin propped on his fists.

'So you technically have had these pictures only a week.'

'I gave a set to Vito Ciccotelli in Philadelphia the day I got them.'

'And that's the one thing that's going to save your ass. Why didn't you come to me?'

Daniel pressed the heels of his hands to his brow bones. 'God. Chase, have you ever done anything so horrible, you were ashamed for anyone to know?'

Chase was silent so long Daniel thought he wouldn't answer. But he finally nodded. 'Yes.' And that appeared to be all Chase planned to say on the topic.

'Then you know why. For *eleven years* I have lived with the knowledge that these girls were victimized. That I *knew* and I said *nothing*. I promised myself I'd find them, that I'd fix this. Then the moment Alicia's ID was dumped in my lap I found every reason not to tell. I didn't want to jeopardize the case. I wanted to atone. I didn't want to hurt Alex.'

'Did you tell Alex?'

Daniel nodded. 'Yeah. She wasn't as mad as I thought she'd be. Are you?'

'What? Mad as you thought I'd be?' Chase sighed. 'I'm disappointed. I thought you trusted me. But I have been in your shoes and it's not a place where right and wrong are black and white.' He looked at the envelope. 'Those are the pictures?'

'Yes. I was thinking Alex might be able to identify some of the other girls. She recognized Sheila from high school.'

Chase put out his hand and Daniel gave him the envelope, feeling as though a weight rolled off his shoulders as he did so.

Chase looked at the pictures, his face tightening in disgust. 'Hell.' He put them back in the envelope and slid it next to his seat. 'Okay. This is what we're going to do from here on out. You're going to put in a formal request for the pictures to Ciccotelli in Philly ASAP. You're going to say you thought Alicia was one of the girls but that you didn't know any of the others until you saw Sheila tonight. So we requested the pictures back.'

'That's not actually untrue,' Daniel said slowly and Chase shot him a rueful look.

'That's why they pay me the big bucks. You will not mention that you made copies and kept the originals. Who else knows you have these, besides Luke?'

'Alex and her cousin Meredith.'

'Can they be trusted?'

'Yes. But Chase, I want to use those originals tonight. I need to find out who the other girls were. Maybe one of them knows who did this to them. Somebody out there doesn't want their identity known.'

Chase shook his head thoughtfully. 'Killing Sheila supports that theory, but killing Janet and Claudia doesn't. Why call attention to themselves?'

'Maybe somebody found out,' Daniel said quietly. 'And we can't forget about the keys. It's important. I just don't know how.'

'And the hair. Did you get Alex's hair down to the lab so they can compare them?'

'I did. Wallin's going to run the PCR on overtime. He thinks he can have a DNA comparison by tomorrow afternoon.' Daniel glanced at his watch. 'I mean, today.'

Chase slapped his own face lightly. 'We need to get some sleep, Daniel. You especially. You've been burning the candle at both ends for three weeks.'

'I want Alex to look at the pictures tonight.'

'Fine. You drive to her bungalow. I'll follow you.'

Daniel lifted his brows. 'You're coming?'

Chase's smile was tight and not terribly friendly. 'Pal, I'm your new partner. You don't go anywhere or do anything without telling me.'

Daniel blinked at him. 'Forever or for just this case?'

'Just this case unless you pull some other dumbass stunt. You only get so many get-out-of-trouble-free cards.'

'Get out of jail,' Daniel corrected with a smile.

'If this had gone a different way, you might've ended up there,' Chase warned, not smiling back. 'No more secrets. You tell me everything.'

'Fine. I'm going to sleep on Alex's sofa tonight.'

Chase leveled him a long look. 'Fine. Just stay on the sofa.'

Daniel lifted his chin. 'And if I don't?'

Chase rolled his eyes. 'Then just lie and tell me you did. Go on. If we're gonna show her the pictures, let's do it before sunup.'

Chapter Thirteen

Dutton, Wednesday, January 31, 2:30 A.M.

They were hideous. Obscene. But Alex forced herself to look at each one even when the sandwich Meredith had forced down her throat threatened to claw its way back up.

'I'm sorry,' Alex said for the seventh time, shaking her head at the picture of a girl being brutalized. *I thought my dreams were bad before* . . . 'I don't recognize her.'

Daniel put another on the table in front of her while Chase looked on in stony silence. Meredith sat on the other side of her while Daniel's friend Luke sat on the sofa in the living room with his computer on his lap, watching in the same thoughtful way he'd watched her at the Underground.

It seems like it's been years. But it had been less than twenty-four hours since she'd nearly been killed.

'Alex?' Daniel murmured and Alex forced herself to look at the eighth picture.

'I'm—' She frowned, the denial forgotten. She pulled the picture from the table and held it close to her eyes, which felt like they'd been rubbed with crushed glass. She studied the girl's face. Her nose. 'I know her. That's Rita Danner.'

'How do you know?' Daniel asked.

'Her nose. It's been broken. Rita hung with the popular crowd, but she had a mean streak, especially if she was jealous of you. She liked to pick on the nerds.'

'Did she pick on you?' Meredith asked.

'Only once. We were at a sleepover and I woke up to find Rita smearing peanut butter into my hair. I took a handful of the peanut butter and shoved it up her nose.'

Daniel blinked. 'You broke her nose?'

'I shoved a little too hard.' Alex sighed. 'I hated her. But this . . . My God.'

'Luke?' Daniel asked.

'I found a wedding announcement. Rita married a Josh Runyan of Columbia, Georgia.' He tapped a few more keys. 'And here's a divorce announcement dated two years ago. But it looks like Rita still lives in Columbia.'

'It's not too far,' Daniel said. 'We can visit her. See what she recalls. What about this one?' He slid another picture on the table. 'Well?'

'I know her, too. Cindy . . . Bouse. She was a nice girl. I didn't break her nose.'

'Then we should try to talk to her first,' Daniel said dryly. 'Luke?'

Luke's expression was stricken. 'She committed suicide eight years ago.'

Alex sucked in a breath. 'Oh God.'

Daniel stroked her back. 'I'm sorry.'

Alex nodded unsteadily. 'Let's see the next one.' She couldn't identify the girl in the tenth picture, or the eleventh. There had been fifteen victims and Daniel had told her from the outset that he would not show her Alicia's picture. For that she'd been grateful. Daniel had already identified Sheila's picture, so Alex had only two pictures to go.

He slid the twelfth picture onto the table.

'Gretchen French,' Alex said immediately. 'We were friends in junior high.'

'I'm looking,' Luke said before Daniel could ask. 'Here's one. She lives on Peachtree Boulevard in Atlanta. She's a nutritionist. Has her own website.' He brought the laptop over to the table. 'Look at her current photo.'

Daniel compared them. 'That's her.'

'Then we start there,' Chase said. Those had been the first words he'd spoken since they began. 'Go ahead and look at the last one.'

Alex focused. 'Carla Solomon. She played in the school orchestra with Bailey.'

'I see a C. Solomon on Third Avenue, here in Dutton,' Luke said. 'That's all I got.'

'What about the nine you didn't know?' Meredith said.

'They may have gone to a different school,' Alex replied. 'Dutton's high school was pretty small. Everybody knew everybody.'

'We'll pull yearbooks from all the local high schools,' Chase said brusquely. 'Daniel, you've got enough leads for now. Everybody go to sleep. I'll see you in the office at eight sharp.' He looked at Alex. 'Thank you. You've been a big help.'

Exhaustion was fuzzing the edges of her mind. 'I wish it would help us find Bailey.'

Daniel squeezed her knee. 'Don't give up,' he murmured.

She lifted her chin. 'I won't.'

Wednesday, January 31, 2:30 A.M.

Mack couldn't stop the chuckle from bubbling out as he nodded at the computer screen. Things were going so well. Gemma was dead and ready for disposal and *I'm a hundred thousand dollars richer*. Then again, it really wasn't about the money at this point. It was about making them pay the money. It meant they were afraid. The one who'd paid the hundred grand was so afraid, he was sitting outside his sister Kate's house watching at this very moment, just in case.

He'd made his point. *I'm here. You're not safe. Your family is not safe.*

And it had worked. Kate's big brother had paid a

hundred grand. Her big brother's whiny friend hadn't paid a penny, but he'd also been afraid.

He smiled. The one who hadn't paid the money had paid in another, far more satisfying, way. He'd been successful with the two he'd chosen for his initial assault. They'd been the weakest. Low-hanging fruit, ripe for the picking. But the other two were also affected. They were getting nervous. Scared.

Things were starting to happen. Things he hadn't had a direct hand in. *Janet, Claudia, Gemma, all mine.* All just pieces of kindling to get the fire going, but now it appeared the fire was going pretty good.

Bailey Crighton had been declared a missing person. Of course Mack now knew exactly where she was, and who had taken her. And why. He actually felt a little sorry for Bailey. She was an innocent bystander, and was now caught up in all this. He knew how that felt. When this was over, if she was still alive, he might go let her out.

He knew someone had tried to kill Alex Fallon. So clumsy. No finesse at all. Now she had a guard, two sharp-eyed GBI agents keeping watch over her little house. And one sharp-eyed agent keeping watch inside. He knew there'd been some kind of gathering at Fallon's house tonight. Vartanian was getting close.

Took him long enough.

He knew there'd been a big brouhaha at the pizza parlor tonight. Three dead. Sheila among them. Yes, Vartanian was getting close.

And the remaining *three* were scared. One of the four was dead, a victim of his own guilt and fear. Of course getting run off the road and left to die in an amazing explosion had helped. Which had only gone to prove what he'd believed all along. The group of upstanding pillars of the community would kill one of their own without blinking an eye.

They'd done it tonight to Rhett Porter. From his desk drawer he pulled the last of his brother's journals. It was half unfinished, because they'd done it five years ago to his brother Jared. Yes, he knew one of the four was dead. By sunrise, everyone in Dutton would know it, too.

Wednesday, January 31, 2:30 A.M.

'Bailey.'

Bailey had heard Beardsley's last five whispers. *I'm here. Please help me*. The words were in her mind, but she couldn't force them to her tongue. Every muscle in her body clenched and ached. *More*. She needed more. Dammit, *he'd* made her need it again. Damn him to hell.

'Bailey.'

She watched four fingers curve under the wall. Beardsley had torn a little more of the floor away. Hysterical laughter welled from somewhere deep inside her. They were trapped. They'd die here. But now Beardsley could wave good-bye.

The fingers disappeared. 'Bailey. Sshh. He'll come.'

He'll come anyway. Her eyes closed and she prayed to die.

Wednesday, January 31, 3:15 A.M.

Mack crept up the stairs silently. Breaking into a cop's house should have been harder to do. He'd passed the impressive gun cabinet on the first floor, wishing he could take what he wished. But tonight was about recon and stealth, not weapons. If he cleaned out the gun cabinet as he was so tempted, the fact that he'd been here would no longer be a secret. And he wanted it to be a secret.

He'd come prepared to knock the man out with a little chloroform on a handkerchief, but he was in luck. His prey was passed out drunk, still wearing his shoes. Carefully he patted the man's pockets, smiling when he felt a cell phone. Quickly he noted the cell's number and all numbers of incoming and outgoing calls.

Knowing how to reach out and touch this man in a way he'd trust was a very important component of Mack's plan. He slipped the phone back down into the man's pocket as carefully as he'd taken it out. He checked his watch. He'd need to hurry to be able to dump Gemma's body and still start his morning deliveries on time.

Dutton, Wednesday, January 31, 5:05 A.M.

Thunder and lightning. I hate you. I hate you. I wish you were dead.

Alex woke with a start, shaking and freezing cold. She sat up in bed, pressing the back of her hand to her mouth. Hope slept soundly and Alex resisted the urge to touch her golden curls. Hope needed to sleep. *I hope she doesn't dream like I do.*

Between them, Riley lifted his head, his sad basset eyes looking up at her. Alex ran a shaky hand over the dog's long back. 'Stay,' she whispered, and climbed out of bed. Pulling her robe over her nightshirt, she left the room, carefully closing the door behind her. She didn't want to wake Daniel.

The man was sleeping on her sofa. He'd refused to leave, even with Agents Hatton and Koenig sitting outside. She stood for a moment, rubbing her arms for warmth, looking down at him, too many thoughts racing through her head.

He's a beautiful man. And he was, with his blond hair and strong jaw and those blue eyes that could be kind, but also ruthless as they bore through her defenses.

He lied to me. No, not really. Intellectually she knew how difficult it must have been for him to know what had happened to Alicia and not to tell her. To know his own flesh and blood had in some way been responsible.

I'll see you in hell, Simon. At least Wade hadn't been

her flesh and blood. She thought about how he'd forced his way between her thighs at that party so long ago. He'd thought she was Alicia. Alex remembered his genuine shock when she'd said no.

Did that mean at one point Alicia had said yes? It was a disturbing thought to mix in with all the others that bombarded her mind. Alex had known Alicia was sexually active and Alex had thought she'd known with whom . . . but *Alicia and Wade*? The mental picture made her skin crawl. What kind of girl had Alicia really been?

What kind of monster had Wade been? She thought of the pictures she'd seen, perverted and horrific. Wade had raped those girls. She'd lived under the same roof with him for years and never suspected he was capable of such . . . depravity. Cruelty.

Alicia. Sheila and Rita. Gretchen and Carla. And Cindy. They'd all been raped. And poor Cindy had killed herself. The depths of depression she must have experienced. Alex knew those depths well. *Poor Cindy. Poor Sheila.*

And the nine others she didn't know . . .

Daniel had carried their faces in his mind for a week. *Poor Daniel.*

His handsome face was stern, even in sleep. He'd removed his suit coat, his only apparent concession to comfort. His muscled chest rose and fell under the shirt he'd unbuttoned only enough to loosen his collar. His tie was tugged away from his throat, knocked askew.

He still wore his gun, holstered at his hip. His shoes were still on his feet. He was ready, even in sleep.

Again, the pictures assaulted her mind. After seeing thirteen of them, it didn't take much imagination to conjure what Alicia's must have looked like. She thought of the first time Daniel had seen her in the GBI office. The utter shock on his face.

She thought about the way he'd looked at her, right before he'd kissed her, tonight and earlier today in his car after she'd nearly been killed. *What do you want from me?* she'd asked. *Not anything you're not willing and . . . anxious to give,* he'd replied.

She'd believed him then. She wasn't sure she believed him now.

He felt guilt. Deep, soul-searing guilt. Daniel Vartanian sought atonement.

Alex didn't want to be any man's atonement. She didn't want to be any man's charity project. She'd done that already, with Richard. And it had been the most abysmal of failures. She didn't want to be a failure again.

She knew the moment Daniel woke. His eyes opened deliberately, as he did everything else. And when he focused that bright blue gaze on her face, she shivered. For a moment he stared, then rolled to one hip and held out his hand.

And she knew it didn't matter what she did or didn't want. It only mattered what she needed, and at that moment, she needed him. He sat up against the corner of the sofa and drew her into his lap. She went, greedily absorbing all his warmth.

'Your hands are like ice,' he murmured, carefully covering them with his own.

She burrowed her cheek against the hard wall of his chest. 'Riley hogs the covers.'

'That's why he doesn't sleep with me at home.'

She lifted her face to look at him, needing to know. 'Who does?'

He didn't try to misunderstand. 'No one. Not in a very long time, anyway. Why?'

She thought of Richard's new wife. 'I need to know if I'd be first or second string.'

She thought she might see his one-sided smile, but his mouth remained completely serious. 'First.' He swept his thumb across her lip, sending a tingle down her body. 'You were married before.'

'And divorced.'

'Were you second string?' he asked, so very quietly.

'More like water boy,' she said with a half smile of her own.

Still he didn't smile. 'Did you love him?'

'I thought I did. But I think I just didn't want to be alone in the night.'

'So he was there for you . . .' His eyes grew intense. '. . . in the night.'

'No. At the beginning he was a resident in the hospital where I worked. We dated a few times. My roommate had moved out and before I knew it, he'd moved in. I saw him at the hospital, but our off-hours didn't seem to mesh well. He wasn't home a lot.'

'But you married him.'

'Yes.' They'd kind of wandered their way into marriage, she and Richard. She honestly couldn't remember the moment he'd proposed.

'Did you love him?'

It was the second time he'd asked the question. 'No. I wanted to. But I didn't.'

'Was he kind to you?'

She smiled then. 'Yes. Richard is . . . he's a nice man. He's good to children and he likes dogs . . .' She stopped when she realized the direction her words were going. 'But I think he viewed me as something of a challenge. His own little Eliza Doolittle.'

He frowned. 'Why would he want to change you?'

For a moment she stared. His words were a sweet balm, easing the disappointment she'd felt at never being quite what Richard needed, or what she'd wanted to be for both of them. 'Most of it was me, I think. I wanted to be . . . interesting. Dynamic. Unbridled.'

He lifted his brows. 'Unbridled?'

She laughed self-consciously. 'You know.' She waggled her brows and he nodded, but still didn't smile.

'You wanted to make him come home to you.'

'I suppose so. But I couldn't be what he wanted me to be. What I wanted me to be.'

'So he left?'

'No, I did. Hospitals are like small towns. Lots of secrets hidden below the surface. Richard had affairs. All very discreet.' She held his gaze. 'He should have just left me, but he didn't want to hurt me.'

Daniel winced. 'Point made. So you left?'

'He met someone, luckily not one of the nurses. I couldn't have stayed then.'

He was frowning. 'I thought you left.'

'I left him. By this point we'd bought a house, and I let him have it. But I wouldn't leave the hospital. I was there first.'

He blinked at her. 'You gave him the house, but not the job.'

'Exactly.' She said it matter-of-factly, because to her, it was. 'He'd finished his residency and had signed on as a full-time ER doc. Everyone expected me to leave, I think. To go to paedes or surgery or something. But I like the ER. So I didn't leave.'

He looked nonplussed. 'I guess that makes for some awkward moments.'

'That's putting it mildly.' She shrugged. 'Anyway, I moved out of the house a year ago and the new wife moved right in behind me. They're . . . good together.'

'That's magnanimous of you,' he said warily, and she laughed ruefully.

'I guess I liked him enough not to want him to be unhappy. Meredith, now, she'd like to see him strung between two anthills and dipped in honey.'

Finally that one side of his mouth lifted, lifting her heart with it. 'Note to self,' he murmured. 'Don't piss Meredith off.'

She nodded once, pleased to have been able to make him smile. 'Exactly.'

But too quickly his smile faded. 'Were you dreaming again tonight?'

Thinking about the dreams made her cold again. 'Yes.' She rubbed her arms to get warm and he took over, pulling her against him, rubbing her back briskly. The man was like a furnace, warm and strong and male, and she snuggled closer, wanting more.

And finding it in the pulse of his hard arousal against her hip.

She sucked in a breath, suddenly much warmer. He wanted her. And she wanted him. But before she could decide what to say or do, he shifted, settling her away from his lap, and all that wonderful, sensual heat disappeared. His arms came hard around her and he tucked her head under his chin. 'I'm sorry,' he murmured against her hair.

She pulled back to see his face. He was wearing a guilty look. 'Why?'

He glanced at Meredith's door. 'Look, I promised you that nothing would happen that you didn't want to happen.'

'Yesterday, in the car. I remember. And so? Nothing *has* happened.' She lifted her chin. 'Not yet anyway. That could change.'

His chest expanded and his blue eyes grew dark. Still he resisted. 'If Hatton hadn't come knocking on that door last night . . . I was trying to . . .' He closed his eyes, his cheeks darkening. 'I wanted you. If we hadn't been interrupted I might have tried to push you into something you weren't ready for.'

Alex considered the most appropriate response. He was trying to take care of her, and while she found it sweet, she was leaning toward being very annoyed. 'Daniel.' She waited until he opened his eyes. 'I'm not sixteen anymore and do not want to be any kind of a victim in your eyes or anybody else's. I'll be thirty on my next birthday. I have a good job. A good life. And the good sense to make my own decisions.'

He nodded, respect in his eyes. It was grim, but it was respect. 'Understood.'

'But, Daniel.' She hooked her finger inside his loosened tie, trying for sultry, but sounding wistful instead. 'I still want to be . . . unbridled.'

His eyes flared. Then he was kissing her and she could feel the heat and power of his mouth. Then he was rolling her beneath him and she could feel the heat and power of his body as he thrust against her, his movements hard and deliberate. His hands held the sides of her face, his fingers shoving into her hair and he moved her head, this way, then that, until he found the perfect fit.

And then he feasted, a low groan that sounded like her name rumbling from deep in his throat. Alex held on, determined to enjoy every minute of the wild ride for as long as it lasted. She met him thrust for thrust and when he nudged her mouth open she complied, learning the varied textures of his lips, his seeking tongue.

Too soon he lifted his head to drag in a lungful of air. He looked down, his eyes dark and hot and slightly dangerous. 'That was . . .'

'Really good,' she whispered, startling a soft laugh from him.

'Really good? I expected more from a woman who comes up with "unbridled."'

She arched her brows. 'That's because I wasn't yet. Unbridled, that is.'

His lips twitched, but his eyes remained intense. 'Next time you will be,' he murmured. 'Now go back to bed.' He started to shift, to lift his body from hers and in a split second of certainty she knew what she wanted. With both hands she grabbed his belt and yanked him back, pressing her heels down into the sofa and her body up into his until she could feel him throbbing against her again, hot and hard. 'I don't want to.'

His eyes widened, then narrowed. 'No. There's no way. Not here.'

Feeling a power of her own, she held on to his belt when he tried to move again, realizing that if he'd really wanted to be gone, he would have been. He wanted this, too. She rolled her hips in what she hoped was a blatant invitation. 'Why not?'

He was looking at her with an incredulity and a . . . carnal craving that made her own desire treble. 'You want a freaking *list*?' he whispered.

'No, I want you to shut up and kiss me again.'

Relief had his shoulders slumping. 'That I can do.' And he did with a kiss that started sweet, but quickly became hot and wet, dragging her back down into the swirling mass of needs and wants that she had no intention of escaping. She tugged at his shirt until she'd pulled the tails free and was free to explore the smooth skin she'd only glimpsed before. He groaned into her mouth. 'Alex, stop.'

Her fingers stopped stroking and she pulled back far enough to see his face. 'You really want me to?' she whispered and held her breath as want and responsibility warred in his eyes. After what seemed like an eternity he shook his head.

'No.'

The breath she held rushed out. 'Good.' Nimbly she freed the buttons up the front of his shirt, then pulled the tie over his head and dropped it on the floor. Finally she had full access to his warm, hard chest, and she fanned her hands, side to side, feeling every flex and ripple. Golden hair covered him and she brushed at it with her fingertips, trailing lower until his abs twitched. 'Daniel, look at you,' she whispered.

He kissed her again, softly this time. When he answered, his whisper was husky. Tender. 'I'd rather look at you.' He pulled at the belt of her robe and caught her nightshirt in one hand. 'Lift up.' She did and he pulled the nightshirt over her hips, continuing until she felt the cool air on her breasts. She shivered.

Then closed her eyes when his body slid down hers and his mouth closed over her. She shivered again, but this time from the heat. He sucked and fondled until she was thrusting against him, her hands in his hair, pulling him closer. He switched to the other breast, and she twisted, knowing she could get no closer, but trying nonetheless.

His hand flattened on her stomach and she sucked in a breath and held it, waiting. But he didn't move it up or down, just kept it lightly resting, and she realized he was waiting for permission. Encouragement, even. Instead she begged. 'Please.'

The single syllable launched him back into motion and his fingers slipped under the cotton that still covered her and she knew she'd been right about how good that thumb of his would feel. He made her shiver and shudder, but when she whimpered for more he shifted his mouth back to hers, swallowing her little moans.

She was so close. Digging her heels into the sofa cushions she surged against his hand until her blood was pounding and every nerve on every last inch of skin was firing. Until finally, light exploded behind her eyelids and she fell back against the cushions, panting and feeling better than she'd felt . . . possibly ever.

He dropped his forehead to her shoulder, his body

rigid, his breathing labored. 'Okay.' His murmur was ragged. 'Now go to bed. Please.'

But his hand was still touching her intimately and she knew there was no way she could sleep now. Her pulse still thrummed and she still . . . needed. Judging from the way his body was still pulsing against her thigh, Daniel felt the same way.

She slid her hands to his belt and he lunged up, his brows crunched in a mighty frown. The hand that had worked such magic caught her wrist, but Alex had nimble fingers and she'd already worked the belt loose.

'What are you doing?' he hissed and she blinked at him.

'What do you think I'm doing?' she countered.

A muscle ticked in his jaw. 'I thought I said go to bed.'

She feathered her fingers along the skin at his waist and his abs convulsed, his body going taut. 'You really want me to?' she whispered once again. She watched his face, his struggle obvious. Then he strained up to look at Meredith's door over the back of the sofa and Alex swallowed her smile even as she grabbed the edges of his shirt and pulled him down on her. He fell with a hard thump and she wrapped her arms around his neck, kissing him as he'd kissed her before. With a growl he took over, his mouth hungry, almost savage. The thrusts of his hips were hard and equally savage.

He ripped his mouth away. 'This is crazy,' he

whispered against her lips. 'We're not teenagers having sex on this sofa.'

'No, I'm almost thirty and I want to have sex on this sofa.' She met his eyes with challenge. 'With you. So do you want me to stop?'

'No,' he said, his answer strangled and hoarse. 'But are you sure?'

'Oh, yes. I'm very sure.' She eased down his zipper. Her first touch was tentative, but his body jerked and he hissed out a curse. Quickly she pulled her hand away. 'But if you're not . . . I don't want you to do anything you're not comfortable—'

He silenced her with a hard kiss, then flipped the snap on his holster and carefully put his gun on the floor. He wrestled his wallet from his back pocket, pulled out a condom and tossed his wallet next to his gun. He looked down into her face, his blue eyes brighter than the core of a flame and twice as hot. 'Be sure, Alex.'

Keeping her gaze on his, she slid the cotton panties down her legs and kicked them away. 'Please, Daniel.' His eyes jerked down to the skin she bared. She watched his throat work as he tried to swallow and suddenly understood this moment was more than a mating between two consenting and extremely attracted adults. It would be the moment she ceased to be a victim in his eyes.

And perhaps in her own. 'Please, Daniel,' she whispered again.

For three hard beats of her heart he stared down at her, then with unsteady hands he ripped the packet and covered himself. Slipping his arms beneath her back, he cradled her head between his palms and settled himself between her thighs. He took her mouth with a quiet authority that was more intense than his most reckless kisses had been. Then he entered her with a slow reverence that stole her breath.

Every roll of his hips was deliberate, and he watched her, gauging her response. Then he shifted and she gasped as unexpected pleasure rippled through her body.

He brushed his lips over her ear, making her shiver. 'Right there?' he whispered.

'Right there is really good.' Her hands covered his buttocks, thrilling in the play of his muscles as they tensed and flexed. He was a well-formed man, hard and honed.

Slowly he began to bring her up again, rocking harder against her until her heart was racing faster than before, rocking faster up into her until his control began to slip. She wanted to see his control slip. She wanted to be the one to break that deliberate restraint, make him forget who he was, where he was, and . . . take her.

She brought her hand around his hip, trailing her fingertips over the sensitive skin of his groin, and his body jolted. With a low groan he froze, trembling against her.

'Daniel, please.' She whispered it in his ear. 'Do it. Now.'

He shuddered as his control shattered. His hips plunged at a frantic pace, as if he couldn't get deep enough fast enough. This, this was what she'd wanted. Him, holding nothing back. She met him at each peak, clutching his shoulders, digging her nails into his back to get closer, to bring him deeper until once again she teetered at the edge. With one last hard twist up into her body he pushed her over. She started to cry out, but his hand clamped across her mouth, muffling her moan.

When the bucking of her body had subsided to quivers, his body went rigid, his back arching as if he'd bay at the moon, but no sound broke free. His jaw clenched as his hips jerked, pressing hard and deep. For a long moment he held himself motionless above her, magnificently male. Then his breath left him in a rush and he collapsed, burying his face in the curve of her neck. He was panting and shudders racked him. Alex smoothed her hands across his back, up under the shirt he still wore.

When his shudders stilled, he lifted his head again, this time leaning up on his elbow so that he looked down into her face. His cheeks were flushed and his mouth was wet and his breathing was still strident. But his eyes . . . She always came back to his eyes.

He looked awed. And Alex felt as if she'd conquered Everest. He drew a deep breath. 'Did I hurt you?'

She shook her head, loving looking up at him. 'No. It was perfect.'

Another shudder shook him, an aftershock, smaller this time. 'You were so tight. I should have done this better, in a bed. I should—'

'Daniel.' She pressed her fingertips to his lips. 'It was perfect. Perfect,' she repeated on a whisper and watched his mouth smile.

'Now that sounds like a definite challenge. Next time I'll—'

'Police! Stop right there!'

The shout came from outside and Daniel was instantly on alert, on his knees. He zipped his pants and rolled to his feet, scooping up his gun. 'Stay down,' he told her. He stood at the side of the window, peeking between the lace curtains.

Alex stayed down until she saw his shoulders relax. 'What?' she asked.

'What?' Meredith echoed, opening her bedroom door a crack.

'It's the paperboy,' Daniel said. 'Hatton took the paper and he's coming up the walk. But he doesn't look happy,' he added, sounding unhappy himself. 'Now what?'

Alex grabbed her underwear from the floor and shoved it into her robe pocket before pulling her belt tight around her waist. Ignoring Meredith's raised brow, she fled to the kitchen, busying herself making coffee while Daniel opened the door for Agent Hatton.

'Sorry, Daniel,' Hatton said. 'Miss Fallon.' He nodded at Alex, then Meredith, apparently not a man to waste words repeating a name when it worked for both women. He turned back to Daniel. 'He drove up in a van. We didn't know he was the paperboy at first. But take a look at the front page. Your friend Woolf has been a busy boy.'

Daniel grabbed the paper, then looked up, his expression grim.

Alex forgot the coffee, hurrying to take the paper from his hands. At first she frowned. Then her eyes widened. 'Rhett Porter's dead?'

'Who is Rhett Porter?' Meredith asked, reading the front page over Alex's shoulder.

'Rhett was one of Wade's friends,' Alex said. 'Rhett's father owned all the car dealerships around here. Wade worked for them, detailing cars.'

'Rhett was also the brother of the boys that discovered Alicia's body,' Daniel said.

Hatton's brows were lifted. 'Coincidence?'

Daniel shook his head. 'Nothing's a coincidence in this town.'

'I wonder how Woolf got this scoop?' Meredith asked. 'It wasn't on the news or on the Internet. I was just online, checking my mail.'

She said it with a pointed look, and Alex knew Meredith had not only been awake but had heard the entire scene on the sofa.

His cheeks darkening, Daniel buttoned his shirt. 'I'll

go have a chat with Mr Woolf.'

'I'll stay inside the house with the Miss Fallons,' Hatton said.

'And I'll make coffee,' Alex said. 'I know I need it.'

Meredith followed her to the kitchen, smirking. '*I* need a cigarette,' she murmured.

Alex glared at her. Neither of them smoked. 'You just shut up.'

Meredith chuckled. 'When you decide to get a wild hair, you really do it right.'

Dutton, Wednesday, January 31, 5:55 A.M.

Daniel was turning onto Main Street when he saw a light come on in the window of the office of the *Dutton Review*. Instinct told him to hold tight, so he pulled his car behind a boxwood hedge, turned off his headlights, and waited. A few minutes later Jim Woolf appeared from behind the building, gliding past Daniel with his headlights darkened as well.

Daniel pulled out his cell phone and called Chase.

'What now?' Chase asked, grumpy.

'Woolf got another big scoop last night. One of the town men was killed when his car went off the road. I came to ask him about it and it looks like our boy is going for another early morning romp.'

'Fuck,' Chase muttered. 'Where's he going?'

'East. I'm going to tail him, but I need backup. I don't want him noticing me.'

'Tell Hatton to stay with the ladies and have Koenig tail him with you. I'll start driving your way. Call me before you confront him.'

'Yes, sir, partner sir.'

Wednesday, January 31, 6:00 A.M.

No, no, no, no, no . . . Bailey rocked herself, the pain from banging her head against the wall a welcome relief from the loathing and disgust that made her want to die.

'Bailey. Stop it.'

Beardsley hissed the command, but Bailey didn't listen to him.

Bang, bang, bang. Her head throbbed and she deserved it. She deserved to be hurt. She deserved to die.

'Bailey.' Beardsley's full hand shot under the wall and grabbed her wrist. He squeezed hard. 'I said stop it.'

Bailey dropped her head, dug her chin into her knees. 'Go away.'

'Bailey.' He wouldn't go away. 'What happened?'

She stared down at the dirty hand that had her wrist in an iron hold. 'I told,' she spat. 'All right? I told him.'

'You can't blame yourself. You held out longer than most soldiers would have.'

It was the smack, she thought heavily, her thoughts a nauseated whirl. He'd held the syringe just out of reach and she'd wanted . . . needed. Craved to the point nothing else mattered. 'What have I done?' she whispered.

'What did you tell him, Bailey?'

'I tried to lie, but he knew. He knew it wasn't in my house.' And he'd kicked and hit and spat on her every time she'd lied. Still she'd been strong. Until the needle.

Now it didn't matter anymore. Nothing mattered.

'So where did you hide it?'

She was so tired. 'I gave it to Alex.' She tried to swallow, but her throat was too dry. She tried to cry, but she had no more water in her. 'Now he's going after Alex, and Alex has Hope. And he'll kill me, and probably you, too. He doesn't need us anymore.'

'He won't kill me. He thinks I wrote down Wade's confession and hid it.'

'Did you?'

'No, but it's buying me time. He'll keep you alive until he checks out your story.'

'It doesn't matter. I wish he'd just killed me.'

'Don't say that. We're going to get out of here.'

She let her head drop back against the wall. 'No, we won't.'

'Yes, we will. But you have to help me. Bailey.' He dug his fingers into her wrist. 'Help me. For your daughter and for all those other girls you hear crying in the night.'

Bailey faltered. 'You heard them, too? I thought I was losing my mind.'

'You aren't. I saw one of the girls when he was taking me to his room.'

His room, where he'd tortured her for days. 'Who is she, the girl?'

'I don't know, but she was young, maybe fifteen.'

'Why does he have them?'

'Why do you think, Bailey?' he countered gravely.

'Oh my God. How many does he have?'

'I counted twelve doors on that hall. Now help me. For those girls and for Hope.'

Bailey drew a breath that hurt inside and out. 'What do you want me to do?'

Releasing her wrist, Beardsley threaded his fingers through hers. 'Good girl.'

Chapter Fourteen

Dutton, Wednesday, January 31, 6:15 A.M.

'Can I get you some more coffee, Agent Hatton?' Alex asked. He sat at her table, calm and unrushed. His partner was gone, giving backup to Daniel.

Hatton shook his head. 'No, ma'am. My wife only lets me have a cup a day.'

Alex lifted her brows. 'You listen to your wife? Really? Very few men that come through the ER listen to their wives, which is why most of them end up in the ER.'

He nodded solemnly. 'I listen to every word she says.'

Meredith scoffed from the kitchen. 'But do you obey her?'

Hatton grinned. 'I listen to every word she says.'

'I thought so,' Meredith said and filled his cup anyway.

Hatton saluted Meredith with his cup, then put it down on the table. 'Hello there.'

Hope stood in the doorway of her bedroom staring at Hatton.

'This is Agent Hatton.' Alex took Hope by the hand. 'Agent Hatton, my niece Hope.' Then Alex stared as Hope touched Hatton's face where a soft gray beard grew.

Hatton leaned forward in his chair so Hope could reach him more easily. 'Everyone says my beard makes me look like Santa,' he said. He opened his arms, and to Alex's shock, Hope climbed into his lap. She stroked his beard with the flat of her palms.

Meredith uttered a small groan. 'Not again.'

Alex looked at Hatton helplessly. 'Hope's had a tendency to fixate on things.'

'Well, she's not hurtin' a thing, so leave her alone for now,' Hatton said, forever endearing him to Alex.

Alex sat down at the table with them. 'You have kids, Agent Hatton?'

'Six. All girls. Eighteen all the way down to eight.'

Meredith looked at the organ, then at Alex. 'Maybe he knows what the song is.'

'I don't want to get her started again,' Alex said, then sighed. 'We have to try.'

'What song?' Hatton asked.

Meredith hummed it and Hatton frowned. 'Sorry, ladies. I can't help you.' He checked his watch. 'Vartanian said you were meeting Dr McCrady and the forensic artists this morning at eight. We should be getting a move on.'

Disappointed that he hadn't recognized the song either, Alex stood up, her knees still stiff from her concrete slide the day before. 'I have to walk Daniel's dog.'

Hatton shook his head. 'I'll take the dog outside, Miss Fallon.' To Hope he said, 'You've got to get ready. Little girls need time to primp.'

'He does have six daughters,' Meredith said wryly.

Hope pressed her hands to Hatton's soft beard, her little face suddenly intense. 'Pa-paw.' It was the first word she'd spoken, her voice small and sweet.

Hatton blinked once, then smiled at Hope. 'Your pa-paw has a beard like mine?'

'Does he?' Meredith asked, and Alex tried to bring Craig Crighton's face to mind.

Quiet. Close the door. When she could think, she shook her head. 'He never had a beard that I remember.' She cupped Hope's cheek. 'Did you see your pa-paw?'

Hope nodded, her big gray eyes so sad Alex wanted to cry. But Alex made her mouth smile. 'When, honey? When did you see your pa-paw?'

'Didn't you say the nun at the shelter said Bailey had looked but hadn't found him?' Meredith murmured.

'Sister Anne said she didn't think Bailey had found him.' Alex frowned. 'You know, Daniel never told me if he'd found Sister Anne. Or Desmond.'

'I know he called it in last night. I'll check it while

you two get ready,' Hatton said. He set Hope on her feet and tipped up her little chin. 'Go with your aunt now,' he said, and Hope obediently put her hand in Alex's.

'We have to keep him,' Meredith said, pointing to Hatton. 'He's got a way with her.'

'Or he needs to give us his magic wand,' Alex countered wryly, and Hope's face shot up, suddenly panicked. Alex glanced at Meredith, then ignoring the protest of her knees, crouched to look Hope in the eye. 'Sweetheart, what is the magic wand?'

But Hope said nothing, her face frozen, terrified. Alex wrapped her arms around her. 'Baby,' she whispered into Hope's golden curls, 'what did you see?' But Hope said nothing and Alex's heart sank. 'Come on, sweetie. Let's get your bath.'

Bernard, Georgia, Wednesday, January 31, 6:25 A.M.

'Agile sonofabitch,' Agent Koenig murmured behind Daniel.

Daniel watched Jim Woolf pull his way up into a tree. 'You wouldn't think he had it in him.' His jaw tightened as he looked through the trees at the ditch by the side of the road. 'He took lots of pictures before he picked his tree. I don't want to know who it is.'

'I'm sorry, Daniel.'

'Me, too.' In his pocket his cell phone vibrated. It

was Chase. 'We just got here,' he said. 'Koenig and I. I haven't checked the scene yet. How far out are you?'

'Not far. I used my lights. Go ahead and check it out. I'll wait.'

Daniel pushed through the trees, cell phone still pressed to his ear, imagining Woolf's stunned expression even as the man snapped his picture. He got to the edge of the ditch and stopped. 'There's another one,' he told Chase. 'Brown wool blanket.'

Chase made an angry sound in his throat. 'Then pull that damn idiot out of his tree and sit tight. I'm exiting the interstate now and CSU and the ME's rig are on the way.'

Dutton, Wednesday, January 31, 6:45 A.M.

He pulled into his own driveway, relieved, exhausted, stiff in all the wrong places. But Kate was safe and that's what counted. He had an hour to shower, eat, and pull himself together before he was due at Congressman Bowie's for an update meeting.

There was tragedy, he thought, and there was politics. Sometimes they were one and the same. He stopped on his front porch to pick up the morning paper, and even though he'd been expecting the news, his heart sank. 'Rhett,' he murmured. 'You dumbass. I warned you.'

His front door opened and his wife stood there, hurt

in her eyes. 'You used to try to hide your late-night romps from the neighbors. Not to mention the children.'

He nearly laughed. After all the times she'd ignored his rolling in late from another woman's bed, she'd picked today to confront him. The one time he wasn't guilty.

Yes, you are. You need to tell Vartanian about the seven other women. It's not enough to keep Kate safe. If one of them dies . . . it's on your head.

His wife's eyes narrowed in scrutiny. 'You look like you slept in your clothes.'

'I did.' The words were out before he could stop them.

'Why?'

He couldn't tell her. He didn't love her. He wasn't sure he ever had. But she was his wife and the mother of his children and he found he still had enough self-respect to admit her opinion of him mattered. He couldn't tell her about Kate, about any of it.

So instead, he held out the paper. 'Rhett's dead.'

His wife drew a shuddering breath. 'I'm sorry.'

She was. Because she was a decent person. She'd never liked Rhett, never understood their 'friendship.' Ha. As if. More like a mutual self-preservation society. Keep your enemies close to your heart; then you'll know if they're about to double-cross you. It was valuable advice he'd received from his father once a long time ago.

His father had meant his political enemies. Not his supposed friends. But the advice worked just the same. 'He . . . um . . . he ran off the road.'

She opened the door a little wider. 'Come on in, then.'

He stepped over the threshold and looked into her face. She'd been a good wife all these years. He didn't want to hurt her. He just never seemed to be able to stop himself. None of his affairs really meant anything, except the last one.

He still felt bad about the last one. Normally he just used women for sex. But he'd used Bailey Crighton to get information. She'd changed since her daughter was born. No longer was she the town slut they'd all had at one time or another.

She'd thought he cared, and on some level he had. Bailey had tried so hard to make a life for herself and Hope and now she was gone. He knew where she was and who had taken her. But he couldn't say anything to help Bailey any more than he could help the other seven women targeted by a killer.

'I'll fix you some eggs while you get showered and changed,' his wife said quietly.

'Thank you,' he said and her eyes widened. It occurred to him he hadn't said that to her nearly often enough. But then, on the list of his many sins, being impolite didn't seem to hold a candle to rape. Or the murder of the women he'd refused to help.

Atlanta, Wednesday, January 31, 8:45 A.M.

Daniel slumped in a chair at the team table. He dragged his hands down his face. He hadn't even had time to shave. Thanks to Luke, he at least had a change of clothes.

Luke had given credit to Mama Papadopoulos, who'd called him every hour the evening before, fretting about 'poor Daniel.' Luke had dropped off one of Daniel's suits on his way to his own office. But Luke's face had been drawn and weary and Daniel knew his friend had troubles of his own. He thought of the pictures Luke had to look at every day as he investigated the slime that peddled children on the Internet.

He thought about Alex. She'd been a child when Wade had assaulted her, whether she'd admit it or not. Primal rage flared within him and he was glad Wade Crighton was dead. Slime like Wade and the predators Luke chased did so much more than physically assault their victims. They stole their trust, their innocence.

Daniel thought of how Alex had looked the night before – vulnerable and fragile. He shuddered where he sat. The sex had been the most amazing of his life. Being with her had rocked him to his very foundation. The thought of losing her scared him to death.

He had to make this insanity stop. Now. *So get to work, Vartanian.*

Chase, Ed, and Hatton and Koenig joined him at the table, carrying cups of coffee and looking grim. 'Here,' Chase said, giving him a cup. 'It's strong.'

Daniel took a sip and winced. 'Victim three is Gemma Martin, twenty-one. We're three for three. All three grew up in Dutton, all graduated from Bryson Academy, same year. Gemma lived with her grandmother, who got worried when she didn't come down for breakfast. She found Gemma's bed unslept in and called us.'

'We ID'd her with her prints,' Ed said. 'Everything at the scene was identical to the others, down to the key and the hair wrapped around her toe.'

'I want to know where he grabbed her,' Chase said. 'Where was she last night?'

'Gemma told her grandmother that she wasn't feeling well and was going to bed early, but the grandmother told me that Gemma often lied. Her Corvette is missing from her garage. We'll start with her usual haunts.'

'What about the tapes from where Janet rented her minivan?' Chase countered.

'I dropped them off at CSU when I brought Hope to see Mary last night. Ed?'

'I had one of the techs review the tapes overnight,' Ed said and slid a photo across the table. 'We got very lucky. Look familiar?'

Daniel picked up the photo. 'It's the guy who bought the blankets.'

'He made no attempt to hide his face this time either. He had the key to Janet's Z.'

'And we have no idea who he is?' Chase demanded.

'We've got his face taped to the visor of every squad car in the city, Chase,' Ed said. 'The next step is to flash his picture on the TV news.'

Daniel looked at Chase. 'If we do that, he could go under.'

'I think that's a chance we have to take,' Chase said. 'Do it. What's next?'

'Yearbooks,' Daniel said. 'We need to track down the women in the pictures.'

'Already started,' Chase said. 'I've got Leigh calling every high school in a twenty-mile radius of Dutton to get their yearbooks from thirteen years ago.'

Ed sat back, puzzled. 'Why high school yearbooks from thirteen years ago? Janet, Claudia, and Gemma would have been nine years old thirteen years ago.'

'I'm getting to that.' From his briefcase Daniel pulled Simon's pictures and told the others the version of the story he and Chase had agreed upon the night before.

'Daniel had surrendered the pictures to the police up in Philly,' Chase said. 'The detective on the case up there was good enough to have them scanned and e-mailed to us first thing this morning. The originals are being couriered down.'

Daniel felt bad about Vito Ciccotelli jumping through the hoop of scanning and e-mailing the photos, but he'd been completely honest with Vito last night when he'd called him. Vito had offered to scan the pictures himself. Daniel hadn't needed to ask.

Vito had rejected any offer of thanks, saying Daniel had given him something more precious – he'd helped Vito save his girlfriend Sophie's life. Daniel thought of Alex and understood how Vito viewed the saving of his Sophie as the all-trumping act.

Ed shook his head. 'Okay. So Simon had these pictures, including one of Alicia Tremaine and another of the waitress who was killed last night, Sheila Cunningham.'

'Yes. Alex was able to identify four of the others. One is dead, suicide. The others we have to match to girls from the local schools. That's why I want the yearbooks.'

Ed blew out a breath. 'You know how to shake things up, Vartanian.'

'I sure don't mean to,' Daniel murmured. 'What else do we have?'

Hatton rubbed his beard absently. 'That nun from the shelter. Sister Anne.'

Daniel's stomach turned over. 'Please don't tell me she's dead.'

'She's not dead,' Hatton said. 'But she's close. The uniforms who went to check on her last night didn't find her at the shelter and she didn't answer her door at home. They didn't get the message that this woman's life might be in danger, only that you were looking for her. They didn't go in her apartment last night.'

'And this morning?' Daniel asked grimly.

'When I called I impressed on them the importance of this matter.' Hatton's voice was still calm, but his eyes were not. 'They busted open the door and found her. She'd been beaten badly. Looks like somebody came through her window. She was taken to County about an hour ago. They told me she's unconscious, but that's all I know.'

'Does Alex know?' Daniel asked.

'Not yet. I thought you might want to tell her.'

Daniel nodded, dreading it. 'I'll tell her. What about the hairdresser, Desmond?'

'He's fine. He'd had no visits, phone calls, no problems.'

'At least I don't have to give her two pieces of bad news.'

'So . . .' Chase drummed his fingers on the tabletop. 'Our only witness to anything is one four-year-old girl who won't talk.'

'Hope's with McCrady and the forensic artist now,' Daniel said.

'She talked,' Hatton said. 'One word anyway. She called me "Pa-paw." Apparently he has a beard like mine.'

Daniel frowned. 'Then Bailey did find him.'

'Does McCrady know this?' Chase demanded.

'Yep.' Hatton looked at Daniel. 'There's also something about a magic wand.'

'Oh, for God's sake,' Chase muttered.

'Chase,' Daniel said, exasperated. 'What about a magic wand?' he asked Hatton.

'Miss Fallon said that the two times they'd said "magic wand" Hope stopped what she was doing and looked afraid. Neither Miss Fallon knew what it meant. I think we should look for Bailey's father. I can scour the streets if you want. I pulled Craig Crighton's last driver's license photo. It's fifteen years old, but it's all we've got.'

'He hasn't got his license renewed in fifteen years?' Daniel asked.

'It expired two years after Alicia died,' Hatton told him. 'You want me to track him?'

'Yeah. Thanks. What else?'

'What about our tree-climbing Woolf?' Koenig asked.

Daniel shook his head. 'I've checked all the devices we have warrants for to see when he got the call about Gemma, but there have been no new calls. What I want to know is how he got the story on Rhett Porter.'

'The car salesman whose car ran off the road last night,' Chase said. 'Connected?'

'This wreck happened down off of US-19, more than seventy miles from Dutton. Nobody saw Porter go off the road. It was reported by a motorist who passed by after the car was already incinerated and the fire was mostly burned out.'

'How did anybody know it was Porter?' Ed asked,

looking at the picture on the front page of the *Dutton Review*. 'I can't imagine there would have been much body left.'

'They haven't actually identified the body yet,' Daniel answered. 'They're hoping to use dental records. But Porter was a car salesman and he drove test models using his magnetic dealer plates. His plate flew off the car as it was rolling down the embankment and that's how he was identified.'

'So how did Woolf know?' Chase asked, and Daniel shook his head in disgust.

'Don't know yet. According to what Woolf told me this morning when I yanked his sorry ass out of that tree, Porter's wife said he'd been upset the last week. And everybody knew the Lincoln that rolled was the model Porter drove. But as for how Woolf arrived on the scene just in time to snap this picture . . . Woolf refused to reveal his source and unless he communicated in a way we're tracking, we got nothin'.'

'So other than the fact that Rhett Porter lived in Dutton, was upset, and the Woolf connection, what else is there to connect him to these three murders?' Chase asked.

'He went to school with Wade Crighton and Simon. Alex remembers him being Wade's friend. And he was the oldest brother of the two boys that found Alicia's body.'

Chase groaned. 'Daniel.'

Daniel shrugged. 'I'm just sayin' the facts. Plus,

don't discount the fact that Jim Woolf was there at the crash site. I asked the field office down in Pike County to keep tabs on the investigation. I want every inch of that car examined. I'd also like a full-time tail on Jim Woolf. He hasn't done anything I can arrest him for yet, but I know he will.'

Daniel drew a breath, not liking what he had to say next. 'And once Leigh gets the yearbooks, we need to figure out who else went to school with Wade, Simon, and Porter. The rapists in Simon's pictures could all be guys from Dutton.'

'Somebody's nervous,' Hatton said in his quiet way. 'They got sloppy when they tried to run Miss Fallon down. It looks like they may have done a better job with Porter.'

'Looks like.' Daniel turned to Ed. 'Bailey's house and the pizza parlor. Anything?'

'We didn't find any more at Bailey's, certainly nothing to point to where Hope was when she saw Bailey taken. We have matched Bailey's blood type to the blood we found soaked into the ground. We took some hair we found in a brush in the bathroom. We'll do a PCR, but I'm pretty sure it's Bailey's blood.'

'And the pizza parlor?'

'We took prints off the gunman and we're running them through AFIS today. We'll also want to get the officer who chased that car that tried to hit Alex yesterday,' Ed added. 'See if he can make a positive ID on either the car or the shooter.'

'I can take that,' Koenig said.

Daniel noted all their next steps in his notebook. 'Thanks. I'm going to interview the rape victims from thirteen years ago. I'll want a female agent to go with me.'

'Take Talia Scott,' Chase said. 'She's good at that kind of interview.'

Daniel nodded. 'Will do. Once Leigh gets the yearbooks from Bryson Academy, have her get me the list of every woman who went to school with Janet, Claudia, and Gemma. We need to figure out why the killer picked them to re-enact Alicia's murder. Maybe one of the classmates can help us tie them to Alicia or the other victims.'

'We should warn them, too,' Ed said, 'if they haven't already taken precautions.'

'I'll take care of warning them,' Chase said. 'We'll have to clear the communication through channels. We don't want to start a panic and we don't have the man-power to give all the potential victims police protection.'

Daniel stood up. 'Then let's go. We meet back here at six.'

Atlanta, Wednesday, January 31, 9:35 A.M.

'Alex, will you sit down?'

Alex stopped pacing to stare at Meredith's reflection in the one-way glass. Meredith sat behind her calmly working on her laptop, while Alex was a bundle of nerves. On the other side of the glass Hope sat with child psychologist Mary McCrady and a forensic artist who seemed to have the patience of Job.

'How can you be so calm? They're not getting *anything*.'

'I was a wreck yesterday. It was that music.' She shuddered. 'Today, no music and I've had my run. I'm good.' She looked at Hope, who was refusing to meet either the psychologist's eyes or the artist's. 'They just started, Alex. Give Hope some time.'

'We don't *have* time.' Alex gripped her fingers, wringing them. 'Bailey's been gone seven days. Four women are dead. We don't have time to wait.'

'And your pacing won't change that.'

Alex rolled her eyes. 'I know,' she gritted furiously. 'Don't you think I know?'

Meredith set her laptop aside and slung her arm around Alex's shoulders. 'Alex . . .'

Alex leaned her head against Meredith's shoulder. 'They found another victim,' she murmured, feeling . . . powerless. For a few moments, with Daniel on the sofa, she'd felt powerful, important. Now, reality intruded and she knew how helpless she really was.

'And if it had been Bailey, Daniel would have told you.'

'I know. But, Mer . . . three women and Sheila. And Reverend Beardsley. This is worse than any nightmare I've ever had.'

Meredith hugged Alex harder and together they watched Hope through the glass. When the door behind them opened, they spun around as Daniel closed the door behind him.

Alex's pulse quickened and her heart lifted at the sight of him. But his mouth didn't smile and she knew what he had to say would not be good. She braced herself for the worst, although she wasn't even sure what could be worse.

'I don't have much time,' he murmured. 'But I need to talk to you.'

'You want me to leave?' Meredith asked, and Daniel shook his head.

'No need.' He squeezed Alex's upper arms. 'I don't how to tell you this, so I'll just tell you. Sister Anne is in the hospital. She was beaten during the night. It's not good.'

Alex's knees buckled and she lowered herself to a chair, suddenly sapped. 'Oh, no.'

He crouched so that he looked up into her face. 'I'm sorry, honey,' he said softly. He took her hands, warming them. 'We sent a CSU team to check out her apartment.'

She swallowed. 'And Desmond?'

'He's okay.'

She sighed, relief and fear combined. 'Sister Anne. My God.'

He squeezed her hands. 'Alex, it's not your fault.'

'I feel so helpless.'

'I know,' he whispered and she could see his eyes were haunted, too. He cleared his throat. 'But I hear Hope called Hatton "Pa-paw."'

Alex nodded, the violent screeching in her mind at any mention of Craig Crighton no longer taking her by surprise. 'We think Bailey found her father. Maybe she gave him the letter Wade had written.'

'Hatton's going to try to track him down today.'

Alex used what little energy she had left to push the screeching back. 'I'll go, too.'

Daniel rose, a forbidding frown on his face. 'No. It's too dangerous.'

'He won't know what Craig looks like.'

'He's got his driver's license picture.'

'I need to go, Daniel.' She grabbed his arm, needing to make him understand. 'Every time someone mentions his name, it starts in my head. He's one of my triggers. I need to see him. I need to understand why.'

His eyes bored into hers and his face went stern. 'I need you to be safe.'

'I need to make this *stop*,' she gritted through her teeth. 'I need to find out why I'm so afraid of him. I need to know if he knows who took Bailey.' She pointed at the glass and her hand shook. 'Hope hasn't spoken in a week. I need to know what happened.'

He tugged at her chin so that she met his eyes. 'Then or now, Alex?' he asked.

'Both. You said I could trust Hatton. If I'm with him I'll be safe. Don't make me stay.' She grabbed his arm harder. 'Daniel, *please*. I feel like I'm losing my mind.'

He held her gaze another long minute while a storm raged in his eyes. Then he pressed a kiss to her forehead. 'If Hatton's okay with it, I won't stop you. I have it on good authority that you're old enough to make your own decisions.'

Her lips curved sadly and he kissed her mouth tenderly. 'Thank you, Daniel.'

He pulled her to him, hard, then let her go. 'I have to change my clothes. I'm going to try to find the women you remembered from the pictures. You call me,' he said fiercely, 'every hour. If I don't answer, leave me a voicemail. Promise me.'

'I promise.'

'I should be with you when you talk to him,' he said.

She leaned up and pecked his stubbly cheek. 'I'll be fine. I'll call you. I promise.'

'Daniel.' Meredith leaned against the wall, watching them. 'You said we could think about a safe house for Hope.'

Daniel nodded. 'I can make that happen today.'

'For Hope and Meredith,' Alex countered.

Meredith's look shouted disagreement, but she nodded. 'Alex won't be alone?'

'No,' Daniel said, his voice again fierce, as was his expression. 'I'll make sure of it.'

One side of Meredith's mouth lifted. 'Somehow, I'm sure you will,' she said dryly.

'That's the first thing I've felt comfortable about in

days.' He started to walk away, but Alex held him back.

'Daniel, the new victim. Who is she?'

'Gemma Martin. Did you know her?'

'No. I know the Martin name, of course, but I never would have babysat for them. The Martins had nannies and butlers. She was the same age as the other two?'

He nodded. 'The other two lived in Atlanta, but Gemma lived here with her grandmother in Dutton. The school seems to be the only link between them so far.' He covered her mouth in one last hard kiss. 'Don't forget to call me.'

'Every hour,' Alex said dutifully. 'I promise.' She thought about what he was about to do, the women he was about to talk to. 'Good luck.'

He gave her a curt nod, then was gone.

For a moment there was only silence, then Meredith spoke. 'So, now you know.'

Alex fixed her eyes on Hope through the glass. 'Know what?' But she knew.

'That thinking about Craig Crighton is one thing that triggers the screams.'

Alex swallowed, too weary to shove the screams back again. 'I've always known there was something about Craig. I never wanted to know what it was.'

'Alex . . . did Bailey's father molest you?'

Reflected in the glass, Alex watched her own head

wag back and forth in slow motion. 'I don't think so. But I don't know. Every time I've tried to remember . . .' She closed her eyes. 'But now the screams won't go away. I can't make them go away.'

'Alex, what do you remember about the day we took you home, away from Dutton?'

Alex leaned her forehead against the glass. 'I remember the horrible old women who were talking about me and Alicia. Aunt Kim bawling you out because you let them.'

'And then?'

'He came.' She made herself say his name. 'Craig. With Bailey. And Wade. He argued with Kim. He wanted to keep me. Said he loved me. Said I called him "daddy."' The word stuck in her throat. Tasted bad on her tongue.

'But you hadn't.'

'No. Never. He wasn't my father. He was Bailey's father. Always.'

Meredith said nothing, patiently waiting. Alex turned her face so that the glass was cool against her hot cheek. 'He was often harsh with us, me and Alicia. He said Mama spoiled us. He may have been right. For so long it was just the three of us after my real dad died. But you're asking if Craig . . . if he made us have sex with him. No. I don't remember anything like that. I think I would remember.'

'Maybe not.' Meredith's voice was calm. 'What else do you remember about that day, Alex? That day we took you from the hospital and brought you home to Ohio?'

Alex opened her eyes. Stared at her clenched fist. 'More pills.' She pivoted her forehead on the glass so she could look at Meredith, a memory shoving its way through the cacophony inside her mind. 'You took them from me.'

'I didn't know what to do about them. I was a sheltered little bookworm. I'd never even seen drugs before. You terrified me, sitting in that hospital, staring at nothing.'

'Like Hope is now.'

'Like a lot of people do after a trauma,' Meredith soothed. 'Dad took you from the hospital wheel-chair and put you in the car. Then you asked for water. We were so thrilled you'd said anything . . . Mom gave you the water and we started driving. And I saw you peeking into your fist. So I watched you. I let you think you were alone and when you tried to take them, I took them from you. And you never said a word.'

'I hated you that day,' Alex whispered.

'I know. I could see it in your eyes. You didn't want to live and I didn't want to let you die. You meant too much to my mom at that point. You were all she had left of Aunt Kathy. There had been so much violence. I couldn't let you do it.'

'So you came to my room every day after school and sat with me. You didn't want me to finish the job.'

'Not on my watch. And then, little by little, you came back to us.'

Alex's eyes stung. 'You all saved me.'

'My parents loved you. I still do.' Meredith's voice trembled and she cleared her throat. 'Alex, do you remember where you got those pills?'

She tried to think. Tried to focus on the quiet. 'No. I remember looking into my hand and there they were. I remember not caring where they'd come from.'

'All three of the Crightons hugged you before we took you away.'

Alex swallowed. 'I know. That I remember.'

'I've always wondered if one of them gave you the pills.'

Alex pushed away from the glass, suddenly cold. 'Why would they?'

'I don't know. But now that we know about Wade and Simon . . . and Alicia . . . we have to consider it. It could be why you've always had this reaction to Craig's name.'

Alex controlled her flinch. 'You always knew?'

'Yes. I always figured you'd deal with it when you were able to deal with it. The easiest thing was just not to say his name. But now . . . we have to. We have to know. For Bailey and for Hope and for you.'

'And for Janet and Claudia and Gemma,' Alex added. 'And Sheila and all those other girls.' A wave of sadness hit her hard. 'So many lives, ruined.'

'You still have your life, Alex. And now you have

Hope. Bailey turned her life around for Hope. Don't let her down now.'

'I won't. I'll find Craig and I'll find out what he knows.' She clenched her teeth. 'And I'll go into that house. And up the stairs. Even if it kills me.' She winced. 'Sorry.'

'Daniel told me about the attack you had on the stairs. Dr McCrady and I were talking last night about using a form of hypnosis with Hope, to try to get past the wall she's built in her mind. As her guardian, you'll need to sign the release forms.'

'Of course.'

'And then I want to do the same thing with you.'

Alex drew a breath. 'In the house?'

Meredith cupped Alex's cheek, determination in her eyes. 'Don't you think it's time?'

Alex nodded. 'Yes. It's time.'

Chapter Fifteen

Atlanta, Wednesday, January 31, 10:00 A.M.

Agent Talia Scott was a down-to-earth woman with a pixie face and a sweet smile that put victims at ease. But Daniel had worked with her before and knew anyone who'd had to face Talia in tactical response gear would never use the adjective 'sweet' again.

She was sitting across from his desk, staring at him as if monkeys had flown out of his ears. 'If I were a Hollywood producer, I'd be snapping up the rights to this one.'

'Don't think they're not already trying,' Daniel said darkly.

'So. We've got six women identified out of these fifteen pictures.' Talia rifled through them, the tightening of her mouth her only visible response. 'Two are dead.'

'Three are dead,' Daniel corrected. 'Alicia, Sheila, and Cindy Bouse, who committed suicide a few years ago. We have three names. Gretchen French is here in

Atlanta, Carla Solomon lives in Dutton, and Rita Danner lives in Columbia.'

'These women are all almost thirty now, Daniel,' Talia said. 'They may not want to talk about this, especially if they've built lives with people who don't know.'

'I know,' Daniel said. 'But we need them to tell us what they know. We need to find out who feels threatened enough by all this to start striking out.'

'You think one of these rapists killed the three women this week?'

'No, but whoever did wants us to look at Alicia's murder and Alicia's in the pictures.'

'As is Sheila.' Talia nodded hard. 'Then let's go.'

Wednesday, January 31, 10:00 A.M.

The Jag was waiting as he slowed to a stop and started rolling the window down.

'You're late,' he snapped before the window fully rolled down. 'And you look like shit,' he added with contempt.

I do. Last night he'd drunk himself into a blessed stupor, then fallen facedown in his bed without taking off his pants or shoes. The buzzing of the cell phone in his pocket had woken him. 'I didn't have time to shave.' In reality, he hadn't wanted to look in the mirror. He couldn't stand the sight of himself.

'It was an unfortunate miscalculation. Pick yourself up and go on.'

An unfortunate miscalculation. His temper spewed, loosening his tongue. 'One of my deputies *died*. That is not a *misfortunate calculation*.'

'He was a trigger-happy hick-faced idiot who wanted to play big-city cop.'

'He was *twenty-one years old*.' His voice broke and he was too angry to care.

'You should have kept more discipline in your ranks.' There was no sympathy. Only contempt. 'Next time your boys will listen before they rush in to vanquish a big, bad boy with a bigger, badder gun.'

He said nothing. He could still see the blood. *All that blood*. He thought he'd see that boy's blood every time he closed his eyes, maybe for the rest of his life.

'Well?' he barked from the Jag. 'Where is it?'

He opened his eyes and wearily pulled a key from his pocket. 'Here.'

Dark eyes narrowed. 'It's not the right key.'

He laughed bitterly. 'Hell. Even Igor was smart enough not to carry it around with him. That's likely a key to his safe-deposit box at the bank.'

He handed the key back. 'Then go open the damn box,' he said, too softly. 'Bring me back the right key.'

'Yeah, sure.' He slipped the key in his pocket. 'Why should you take any risk?'

'Excuse me?' he said silkily.

He met the dark eyes without flinching. 'I find the

girls and bring them to you. I grab Bailey for you. I kill Jared and Rhett for you. Now I go to the bank for you. I take the risks. You get to sit in your fancy car lurking in the shadows like you always do.'

For a moment he only stared, then his mouth curved. 'Every now and again, you prove you do have balls after all. Get the correct key and bring it to me.'

'Fine.' He was too weary to argue. He started to put his car in gear.

'I'm not finished yet. I know where Bailey put Wade's key.'

He dragged in a breath. 'Where?'

'She sent it to Alex Fallon. That woman's had it all the time.'

Fury sputtered, then fanned into a flame. 'I'll find it.'

'See that you do. Oh, and assuming Fallon is a bit smarter than Igor, she probably isn't carrying it on her person either.' The Jag's window rolled up and he drove away.

Atlanta, Wednesday, January 31, 11:00 A.M.

Gretchen French was a pretty woman with very careful eyes, Daniel thought. He kept quiet, allowing Talia the lead.

'Please sit down,' Gretchen said. 'What can I do for you?'

'Agent Vartanian and I are investigating a series of sexual assaults.'

'Vartanian?' Gretchen's eyes widened, then narrowed in recognition. 'You're Daniel Vartanian. You're working on the murders of Claudia Barnes and Janet Bowie.'

Daniel nodded. 'Yes, ma'am. I am.'

'But that's not why we're here, Miss French,' Talia said. 'As we've been investigating the recent murders of Claudia Barnes and the others—'

Gretchen held up her hand. 'Wait. Others? Besides Janet and Claudia, there are others?'

'We found the body of Gemma Martin this morning,' Daniel said quietly, and Gretchen collapsed back into her chair, her face blank with shock.

'What's happening here? This is insane.'

'We understand your shock.' Talia's tone was calm without being condescending. 'But as I said, we're not here to talk about the recent murders. During the course of our investigation, we've discovered evidence of a series of sexual assaults.' Talia leaned forward. 'Miss French, I wish I knew a way to say this to make it easier to bear, but I don't. A series of sexual assaults occurred around the time of Alicia Tremaine's murder. You were the same age as Alicia. You went to her high school.'

Daniel saw a flicker of fear in Gretchen's eyes. 'I don't know what you mean.'

Talia glanced down, then back up. 'We found

pictures of girls being raped. Your picture was among them, Miss French. I'm sorry.'

Daniel's heart squeezed in helpless pity as he watched Gretchen's expression change. Every drop of color drained from her face until she was ashen. Her lips dropped open and moved, as if she was trying to speak. Then her eyes skittered away, cast down, ashamed. Daniel saw Talia's expression had also changed. There was acute sympathy, but there was also strength, and Daniel understood why Chase had handpicked her for this interview.

Talia put her hand over Gretchen's. 'I wish I didn't have to ask you to live that moment again, but I do. Can you tell us what happened?'

'I can't remember.' Nervously she moistened her lips. Her eyes were conspicuously dry. 'I'd tell you if I could. I wanted to tell when it happened. But I couldn't remember.'

'We think whoever did this to you, drugged you,' Daniel murmured.

Gretchen's chin jerked up, her eyes devastated, but still dry. 'You don't know who?'

Daniel shook his head. 'We're hoping you can tell us.'

Gretchen sat, barely breathing. 'I . . . I was only sixteen. I remember waking up, in my car. It was dark and I was . . . so scared. I knew . . . I mean, I could feel . . .' Her throat worked convulsively. 'It hurt. A lot.'

Talia kept holding Gretchen's hand. 'Had you been with anyone before?'

Gretchen shook her head. 'No. Some of the boys tried, but I'd always said no.'

Daniel bit back the fury that exploded within him. And said nothing.

'After that . . . I never dated. I was so afraid. I didn't know who . . .' She closed her eyes. 'Or why. If I could have avoided it. I knew I should have been more careful.'

The rage was hot and so hard to control. But control it, he did. 'Miss French,' he asked when he could trust his voice, 'do you remember where you were coming from, going to, was anyone with you?'

She opened her eyes, a modicum of composure restored. 'I was driving home from my job. I washed dishes at the Western Sizzlin' back then. I was trying to earn money for college. I was by myself. It was late, maybe ten-thirty. I remember being tired, but I was studying all the time and working and helping out on the farm . . . I was always tired. I remember thinking I'd stop and get out. Get some air, before I fell asleep at the wheel.'

Talia smiled reassurance. 'You are doing great,' she said. 'Can you remember drinking anything before you left your job or stopping on the way?'

'I worked in the kitchen. We were allowed to drink as much Coke as we wanted. And I washed dishes, so I wasn't going to mess a glass every time I got thirsty. I just used the same one.'

'So someone could have put something in your drink,' Talia said quietly.

Gretchen bit the inside of her cheek. 'I guess so. That was pretty stupid of me.'

'You had the expectation of being safe at your job,' Daniel said, and the look of gratitude she flashed him made him want to scream. She'd been violated, but she was grateful to be told she wasn't stupid.

'Agent Vartanian's right. You did nothing wrong or stupid. When you woke up, what do you remember?'

'I had a headache and I was sick. And sore. I knew . . . I was bleeding.' She swallowed hard and her lips trembled. 'I had these new white pants. I'd saved my money to buy them. They were ruined.' She looked down. 'I was ruined.'

'You woke up in your car,' Talia prompted softly, and Gretchen nodded. 'Your pants were ruined, so you had your clothes on. All of your clothes?'

Gretchen nodded again, dully. 'The pictures you have. Am I . . . ?' Tears filled her eyes and Daniel's eyes stung. 'Oh God.'

'Nobody will see the pictures,' Daniel said. 'No newspapers will get them.'

She blinked, sending tears down her cheeks. 'Thank you,' she whispered. 'And there was the bottle.'

'What bottle?' Talia asked, slipping a tissue into Gretchen's hand.

'A bottle of whiskey. Empty. There was whiskey on my clothes and in my hair. And I knew if I went to the sheriff it would look like I'd been drinking. That I'd asked for it.'

Talia's jaw tightened. 'You didn't.'

'I know. If it happened today, I'd call the police so fast . . . But that was then and I was sixteen and scared.' She lifted her chin, making Daniel think of Alex in so many ways. 'You're saying this happened to more than just me?'

Daniel nodded. 'We can't tell you how many. But it was more than just you.'

Her lips turned up, so sadly. 'And if you catch them you can't do anything, right?'

'Why?' Talia asked.

'It's been thirteen years. Hasn't the statute of limitations long since run out?'

Daniel shook his head. 'The clock doesn't start until we file charges.'

Gretchen's eyes hardened. 'So if you catch them, you can prosecute?'

'To the fullest extent of the law,' Talia said fiercely. 'You have our word.'

'Then put me on your list of witnesses. I want my day in court.'

Talia's smile was sharp. 'And we'll do our damndest to give it to you.'

'Miss French,' Daniel said. 'You mentioned some of the boys trying things and you saying no. Do you remember who you refused?'

'I didn't have that many boyfriends. My mother

made me wait until I was sixteen to date and that had only been a few months before. The boy I remember was Rhett Porter. I thought maybe he'd done it, but . . .'

Finally. But it was a connection one day too late. 'But what?' he asked gently.

'But he ran with a mean crowd. I was afraid if I said anything . . .'

'You thought they'd hurt you?' Daniel asked.

'No.' She laughed bitterly. 'He would have told everyone I asked for it and people would have believed him. So I kept my mouth shut and was grateful I wasn't pregnant.'

'One more question,' Daniel said. 'When was this?'

'May. The year before Alicia Tremaine was killed.'

Daniel and Talia stood up. 'Thank you for your time, Miss French,' Talia said. 'And your candor. I know this was difficult.'

'At least now I know I didn't imagine it. And maybe whoever did it will be caught.' She frowned. 'Are you going to talk to Rhett Porter?'

Daniel cleared his throat. 'Probably not.'

Talia's eyes grew huge with question.

Gretchen drew herself rigid. 'I see.'

'No, Miss French,' Daniel said, 'I don't think you do. Rhett Porter's car ran off the road last night. He's believed to be dead.'

'Oh. I guess I do see. You've got yourself one hell of a mess, Agent Vartanian.'

Daniel nearly laughed at the understatement. 'Yes, ma'am. I do at that.'

'You might have told me about Porter,' Talia said when they got to his car.

'I'm sorry. I thought I'd told you everything.'

'Well, as Gretchen French said, you have one hell of a mess. I suppose leaving out one thing is to be expected.'

They buckled up and Daniel started the car, then met her eyes. 'You were good in there. I hate interviewing the rape victims. I never know what to say, but you did.'

'You do a lot of homicides. That can't be easy either.'

Daniel winced as he pulled into traffic. 'I wouldn't say I do a lot of homicides.'

She grimaced. 'Sorry. Bad choice of words.'

'Recently, especially.'

'Daniel, do you think your brother killed Alicia Tremaine thirteen years ago?'

'I've done nothing but wonder about that. But they arrested someone else, some drugged-out drifter. They found Alicia's ring in his pocket and her blood on his clothing and the tire iron he was brandishing when they caught up with him.'

'So what are you thinking, then? Did this rape happen at the same time she was murdered or another time?'

Daniel tapped the steering wheel in an even rhythm

as he pondered. 'I don't know.' But now, something else was bothering him. Something he should have considered before, but hadn't. Something he'd pushed aside, until the pain and fear in Gretchen French's eyes dragged it front and center.

'Daniel? Think out loud, please. And stop tapping. That's making me crazy.'

Daniel sighed. 'Alicia Tremaine has a twin sister. Alex.' He focused on the road to keep the fear from crowding his mind. 'Alex has these bad dreams and panic attacks. They've gotten worse since she came back to Dutton a few days ago.'

'Oh.' Talia twisted so that she faced him. 'You're wondering which sister got raped.'

'Alex denies anything happened to her.'

'Not unusual. You have anything more than this picture? Any forensics?'

'No. Like I told you, Dutton's sheriff and his staff have been less than forthcoming.'

'Which makes you wonder about the arrest of this drugged-out drifter.'

He nodded. 'Yes.'

'Sounds like you need to pay a visit to the state pen, Daniel.'

'I know. I need to separate out the facts on Alicia's murder from her rape.'

Talia bit her lip thoughtfully. 'I once had a case with identical twins, where one was a rape victim who later died from injuries sustained in the assault. We had her hair in the perp's apartment, but the asshole's defense attorney kept throwing out that we couldn't prove which twin the hair had belonged to. Created one hell of a reasonable doubt.'

'Because DNA on identical twins is identical.'

'In this case genetics was not our friend. It looked really bad for the state until the DA put the surviving twin on the stand. It was like the accused had seen a damn ghost. He went white as a sheet and started shaking so hard his shackles sounded like Jacob Marley haunting Scrooge. It made an impact on the jury and they found him guilty.'

'Alex has been all over Dutton getting double-takes. Hell, I did a double-take when I first saw her. That's not going to help me figure out who's involved.'

'No,' she said patiently, 'but it could startle the guy who's sitting in a cell for killing her sister into saying some interesting things. Just a thought.'

It was a damn good thought. Daniel pulled into a side road to turn around. 'I have the suspicion that every woman we talk to is going to have a story like Gretchen's.'

'I'd say you're probably right. You want to let me take over the interviews? You can get your Alex and take her up to visit the drugged-out drifter, whatever his name is.'

'Gary Fulmore. You don't mind finishing the interviews yourself?'

'Daniel, this is what I do. I'll get another agent to go with me for backup. You need to focus your efforts on what's important to this case. At this point, unless any of these women remembers a name or a face, you're not going to get anything new.'

'But they're all still important,' he protested.

'Of course they are. And each of these women needs to be told she's not alone, just like Gretchen. But I can do that, just as well as you can.'

'Probably better.' He glanced at her. 'My Alex?'

Talia smiled. 'It's written all over your face, honey.'

He felt a trickle of warmth break through the bleakness in his mind. 'Good.'

Atlanta, Wednesday, January 31, 12:45 P.M.

Alex leaned against a light post while Agent Hatton talked to Daniel on the phone. They'd only been looking for Bailey's father for two hours and already Alex was weary, in body, but mostly soul. So many faces with so much pain and too little hope. So much noise in her mind. She'd given up trying to still it, instead keeping Craig's face at the front of her mind. She tried to imagine him thirteen years older with a soft beard like Hatton's.

So far no one had seen Craig Crighton, or would admit to it anyway. But they had blocks to cover still. If her knees didn't give out first. She was still stiff from her fall the day before and standing still wasn't helping matters.

Finally Hatton hung up and said, 'Let's go.'

She pushed herself away from the light pole. 'Where to?'

'My car. Vartanian's picking you up. You're going to visit Macon State.'

She frowned. 'College?'

'Um, no. Macon State Penitentiary. You're going to visit Gary Fulmore.'

'Why?' But as soon as the word flew from her mouth she shook her head. 'Stupid question. Of course we'd have to see him sooner or later. But why this afternoon?'

'You'll have to ask Daniel. Don't worry. I'll keep looking and I'll call you if I find him.'

She winced as her knees creaked. 'But first I want to stop by Sister Anne's shelter. I have a package to drop off.' Hatton took her arm, steadying her. 'You're probably glad to get rid of me. I'm just slowing you down.'

'I wasn't planning on racing through the streets, Miss Fallon. You're doing fine.'

'You know, you could call me Alex.'

'I don't know. Miss Fallon was economical. I'd have to remember two names.'

He was teasing her and she smiled. 'Do you have a first name, Agent Hatton?'

'I do.'

She looked up at him. 'Are you going to tell me what it is?'

He sighed. 'George.'

'George? That's a perfectly fine name. Why the sigh?'

He rolled his eyes tolerantly. 'My middle name is Patton.'

Her lips twitched. 'George Patton Hatton. Interesting.'

'Just don't tell anybody.'

'I won't breathe a word,' she promised, feeling a little lighter in spirit – until they reached Sister Anne's shelter, and her spirit sagged. Sister Anne was critical. The ICU nurses at Atlanta's County General had given Alex the prognosis, and it was not good.

Another one of the nuns met them at the door with a smile. 'Can I help you?'

'My name is Alex Fallon. I was here two nights ago, talking to Sister Anne about my stepsister, Bailey Crighton.'

The nun's smile disappeared. 'Anne said you were coming back last night.'

'We couldn't come last night. We took Hope to a doctor. Did Sister Anne say anything yesterday, anything to let you know who might have done this to her?'

The nun hesitated, then shook her head. 'She wasn't here yesterday. She went out looking for Bailey's daddy. Because you told her you were coming back last night.'

Alex's heart sank. 'Did she find him?'

'I don't know. I expected her back this morning and she probably would have told me then. But she didn't come in.' The nun's lips trembled and she firmed them.

'I was just at the hospital,' Alex said. 'I'm sorry.'

The nun nodded brusquely. 'Thank you. Now, if that's all, I have supper to get on.'

'Wait.' Alex held the door open. 'Will you see Sarah Jenkins tonight?'

'Why?' the nun asked suspiciously.

Alex held out the sack filled with the samples of prescription-strength antibacterial cream the nurses at the Atlanta ER had given her. 'Her little girl has impetigo and this will fix it. There are also a few other supplies in there.'

The nun's face softened. 'Thank you.' She started to close the door again.

'Wait. I have one more question. Do you know this song?' She hummed the six bars Hope had been fixated upon the day before.

The nun frowned. 'No, but I don't get out much lately. Hold on. I'll be back.' She shut the door and Alex and Hatton waited for a long time.

Hatton checked his watch. 'We need to go. Vartanian will be here soon.'

'Just another minute. Please.' A minute came and went and Alex sighed. 'I guess she's not coming back. Let's go.' They were almost out to the street when the door opened and the nun stuck her head out, a scowl on her face.

'I *said* I'd be back.'

'We waited. We thought you weren't coming,' Alex said.

'I'm eighty-six years old,' the nun snapped. 'Turtles move faster'n me. Here. Talk to this one.' She opened the door wider, revealing another nun who was only slightly younger and who looked very worried. 'Tell them, Mary Catherine.'

Mary Catherine glanced up the street, then whispered. 'Check Woodruff Park.'

Alex looked up at Hatton. 'What's that?'

'It's one of the areas where musicians gather,' he said. 'Anybody we should talk to in particular, Sister?'

Mary Catherine pursed her lips and the first old nun gave her a nudge. 'Tell her.'

'You've heard the song before?' Alex asked, and Mary Catherine nodded.

'Bailey was humming it on the last Sunday she was here, while she was making the pancakes. She looked so sad. The song sounded sad. When I asked her what the song was, she got this scared look and said it was just a song she'd heard on the radio. But Hope said no, that it wasn't the radio and didn't her mama remember it was her Pa-paw and he was playing the song on his flute.'

Alex stiffened. *Hope's magic wand.*

'What did Bailey do then?' Hatton asked, and she knew he thought the same thing.

'She got real flustered and sent Hope off to help set the tables, saying Hope thought every man with a beard was her Pa-paw. She said it just some poor drunk on the street corner playin' a flute, that was all.'

Alex frowned. 'But Sister Anne said she didn't think Bailey had found her father.'

The first nun nudged Mary Catherine again. 'Go ahead.'

Mary Catherine sighed. 'Anne wasn't in the kitchen at the time. I told her about it Monday night after you left. That's when she decided to go lookin' for him yesterday.'

Alex's shoulders sagged. 'She should have called me. I would have gone looking for him myself. Why did she go alone?'

The first nun sniffed. 'Anne's been ministering on these streets for years. She ain't afraid to walk around herself.' Then she sighed. 'I guess she shoulda been. At any rate, she didn't want to get your hopes up. She said she'd check it out, then tell you when you came back last night. But you didn't come back and neither did she.' The old nun shook herself back to brusque. 'Thanks for the medicine. I'll make sure it goes to good use.' She shut the door in Alex's face.

Alex looked up and down the street. 'Which way to Woodruff Park?'

But Hatton took her arm. 'You don't have time to

look. I'll find the flute player, and even if he's not Crighton, I'll bring him in. Now come on. You have a date.'

Atlanta, Wednesday, January 31, 3:30 P.M.

Daniel had parked his car in the prison lot, but he still sat behind the wheel. He'd told her about the interview with Gretchen French, about the assault and the empty whiskey bottle. He'd told her his plan to startle Fulmore with her face, that neither Fulmore nor his lawyer knew she was coming. All that conversation had eaten up about twenty minutes. The rest of the drive, he'd been withdrawn, deep in thought. She'd let him brood, hoping he'd eventually say something, but he'd said nothing at all.

Finally she broke the silence. 'I thought we were going inside the prison.'

He nodded. 'We are, but we need to talk first.'

Dread had her stomach clenching. 'About?'

Daniel closed his eyes. 'I don't know how to ask you this.'

'Just *ask*, Daniel,' she said, her voice trembling.

'Is the picture I found of Alicia . . . or of you?'

Alex shrank away. 'No. It's not me. How . . . why would you even ask me that?'

'Because you have nightmares and hear screams and there are things you can't remember. I assumed that Alicia was raped the same night she was killed, but the MO is too different. I wondered if they'd happened at different times, by different perps. And then I started to wonder . . .' He opened his eyes, and they were filled with pain and guilt. 'What if the victims were different, too? What if Simon and the others hurt *you*?'

Alex pressed her fingers to her lips and for a moment simply focused on breathing.

'I'm sorry,' he whispered. 'So sorry.'

Alex dropped her hands to her lap and made herself think. *Could it be?* No. She'd remember something like that. *Maybe not*. Meredith had said so in response to her exact same declaration earlier in the day.

'You're the second person today to ask if I've been molested. I don't know how to answer you except to say I don't remember it happening, but I don't remember the night she died, either. I started feeling sick on the way home from school and went right to bed. The next thing I remember was my mother shaking me awake the next morning, demanding to know where Alicia was. But I wasn't bleeding and I don't remember any whiskey bottle. I would think details like that would be harder to forget.'

For a moment the two of them were silent. Then Alex lifted her chin. 'You never showed me the picture of Alicia,' she said.

He looked horrified. 'You want to see it?'

Quickly she shook her head. 'No. But there is one

feature we had that was different.' She lifted the left leg of her slacks. 'Can you see it through the hose?'

Daniel leaned over the gearshift. 'The sheep tattoo. You said Bailey had one. No, you said you all had one, on Monday morning when you were viewing Janet's body.'

'It's actually a lamb. We thought it was cuter than a sheep. My mother called us her little lambs. Bailey, Alicia, and Alex. Baa. On our sixteenth birthday, Alicia got the idea to get the tattoos. Looking back, I think she was a little high. But Bailey was going, too, and it was our birthday, Alicia's and mine, and I didn't want to be alone.'

'A tattoo parlor gave sixteen-year-olds tattoos?'

'No, Bailey knew a guy. She told him we were seventeen. I tried to chicken out at the last minute, but Alicia triple-dog-dared me.'

One side of his mouth lifted. 'The dreaded triple-dog-dare.'

'I never did anything exciting or fun. That was always Alicia. So I went along. In the picture of Alicia that you have, can you see her tattoo?'

'I didn't look at her ankle.'

'Then look, at her right leg.'

He lifted his brows. 'You didn't get the same leg?'

Alex's mouth quirked in a tiny smirk. 'No. Bailey went first, then Alicia, which was the usual way of it. They were admiring their tattoos when the guy started mine. I purposely gave him my left foot. I was tired of getting in trouble for Alicia's wildness.'

'You wanted people to be able to differentiate. What did Alicia say?'

'By the time she noticed me, he was already halfway done and it was too late. But oh, was she mad. And my mom, she was livid. She punished all three of us and for the first time in a long time Alicia had to take responsibility for her own actions instead of blaming me. I finally felt like I'd gotten the upper hand for once.' But then, Alicia had been murdered and all their lives had gone to hell. Her little smirk faded. 'Look at the picture again, Daniel, and tell me what you see.'

'All right.' He found the photo in his briefcase and held it so that she couldn't see, then pulled a small magnifying glass from his pocket.

When he sighed in relief, Alex did, too, unaware until that moment that she'd been holding her breath. He put the picture away, then met her eyes. 'Right ankle.'

Alex moistened her lips, then pursed them until she was confident her voice wouldn't shake. 'Then that's settled at least.' It didn't answer Meredith's concern, but she'd cross that bridge when she came to it. 'So let's go.'

Chapter Sixteen

Dutton, Wednesday, January 31, 3:45 P.M.

Well, well. He stood in the bank's vault staring into Rhett Porter's safe-deposit box. His chuckle was bitter as he read the letter Rhett had left behind.

My key is being held by an attorney you've never met, in a place you've never been, along with a sealed letter detailing our sins. If anything happens to my wife or kids, the letter gets mailed to every major newspaper in the country, and my key will be turned over to the state's attorney. See you in hell.

It was dated less than a week after he'd fed DJ to the gators. He guessed Rhett Porter wasn't so dumb after all.

He pocketed the note and left the vault, nodding to old Rob Davis, who waited outside. Davis owned the bank and normally would have delegated tasks such as safe-deposit boxes to a lowly employee. But this was a delicate matter, and he'd come without a warrant. He'd known Davis wouldn't question his request, because he knew more about old Rob Davis than Davis knew about him. That was power.

'I'm done.'

Davis gave him a look of contempt. 'You abuse your position.'

'And you don't? Give my regards to your wife, Rob,' he said deliberately. 'And if Garth asks, tell him I have it.'

Rob Davis's cheeks went hollow. 'It?'

'Your nephew will understand. Garth's smart that way.' He touched his hat. 'Bye.'

Macon, Georgia, Wednesday, January 31, 3:45 P.M.

'We're late,' Alex said as Daniel signed them in.

'I know. I wanted Fulmore and his lawyer to get here first. I want a grand entrance.'

'He's just going to say he didn't kill her, like he's been saying for thirteen years.'

'Maybe he did and maybe he didn't. Between your memory and the yearbooks we've gathered, we've identified ten of the fifteen pictures. Only Alicia was murdered.'

'And Sheila,' she corrected, 'but I get your drift. Daniel, I've read about the trial. They had evidence on Gary Fulmore that tied him to Alicia's body. Her blood was on his clothes. It's not like they railroaded him for murder.'

'I know. One of the things I'm hoping to get out of this is some way to determine if that picture of Alicia was taken the same night she was killed or a different night. If it was the same night and the rapists followed the same MO, maybe they left her somewhere and Fulmore came along and found her.'

'I wish I remembered that night,' she gritted out. 'Dammit.'

'It'll come. You said you were sick that night.'

'Yeah. I had stomach cramps and went to bed. It was awful.'

'Were you sick often?'

Her step faltered and she looked up at him, wide-eyed and miserable. 'No. Hardly ever. It's another coincidence, isn't it? Do you think I was drugged, too?'

He slid his arm around her for a hard hug as they arrived at the small room in which she'd come face-to-face with the man accused of suffocating her sister before beating her face with a tire iron. 'Let's take one thing at a time. Are you ready?'

She swallowed hard. 'As I'll ever be.'

'Then you walk in first. I want to watch him when he sees you.'

Her shoulders grew rigid as she took a deep breath. Then, with determination, she twisted the doorknob and pushed her way inside where a man in orange coveralls and a man in a cheap suit waited. The cheap suit was Jordan Bell, the defense counsel.

Bell stood up, annoyed. 'It's about time you—' He

stopped at the clatter beside him. Gary Fulmore had shoved back from the table, his chair bouncing against the concrete floor and his shackles clanging. His mouth was open, his face instantly pale.

Bell's eyes narrowed. 'What the hell is this?'

Fulmore backed away when Daniel pulled out Alex's chair and she slowly sat.

As pale as Fulmore was, Alex was paler. She was pale . . . as a ghost. Daniel felt like the biggest heel in the universe for putting her through this. But she'd wanted to find Bailey. She'd wanted to help him get justice for the three murdered women.

Somehow, some way, Alicia's murder was the linchpin that held it all together.

'I said' – the lawyer hissed through his teeth – 'what the hell is this?'

'M-m-make her g-g-go aw-w-way,' Fulmore stammered, his breath coming in shallow pants. 'Go aw-way.'

'I came to see you,' Alex said, her voice calm. 'Do you know who I am?'

Bell was frowning to beat all hell. 'You never said you would bring her.'

Alex stood up and leaned forward, bracing her fists on the table. 'I asked you a question, Mr Fulmore. Do you know who I am?'

Who she was, was magnificent, Daniel thought. Calm, cool, and collected under extreme stress. Quite simply, she took his breath away.

She had the same effect on Fulmore, who was nearly hyperventilating.

Daniel moved so that he stood between Fulmore and Alex. She was still as pale as death, her eyes wide and intense, and he realized she wasn't calm and collected. She was only cool, which meant she was terrified. But she was holding it together.

'Alicia Tremaine was my sister. You killed her.'

'No.' Fulmore shook his head vehemently. 'I did not.'

'You killed her,' Alex continued as if Fulmore hadn't spoken. 'You put your hands over her mouth and smothered her until she *died*. Then you beat her face again and again until even her own *mother* didn't recognize her.'

Fulmore was staring at Alex's face. 'I didn't,' he said, desperation in his voice.

'You *did*,' she spat. 'Then you dumped her in a ditch like she was garbage.'

'No. She was already in the ditch.'

'Gary,' Bell said. 'Stop talking.'

Alex jerked her face to glare at Bell with loathing and contempt. 'He's serving a life sentence. What more can I possibly do to hurt him?'

Fulmore hadn't taken his eyes off Alex. 'I didn't kill her, I swear. And I didn't dump her in that ditch. She was already dead when I found her.'

She turned back to him, her contempt now focused and cold. 'You killed her. Her blood was on your clothes. On that tire iron they found in your hand.'

'No. That's not what happened.'

'Maybe you could tell us what did happen,' Daniel said softly.

'Gary,' Bell warned. 'Shut up.'

'No.' Fulmore was trembling. 'I see her face, still. I see her when I try to sleep.' His eyes locked on Alex's, filled with misery. 'I see her face.'

Alex made no move to comfort, her expression now set in stone. 'Good. So do I. Every time I look in the mirror, I see her face.'

Fulmore swallowed, his Adam's apple bobbing up and down in his bony throat.

'What happened, Gary?' Daniel repeated, and when Jordan Bell would have protested, Daniel froze the lawyer with a look. Alex was trembling, and he gently pushed her back into her chair, Fulmore's eyes following her down.

'It was warm,' Fulmore murmured. 'Hot, even. I was walking. Sweatin'. Thirsty.'

'Where were you walking?' Daniel prompted.

'Nowhere. Anywhere. I was high. PCP. That's what they told me anyhow.'

'Who told you?' Daniel asked, still softly.

'The cops that took me in.'

'Do you remember who took you in?'

Fulmore's lips thinned. 'Sheriff Frank Loomis.'

Daniel wanted to ask more about Frank, but held those questions back. 'So you were high and you were walking and you were hot and thirsty. What then?'

He gave a facial shrug. 'I smelled it. Whiskey. And I remember wanting some.'

'Where were you?'

'On the side of some road outside of some bumfuck town in the middle of nowhere. Dutton,' he spat it out. 'I wish I'd never heard of the place.'

That makes two of us, Daniel thought, then looked at Alex. *Three of us*. 'Do you remember what time it was?'

He shook his head. 'I didn't never carry a watch. But it was bright again, all the time. I could finally see where I was. I'd wandered . . . I guess I was lost.'

Bright again? Daniel made a mental note to check the phase of the moon on the night Alicia was murdered. 'All right. So you smelled whiskey. And then?'

'I followed my nose to the whiskey down into this ditch. There was a blanket and I thought I'd take it. My blanket was nasty.' He swallowed hard, his eyes still focused on Alex. 'I grabbed the blanket and yanked. And she just . . . fell out.'

Alex flinched. Her skin was ashen, her lips bright pink from her lipstick, and Daniel thought of Sheila, dead in the corner, her hands still gripping her gun. He considered stopping the whole interview and rushing Alex out of this place where she'd be safe. But they'd come this far and he knew she was made of sterner stuff. So he swallowed the emotion and kept his voice level. 'What do you mean, Gary, "she fell out"?'

'I grabbed the blanket and she rolled out of it,

naked. Her arms were all limp and rubbery and they flopped, all spread out. One of her hands landed on my foot.' His tone had gone hollow. His eyes never left Alex's face. 'Then I saw her face,' he said, pain in every word. 'Her eyes were starin' at me. Empty. Like empty holes.' Just like Alex's stared at him now. Empty and blank. 'I was . . . wild. Scared out of my mind.'

He said nothing, lapsing back into a memory that still obviously had the power to scare him out of his mind. 'Gary, what did you do?'

'I don't know. I wanted her to . . . stop lookin' at me.' His clenched fists punched at the air twice, hard and fast, sending chains jangling. 'So I hit her.'

'With your hands?'

'Yes. At first. But she wouldn't stop lookin' at me.' Fulmore was rocking now, and Alex continued to stare at him blankly.

Daniel poised himself to hold Fulmore back in the event he became unable to distinguish Alex in the now from Alicia in the then. 'Where did you get the tire iron?'

'In my blanket. I carried it with me always, in my blanket. But then it was in my hands and I was smashing her face. I hit her again and again and again.'

Visualizing it, Daniel drew in a quick breath. And in that moment knew this man had not killed Alicia Tremaine.

Tears streaked Fulmore's face, but his clenched fists stayed frozen in front of him. 'I just wanted her to stop lookin' at me.' His shoulders sagged. 'And then, finally, she did.'

'You'd beaten her face.'

'Yes. But just her eyes.' He looked childishly beseeching. 'I had to close her eyes.'

'So then what did you do?'

Fulmore wiped his face with his shoulder. 'I wrapped her up. Better.'

'Better?'

He nodded. 'She was kind of loose in the blanket before. I wrapped her up tight.' He swallowed again. 'Like a baby, only she weren't no baby.'

'What about her hands, Gary?' Daniel asked, and Fulmore nodded absently.

'She had pretty hands. I folded them across her belly before I wrapped her up.'

They'd found Alicia's ring in his pocket. A glance at Bell from the corner of Daniel's eye told him the lawyer was thinking the same thing.

'Did she have anything on her hands?' Bell asked him, using the same soft tone.

'A ring. It was blue.'

'The stone was blue?' Daniel asked, and watched Alex stretch out her hands and stare at her fingers, then slowly curl her hands into fists.

'Yeah.'

'And you wrapped her up with the ring on her hand,' Bell murmured, and Fulmore's eyes shot up to meet Daniel's, panicked and angry.

'Yeah.' The faraway tone was gone. 'They said I took it, but I didn't.'

'Then what happened, Gary?'

'I don't remember. I must have taken some more PCP. The next thing I knew, I had three guys on top of me and they were beating me with their clubs.' Fulmore's chin jutted out. 'They said I killed her, but I didn't. They wanted me to take a plea, but I wouldn't. I did a terrible thing to that girl, but I did not kill her.' His final words were evenly spaced and very deliberate. 'I did not.'

'Do you remember going to the autobody shop?' Bell asked him.

'No. Like I said, I woke and three guys were holding me down.'

'Thank you for your time,' Daniel said. 'We'll be in touch.'

Fulmore looked to Bell, a glimmer of hope in his eyes. 'Can we get a new trial?'

Bell's eyes met Daniel's. 'Can we?'

'I don't know. I can't make promises, Bell, you know that. I'm not a DA.'

'But you know the DA,' Bell said cagily. 'Gary's told you what he knows. He's cooperating without guarantee of recourse. That should mean something.'

Daniel's eyes narrowed at Bell. 'I said I'd be in touch. Now I have to get back to Atlanta for a meeting.' He urged Alex to her feet. 'Come on, let's go.'

She came willingly, more like a doll than a live

person, and once again Daniel's mind was assaulted with the memory of Sheila's dead body in that corner. He put his arm around Alex's shoulders and propelled her from the room.

They were almost to Daniel's car when Bell shouted for them to wait, then jogged the length of the parking lot, breathing hard. 'I'm going to file for a new trial.'

'Premature,' Daniel said.

'I don't think so and neither do you, or you wouldn't have driven all the way down here and put her through that.' He pointed to Alex, who lifted her chin and gave him a cool look. But she said nothing and he nodded, satisfied he'd hit the truth. 'I've been following the news, Vartanian. Somebody's recreating these murders.'

'Could be a copycat,' Daniel said, and Bell shook his head.

'You don't think so,' he said again. 'Look. I know your sister was killed, Miss Fallon, and I'm sorry, but Gary's lost thirteen years of his life.'

Daniel sighed. 'When this is over, we'll meet with the state's attorney.'

Bell nodded briskly. 'That's fair.'

Atlanta, Wednesday, January 31, 5:30 P.M.

They were close to Atlanta when Daniel finally spoke. 'Are you all right?'

She was staring at her hands, a frown puckering her brow. 'I don't know.'

'When he said Alicia "fell out" of the blanket, it was like you went into a trance.'

'I did?' Abruptly she turned to look at him. 'Meredith wants to try hypnosis.'

He agreed with Meredith, but in his experience the person undergoing hypnosis had to be open. He wasn't sure Alex was open right now. 'What do *you* want?'

'To make this all go away.' She whispered it fiercely.

He reached for her hand. 'I'll go with you.'

'Thank you. Daniel . . . I . . . I didn't expect to feel that way when I finally saw him. I wanted to kill him myself.'

Daniel frowned. 'You mean you'd never seen Fulmore?'

'No. I was in Ohio the whole time of the trial. Aunt Kim and Uncle Steve wanted to protect me. They were good to me.'

'Then you're lucky.' The words came out more bitterly than he'd expected. He kept his eyes on the road, but he could feel her eyes studying his profile.

'Your parents weren't good to you.'

It was such a simple statement, he almost laughed. 'No.'

Her brows lifted. 'What about your sister, Susannah? Are you two close?'

Suze. Daniel sighed. 'No. I'd like to be, but we're not.'

'She's hurting. You've both lost your parents and even though they died a few months ago, for you, it was really just last week.'

Daniel huffed a mirthless laugh. 'Our parents were dead to us a long time before Simon killed them. We were what you'd call a dysfunctional family.'

'Does Susannah know about the pictures?'

'Yeah. She was there when I turned them over to Ciccotelli up in Philly.' Suze knew a lot about Simon, more than she'd told him, of that Daniel was certain.

'And?'

He looked at her. 'What do you mean?'

'You look like you want to say more.'

'I can't. I'm not sure I could even if I knew.' He thought about his sister, working long hours as a New York City assistant DA, living alone, with only her dog for company. He thought about the pictures and the pain on Gretchen French's face.

It was the same pain he'd seen on Susannah's when he'd asked her what Simon had done to her. She hadn't been able to tell him, but Daniel was terrified that he already knew. He cleared his throat and focused on the matter at hand. 'I'm thinking Gary Fulmore did not kill your sister.'

Alex regarded him levelly, no surprise on her face. 'Why do you think that?'

'First, I believed his story. You said yourself, he's serving a life sentence, so at this point how can we hurt him any more? What does he gain from lying now?'

'He's hoping for a new trial.'

He heard the thread of panic in her voice and made his response as gentle as he could. 'Alex, honey, I think he might deserve one. Listen to me. He said he hit her face, repeatedly. Try to think past the fact that this was Alicia and think about what you know. Be a nurse for me now. If Alicia had been alive, or even if he'd just killed her, and he'd hit her that viciously and repeatedly . . .'

'There would have been a lot of blood,' she murmured. 'He would have been covered in her blood.'

'But he wasn't. Wanda at the sheriff's office told me there was blood on the cuffs of his pants. Alicia had been dead for a while by the time he hit her.'

'Maybe Wanda was wrong.' Her voice was desperate, and he realized Alex wanted Fulmore to be guilty. And he wondered why it was so important to her.

'I'll never know,' he replied carefully. 'All of the evidence is gone. The blanket, Fulmore's clothes, the tire iron . . . all gone. I have to assume Wanda is right, until I can prove otherwise, and if Wanda is right, Alicia was already dead when Fulmore hit her.'

She moistened her lips. 'He still could have killed her, waited, then come back to hit her face later.' But there was no conviction in her words. 'But that doesn't make sense, does it? If he killed her, he'd probably run, not come back, beat her, then wander into an autobody shop. What else is bothering you about his story?'

'Plenty. If her arm flopped like that—' Daniel stopped when he sensed a stillness come over her. 'Alex, what is it?'

She closed her eyes and clenched her teeth. 'I don't remember.'

'But it makes the screams come, right?' She nodded tightly and he brought her hand to his lips. 'I'm sorry to make you go through this.'

'There was thunder,' she said unexpectedly. 'That night. Thunder and lightning.'

It was bright again, all the time, Fulmore had said. It must have stormed before. He'd have to check. 'It was April,' he said quietly. 'Storms are common then.'

'I know. It was hot outside that day. It was hot that night.'

Daniel glanced at her, then back at the road where traffic was starting to snarl. 'But you slept through the night that night,' he said very softly. 'From the time you got home from school until the next morning when your mother woke you up. You were sick.'

Her mouth opened, then closed. When she spoke, her voice was cool. 'If Alicia's body was limp, rigor hadn't set in. If he's telling the truth, Alicia hadn't been dead more than a few hours by that point.'

'You still think he's lying.'

'Maybe. But if he didn't kill her . . . Gary Fulmore's been in prison a long time.'

'I know.' He tapped his steering wheel as traffic came to a complete halt, with him stuck in the far left lane. His meeting started in less than twenty minutes. He was going to be late again. He turned his mind from the traffic back to Gary Fulmore. 'Fulmore has a damn good memory of that night for someone who was flying high on PCP.'

'Maybe he's made that whole story up in his mind,' Alex said, her chin lifting. Then her shoulders slumped. 'Or maybe he wasn't on PCP at all.'

Which was one of the things that was bothering him the most. Frank Loomis had made that arrest, and too many things weren't adding up. 'Randy Mansfield said it took three men to take him down. That sounds like somebody on PCP.'

'But that was hours later. After they'd found Alicia.'

'Alex, what happened after they found Alicia? At your house? Among your family?'

She shuddered. 'My mother had been calling everyone in town, all morning after she found Alicia's bed empty.'

'Empty or un-slept-in?'

'Un-slept-in. They figured she'd snuck out some time the night before.'

'Did you share a room?'

Alex shook her head. 'Not at that point. Alicia was still mad about the tattoo. She'd moved out of our room into Bailey's room. I was getting the silent treatment.'

'How long had it been since your birthday, when you all got the tattoos?'

'A week. She'd been sixteen for only a week.'

So had you, baby. 'Do you think Bailey knew she'd left the house that night?'

She moved her shoulders, not quite a shrug. 'Bailey insisted she didn't. But Bailey was wild then. She was good at lying on the fly to get out of trouble. So I don't know. I remember still feeling sick, kind of . . .' She stilled again. 'Kind of hung over.'

'Like you'd been drugged?'

'Maybe. But nobody ever asked me about it, because of what happened . . . later that night.' She closed her eyes on a grimace. 'You know.'

When she'd overdosed on tranquilizers prescribed for her hysterical mother. 'I know. How did you learn Alicia's body had been found?'

'The Porter boys found her body and went running to Mrs Monroe's house for help. Mrs Monroe knew Mama had been looking for Alicia, so she called her. My mother got there before the police.'

Daniel grimaced. 'Your mother found her like that?'

Her swallow was audible. 'Yes. Later they went to the morgue to . . . to identify her.'

'They?'

She nodded. 'My mother.' She turned her face to look out the car window at the stopped traffic, her body tensing, her face ashen once more. 'And Craig. When they came home, my mother was hysterical, crying, screaming . . . *He* gave her some pills.'

'Craig?'

'Yes. Then he went to work.'

'He went to work? After that? He left you all alone?'

'Yeah,' Alex said bitterly. 'He was a real prince.'

'So he gave your mother some pills. Then what happened?'

'Mama was crying, so I climbed into bed with her and she went to sleep.' She was pale and trembling again. Traffic hadn't moved an inch, so Daniel put the car in park and leaned over the gearshift to pull her close.

'And then what, honey?'

'Then I woke up and she wasn't there. I heard her screaming and came down the stairs . . .' Abruptly she lunged from the seat and bolted from the car.

'*Alex*.' Daniel jumped from the car as she darted to the side of the road, where she fell to her knees, heaving. He knelt beside her, rubbing her back as she shuddered.

Motorists were watching, intrigued by the sudden excitement. One man rolled down his window. 'Do you need help? I can call 911.'

Daniel knew that as soon as anyone recognized Alex, the cell phone cameras would come out, so he made his smile rueful. 'Thanks, but no. Just a little morning sickness a little late in the day.' He leaned over to whisper in her ear. 'Can you stand?'

She nodded, her face clammy. 'I'm sorry.'

'Sshh. Hush.' He put his arm around her waist and physically lifted her to her feet. 'Come on. We're getting out of here.' He looked up the road. 'The nearest exit is three miles up the road. I could use my lights, but that'll draw attention to us.'

'I think I just did draw attention to us,' she murmured.

'You drew attention to a pregnant couple. Just keep your head down and we can keep it that way.' Gently he led her back to the car and put her in, pushing her head between her knees. 'Head down.' He slid behind the wheel and pulled his car onto the left shoulder, ignoring the glares of the motorists he passed.

'You're going to get a ticket,' Alex muttered, and he smiled, then reached over to stroke the back of her neck and felt her muscles begin to soften.

'You pregnant women get testy,' he said, and she chuckled once. He turned into the first emergency access he came to, then pulled into the opposite bound lanes where traffic was moving more smoothly. He put on his lights and traffic parted like the Red Sea. 'We'll use the back roads for now. You want me to stop and get you some water?'

A little color had returned to her cheeks. 'That'd be good. Thank you, Daniel.'

He frowned, wishing she'd stop thanking him. Wishing she'd stop having occasion to do so. Wishing he could see inside her head to understand exactly what it was that was causing that visceral, very physical response. Her cousin was right. They needed to get to the bottom of this and hypnosis might be the best way.

Wednesday, January 31, 6:15 P.M.

Well, that took them long enough, he thought, looking at the TV screen. The news anchor had flashed a picture of the boy, saying he was wanted for questioning by the police. He wasn't such a bright kid, but he'd done everything he'd been asked to do.

Shame he'd have to die now, but . . . *so it goes.* The kid had grown up with all the luxuries money could buy. Now it was time to pay the piper, or at a minimum, pay for the sins of his father. In the kid's case, his grandfather.

Who knew a kid that rich would be lonely? But he had been. He'd been excited to have a friend, and eager to help in any way he could. He'd make it painless for the kid. One bullet, right through the head. The boy would be dead before he hit the ground.

Chapter Seventeen

Atlanta, Wednesday, January 31, 6:45 P.M.

Chase was waiting at the team table when they arrived. 'Are you okay, Alex?'

'Just a little morning sickness a little late in the day,' Alex murmured ruefully.

Chase's eyes widened. 'You're *pregnant*?'

He said it so loudly Daniel winced. 'No. Hush.' Daniel pulled a chair out for Alex and gently pushed her into it. 'Alex got a little sick on the highway and I didn't want to call any more attention to us. It seemed like the right thing to do at the time.'

Daniel began massaging Alex's neck and shoulders. By now he knew where she liked to be touched. Well, maybe not all the places. He'd rushed this morning. He wouldn't make that mistake again. When he got her in a proper bed, he'd take his time and seek out every one of those places. It paid to be thorough, after all.

Chase cleared his throat. 'I'm so glad you kept a clear head,' he said dryly.

Daniel flushed at the knowing look that accompanied Chase's double-barbed jab. 'Where is everyone? We're late.'

'Everyone was running late. I pushed the meeting to seven.'

'Where is Hope?' Alex asked. 'Did Dr McCrady get anywhere today?'

'A little.' Chase leaned against the team table, his arms crossed. 'We know the "magic wand" is a flute. Mary McCrady put one on the table and the little girl started to hum the tune. The forensic artist mocked some pictures of your stepfather, Miss Fallon. He aged Crighton and gave him a beard, then he mixed up the mock-up with a half-dozen other pictures of old men and Hope picked Crighton right out.'

Alex clenched her jaw and swallowed hard, but she kept her eyes open and her focus on Chase. 'Did Agent Hatton find him at Woodruff Park?'

'No. From what Hatton could learn, Crighton's got a terrible temper and gets into a lot of brawls. Most of the other winos were terrified to even talk about him.'

'Has he ever been picked up?' Daniel asked.

'No record that I could find.' Chase aimed a hesitant look at Alex. 'One of the winos said he saw Crighton arguing with a nun late yesterday evening.'

Beneath his hands, Alex's shoulders sagged. 'Oh God. Craig beat Sister Anne?'

'I'm sorry,' Chase said gently. 'I think Crighton does not want to be found.'

She shook her head wearily. 'I keep thinking it can't get worse and it does. Where are Hope and Meredith?'

'Having supper in the cafeteria,' Chase said. 'When they're done, I have two female agents waiting to take them to their safe house. One of the agents will stay with them there and the other will meet you at your house in Dutton to get their things.'

'Thank you. You all have work to do. I'll go sit with Meredith and Hope.'

Daniel watched her go, wishing he could make her sorrow and fear go away and a little guilty that he couldn't quite get the picture of her in a proper bed out of his mind. He turned back to find Chase looking at him with scornful disbelief.

'You just couldn't stay on that sofa, could you?'

Daniel couldn't stop the grin that seemed to take over his face. 'Actually, I did.'

Chase rolled his eyes. 'Oh, for God's sake, Daniel. On the *sofa*?'

Daniel shrugged. 'It seemed like the right thing to do at the time.'

'What did?' Ed said, coming through the door, a folder in one hand.

Chase's lips twitched. 'Never mind.'

'Then it was good,' Talia grumbled, following Ed in. 'I passed Drs McCrady and Berg in the parking lot and Hatton and Koenig are on their way in, too.'

In five minutes they were all seated around the table. Mary McCrady sat at the far end, working on other cases until they needed her, and Daniel noticed Felicity had seated herself next to Koenig, as far away from Daniel as she could get and still be seated with the group. It made him a little sad, but he wasn't sure what he could do about it, so he focused on the work. 'Koenig, you go first.'

'The gunman in the pizza parlor last night was Lester Jackson. Sheet as long as your arm. Assault with a deadly, B&E, armed robbery. Been in jail more than he's been out. That cop from the Underground said he was about 75 per cent sure it was the guy that tried to run Alex down. He was surer about the car itself.'

'Do we know how Jackson ended up in Dutton last night?' Chase asked.

'We found a cell phone in his car,' Ed said. 'Log showed he got three incoming calls from the same number yesterday and one outgoing to that same number.'

'So what exactly happened there?' Chase asked.

'I took Deputy Mansfield's statement this morning,' Koenig said. 'He said that they were notified the alarm at the pizza parlor had been triggered. Mansfield said he ordered the first responder to wait for backup before going in. Officer Cowell didn't. Mansfield heard the shots as he drove up. He ran inside just as Lester Jackson shot Cowell. When Jackson pointed the gun at Mansfield, Mansfield shot him.' Koenig lifted his brows. 'But Mansfield's story doesn't play. That's why Felicity is here.'

'CSU recovered four weapons,' Felicity said. 'Jackson's .38, Sheila's .45, and the two nine-millimeters belonging to Deputies Cowell and Mansfield. Deputy Cowell had been hit twice by Jackson's .38. Either one would have killed him instantly. In fact, the first one did. The first one hit him in the throat, from about ten feet away.'

'The distance from where Jackson stood behind the counter to where Deputy Cowell fell,' Daniel said. 'What about the second bullet?'

'He was dead when it entered his heart,' Felicity said, 'from very close range.'

'So Jackson was standing at the cash register, shot Cowell the first time, then came around, stood over him, and shot him again.' Daniel shook his head. 'Cold bastard.'

'Cowell hit Jackson in the arm,' Koenig said. 'Sheila never fired her gun.'

Daniel remembered the haunting sight of Sheila sitting in the corner, both hands still wrapped around her gun. 'She must have gotten scared or frozen up.'

'Jackson shot her twice,' Felicity said. 'But from the angle, he wasn't behind the counter. He was standing by the fallen deputy.'

'So Mansfield's story doesn't play,' Koenig said, 'because he said he shot Jackson as soon as he came in the door because Jackson had just shot Cowell.'

'But Jackson wouldn't have been behind the counter then.' Daniel rubbed his head. 'So either Mansfield was wrong about the timing or he waited for Jackson to go back behind the counter to shoot him.'

Felicity nodded. 'The bullet that killed Jackson came up at an angle. It was a straight in and out, so Mansfield was crouching when he fired.'

'And,' Koenig added, 'the angle of the entry into Jackson says the bullet didn't come from the door. Mansfield was crouched next to Cowell when he fired.'

'Why would he lie?' Talia asked. 'Mansfield's a deputy sheriff. He would have known the ballistics would tell the truth.'

'Because he expected it to be handled internally,' Daniel said heavily. 'He expected Frank Loomis to be investigating, not us.'

Chase looked grim. 'So we're saying the Dutton sheriff is rotten?'

Daniel was still unwilling to accept that. 'I don't know. I do know nothing was done right on the Tremaine murder investigation. No photos of the scene, evidence stored improperly so it was ruined in the flood, no reports in the file. I think Fulmore might have been framed. At the very least, somebody's hiding something.'

'And I wasn't successful in getting the coroner's report,' Felicity said. 'Dr Granville told me that his predecessor didn't file required paperwork.'

'But it would be in the court records,' Talia said.

'It's not,' Daniel told her. 'I had Leigh pull the court transcripts and all the filed paperwork. She got it this morning. It's a pretty empty file. None of that stuff is in there.'

'What about the prosecutor and the judge?' Talia pushed.

'Dead and a retired hermit, respectively,' Daniel answered.

'This doesn't look good for Loomis,' Chase said. 'I'm going to have to alert the state's attorney's office.'

Daniel sighed. 'I know. But we still need to know what or who brought Jackson to Dutton last night. That person ties to the attempted hit-and-run yesterday.'

'Jackson's one outgoing call on his cell was made right after Alex was almost hit,' Koenig said. 'I think it was to tell whoever hired him that he'd missed.'

'We need to find out who that other number belongs to,' Chase said.

'I'll work it tomorrow,' Koenig said, stifling a yawn. 'Between being up all night watching Fallon's house and working all day, I'm beat.' He poked Hatton, who'd nodded off. 'Wake up, sweetheart.'

Hatton gave Koenig a dirty look. 'I wasn't asleep.'

'I already told Daniel what you found out about Craig Crighton,' Chase said. 'If you don't have any more, why don't the two of you go home and get some sleep?'

'I'll catch a nap,' Hatton said, 'then I'm going back down to Peachtree and Pine to look for Crighton. I have a lead on one of his haunts. I'm going to dress for the occasion, see if I can't blend in a little better than I did today.'

'I should go with you, then,' Koenig said. 'Let me get a little sleep and I'll go hobo, too. I'll follow ten paces behind and watch your back.'

Chase smiled. 'I'll let the patrol in the neighborhood know you're there and hobo.'

Felicity Berg also rose. 'The bullet entry wounds on Jackson were all I had that was new, also. I'm headed out.'

'Thank you, Felicity,' Daniel said sincerely, and she gave him a small smile.

'You're welcome. Don't bring me any more bodies, Daniel.'

One side of his mouth lifted. 'Yes, ma'am.'

When they were gone, Chase turned to Ed. 'The hair.'

'Exact match to Alex's DNA,' Ed said without blinking.

Daniel's heart sank. Now he'd not only have to tell Alex about the hair they'd found on the bodies, he'd have to tell her that he'd taken her hair without permission.

'Crap,' Chase muttered.

'We should have told her before,' Daniel muttered back. 'Now I'm up shit creek.'

'What did you do?' Talia asked.

'He took Alex's hair for me to test without her knowing,' Ed said and Talia grimaced.

'Bad move, Danny. You *are* up shit creek.'

'You'll think of something to tell her,' Chase said.

'You could try the truth,' Mary McCrady called from the end of the table. Chase gave her a disgruntled glare and she shrugged. 'Just sayin',' she said.

'Hell,' Daniel grumbled. 'I should never listen to you, Chase.'

'But you always do. So now we know that whoever killed Claudia, Janet, and Gemma has access to hair from one of the twins. How?'

'An old hairbrush, maybe,' Talia said. 'Who got Alicia's things after she died?'

'That's a good question,' Daniel said. 'I'll ask Alex. Talia, what do you have?'

'I talked to Carla Solomon and Rita Danner. Their stories agreed completely with Gretchen French's. Everything was the same down to the whiskey bottle. When I got back, I helped Leigh go through the high school yearbooks and we identified the other nine victims. All went to three of the public schools between Dutton and Atlanta. Not one went to the private school the murdered women attended, so there's no tie there.'

Daniel thought of his sister, Susannah, and wondered if there might not be just one victim who had attended Bryson Academy. *I need to talk to Suze. Tonight*.

'Are the other rape victims still living?' Daniel asked, and she nodded.

'Four have moved out of state, but the others are still in Georgia. I'll need travel money to get out to the four out of state. So, Daniel, what happened up at the prison?'

Daniel filled them in on the details and Mary moved to join the group.

'So you think this Gary Fulmore might be innocent?' Mary asked.

'I don't know, but things don't add up. And Alex seems more panicked at the thought of Fulmore not being guilty than she was about her own sister's assault.'

'It's the only closure she got out of all this, Daniel,' Ed said sympathetically.

'Maybe.' Daniel looked at Mary. 'All the time Fulmore was talking about that ring he'd left on Alicia's finger, Alex was staring at her hands. She was almost in a trance.'

'Did Alex tell you her cousin and I talked about hypnosis?'

Daniel nodded. 'Yeah. I think it's a good idea, if it doesn't make things worse.'

'All hypnosis will do is relax her enough so that her defenses don't come up. I think we should try it as soon as possible.'

'How about tonight?' Daniel asked.

'Her cousin is broaching the subject as we speak.'

'All right. So after we're done here, we drive to Bailey's house. But first,' Daniel said, 'let's start lining up possible members of this rape posse. We suspect Wade, Rhett, and Simon. They graduated the same year. They would have been in the eleventh grade the spring Alicia was murdered.'

'But Gretchen's rape happened almost a full year earlier,' Talia reminded him.

Daniel sighed. 'The year Simon was expelled from Bryson Academy and sent to Jefferson High. It fits. He would have been sixteen himself then.'

Chase produced a stack of paper from one of the boxes on the table. 'Leigh made copies of the yearbook pictures of every boy who went to Simon's public high school. These' – he produced a thicker stack – 'are the boys who went to the other high schools, including the fancy private school you went to, Daniel.' Chase lifted an amused brow. 'You were voted most likely to become the president of the United States.'

Daniel huffed a tired laugh. 'There are too many files to even know where to start.'

'Leigh's been entering them in spreadsheets so we can sort them better and she's running last knowns on them all. We can already cross out a few who've died. All the perps in Simon's pictures were white boys, so I eliminated all minorities, too.'

Daniel stared at the stack, half dazed at the thought of the man-hours it would require to comb through. He blinked hard and put the stack out of his mind for the moment. 'Chase, what about the rich girls?'

'I got a list of all the girls who graduated from Bryson Academy the same years as Claudia, Janet, and Gemma, plus a year on either side. Leigh and I called as many as we could reach, to tell them to be careful. Most of them had already heard the news and figured it out. Some of them can afford bodyguards and a few have hired one. We'll try to get in touch with the others tomorrow.'

Mary leaned over to squeeze Daniel's forearm. 'Dr Fallon and Hope should be done eating supper by now. Are you ready to see if Alex wants to try hypnosis tonight?'

He nodded grimly. 'Yeah. Let's get this done.'

Dutton, Wednesday, January 31, 9:00 P.M.

'Hope's asleep in the car with Agent Shannon,' Meredith said, climbing up into the surveillance van. Meredith had refused to let Alex go through hypnosis alone, and Hope had become agitated when Agent Shannon tried to take her to the safe house alone, so they'd brought Hope along. 'Luckily Hope fell asleep on the way. I don't know how she'd react to seeing her house again. Have you ever done this before?'

Meredith sat in one of the folding chairs next to Daniel. Ed was manning the video controls and Mary McCrady stood on Bailey's front porch with Alex, who looked eerily calm. Meredith, in contrast, was a bundle of nerves.

'Relax, Meredith,' Daniel said. 'She'll be fine.'

'I know. I just wish I could be in there with her.' She

clenched her hands in her lap. 'I'm supposed to be the calm one, Daniel. I have done this before.'

Procedure was that only the therapist and the subject were to be present during forensic hypnosis. It was the way it was done. But Daniel understood how Meredith felt. 'I wanted to be with her, too. We'll both do the next best thing and stay here.'

With his characteristic expression of sympathy, Ed twisted the monitor so that Meredith had a better view. 'Can you see?'

She nodded. 'I feel like a voyeur,' she said glumly.

'Wouldn't be the first time,' Daniel muttered.

After a beat of shocked silence, she snickered. 'Thank you, Daniel. I needed that.'

Ed cleared his throat. 'Looks like they're ready to go.'

Mary and Alex appeared on the monitor, walking into the living room. For more than a minute Alex stood rigid and trembling and Daniel had to force himself to stay where he sat. Mary's voice came through the speaker, low and soothing, and eventually Alex moved to the leather reclining chair Mary had brought into the room an hour before.

'She might need to bring Alex in and out of it a few times,' Meredith murmured. 'If she's going to get her under enough to move around.'

In the living room, Alex was sitting in the chair, her feet up and her eyes closed. But she was still rigid and Daniel's chest tightened. She was scared. But he sat and watched as Mary, in a soothing voice, told Alex to find a peaceful place and to go there.

'What if I can't?' Alex asked, panicked. 'What if I can't find a peaceful place?'

'Then think of a place you felt safe,' Mary said. 'Happy.'

Alex nodded and sighed and Daniel wondered where she'd finally gone.

Mary continued her slow, soothing routine, taking Alex deeper into a relaxing state.

'So, do you use hypnosis often with your homicide cases?' Meredith asked.

Daniel knew she needed to talk and the distraction would be a good thing for them both. 'From time to time, mainly to generate leads. I've never gone with a case solely on a retrieved memory, though. Not unless I could independently verify it. Memories are fragile things, so easily manipulated.'

'That's wise,' Meredith returned. Both of them had their eyes on the screen where Mary had progressed to determining how deeply under Alex had gone. Alex was watching as her arm lifted and stayed lifted. 'Alex was already a believer in hypnosis from her work. That's making Mary's job easier.'

'Daniel.' Ed was pointing to the monitor. 'I think Mary's got her under.'

Alex had both arms in the air and was looking from arm to arm with detached curiosity. Mary told her to lower them and she obeyed.

'Now let's walk to the stairs,' Mary said, taking Alex by the hand. 'I want you to think back, go back to the day Alicia died.'

'The next day,' Alex said quietly. 'It's the next day.'

'All right,' Mary said. 'It's the next day. So tell me what you see, Alex.'

Alex made it to the fourth stair and stopped, her hand gripping the banister so hard Daniel could see her white knuckles on the video.

'That's how far she went yesterday,' he murmured. 'I thought she'd have a heart attack, her pulse went so high.'

'Alex,' Mary said with quiet authority. 'Keep going.'

'No.' Panic had edged into Alex's voice. 'I can't. I can't.'

'All right. So tell me what you see.'

'Nothing. It's dark.'

'Where are you?'

'Here. Right here.'

'Were you coming up? Or down?'

'Down. Oh, God.' Alex's breath began to hitch rapidly and Mary gently pressed her down until she sat on the stair. Mary then brought her out, then took her under again.

When Alex returned to a hypnotic state, Mary began again. 'Where are you?'

'Here. That stair creaks.'

'All right. Is it still dark?'

'Yes. I haven't turned on the hall light.'

'Why not?'

'I didn't want them to see me.'

'Who, Alex?'

'My mother. And Craig. They're downstairs. I heard them downstairs.'

'Doing what?'

'Fighting. Yelling.' She closed her eyes. 'Screaming.'

'What are they screaming?'

'I hate you. I hate you,' Alex said, her voice even and level, disturbingly so.

'I wish you were dead,' Daniel murmured just as Alex said the same words in that even monotone. 'She thought her mother was saying it to her.'

'But she said it to Craig,' Meredith said quietly.

'Who's saying this?' Mary asked.

'My mother. My mother.' Tears were running down her face, but her expression stayed calm. Doll-like. A shiver of apprehension raced down Daniel's back.

'What is Craig saying?' Mary asked.

'She was asking for it with her short shorts and halter tops. Wade gave her what she wanted.'

'And your mother? What's she saying now?'

Alex stood abruptly and Mary stood with her. 'Your bastard son killed my baby. You let him. You didn't stop him.' Her breath quickened and her voice hardened. 'Wade did not kill her.' She walked down a step and Mary held out her hands in case she stumbled. 'You took her. You took her and dumped her in that ditch. Did you think I wouldn't see the blanket, that I wouldn't know?'

She stopped and Daniel realized he was holding his breath. He made himself exhale and draw another breath. Beside him, Meredith was trembling.

'What are they saying?' Mary asked.

Alex shook her head. 'Nothing. She broke the glass.'

'What glass?'

'I don't know. I can't see.'

'Then come to where you can see.'

Alex came down the remaining stairs and walked to the doorway to the living room.

'Can you see now?'

Alex nodded. 'There's glass on the floor. I'm standing in it. It hurts my feet.'

'Do you cry?'

'No. I don't want him to hear me.'

'What glass did your mother break, Alex?'

'From his gun cabinet. She has his gun. She's pointing it at him and screaming.'

'Oh, God,' Daniel murmured. Meredith clutched his hand, hard.

'What is she screaming, Alex?'

'You killed her and wrapped her in Tom's blanket and dumped her, like garbage.'

'Who is Tom?' Daniel hissed.

'Alex's father,' Meredith whispered, horrified. 'He died when she was five.'

Alex had gone still, her hand on the door. 'She has his gun, but he wants it back.'

'What is he doing?' Mary asked, her voice very calm.

'He's grabbing her wrists but she's fighting.' New tears began to flow down Alex's cheeks. 'I'll kill you. I'll kill you like you killed my baby.' Her head wagged from side to side. 'I didn't kill her. Wade didn't kill her. You can't tell. I won't let you tell.' She drew a deep breath.

'Alex?' Mary asked. 'What's happening?'

'She saw you. She told me she saw you.'

'Who saw, Alex?'

'Me. She says, "Alex saw you with the blanket."' Then she flinched. 'No, no, no.'

'What happened?' Mary asked, but Daniel already knew.

'He turned the gun under her chin. He shot her. Oh, Mama.' Alex leaned her temple against the door, wrapped her arms around her own body, and rocked. 'Mama.'

Meredith shuddered out a sob, tears running down her face. Daniel squeezed her hand tighter, his throat too tight to breathe.

Alex stopped rocking, again going statue still.

'Alex.' Mary returned to her quietly authoritative tone. 'What do you see?'

'He sees me.' Panic sharpened her voice. 'I'm running. I'm running.'

'And then?'

Alex turned her head to look at Mary, her face pale and haunted. 'Nothing.'

'Oh my God.' Next to him, Meredith was sobbing quietly, her fist pressed to her mouth. 'All this time . . . She's carried that all this time and we never helped her.'

Daniel pulled her to his side. 'You didn't know. How could you know?' But his voice was hoarse, and when he touched his face, his cheeks were wet.

Meredith turned her face into his shoulder and wept. At the console Ed swallowed audibly and kept taping. Serene and outwardly composed, Mary led Alex back to the chair and began the process of bringing her back. But when Mary looked up into the camera, her eyes were stark and horrified.

His arm still around Meredith's shaking shoulders, Daniel pulled out his cell phone and dialed Koenig's number. 'It's Vartanian,' he said, his voice cold, his rage barely leashed. 'Have you found Crighton yet?'

'No,' Koenig said softly. 'Hatton's sitting with a group of bums now. One of them says they saw him two hours ago. Why? What's wrong?'

Daniel swallowed. 'When you find him, arrest him.'

'Yeah,' Koenig said slowly. 'For beating that nun.' He paused. 'What else, Danny?'

Daniel had nearly forgotten about Sister Anne. 'For the murder of Kathy Tremaine.'

'Ah hell. You're kidding. Dammit.' Koenig sighed.

'Will do. I'll call you when Hatton has a fix on his location.'

'Get backup before you go in.'

'You bet. Daniel, tell Alex I'm sorry about her mom.'

'I will.' He slipped his cell back into his pocket, then nudged Meredith into motion. 'Come on. Mary's almost done. We'll be there when Alex comes out of the house.'

Chapter Eighteen

Dutton, Wednesday, January 31, 10:00 P.M.

It was, Alex thought, surreal. Now that it was over, now that she knew . . .

But perhaps on some level she'd always known.

She looked over at Daniel, who drove from Bailey's house toward Main Street with both hands clutching the wheel in a white-knuckled grip. He'd been stealing what he probably thought were surreptitious glances at her since he'd put her in the car and buckled her in with such gentleness she wanted to weep.

He had been. Weeping. She could see it in his eyes the moment she'd walked out of the house with Mary McCrady straight into his arms. He'd held her so tight . . . and she'd clung, needing him. Meredith had still been crying as she waited to wrap Alex in her arms. She'd begged forgiveness, when there was nothing to forgive.

It just was. And had always been. She just hadn't wanted to remember.

Now she remembered, every last second of it, up until Crighton grabbed her by the collar and the world had gone black. The next thing she knew she'd been in the hospital, her stomach pumped of the tranquilizers the police told her she'd taken.

But she didn't remember doing that. Before, she hadn't questioned. Now . . .

How could I not?

She might never know. All she knew was that her mother had not taken her own life. At the same time, she'd had in her hands a weapon that could have saved her life.

That was the image that haunted Alex the most.

'She just stood there,' she murmured. 'She had the gun in her hand and she just stood there until it was too late. If she'd fired, she might be alive right now.'

Daniel's throat worked as he swallowed hard. 'Sometimes people freeze. It's hard to know what you'll do in that situation. But it's hard not to blame them after the fact.'

'I feel a little . . . detached, you know?'

'Mary said you would.'

She studied his profile. He was tired and worn. 'Are you all right?'

He huffed a chuckle. 'You're asking *me*?'

'I'm asking you.'

'I . . . I don't know, Alex. I'm angry and I'm . . . sad. I feel so helpless. I want to make this all go away for you, but I can't.'

She laid her hand on his arm. 'No, you can't. But it's awfully nice of you to want to.'

'Nice.' He drew a breath. 'I'm not feeling very nice right now.'

She tugged his hand from the wheel, then brought it to her cheek. It felt good there. Solid and warm and safe. 'At the beginning I panicked. I couldn't think of a safe place to go and I thought, "What if we went to all this trouble and Mary can't hypnotize me?" '

'I know. I wondered where you'd finally gone. I hoped it was someplace nice.'

She rubbed her cheek against his hand. 'There was a moment this morning, after we'd . . . you know . . . *finished*. I looked up at you looking down at me and thought it might have been the most wonderful moment of my life. That's where I went.'

His fingers tightened around hers. 'Thank you.'

She kissed the back of his hand. 'You're welcome.'

They arrived at her bungalow, passing the unmarked GBI vehicle parked on the street. Meredith had left Bailey's house with the two agents who would take her and Hope to the safe house after she'd gathered their things. One of the agents sat in the backseat, guarding Hope as she slept.

Daniel came around to open her door, then pulled her to her feet and into an embrace so tight, so huge, that Alex wished she could just stand there with him forever. She slipped her arms under his coat, around his waist, and held on. His heart was thundering beneath her ear and she understood she'd affected him on a level that was entirely new. *Unfamiliar ground*, he said . . . Could it have been only two days before?

Alex felt like she'd lived a lifetime in those two days.

Daniel pushed her hair away from her face, his lips grazing her cheek, making her shiver. Then he whispered in her ear, husky and hot. 'This morning, Alex, what we did was not *you know*. We made love. And I'm not even close to being finished.' He tipped up her chin and pressed a hard fast kiss to her mouth. 'If that's okay with you.'

This was the bright light at the end of the tunnel. They had a chance to make something good out of so much darkness. 'It is.'

'Then let's go in.' He pulled away with a grimace. 'I forgot all about Riley today. I've never left him alone so long before. He may have had an accident in your house.'

She smiled up at him. 'It's okay. I have renter's insurance.'

His arm wrapped possessively around her, they walked to the front porch. Then as one, their steps slowed. Meredith stood in the middle of the living room, her arms crossed over her chest, scanning the room with weary futility. Everything had been ripped apart – drawers dumped, crayons littered the floor, and the sofa where they'd made love had been slashed, the stuffing everywhere.

'I don't think my renter's insurance will cover this,' Alex murmured.

Meredith looked up, her eyes narrowed. 'Somebody was looking for something.'

Daniel stiffened. 'Where's Riley? Riley!' He ran into Hope's room, Alex on his heels. The other agent was in there surveying a similar state of disaster. 'Where's my—?'

The agent pointed down where only a tail could be seen sticking out from under the bed, wagging like a metronome in slow motion. Daniel heaved a sigh of relief as he gently pulled Riley out. Riley gazed up with his sad basset eyes and Daniel cupped the dog's head in both hands, scratching behind his ears. 'What happened to you, boy?'

'I found a bowl on the floor in the bathroom, under the window,' the agent said. 'The window was open and the bowl still had a little canned dog food in it.'

'I left a bowl of dry food in the kitchen. Riley can't have canned food. It's bad for his stomach.' Daniel's jaw clenched. 'Whoever did this drugged him.'

Alex checked Riley's eyes. 'He looks dazed. Would he have barked at an intruder?'

'Loud enough to wake the dead,' Daniel answered. 'We need to get the food in that bowl tested.'

'Well, there's quite a mess in the bathroom,' the agent said. 'Doesn't look like too much of the canned food stayed in him.'

Alex met Daniel's eyes. 'Could have saved his life.'

Daniel frowned. 'What could they have been looking for?'

Alex stood and looked around the trashed bedroom with a sigh. 'I have no idea.'

'They did the same thing in my room,' Meredith said. 'Thank goodness I had my laptop with me. Where's yours?'

'It was in the closet. Daniel, can you open it?'

He'd already pulled a pair of gloves from his pocket and slid the closet door open with one hand. It was completely empty. 'What was on your computer, Alex?'

'Nothing, really. Maybe old tax returns, so they have my social and my address.'

'We can report it to the credit agencies tomorrow,' Daniel said.

Meredith cleared her throat. 'Alex, where's your *thing*?'

Alex looked at Daniel. 'Is my gun still locked in your trunk?'

He nodded grimly. 'Yeah. Although I'm sure they brought their own, just in case.'

Alex's shocked gaze flew to Meredith's. 'If we'd been here . . .'

Meredith nodded unsteadily. 'But we weren't. And Hope's safe. She may have to wear the same clothes for a few days, but she's safe.'

'We can pick up what you need on the way to the safe house,' the agent said. 'Everything here's going to need to stay the way it is until we can process the scene. You want to call CSU, Vartanian, or should I?'

Daniel rubbed his head and Alex could see the headache lurking in his eyes. 'If you would, I'd appreciate it, Shannon. I need to get Riley to the vet. There's an all-night emergency clinic near my house.'

'I'll make the call,' Shannon said. 'You need help getting the pooch to your car?'

'No.' Daniel scooped Riley into his arms, settling the dog's head on his shoulder like a baby's. 'He's a lead butt, but I got him. Call when you get to the safe house, Meredith.'

'I will.' Meredith pulled Alex to her in a fierce hug. 'When will I see you again?'

'Tomorrow morning. You're bringing Hope in to do her hypnosis, right?'

Meredith's nod was shaky. 'I hope I can make it through another one.'

'You will. Thank you for being there with me tonight.'

Meredith faltered. 'Alex . . .'

'Sshh. Hush now. You couldn't have known. So let it go.'

'You call me when you get to Vartanian's. I assume that's where you'll be tonight.'

'Yes. That's where I'll be.'

Athens, Georgia, Wednesday, January 31, 11:35 P.M.

Mack flinched, the buzzing of his cell phone startling him. Careful not to reveal his hiding place, he checked his phone and frowned. It was a text message from Woolf. He wondered if Woolf had followed him here. But he'd been careful. No one had followed him. And Woolf should be busy right now.

He opened the text message. *Thanks for tip. Here at scene. Who is he? 2 much blood 2 see face. Need ID before 12 for a.m. edition.*

He hesitated, then shrugged. Up until now the Woolfs had been able to reason that he might just be an anonymous tipper and not necessarily a murderer. It was his experience that people could tell themselves all kinds of things to make themselves feel better, and the Woolfs were no exception. *Romney, Sean,* he texted back and hung up.

The Woolfs might not leap to his command anymore. But he was almost finished with them anyway. He heard footsteps. A male voice. Female laughter.

'You should let me drive you home,' the man said.

'I'm fine. I'll see you in class, okay?'

There were sounds of kissing, then a male groan. 'I want you. It's been three days.'

She laughed lightly. 'I have a paper due tomorrow, so not tonight, big boy.'

Mack hadn't anticipated she'd have companionship. Stupid move on his part. He fingered the safety on his

Colt, prepared to do what he needed to do to get away. But the man just groaned and after another kiss, left.

Lisa got in her car, humming. She checked her rearview and pulled her car away from the curb. He let her drive a few blocks before coming up behind her like a thief in the night. He stuffed the handkerchief in her mouth and pressed his knife to her throat. *I'm getting good at this.* 'Drive,' he said. Now *this* was going to be fun.

Atlanta, Wednesday, January 31, 11:55 P.M.

'Why are we here?' Alex asked. 'I thought we were going back to your house.'

'Here' was Leo Papadopoulos's firing range. 'Luke's brother runs this place. He gives a discount to all Luke's friends from the bureau.'

'That's very nice,' she said. 'So why are we here?'

'Because . . . Dammit, Alex, Sheila Cunningham was holding a gun when she died.' And he couldn't get the picture out of his mind. 'She never fired.'

'Like my mother,' she murmured. 'Is it a woman thing?'

'No, men do it, too. It's a training thing. When you get scared you freeze up. You have to have all those behaviors, those habits, ingrained. You do the same thing in the ER. When a crisis hits, you go into autopilot mode on some things, don't you?'

'Some things, yes. So are you going to train me, Daniel?'

'Not in one day. But we'll come back every day until either you've built up some reflexes or this is over and you don't need it anymore.'

'Is this place always open at night?'

'No. Leo opened it up for us. He owed Luke a favor. I called Luke to ask if we could come by while I was waiting for the vet to see Riley.' That the vet believed his dog was suffering from being poisoned simply added to the fury churning in Daniel's gut. He'd benefit from a little target practice himself. 'Come on, let's go.' He came around and helped her from the car, then took her satchel from the trunk. 'You still can't carry this around town, you know.'

She nodded. 'I know.'

'But you didn't say you'd obey.'

She smiled, though it didn't reach her eyes. 'I know.'

He shook his head and held the front door open. 'Just go inside.'

Inside, Leo Papadopoulos stood behind the counter. 'Danny! And who is this?'

Leo was a few years younger than Luke and just as popular with the ladies. 'This is Alex. Hands off, Leo.' He meant it as a friendly jab, but instead it sounded ominous.

Leo just grinned. 'Hell, I already knew that. Mama told me all about Miss Alex.'

Alex looked up at him. 'And how does Mama know? She's never met me.'

'Oh, she will, don't worry.' Leo flashed a dazzling smile. 'She will. You can go on back. Luke's back there already.' Leo's smile faded. 'I think he had a really bad day.'

'Yeah, well, that's goin' around,' Daniel muttered. 'Thanks, Leo. I'll owe you one.'

Back in the range, Luke stood in one of the stations, his ears covered and his face creased in a feral snarl. Alex frowned. 'What's wrong with him?'

'Luke works Internet sex crimes. Lately he's been on a child protection task force. He's been deep into a case the last two months. It's not looking good.'

'Oh.' She sighed. 'I'm sorry.'

'It's the job,' Daniel said with a shrug. 'Yours, mine. We have to flow with it, and Luke will, too. Here, put these on.' He handed her goggles and earmuffs, then opened her satchel and examined her gun. It was an H&K nine-mil, small enough to fit her hand comfortably. 'This is a good gun. You know how to load it?' When she nodded, he added, 'You know how to load it *fast*?'

Her chin lifted. 'Not yet.'

'We can work on that later. For now, shoot.' He handed her the gun and stepped back and watched. In the station next to Luke, she took aim and fired methodically – and missed the target each time. He found himself justifiably concerned . . . and undeniably aroused. It was a hell of a thing to watch a beautiful woman with a good gun. Especially one who'd told you that making love with you was her happiest memory. Especially when you'd thought the same thing. He frowned, concern overriding his arousal. Especially when she couldn't hit the broad side of a barn.

Luke stopped to watch. 'Don't close your eyes,' he said.

She lowered the gun and blinked. 'Was I? Well, that's scary.' She blew out a breath and set herself up to try again.

Luke came over, his eyes full of questions. 'How is she?' he asked, low so Alex couldn't hear. The question made Daniel angry – not at Luke, but angry just the same.

'Given that in the last few days she found out her sister was gang-raped and that her mother was murdered, not too bad.' Luke's eyes widened and Daniel filled him in.

'Shit. Well, how's Riley?'

'The vet said he'll be okay.' He studied Luke's eyes. 'So, what happened?'

Luke's expression smoothed to one of careful blankness. 'It all went down today. We got a fix on three of the kids we'd been tracking through that kiddie-porn site.' He fixed his eyes on Alex, who'd managed to hit the target twice. 'We didn't get there in time.'

'I'm sorry, Luke.'

Luke nodded again. 'Two girls and a boy,' he said,

his voice steady, but without any emotion. 'Sisters and a brother. Fifteen, thirteen, and ten. Shot in the head, all of them.'

Daniel swallowed, able to picture it only too well. 'God.'

'We'd missed the perps by at least a day. We shut down the site, but they'll just reopen somewhere else.' He was staring into space now and Daniel didn't want to think about what he was seeing. 'I need a break. Chase said you had a shitload of names to go through to get a profile on this posse.'

'We can definitely use you.' He clasped Luke's shoulder. 'Do you need anything?'

Luke's lips twisted. 'A key to hell. There's no other place bad enough for those guys.' A muscle in his clenched jaw spasmed. 'I see too many faces in my dreams.'

The fury that roiled inside him bubbled higher. 'I know.'

Luke turned, his eyes bright with tears. 'I have to go. Leo says you can stay as long as you want. When's the morning meeting for your case?'

'Eight,' Daniel said. 'In the team room.'

'Then I'll see you tomorrow.' Luke packed up his gun and ammo and was gone.

Alex lowered her gun and pulled the muffs from her ears. 'He's not okay, is he?'

'No. But, like you, he will be. Put those back on.' He stepped behind her and positioned her arms. 'Aim like this.' He showed her, keeping his arms wrapped tightly around her. 'Now squeeze the trigger and keep your eyes open.'

She obeyed, nodding sharply when her shot hit the paper target's chest. 'Aim for the chest,' she said. 'More area, more room for error. I remember a cop once told me that when he brought a stabbing victim into the ER. Her husband had come at her with a knife. She had a gun, but she'd aimed for his head and missed.'

'What happened to her?'

'She died,' she said flatly. 'Show me how again.'

So he did, holding her arms firmly in place. Her focus on the paper target was absolute as she emptied her magazine into its chest. But each shot pushed her body back against him, wreaking havoc with his own concentration. He made himself remember Sheila Cunningham, sitting in the corner, dead. *Focus, Vartanian*.

'Load,' he gritted, taking a step back as she followed his direction. Her hands were nimble and she completed the task more quickly than he'd expected. 'That was good.'

She lifted the gun, but without his arm guiding hers, her aim was off and by the third shot she was completely off the target again.

'You're closing your eyes again. Keep them open, Alex.' He covered her arms with his again, righting her aim. Accepting the torture of her body rubbing against his when she settled back into him and emptied another magazine. In the quiet, he shuddered out the breath he'd held. 'Load, dammit.'

She twisted to look up at him over her shoulder, her eyes wide with question at his terse command. Then her whiskey-colored eyes darkened with understanding and a need of her own. She turned back and loaded, her fingers just as steady as before. The steadiness, he knew, came from years of functioning under stressful situations. He wished he could watch her in action in her own domain, and realized with a jolt that he wouldn't be able to. Because when this was over, she'd go back. Back to Ohio. Back to the job she wouldn't leave and the 'nice' ex-husband she saw every damn day.

Another pulse of fury bubbled up. He knew his jealousy was totally irrational, but the other . . . when this was over she would leave. *No, she won't. I won't let her.*

You can't stop her. But he knew he couldn't let her slip away. He'd deal with her leaving when the time came. Until then, he had to keep her alive. 'Try it yourself.'

She'd improved, but her aim drifted and he brought his arms back around her. She shifted, her butt rubbing hard against his groin, once, then twice, before she settled into him and began squeezing the trigger again. The move had been deliberate and had what blood was left in his head pounding a fast steady beat. Then she was done.

She put the gun on the waist-high counter, slipped off the glasses and the earmuffs, and he did the same. For a moment she stood, regarding the target with an icy stare. There was very little of it left. Three rounds from her H&K had ripped it to shreds.

'I think I killed it,' she said evenly, no hint of amusement in her tone.

'I think you did,' he answered, his voice rough and gravelly.

She turned in his arms and lifted her chin, meeting his eyes with cool challenge. Then she pulled his head down for the hottest kiss he'd ever experienced. In seconds it exploded and they were dueling for control, openmouthed and frantic. His hands covered the butt that had tantalized him, pulling her up and into him, rubbing her up and down his length, trying to get some relief. She tightened her arms around his neck and fought to get closer, lifting one knee to buttress his hip. He ran his hands down her thighs and lifted her, groaning into her mouth when she wrapped her legs around him.

'Stop.' He ripped his mouth from hers, panting. She was panting, too, and the sound made him want to rip her clothes off and drive deep into her, right here, right now. But they stood in Leo Papadopoulos's target range and Daniel suspected even Leo would have a problem with that. He let her legs slide down his body, trying to get his heart back to a normal rhythm. 'I have to clean up your shells before we go.'

'I'll do that!' Leo called from the front in a singsong voice. 'You two can just go home and do . . . whatever.'

Daniel snorted a laugh. 'Thank you, Leo,' he called back dryly.

'Any time, Daniel.'

Daniel put Alex's gun back in her satchel and took her hand. She hadn't dropped her gaze since he'd broken the moment and the look in her eyes had his heart racing again. She looked determined. Dangerous. *This was going to be* really *good.*

Atlanta, Thursday, February 1, 12:50 A.M.

Luckily Leo's place was not too far from his house. Luckily it was well after midnight and there were few cars on the highway or Daniel would have been tempted to use his lights for personal reasons for the first time ever.

She'd said nothing the entire way home and every minute of silence took the heat higher and higher until Daniel thought he'd lose it like a teenager before he ever got her clothes off. By the time he pulled into his driveway, he was shaking. But if there was any justice in the world, so was she. He grabbed her satchel and hauled her to his front door, his hand trembling as he tried to get the key in the lock. He missed twice before she hissed, 'For God's sake, hurry, Daniel.'

He got the door opened and yanked her inside. Her

arms were around his neck and her mouth was kissing him before he got the front door shut. Blindly he closed it, locked it, threw the deadbolt. 'Wait. The alarm. I have to set it.'

She withdrew and he turned to the alarm panel. When he looked back, his mouth went dry. Those nimble fingers of hers had made short work of the buttons on her blouse and she was pulling it from her slacks with impatient jerks. Her eyes narrowed.

'Hurry' was all she said.

The single word was like a cracked whip. Roughly he backed her against the door, taking her mouth with desperate ferocity as he pulled her jacket and blouse off her shoulders. Her fingers were quicker and she had his shirt unbuttoned before he could manage the hooks on her bra. Finally he twisted and ripped and her breasts were free and he filled his hands with them, plucking at her nipples, already pebbled hard.

'Alex.' He tried to step back but she was pushing her slacks and panties over her hips and kicking them away, all while her mouth ate at his. 'Come to bed.'

'No, do it here.' She stood before him, nude and perfect. 'Do it like you wanted to back there.' Then she gave him no choice when she threw her arms around his neck and launched herself high, twining her legs around his waist. 'Do it now.'

His pulse rocketed through the top of his head and he yanked at his belt. His knuckles caressing her hot, incredibly wet warmth as he pulled and twisted, making her moan. He dropped his pants, pushed her against the door, and thrust as hard as he could. Finally all that wet warmth was surrounding him, pulling him deeper, driving him insane.

She cried out, but there was no pain in her eyes, only heat and need and want and he knew he needed to see those eyes glaze over in mindless satisfaction.

'Keep your eyes open,' he muttered and she nodded once, hard. Her fingers dug into his shoulders and his dug into her hips and held on as he pounded into her, giving free rein to the beast that roared inside his head. He pounded until he couldn't remember anything about the day, until all the fear was gone from her eyes, leaving only dazed passion. Her body arched and she cried out again as she came, gripping him, dragging him with her.

He plunged a final time, and the pleasure was like a brick to his head. He slumped against her, pressing her into the door. His lungs pumped as he gasped for air, certain that if he died right then and there, he could want no more. Then he pulled back to see her face, and knew he had to have her again. And again. She was panting, but her mouth curved. And she looked . . . proud. Incredibly satisfied, but proud, just the same.

'That was really, *really* good,' she said.

He laughed, then wheezed in another breath. 'I think three reallys would about kill me, but I'm willing to risk it if you are.'

'I'm living life on the edge lately. I say we go for it.'

Thursday, February 1, 1:30 A.M.

Someone was crying again. Bailey could hear the plaintive wail through the walls. A door opened down the hall, followed by a hollow thud, then silence. It happened about two or three times every night.

Then her door flew open, bouncing back against the concrete wall. *He* came in and grabbed her by the blouse that was now tattered and rank. 'You lied to me, Bailey.'

'Wh—?' She cried out when the back of his hand connected with her cheek.

'You lied to me. Alex's key is not in her house.' He shook her, hard. 'Where is it?'

Bailey stared at him, unable to speak. She'd told Alex to hide the key. She had no idea where it could be. 'I . . . don't know.'

'Then let's see if we can make your brain work a little better.' He yanked, dragging her from the room, and she tried to make her mind shut down. Tried to keep herself from saying anything more. Tried to keep herself from praying to die.

Atlanta, Thursday, February 1, 2:10 A.M.

Alex's body was sore in all the right places. She rolled her head on the pillow to look at him, the only movement she could muster. Daniel lay on his back as, openmouthed, he struggled to fill his lungs.

'I hope you don't need CPR,' she muttered, 'because I don't think I can move.'

His laugh was half groan. 'I think I'll live.' He rolled to his side and pulled her against him, so that they lay spooned together. 'But I needed it,' he added quietly.

'So did I,' she whispered. 'Thank you, Daniel.'

He pressed a kiss to her shoulder, reached to turn off the light, and pulled the blanket over them. She'd started to drift off when he sighed. 'Alex, I need to talk to you.'

She'd figured this was coming. 'Okay.'

'Tonight you said your mother told Crighton that you'd seen him with Tom's blanket.'

Alex swallowed. 'Tom was my dad. He died when I was five.'

'Meredith told me. What was so special about the blanket?'

'It was my dad's camping blanket. We didn't have a lot of money, but camping was cheap and he liked being outside. Sometimes we'd all pile in the car and go to the lake and fish and swim . . . Then at night he'd make a fire and he'd wrap me and Alicia up in that old blanket and hold us on his lap while he told us stories. My mom kept all of his stuff out in Craig's garage in case Alicia and I wanted it someday. I remember Craig didn't like that very much. He was very possessive of my mother.'

'So what did you see, honey?'

'I don't know, but I know there's something. I keep remembering thunder and lightning. Mary said she was a little surprised when I insisted starting the day after Alicia died. We just need to go back another day. That's all.'

'No, that's not all.' His arm tightened around her waist. 'You're going to be mad, and I don't blame you. Just remember, I was trying to do the right thing at the time.'

Frowning, Alex rolled to look up at him. 'What?'

He stayed on his side, his expression grim. 'This hasn't been in any of the press releases and we've been able to keep it quiet. But two of the three bodies we found in ditches had a hair wrapped around the big toe. The hairs are at least ten years old.' His chest expanded, then fell. 'And they match your DNA exactly.'

Alex was stunned. 'My DNA? How do you know? I've never given you a sample.'

He closed his eyes. 'Yes, you did. Remember Tuesday when you were leaving to go with Ed to Bailey's house and I kissed you and pulled your hair?'

Alex's jaw tightened. 'You did it on purpose. Why? Why didn't you just ask me?'

'Because I didn't want to worry you. I was trying—'

'Not to hurt me,' she finished. 'Daniel . . .' She shook her head, wanting to be annoyed, but he looked so miserable that she couldn't find it in her. 'It's okay.'

He opened his eyes. 'It is?'

'Yeah. You were trying to do the right thing. Just don't do it again, okay?'

'Okay.' He pulled her back against him. 'Let's go to sleep.'

She snuggled back into him. Then the full import of his words struck her, and despite the heat radiating from his body, she felt cold. 'He has her hair,' she whispered.

'I know, baby.'

Fear snaked its way into her gut. 'Where did he get it, Daniel?'

His arm tightened around her protectively. 'I don't know yet. But I'll find out.'

Thursday, February 1, 2:30 A.M.

'Bailey,' Beardsley whispered. 'Are you alive?'

Bailey drew in a shallow breath, testing. 'Yes.'

'Did you tell him anything more?'

'I don't know anything more,' she said, her voice breaking on a sob.

'Sshh. Don't cry. Maybe Alex just hid it.'

Bailey tried to make her brain think. 'I told her to, in the letter.'

'Letter? You mean you mailed it?' he murmured. 'To Ohio? When?'

'The day they took me. Thursday.'

'She might not have gotten it then. She got here on Saturday.'

Bailey drew in another, faster breath. 'Then she might not know about the key.'

'We need to buy some time. If you have to tell him, say you sent it to her in Ohio. She's not there if they look, so she and Hope will be safe. Do you understand?'

'Yes.'

Dutton, Thursday, February 1, 5:30 A.M.

He rolled by Alex Fallon's little bungalow, his eyes narrowing. Crime scene tape was stretched across her front door. He wondered if the assholes who'd tried to run her down two days before had finally been successful at snuffing her out. They better not have. He needed her alive so he could kill her himself. Otherwise his circle would not be complete, and that would be a damn shame.

He kept rolling along at his snail's pace, doing what he'd been paid to do. A few doors down, old Violet Drummond hobbled out to the street and he handed her a paper through the window. 'Mornin', Miz Drummond.'

'Mor-nin',' she said auspiciously.

'What happened at the bungalow?' he asked nonchalantly.

Her lips pursed as if she'd sucked a lemon. 'Break-in. Somebody ransacked that Tremaine girl's things and poisoned her dog. Tore up the house, too. I knew she was trouble the minute she walked back into town. She should have just stayed away.'

He looked back at the bungalow through his side mirror. Somebody had been sloppy. Somebody was getting scared. Inside he grinned. Outside he made his face frown. 'Yes'm. Have a nice day, Miz Drummond.'

He rolled away, relieved Alex Fallon still lived, but annoyed that now she'd be more on her guard than ever – and no longer conveniently located on Main Street. But he knew where she'd be staying. She and Vartanian were practically joined at the hip. But he and Vartanian would meet soon and he'd grab Alex then.

For now, he'd finish his job, then go get some sleep. He'd had a very busy night.

Atlanta, Thursday, February 1, 5:55 A.M.

The phone woke her and groggily Alex answered it. 'Fallon. What is it, Letta?'

'Um, I'm not Letta and I want to talk to Daniel. Is he there?'

Alex sat up, awake now. 'I'm sorry. Wait.' She poked Daniel's arm. 'I think it's Chase. I was so sleepy I thought I was at home and my charge nurse was calling.'

Daniel lifted his head, his eyes still heavy with sleep. 'Oh, hell. Give it here.'

She handed it over, wondering if they would have any trouble over their . . . sleeping arrangements. She glanced at the clock with a wince. They hadn't done much sleeping.

'I'm sorry. I did call you about her mother.' Daniel sat up and hunched over, his free hand massaging his temples. He had a headache already. 'I should have called you about the break-in at the bungalow, but I had to take Riley to the vet.' He looked up at her with a hopeful grimace, then rolled his eyes. 'Well, yeah, there was that, too.'

Alex scooted over so that she knelt next to his hip and lifted his chin. His eyes were shadowed with pain. She pressed her thumbs to his temples and her lips to his brow until she felt him relax. She leaned back and he nodded, but his lips didn't smile.

'When?' he said. 'Who? . . . Never heard of him. Why didn't APD call us? I thought we had a picture of that kid on the visor of every patrol car in the city.' He sighed. 'I guess that would make it hard to see his face. All right.' He sat up straighter and looked at his clock. '*Again?* Then there's another one. Who's his tail? . . . Good. Have him call me when Woolf stops. I'll be there as fast as I can.' He started to hang up, then paused, looking at Alex. 'I'll tell her. Thanks, Chase.' He handed her the phone and she hung it up, her stomach already starting to churn.

'Who did APD have a picture of on their visors?'

'A kid we've been looking for. They found him dead in an alley, a few blocks from his car.' He scrubbed his palms over his face. 'Shot in the head with his face covered in blood. Nobody recognized him until they'd gotten him to the morgue and cleaned up his face. They found his car, ran the plates. But I've never heard of him.'

'What's his name?'

'Sean Romney.'

'I've never heard of him either.' She made herself ask the harder question. 'Woolf's on the move again?' she asked, and he nodded.

'I've gotta get out there and you can't stay here alone.'

'I can be ready in ten minutes,' she said, and he looked impressed. 'When you work level one trauma, you have to be ready to go in whenever there's a major crisis. We get all the chopper cases in a seventy-mile radius. So I can move when I need to.' She rolled out of bed, but he stayed for a moment, watching her. 'What?'

His eyes were that piercing blue that made her shiver. 'You're beautiful.'

'So are you. I hope I didn't get you into any trouble, answering the phone like that.'

He got out of bed, stretching his shoulders one way and then the other while she watched for the simple pleasure of doing so. 'No,' he drawled. 'Chase already knew.'

Her eyes widened. 'You *told* him? *Daniel!*'

'No,' he drawled again. 'I'm a guy, Alex. When we have headbanging sex on a sofa, it's written all over our faces. *Everybody* knows.'

'Oh. Well, okay.' She felt her cheeks heat. 'So what did Chase tell you to tell me?'

Daniel sobered abruptly. 'That he's sorry about your mother. Hurry. We need to go.'

Chapter Nineteen

Tuliptree Hollow, Georgia, Thursday, February 1, 7:00 A.M.

Daniel walked to the ditch, the *Review* tucked under his arm. Ed was already down in it, watching as Malcolm and Trey lifted the newest body to a stretcher.

'Ed, come on up,' Daniel called. 'I need to show you something.'

Ed scrambled up the wooden ramp they'd placed against the side of the ditch. 'You know I'm fucking tired of finding bodies in blankets,' he said. He looked over at Daniel's car where Alex sat huddled in one of Daniel's overcoats. 'How is she?'

Daniel looked over his shoulder. 'She'll be okay.' He handed Ed the paper. 'Look.'

Ed's eyes immediately widened. 'Dammit. It's the kid who bought the blankets.'

'And picked up Janet's Z.' Daniel tapped the page. 'Byline is you know who.'

Ed glared. 'He's up in that tree. I thought you might want to yank him down again.'

'That'll be a pleasure. Take a look at the kid's name.'

'Sean Romney, of Atlanta. So?'

'So . . . Woolf says here that Sean Romney is the grandson of Rob Davis of *Dutton*, who owns the damn Bank of *Dutton*. That makes Romney a second cousin to Garth Davis, the mayor of *Dutton*. That enough *Duttons* for you yet? I don't want to make any accusations,' Daniel added in a whisper, 'but Garth Davis graduated a year before Simon and Wade, but from Bryson Academy.'

Ed puffed out his cheeks. 'The mayor? That's going to be fun to prove.'

'We'll talk more back at the office. Now I'm going to pull Woolf out of his tree.'

Woolf was climbing down when Daniel approached. 'Goddammit, Jim. What's gotten into you? Climbing trees like you're twelve years old.'

Woolf shrugged. 'I'm on public property, so you can't make me leave. This is a fascinating story, Daniel. It needs to be told.'

Fascinating. Anger shot up in Daniel's head like a geyser. 'Damn you. *Fascinating story*. You tell that to the victims and their families. You're getting your damn pictures from up in a tree. How sanitary, how damn *nice*. You come with me. You're going to meet a victim up close and real personal.' He started walking, then turned. Woolf hadn't budged. Daniel's eyes narrowed. 'Don't make me drag you, Jim.'

Slowly Woolf followed, a mix of curiosity and

apprehension on his face. Malcolm and Trey were lifting the body from the stretcher to the body bag on the gurney. 'Peel back the blanket, Malcolm,' Daniel ordered sharply.

Malcolm complied. 'It's the same. Face beaten, bruises around the mouth.'

'This one's got some serious hardware,' Trey said. 'Earrings up and down both ears. A nose ring and a tongue stud.' He pointed to the victim's shoulder. 'And a tat. This one says L-A-L-L. Live and let live.'

There was a thud behind him. Daniel turned to find Jim Woolf frozen where he stood, his camera on the ground, and Daniel suddenly had a very good idea of who this woman was. He should feel guilty for making Jim look, but all he felt was pity for the young woman who'd never have a life. For all the young women who'd never have lives. It was, he thought bitterly, a *fascinating* turn of events. 'Jim?'

Woolf's mouth opened in horrified silence. He said nothing, just stared.

Daniel sighed. 'Ed, can you put Mr Woolf in your vehicle? This is his sister, Lisa.'

Atlanta, Thursday, February 1, 8:35 A.M.

Daniel and Ed both sank into chairs at the team table. Chase and Luke were already there. Talia had left to interview the rape victims they'd identified from the yearbooks. Daniel hoped her luck was better than his.

'We've got two more bodies,' Daniel said. 'Sean Romney and Lisa Woolf. Seeing his sister like that loosened Jim's tongue a little bit. He told me that a man called him with the "tips" on Janet's and Claudia's bodies. All the other "tips" were text messages that came in on a disposable cell. It wasn't registered to any of his accounts, so we didn't know to include it with the warrant.'

'And all the incoming text messages were untraceable,' Ed said with a sigh.

'Maybe he'll be a little less interested in pimping stories for this killer now that his sister's a victim,' Chase said darkly.

Luke was reading the front page of the *Dutton Review* Daniel had brought back with him. 'Who is this Romney kid?'

'APD received an anonymous 911 telling them a young man was dead in an alley,' Daniel said. 'They found Sean Romney with a bullet in his head. Apparently they didn't recognize him as the picture they'd posted on their visor because he was too bloody. They didn't get a positive ID until they'd cleaned up at the morgue at about five this morning. They called Chase and Chase called me.'

'He was only eighteen years old,' Luke noted. 'He was only in kindergarten when Alicia was killed and those girls were raped. And he grew up in Atlanta.'

'But he's connected to Dutton,' Daniel said wearily.

'Sean is the grandson of Rob Davis, who owns the bank in Dutton. Rob Davis is Garth Davis's uncle. Garth's dad was the mayor for years and best friends with Congressman Bowie. I think Sean is like the keys he tied to the victims' toes. A definite message.'

'And you're thinking the message was addressed to Garth Davis,' Chase said.

Daniel nodded, troubled. 'Garth's the *right* age, only a year ahead of Simon and Wade. Garth knew Simon. We can't dismiss the connection to Simon's pictures.'

'You knew Garth,' Ed said. 'Was he capable of the depravity in those pictures?'

'I wouldn't have thought so. I still hope not. I was a senior and he was a freshman, so I didn't know him all that well. I do remember him coming by our house a few times though, looking for Simon. I wouldn't say they were friends, exactly, but they hung out.'

Luke shook his head. 'He might have known Simon, but did he kill these women?'

Daniel brought his focus back to the present. 'Garth couldn't have killed Claudia. He was at Congressman Bowie's house Monday night during the time frame Felicity said Claudia died. But Garth is the first person we can connect to both Simon and one of these victims.'

'No, Jim Woolf is connected to all the victims,' Chase corrected. 'He's taken every one of their pictures for his damn paper. He gets all these leads handed to him on a silver platter. The perp has to know we're watching

Woolf. Why does he continue to feed him leads if he knows Woolf's going to be followed by us?' Chase lifted his brows. 'Unless he wants us to watch Woolf.'

'He sent Jim to his own sister's grave,' Ed said. 'Pretty powerful message.'

'This guy went to a lot of trouble to get Lisa Woolf,' Daniel said thoughtfully. 'She was a student at the university up in Athens. He had to either drive up there or lure her here. I've requested her phone records and I called the Athens field office. They're going to search her apartment and interview her friends. Maybe somebody saw him following her last night.'

Chase pointed to the *Review*. 'I want to know how Woolf got this picture. His tail said Woolf was in the newspaper office from nine till two last night. How did Woolf get to Atlanta to snap this photo of Romney? He must have sent someone else.'

'He wouldn't have trusted just anybody,' Daniel said. 'I'm betting good old Marianne had something to do with it. That's Jim's wife. Of course, Jim neglected to mention that when he was unburdening his soul.'

Ed was still frowning at the paper. 'Wait. APD didn't make a positive ID until about five this morning, after they'd gotten the body cleaned up at the morgue. Woolf had to have this story by press time. Even on a diddly paper like the *Review*, that's gotta be around midnight. I mean, the papers are hittin' Dutton doorsteps by six.'

Daniel remembered the paperboy's delivery the

morning before as he and Alex still lay on her sofa, panting and trembling, and felt his cheeks heat. 'Right at five-thirty,' he agreed. 'So Jim Woolf somehow knew who Romney was before the cops did. That's more than a tip. That could be conspiracy.'

'You're right,' Chase said. 'Let's pick him up. Maybe the threat of real jail will loosen his tongue a little more. Daniel, you'll talk to this Marianne woman?'

'As soon as we're done. Have we heard from Koenig and Hatton?'

Chase nodded. 'Koenig called in about an hour and a half ago. He said they'd looked all night but couldn't find Crighton. They were going to hit the shelters during breakfast, then call it a night and go home and sleep and try again tonight.'

'Damn.' Daniel squared his jaw. 'I was really hoping to arrest that slimy SOB.'

'I watched the tape we made of Alex and McCrady again last night,' Ed said, 'and I was thinking. Alex remembered Crighton saying that Alicia "asked for it with her short shorts." Sounds like he might have known about the rape.'

'You're right,' Daniel said. 'He said Wade didn't kill Alicia, but of course he would. If Wade raped Alicia, that was probably what he confessed to Reverend Beardsley before he died, and maybe what he wrote in the letters to Bailey and Crighton.'

'I checked up on Crighton,' Luke said. 'After Alicia died and Crighton killed Alex's mother, Crighton went downhill fast. He had a good job before, but he's been MIA for almost thirteen years. No income taxes, no record of credit cards. Nothing.'

'Instead he's been living on the streets playing the flute for quarters,' Daniel said with contempt. 'And beating up poor old nuns.'

'Oh.' Ed shook his head hard. 'Flute. I was looking at the inventory of stuff we found at Bailey's house and it included one empty flute case. It looked really old, like it hadn't been used in years. Huge dust buildup in the case crevices and hinges, but the inside was clean, like it had just been opened. Did Bailey play the flute, too?'

Daniel frowned. 'I would've thought Alex would have mentioned that right away. I'll ask her.'

'Did you tell her about the hair?' Chase asked.

'Yeah, I did. On the way to the scene this morning I asked her what happened to all of Alicia's stuff. She said her aunt Kim had it shipped to Ohio and the boxes have been in storage ever since. But she also said that she and Bailey and Alicia shared clothes and makeup and hairbrushes, and Bailey and Alicia were sharing a bedroom at the time because Alicia was mad at Alex about something. That hair could still have come from Bailey's house recently.'

'I don't think so,' Ed said. 'If it had been tangled in a brush all this time, it would be kinked, but it's straight – and free of dust. It's been kept sealed up.'

'A souvenir of the rape,' Chase said slowly. 'Damn.'

'And, uh, there is one other thing.' Ed put a plastic bag on the table.

Daniel held it up to the light. 'A ring with a blue stone. Where did you find this?'

'In the bedroom Alex told us used to be hers, right under the window.'

'She stared at her hands when Gary Fulmore talked about the ring Alicia wore,' Daniel said quietly. 'Gary said it was on Alicia's hand when he wrapped her up, but Wanda in the sheriff's office said they found it in Fulmore's pocket.'

'If the ring was on her finger when she was discovered, the Dutton sheriff's office tampered with evidence,' Chase said, just as quietly.

Daniel sighed. 'I know. We need to know if that ring was on her finger when she was found or not. I'm going down to Dutton this morning to talk to Garth and his uncle about Sean Romney's death. I'll stop by and talk to the Porter boys while I'm there. They found Alicia. I'll see if I can find out if they remember a ring. Luke, will you process all the names Leigh got from the yearbooks?'

Luke looked at the printouts their clerk had produced the day before with a grimace. 'Where do you want me to start?'

'For now, focus on the public school where Simon, Wade, and Rhett graduated and the private school where Garth and I graduated. See if any of them have records or histories of violent behavior. See if any of them have been . . . I don't know, involved in anything weird.'

Luke gave him a dubious look. 'Weird. Okay.'

'And I'll finish calling all the potential targets I didn't talk to yesterday,' Chase said with a sigh. 'Maybe we can head him off at the pass before he bags another one.'

Dutton, Thursday, February 1, 8:35 A.M.

He stepped onto his front porch, bone-tired after another night of watching over Kate. He'd actually fallen asleep sometime after 4:00 a.m. When he'd woken, the sun was shining and Kate was pulling out of her driveway to go to work. She'd nearly seen him, and then he would have had to explain. Given the three dead women, he could probably just say he was worried, but Kate was too smart for that. She'd suspect more.

This had to be over soon. One way or the other. His wife met him at the door, her eyes red from weeping, and his heart started to race. 'What happened?'

'Your uncle Rob's here. He's been waiting for you since six. Sean's dead.'

'What? *Sean's* dead? When? How?'

She looked at him, her lips trembling. 'Who did *you* expect to be dead?'

He hung his head, too exhausted to think. 'Kate.'

She let out a quiet breath. 'Rob's in the library.'

His uncle sat by the window, his face gray and haggard. 'Where have you been?'

He took the chair next to Rob. 'Watching over Kate. What happened?'

'They found him in an alley.' His voice broke. 'They couldn't even identify him at first. There was too much blood on his face. The police said they'd been looking for Sean, that they'd put his picture on the news. My grandson, on the news.'

'Why were they looking for him?'

Rob's eyes filled with rage. 'Because,' he gritted out, 'they said they had proof he was helping the person who killed Claudia Silva and Janet Bowie and Gemma Martin.'

'And Lisa Woolf,' his wife added from the library doorway. 'I just saw it on CNN.'

Rob turned to him, bitterness in every line of his face. 'And Lisa Woolf. So you tell me what you know. And you tell me *now*.'

He shook his head. 'I don't know anything.'

Rob lurched to his feet. '*You lie!* I know you *lie*.' He pointed a trembling finger. 'You wire a hundred thousand dollars to an offshore account Tuesday night. Then yesterday I get a visitor in the bank, checking out Rhett Porter's safe-deposit box.'

He felt the color drain from his face. Still, he lifted his chin. 'So?'

'*So*, when he left he said, "Tell Garth I have it." What does he mean?'

'You paid someone a hundred thousand dollars?' His wife's expression was one of stunned shock. 'We don't have that kind of money, Garth.'

'He took it from the kids' college fund,' Rob said coldly.

His wife's mouth dropped open. 'You sonofa*bitch*. I have taken a lot from you over the years, but now you steal from your own *children*?'

It was unraveling. All of it. 'He threatened Kate.'

'Who?' Rob demanded.

'Whoever's killing all these women. He threatened Kate and Rhett. So I paid to keep Kate alive. The next morning Rhett was dead.' He tried to swallow, but his mouth was too dry. 'And to keep Kate safe, I'll pay again.'

'You will not,' his wife screeched. 'My God, Garth, are you *crazy*?'

'No,' he said quietly. 'I'm not crazy. Rhett is dead.'

'And you think this guy killed him,' Rob said calmly. 'Like he killed Sean.'

'I didn't know about Sean,' he said. 'I swear. He didn't send Sean's picture.'

Rob lowered himself to the chair. 'He sent you pictures,' he said thinly.

'Yes. Of Kate. And Rhett.' He hesitated. 'And of others.'

His wife slowly sat on the loveseat. 'We have to tell the police,' she said.

He laughed bitterly. 'That we definitely will not do.'

'He could come after our children. Have you considered that?'

'In the last five minutes? Yes. Before I heard about Sean, no.'

'You know why this killer is doing all this,' Rob said coldly. 'You will tell me and you will tell me now.'

He shook his head. 'No, I won't.'

Rob's eyes narrowed. 'And why not?'

'Because I don't know who killed Rhett.'

'Garth, what's going on here?' his wife whispered. 'Why can't we go to the police?'

'I'm not going to tell you. Believe me, you're safer not knowing.'

'You don't care about our safety. You've gotten yourself sucked into some mess that involves *us*. Me and *your children*. So don't give me that . . . *bullshit*. Tell me or I'm walking out of here and going to the police right now.'

She was serious. She would go to the police. 'Do you remember Jared O'Brien?'

'He disappeared,' Rob said, his voice flat and detached.

'Well, yeah. He probably got drunk and ran himself off a road one night and . . .' She went pale. 'Like Rhett. Oh my God. Garth, what have you done?'

He didn't answer. Couldn't answer.

'Whatever it was, someone's coming after you because of it,' Rob said. 'If it was only you, I'd let them. But by God, this is destroying my family. We all know Sean wasn't as bright as the rest of you. He used him, *used him* and *killed him* to send *you* a message.' He stood. 'No more, Garth.'

He looked up at his uncle. 'What are you going to do?'

'I don't know yet.'

'Are you going to the police?' his wife asked, crying now.

Rob scoffed. 'Not in this town.'

Garth stood. Looked his uncle in the eye. 'I wouldn't say anything if I were you, Rob.'

Rob's eyes narrowed to slits. 'And why not?'

'You have a few hours? Actually, it would only take me a few minutes. A few well-placed calls and you'll have a bank examiner down your shorts so fast . . .'

Rob's pale face mottled with angry color. 'You have the nerve to threaten *me*?'

'I have the nerve to do anything I need to do,' he said calmly.

His wife covered her mouth with her hand. 'I don't believe this. This is a nightmare.'

He nodded. 'True. But if you keep your mouth shut and your head down, we just might live to wake up when it's over.'

Atlanta, Thursday, February 1, 9:15 A.M.

The little room with the two-way mirror was quiet as they sat waiting for Dr McCrady. Alex propped her elbow on the table, leaned her cheek on her fist, and watched Hope color. 'At least she's using other colors now,' she murmured.

Meredith looked up, a sad smile on her face. 'Black and blue. We make progress.'

Something in Alex snapped. 'But not enough. We have to push her, Mer.'

'Alex,' Meredith warned.

'You didn't see them pull that woman from the ditch this morning,' Alex shot back, her voice shaking with fury. 'I did. My God. Including Sheila, five women are dead. This has to stop. Hope, I need to talk to you and I need you to listen.' She tugged at Hope's chin until the child's hand stilled and wide gray eyes looked up at her. 'Hope, did you see who hurt your mommy? Please. Sweetheart, I need to know.'

Hope looked away and Alex tugged her face back, desperation clawing at her throat. 'Hope, Sister Anne told me how smart you are, how many words you know, and how well you talk. I need you to talk to me now. You're smart enough to know your mommy's gone. I can't find her.' Alex's voice broke. 'You have to talk to me so I can find her. Did you see the man who took your mommy away?'

Slowly Hope nodded. 'It was dark,' she whispered, her voice tiny.

'Were you in bed?'

Hope wagged her head no, misery filling her eyes. 'I snuck out.'

'Why?'

'I heard the man.'

'The man that hurt her?'

'He left and she cried.'

'Did he hit her?'

'He left and she cried,' she said again. 'And played.'

'With toys?' Alex asked.

'The flute.' The words were only a breath.

Alex frowned. 'Your mom played a big shiny horn. That's different than a flute.'

Hope's mouth set stubbornly. 'The flute.'

Meredith put a blank piece of paper in front of Hope. 'Draw it for me, baby.'

Hope picked up her black crayon and drew a round face in a childish style. She added eyes, nose, and a thin rectangle that went sideways from where the mouth would have gone. She then chose a silver crayon from the box and colored the thin rectangle.

She looked up at Alex. 'Flute,' she said.

'It is indeed a flute,' Meredith said. 'That's a good picture, Hope.'

Alex hugged Hope. 'It's a wonderful picture. What happened to the flute?'

Hope's eyes dropped again. 'She played the song.'

'Your pa-paw's song. Then what happened?'

'We runned.' Her words were barely audible.

Alex's heart was thumping hard. 'Where did you run?'

'The woods.' Hope whispered it, then scrunched into the smallest space she could.

Alex lifted Hope to her lap and rocked her. 'In the woods, were you with Mommy?'

Hope began to cry, with a low mewling sound that tore at Alex's heart. 'I'm here, Hope. I won't let anyone hurt you. Why did you run to the woods?'

'The man.'

'Where did you hide?'

'The tree.'

'Up a tree?'

'Under the leaves.'

Alex drew a breath. 'Mommy covered you with leaves?'

'Mama.' It was a frightened little plea.

'He hurt your mama?' Alex whispered. 'The man hurt your mama?'

'She runned.' Hope's hands clutched Alex's blouse frantically. 'He was coming, so she runned. He g-g-got her and he hit her and hit her and—' Hope was rocking as she chanted the words. Now that she was talking she seemed unable to stop.

Unable to listen to any more, Alex cupped the back of Hope's head and pressed Hope's mouth into her shoulder while the child sobbed. Meredith's arms came around her and they sat, listening to Hope's choked sobs. 'Bailey hid Hope so he wouldn't find her,' Alex whispered. 'I wonder how long you stayed under those leaves, baby.'

Hope said nothing, just rocked and sobbed until finally she quieted, breathing hard, her little forehead covered in sweat, her cheeks drenched. The front of Alex's blouse was soaking wet and Hope still clutched the fabric in her hands. Alex shifted her, prying her fists away, cradling her.

The door behind them opened and Daniel and Mary McCrady came in, looking sober. 'You heard?' Alex said, and Daniel nodded.

'I came into the back room when she started drawing the flute. I called Mary.'

'I was already on my way for our session.' Mary brushed her hand over Hope's hair. 'That was hard, Hope, but I'm so proud of you. So's your aunt Alex.'

Hope burrowed her face into Alex's chest and Alex's arms tightened around her protectively. 'Can she be done for now?'

'Yes,' Mary said, sympathy on her face. 'You hold her for a while. But let's not wait too long, okay? I think we might be able to get somewhere with the artist now.'

'A little longer,' Alex insisted. She looked up at Daniel, whose eyes were resting on her in an almost palpable caress. Then he spread his big hand over Hope's thin back in a gesture so tender it stole her breath.

'You did well, Hope,' he said softly. 'But, honey, can I ask you one more question? It's important,' he added, more for her own benefit, Alex thought, than for Hope's.

Hope nodded, her face still pressed against Alex's chest.

'What happened to your mommy's flute?'

Hope shuddered. 'In the leaves,' she said, her voice muffled.

'Okay, sweetheart,' Daniel said. 'That's all I needed to know. I'm going to have Ed go over that area in the woods again. I'll be back in a little while.'

Atlanta, Thursday, February 1, 9:15 A.M.

Daniel had barely hung up after talking to Ed when Leigh appeared in his doorway.

'Daniel, you have a visitor. Michael Bowie, Janet's brother. He's not happy.'

'Where is Chase? He's supposed to be handling communications.'

'Chase is in a meeting with the captain. You want me to tell Bowie you're not here?'

Daniel shook his head. 'No. I'll come talk to him.'

Michael Bowie looked like exactly what he was – a man whose sister had been viciously murdered days before. He stopped pacing when Daniel stopped at the counter. 'Daniel.'

'Michael. What can I do for you?'

'You can tell me you've found the man who killed my sister.'

Daniel steeled his spine. 'No, I can't. We're following leads.'

'You've been *saying* that for *days*,' Michael gritted.

'I'm sorry. Have you thought of anyone who hated Janet enough to do this?'

Michael's ferocity seemed to wilt. 'No. At times Janet was selfish and arrogant. Sometimes she could be devious and just plain mean. But nobody hated her. She and Claudia and Gemma . . . They were just girls. They didn't do anything to deserve this.'

'I'm not saying they deserved this, Michael,' Daniel said gently. 'But someone has targeted Janet and the girls she knew.' *To be pawns in a bigger game.* 'Anything you can remember. Any person she'd annoyed.'

Michael made a frustrated noise. 'You want a *list*? The girls were spoiled and probably pissed people off every day of their lives. But *this*. They did nothing to deserve this.'

Michael was grieving, Daniel knew. That the girls hadn't deserved their fate was a break in logic he couldn't yet absorb. He would, in time. Victims' families usually did.

'I can't tell you what you want to hear, Michael. Not yet. But we will catch him.'

Michael nodded stiffly. 'You'll call me?'

'As soon as I have news to share. I promise you that.'

Chapter Twenty

Atlanta, Thursday, February 1, 10:15 A.M.

'I can take her, Alex,' Meredith said, looking up from her laptop. 'You haven't moved from that position in an hour. Your arms have to be breaking by now.'

Still sitting at the table in the room with the two-way mirror, Alex pulled Hope a little closer. 'She's not that heavy.' Even asleep, Hope grabbed at Alex's shirt as if she was afraid Alex would leave her. 'I should have been with her all this time,' Alex murmured.

'Ideally, yes,' Meredith said logically. 'But this is far from ideal. You've been looking for Bailey. You needed to see Fulmore and all the other people, so stop feeling guilty.'

But as she held Hope, Alex knew it was more than simple guilt. She'd been quick to accept the responsibility for Hope's physical care and safety, but until Hope had sobbed against her, she hadn't opened her heart to this little girl who'd needed her. She hadn't opened her heart to many people over the years.

Certainly not to Richard, and if she was honest, not even to Bailey. Again, she'd been quick to offer help to get Bailey into rehab, but she hadn't offered her heart.

Maybe she hadn't known how. Deep down she was afraid she still didn't. But then the door opened and Daniel came in, and every dark and heavy thing inside her heart lightened at the sight of him. Maybe there was hope for her after all. It was a light in the midst of all the darkness.

'Is it time for Hope to go with Mary?' she asked softly, but he shook his head.

'Not yet. I didn't mean to make you wait here so long. There's a sofa in the break room. Hope can sleep there until Mary comes back.'

Alex started to rise, Hope in her arms, but Daniel stopped her. 'I'll take her.' And he did, holding Hope much like he'd held Riley the night before. Hope didn't wake, though she snuggled against him, and Alex was hit with a wave of longing so strong it almost knocked her over.

This is what I want. This child. This man. She stood unsteadily, a wave of panic following in the wake of the longing. *What if he doesn't want the same? What if I can't give him what he needs?*

Meredith was watching her with a frown. 'Come on.' She put her arm around Alex's shoulders as they followed Daniel.

Daniel stopped at the sofa in the break room, Hope nestled on his shoulder. He gently rocked from side to side, his brows bunched, his mind obviously somewhere else. Alex was certain he didn't realize what a picture he made, strong golden-haired man holding the small golden-haired child.

He settled Hope on the sofa and shrugged out of his jacket to cover her, then glanced at Alex and gave her that half smile. 'Sorry, my mind wandered.'

'Where did it go?' she said, her voice low.

'To the day your mother died.' He slid his arm around her waist and walked her to a table by the coffee machine. 'I need to talk to someone who talked to your mother after she found Alicia.' He pulled out chairs for her and Meredith.

'That would have been Sheriff Loomis, Craig, the coroner, and me,' Alex said, sitting down.

'And me,' Meredith added.

Daniel's hands stilled on the coffeepot. 'You talked to Kathy Tremaine that day?'

'Several times,' Meredith said. 'Aunt Kathy called that morning to say Alicia was missing and my mom packed her suitcase. Her car wasn't too reliable, so she decided to fly.' Meredith frowned. 'My mom was guilty about that decision until the day she died.'

'Why?' Alex asked and Meredith shrugged.

'Her flight kept getting delayed because of storms. If she'd driven, she would have arrived hours earlier and your mom would have still been alive. And if Aunt Kathy had been alive, you would never have taken those pills.'

'I wish Aunt Kim were here to know the truth,' Alex said sadly.

Meredith patted her hand. 'I know. Anyway, Aunt Kathy called later, hysterical, and that's when I started talking to her. Mom had left for the airport already and back then nobody had cell phones. I was the go-between. Mom called from a pay phone at the airport every half hour and I'd tell her what Aunt Kathy had said. The first time I talked to Aunt Kathy, she'd gotten a call from a neighbor saying some boys had found a body.'

'The Porter boys,' Daniel said.

Meredith nodded. 'Aunt Kathy was leaving to check it out.'

'And that's when she found Alicia,' Alex murmured.

'When did you talk to her again, Meredith?' Daniel asked.

'When she came home from finding Alicia, before she went to identify the body. She was . . . past hysterical. She was sobbing, crying.'

'Do you remember what she said?'

Meredith frowned. 'She was crying that her baby had been left in the rain.'

Daniel frowned as well. 'It didn't rain the night before. There was thunder and lightning, but no rain. I checked the weather report after we talked to Gary Fulmore.'

Meredith shrugged. 'That's what she said. "Just asleep in the rain." Over and over.'

Alex tensed, remembering the phrase. 'No, that's not what she said.'

Daniel sat beside her, looking her square in the eye. 'What did she say, Alex?'

'When Mama came back from identifying Alicia, Craig gave her a sedative, then went to work. I put her to bed. She was crying so hard, and so was I . . . so I climbed in bed with her and just held on.' Alex pictured her mother lying in bed, a steady stream of tears running down her face. 'She kept saying, "A sheep and a ring." That's all she had to identify Alicia because her face was so destroyed. "Just a sheep and a ring."'

Daniel's eyes narrowed, and she saw the flash of triumph. 'All right then.'

Alex looked down at her hands. 'Alicia had a ring. So did I. Our birthstones. Mama gave them to us for our birthday.' Her mouth curved bitterly. 'Sweet sixteen we were.'

'Where is your ring, Alex?' he asked softly, and her stomach turned over.

'I don't know. I don't remember.' Her heart was suddenly racing. 'I must have lost it.' She looked up, studied his eyes, and knew. 'You know where it is.'

'Yes. It was in your old room. On the floor, under your window.'

A sense of dread stole inside her, darkening everything. Inside her mind, thunder rolled and a single voice screamed. *Be quiet. Close the door*. 'That's it, isn't it? What I don't want to remember.'

His arm tightened around her. 'We'll find out,' he promised. 'Don't worry.'

But she did.

Atlanta, Thursday, February 1, 10:55 A.M.

Daniel stopped by the team room, where Luke pored over a stack of spreadsheets.

'A sheep and a ring,' Daniel said with a nod.

Luke looked up, his eyes narrowed. 'That sounds nasty, Daniel.'

'But it's not.' He sat down at the table and pushed a stack of yearbooks out of the way. 'Alex's mother said it the day Alicia died. She meant because Alicia's face was smashed, she could only identify her by her sheep tattoo and the ring on her finger. And she saw Alicia before the cops got there.'

Luke frowned. 'Alicia had a sheep tattoo?'

'On her ankle. They all did – Bailey, Alicia, and Alex.'

'And a ring on her finger. So now you have independent corroboration that Fulmore was telling the truth,' Luke said. 'And that the Dutton sheriff's office wasn't.'

Daniel nodded grimly. 'Looks like. So what have you found?'

Luke pushed a sheet of paper across the table. 'I've compiled the names of every male to graduate the same year as Simon, a year ahead and a year behind, from the public and the private schools.'

Daniel scanned the list. 'How many?'

'After we cut minorities and dead people?' Luke asked. 'Roughly two hundred.'

Daniel blinked. 'Shit. Do all two hundred still live in Dutton?'

'No. Culling out everyone that's moved away leaves only about fifty.'

'Better,' Daniel said. 'But still too many to show to Hope.'

'Why would you show them to Hope?'

'Because she saw the man who abducted her mother. I have to assume whoever took Bailey did so because of the letter she got from her brother, Wade, or else Beardsley wouldn't be missing now.'

'That makes sense. But then what? I hate to be a broken record, but we're trying to solve the murders of four women left in ditches. How are you going to connect whoever took Bailey to whoever's killing the women?'

'You assume it's not the same person.'

Luke blinked. 'I guess I did.'

'And you're probably right. Whoever took Bailey doesn't want anyone to know about the rapes and the pictures. Whoever's killing the women wants us to focus on Alicia Tremaine. I don't know how I'll connect them. All I know is that this SOB doesn't leave anything behind on the body or at the scene that can identify him. If I can find out who took Bailey, something else might shake out.'

'Fair enough,' Luke said. 'So you want me to get these fifty photos down to five or six so we can show them to Hope. You're going to have her talk to an artist, right? If she can give the artist some basic description, we can cherry-pick from the fifty.'

Daniel stood up. 'I'll tell Mary to get you whatever they come up with. I've got to get down to Dutton to talk to Rob Davis and Garth. But first I have to call the SA. Fulmore was telling the truth about the ring and he didn't hit Alicia while she was alive, so the man is not guilty of murder. Abuse of a corpse, but not murder.'

'Chloe's gonna love you,' Luke said, shaking his head. 'Not.'

'As long as—' Daniel stopped himself short. *As long as Alex does*, he'd been about to say. But that was premature. Maybe. But he was still warm from the . . . rightness of holding her in one arm and a little girl in the other. It was certainly more than he'd ever had before. It could end up being nothing more than good sex.

Really, really, really good sex.

But he didn't think so, and Daniel was a man to trust his instincts.

'As long as what?' Luke asked, one side of his mouth quirking up.

'As long as Chloe does the right thing by Fulmore,' Daniel said quietly. 'But that's not the biggest thing. If

Fulmore is telling the truth about that ring, then the Dutton police planted evidence.'

'Chase already gave Chloe the heads-up on Frank Loomis,' Luke said.

'I know. They're going to open a formal investigation.'

'Are you okay with that? I mean, the guy was your friend.'

'No, I'm not okay with that,' Daniel snapped, 'but if he planted evidence, he sent an innocent man to prison for thirteen years and let a killer walk free, and I'm even less okay with that.'

Luke held up his hands. 'Sorry.'

Daniel realized he was grinding his teeth and forced himself to relax. 'No, I'm sorry. I shouldn't bark at you. Thanks for all of this. I gotta go.'

'Wait.' Luke pushed two yearbooks across the table, one stacked on the other, opened to the senior graduation pictures. 'Yours and your sister's. I thought you might like to have them.'

Daniel looked at the photo on the bottom row and his heart hurt. Susannah Vartanian maintained a cool, sophisticated air in her senior picture, but he knew she'd been silently miserable. He needed to call her before the press got wind of the rapes Talia Scott was investigating. He owed her that much. He owed her a great deal more.

Atlanta, Thursday, February 1, 11:15 A.M.

Most likely to be president of the United States. Daniel traced a finger over his senior picture in his high school yearbook. His classmates had voted him so because he'd been so serious and sober. So studious and sincere. He'd been the class president and captain of the debate team. He'd lettered in football and baseball every single year. He'd had straight As. His teachers had seen him as having integrity. Ethics. The son of a judge.

Who'd been a sonofabitch.

Who'd been the reason Daniel had pushed himself so hard. He'd known his father was not all everyone believed. He'd overheard the whispered conversations between Judge Arthur Vartanian and the late-night visitors to his office on the first floor of the house in which Daniel had grown up. He knew where his father had hidden things all over their old house. He knew his father kept a whole cache of unregistered guns and stacks of cash. He'd always suspected his father had been on the take, but he'd never been able to prove it.

He'd lived his life trying to make up for being Arthur Vartanian's son.

His eyes moved to the other yearbook and stared sadly at his sister Susannah's picture. She lived her life trying to forget she was Arthur Vartanian's daughter. She'd been voted most likely to succeed and she had, but at what cost? Susannah harbored secret pain she'd share with no one . . . *even me. Especially me.*

He'd gone away to college, then he'd gone away to the police academy. Then after his father had burned Simon's pictures, he'd just gone away. And left Susannah in that house. With Simon.

Daniel swallowed. And Simon had hurt her. Daniel knew it was true. He was afraid he knew how. He had to find out. With fingers that trembled, he dialed Susannah's number at work. He knew all her numbers by heart. After five rings, he heard her voice.

'You've reached the voicemail of Susannah Vartanian. If this is urgent, please—'

Daniel hung up and called her assistant. He knew the assistant's number by heart, too. 'Hi, this is Agent Vartanian. I need to speak to Susannah. It's urgent.'

The assistant hesitated. 'She's not available, sir.'

'Wait,' Daniel said before the woman hung up. 'Tell her I have to speak to her. Tell her it's a matter of life and death.'

'I'll tell her.'

A minute later, Daniel heard Susannah's voice again, live this time. 'Hello, Daniel.' But there was no joy in her greeting. Only wary distance.

His heart hurt. 'Suze. How are you?'

'Busy. Being out of the office for so long, I had stacks of work waiting for me when I got back. You know how that goes.'

They'd buried their parents, but immediately after

the funeral Susannah had flown back to New York and he hadn't talked to her since. 'I know. Have you seen the news from down here?'

'Yes. Three women, found dead in ditches. I'm sorry, Daniel.'

'Four, actually. We just found the fourth. Jim Woolf's little sister.'

'Oh, no.' He heard pain and surprise in her voice. 'I'm sorry, Daniel.'

'We have something the news hasn't reported yet, but will soon. Suze, it's the pictures.'

He heard her exhale. 'The pictures.'

'Yes. We've identified all the girls.'

'Really?' She sounded truly shocked. 'How?'

Daniel drew a breath. 'Alicia Tremaine was one of them. She was the girl murdered thirteen years ago, the one all these new murders are copying. Sheila Cunningham was another. She died in what we're supposed to think was a robbery of Presto's Pizza two nights ago. Some of the others Alicia's sister has identified.' He'd tell her about Alex a different time. This call would not be one either he or Susannah would want to remember. 'We've started interviewing them. They're all around thirty years old now.' *Same as you,* he wanted to say, but didn't. 'They're all telling the same story. They fell asleep in their cars. When they woke they were fully clothed, and—'

'And holding a whiskey bottle,' she finished woodenly.

His throat closed. 'Oh, Suze. Why didn't you tell me?'

'Because you were *gone*,' she said, her voice suddenly angry and harsh. 'You were *gone*, Daniel, and Simon *wasn't*.'

'You knew it was Simon?'

When she spoke again, she was back in control. 'Oh, yes. He made sure of it.' Then she sighed. 'You don't have *all* the pictures, Daniel.'

'I don't understand.' But he was very afraid he did. 'Are you saying there was one of you?' She said nothing and he had his answer. 'What happened to it?' he asked.

'Simon showed it to me. He told me to stay out of his affairs. He told me I had to go to sleep sometime.'

Daniel closed his eyes. Tried to speak past the constriction in his chest. 'Suze.'

'I was afraid,' she said, speaking now in a logical, cool voice, and he thought of Alex. 'So I stayed out of his way.'

'What affairs of his had you been in before?'

She hesitated. 'I really need to go now. I'm late for court. Bye, Daniel.'

Daniel carefully hung up the phone, wiped the moisture from his eyes, then got up and prepared his mind to talk to Jim and Marianne Woolf. Jim would be grieving his sister, but grief or no grief, Daniel was going to get some answers.

Atlanta, Thursday, February 1, 1:30 P.M.

Alex stood at the glass, Meredith beside her. On the other side of the glass, Mary McCrady had relaxed Hope so that she was actually speaking in full sentences.

'Maybe she was finally ready to talk,' Alex said.

Beside her, Meredith nodded. 'You helped.'

'I could have made things worse.'

'But you didn't. Every child is different. I'm sure Hope would have been ready to talk soon either way. But she needed to feel safe and loved and you did that.'

'I should have made her feel safe and loved before.'

'Maybe *you* weren't ready before.'

Alex turned her head to study Meredith's profile. 'Am I now?'

'Only you can answer that, but if the look on your face was any indication . . . I'd say yes.' She chuckled softly. 'Heck, if he hadn't looked back at you the same way, I might have wrestled you for him.'

'It was that obvious?'

Meredith met her eyes. 'In the dark wearing a blindfold. You got it bad, girl.' She turned back to the glass. 'At least Hope's talking to the artist this time. Between her description and the pictures Mary got from that guy who works with Daniel, we might at least get a lead on who did this.'

Alex drew a breath. 'Even if we never get Bailey back.'

'We may not, Alex. You need to start coming to grips with that.'

'I am. I have to. For Hope.' Her cell phone jingled in her purse and Alex grabbed it, frowning at the caller ID. It was an Atlanta number, but no one she knew. 'Hello?'

'Alex, this is Sissy, Bailey's friend. I couldn't talk to you before. Not on my phone. I had to wait until I could use a pay phone. Bailey told me that if anything happened to her that I should talk to you.'

'Then why didn't you?' Alex asked, more sharply than she'd intended.

'Because I have a daughter,' Sissy hissed. 'And I'm scared.'

'Has someone threatened you?'

Her laugh was bitter. 'Does a letter under my front door saying "Don't say a word or we'll kill you and your daughter" count?'

'Did you contact the police?'

'Hell no. Look, I told Bailey to pack her things and move in with me. She was going to, the next day. She called me Thursday night, said she had their things packed and loaded in her car. She said she'd see me the next day. But she never came to work.'

'So you went to the house and found Hope in the closet.'

'Yes. The house was trashed and Bailey was gone. There's one other thing. Bailey told me that she'd mailed you a letter. That I was supposed to tell you that.'

'A letter. Okay.' Alex's mind was spinning. 'Why didn't she just come that night?'

'She said she was meeting someone. That she'd come when she finished.'

'You don't know who she was meeting?'

Sissy hesitated. 'She was seeing a man. I think he might have been married. She said she needed to say good-bye. I have to go now.'

Alex looked at Meredith, who was impatiently waiting. 'Bailey mailed me a letter the day before she disappeared.'

'Who's been getting your mail?'

'One of my friends from the hospital.' She hit Letta's speed dial on her cell phone. 'Letta, it's Alex. I have a favor to ask.'

Dutton, Thursday, February 1, 2:30 P.M.

Daniel's conversation with the Woolfs had not gone well. Jim Woolf had lawyered up and Marianne had just slammed the door in his face. He'd gotten back to his car when his phone buzzed. 'Vartanian.'

'Leigh told me you called,' Chase said. 'I've been in a meeting with the captain for the last two hours. What's the news?'

'I went to Sean Romney's house and interviewed his mother. Apparently Sean was below average in cognitive ability as the result of a birth defect. He was too trusting and willing to please, according to Mrs Romney. Because of this, she kept closer tabs on him than her other kids. Guess what she found in his room two days ago?'

'I have no idea, but you're going to tell me right now, aren't you?'

Chase sounded cranky and Daniel guessed his meeting with the captain had gone even less well than his visit with Marianne Woolf.

'A disposable cell phone. It wasn't in his room and the cops didn't find it on his body, but Mrs Romney had written down the numbers in his call log. The number for his incoming calls matches the call Jim Woolf got Sunday morning.'

'Yes,' Chase hissed. 'Does it match any of the incomings on the cell you found on the pizza parlor guy, Lester Jackson?'

'Unfortunately no, but we finally have a solid connection.'

'I wish you'd told me this before I went into my meeting,' Chase grumbled.

'Sorry,' Daniel said. 'How bad is it?'

'They wanted you off the case, but I convinced them otherwise,' Chase said dryly.

Daniel let out a breath. 'Thanks. I owe you.' His phone beeped and he glanced at the caller ID. 'It's Ed. I gotta go.' He switched calls. 'Hey, Ed. What do you know?'

'Lots,' Ed said, clearly pleased. 'Come to Bailey's and you'll know lots, too.'

'I'm just leaving the Woolfs', so I'm not far. I'll see you in twenty.'

Atlanta, Thursday, February 1, 4:50 P.M.

'Alex. Wake up.'

Alex twisted out of sleep, a warm mouth meeting hers. 'Umm.' She kissed him back, then leaned back against the sofa in the break room where she'd drifted off. 'You're back.' She blinked her eyes open. 'What time is it?'

'Almost five. I have a team meeting, but I wanted to find you first.'

Kneeling on one knee next to the little sofa, he gave her an appraising glance. 'Did you get your clothes back from the bungalow?'

'No. Shannon, the agent who was there last night, said they'd been slashed.' She shrugged. 'So I went shopping.'

He frowned. 'I thought—'

She patted his cheek. 'Relax. Chase had one of the agents "accompany" me.'

'Which one?'

'Pete Haywood.'

Daniel smiled, relieved. 'Nobody messes with Pete.'

'I should think not.' The man had been bigger than Daniel and built like a tank.

'Nobody tried anything?'

'Nobody even looked at me cross-eyed.' She struggled to sit up and he easily lifted her. 'I got a call from my friend Letta.' Alex had called him with Sissy's revelation earlier in the afternoon. 'She said there was no letter from Bailey.'

'It should have arrived already.' His brow creased. 'How long since you moved?'

'A little more than a year. Why?'

'The post office only forwards mail for about a year. Did Bailey know you'd moved?'

'No.' She rolled her eyes. 'It's probably at Richard's house. I'll call him.'

'Where are Hope and Meredith?'

'Back at the safe house. Hope was exhausted after she and Mary were done, so Meredith took them both back. Hope was able to pick out two of the pictures, then Mary showed her a bunch of different hats and asked Hope to pick out one that matched the hat she drew on Bailey's assailant the other night. Hope picked a hat just like the one they wear in the Dutton sheriff's office.'

He nodded soberly. 'I know. I stopped by the team room on my way to find you.' He rose and held out his hand. 'Come. We need to talk to you.' He pulled her to her feet and, sliding his arm around her waist, walked her to a conference room with a big table. Around the table were Luke, Chase, Mary, and a woman she hadn't yet met. 'I think you know everyone except Talia Scott.'

Talia was a little woman with a sweet smile. 'It's nice to meet you, Alex.'

'Talia's been interviewing all the women in the pictures.'

And Alex could see the day had taken its toll. Although Talia's smile was sweet, her eyes were weary. 'It's nice to meet you, too.' She looked at the table and saw the two pictures Hope had identified.

Garth Davis, the mayor, and Randy Mansfield, the police deputy.

'What did they say when you arrested them?'

Chase shook his head. 'We haven't arrested them.'

Alex's mouth fell open in disbelief, then anger started to rise. 'And why not?'

Daniel smoothed his hand over her back. 'That's what we wanted to talk to you about. We don't know which of them abducted Bailey. Maybe both.'

'So arrest them both and sort it out later,' she said from between gritted teeth.

'At this point,' Chase said patiently, 'it's the word of a four-year-old against two men who are respected in the community. We need evidence before we can bring them in.'

He said the words as if she were four years old herself. 'This is *insane*. Two men can abduct a woman and beat her head in and you won't do *anything*?' She whipped her gaze up to Daniel. 'You were there at the pizza parlor. Garth Davis walked up to our table and a minute later, Hope's smearing sauce all over her face like blood.' The memory had surfaced as soon as she'd seen the picture. 'Garth Davis kidnapped Bailey. Why is he walking free? Why haven't you even brought him in for questioning?'

'Alex—' Daniel started, but she shook her head.

'And Mansfield . . . he's a cop. He has a badge and a gun. You can't just let him roam free while you figure all this out. Everything he's ever done has to be suspect. I mean, he shot the guy who tried to kill me after the guy killed Sheila Cunningham. Isn't that enough *evidence*? What does it take to get arrested in this goddamn state?'

'Alex.' Daniel's voice was sharp, then he sighed. 'Just show it to her, Ed.'

Ed moved a box filled with books, revealing a silver flute. Alex's mouth dropped open. 'You found the flute Bailey was playing.'

Ed nodded. 'We sent out a team with metal detectors and found it behind a fallen log. It had been buried under about a half inch of dirt and a pile of leaves.'

'Where Bailey hid Hope.' She glared at them all, her breath hitching in her chest. 'While those men beat her senseless, until her *blood* soaked the *ground*.'

'Alex.' Daniel bit her name out. 'If you can't hold it together, you'll have to leave.'

She stopped, still furious, but now embarrassed as well. Chase only talked to her like a four-year-old. Daniel treated her like one. But perhaps he'd had a right. She was closer to hysteria than she'd ever been.

She drew on her control and nodded. 'I'm sorry,' she said coolly. 'I'll hold it together.'

Daniel sighed again. 'Alex, please. The flute isn't what we wanted you to see.'

Ed held out a pair of gloves and obediently Alex pulled them on. Then her eyes widened when he handed her a piece of paper, creased where it had been folded longways multiple times like a child's fan.

'Ed found the note inside the flute,' Daniel said. 'It's from Wade to Bailey.' He held a chair out for her and she sank into it, her eyes fixed to the page as she read aloud.

'Dear Bailey, after years of trying, I've finally succeeded. I've been hit and I'm dying. Don't worry. There's a chaplain here and I've done my confession. But I don't believe God will forgive me. I haven't forgiven myself. Years ago you asked me if I killed Alicia. The answer was no then and it still is. But I did other things and so did Dad. I think some you guessed. Some you never will and that's for the best.

'Some of the things that I did, I did with others. They won't want anyone to know. At first there were seven of us, then six, then five. When I die, there will still be four men who share the secret. They live in fear and distrust, always watching each other, wondering who will be the first to fall. The first to tell.

'I'm enclosing a key. Do not carry it with you. Put it somewhere safe. If you're ever threatened, tell them you'll turn it over to the authorities. But not to the police. Not in

Dutton, anyway. The key will unlock a secret that some of the four would pay to keep and some would kill to keep. Two have already been killed to keep the secret.

'I won't tell you the names of the four, because you'd feel you had to report them. Once you go down that road, you'd be as dead as me. Them knowing that you have the key will be the only thing that will keep you alive.

'I know you've stayed in the house, waiting for Dad to come back. I've told you before, he won't. He's not capable of the goodness you want him to have. If you see him, give him the other letter. If you don't, then burn it. Then let Dad go. Let him kill himself on booze and drugs, but don't let him drag you down with him. Leave the house. Leave Dutton. And for God's sake, don't trust anyone.

'Least of all me. I've never earned it, although God knows I've died trying.

'Take Hope and leave Dutton and never look back. Promise me that. And promise me you'll have a good life. Find Alex. She's the only family you have left now. I never told you before, but I love you.'

Alex drew a breath. '*Lt. Wade Crighton, United States Army.*' She looked up. 'He sent her a key. Do you think that's what Bailey sent to me?'

Daniel sat in the chair next to her. 'We think so. Three of the four victims this week were found with keys tied to one of their toes. Now we know why.'

'Do you think the keys tied to their toes are the same as Wade's key?'

'No. The keys we found this week are brand-new.

It's a sign, a message. Like the hair he tied around their toes.'

'Alicia's hair.' She stared at the note, trying to focus. 'He says there were seven. Two died before him. Both killed to keep the secret. But Simon died in Philadelphia.'

'Wade didn't know that when he wrote the letter,' Daniel said. 'He died a few weeks before Simon. He thought Simon was still dead from the first time.'

'So they all thought that Simon's first "death" was done by one of them,' she murmured. '*They live in fear and distrust*. So one of the dead men he's talking about is Simon. Who is the other?'

'We don't know yet,' Chase said, 'but we have an idea of three of the remaining four.'

'Garth Davis and Randy Mansfield,' she said. 'And I guess Rhett Porter would have been the third.'

'That means we still have to identify two,' Daniel said. 'One living, one dead.'

'What will you do?'

'Try to use the two we know to turn on the one we don't,' Chase said. 'But in the meantime, we still don't know who's behind all of this.'

'It's revenge,' Daniel said. 'We figure that much. Someone is using Alicia's death to get us to focus on these men. We have to be careful, Alex. We can't let them know what we know until we know what it all means, or at least until we know more. If Garth Davis or Randy Mansfield had something to do with Bailey's disappearance, we'll find out and they'll answer for it. I promise you that. But, Alex, I've got six women and four men in the morgue. At this point nothing else is more important than *making this stop*.'

Alex dropped her eyes, ashamed. She worried about Bailey. Daniel worried about all the victims. Six women. Four men. Rhett Porter, Lester Jackson, Officer Cowell, and Sean Romney. That was four. But *six* women . . . Janet, Claudia, Gemma, Lisa, and Sheila. *That was only five*. Slowly she lifted her eyes. '*Six* women, Daniel?'

He closed his eyes, drained. 'I'm sorry, Alex. I meant to tell you . . . differently. Sister Anne died this afternoon. Even though we think Crighton is responsible, we're counting her among the fatalities. She would be the tenth.'

Alex let out a breath. Pursed her lips. Felt the sympathy from everyone in the room. 'No, I'm sorry. You were right. I wasn't helping. What do you want me to do?'

His eyes flashed approval and appreciation. And respect. 'For now, just try to be patient. We're getting warrants for phone and financial records on both Davis and Mansfield to try to tie them to each other or to the other two Wade mentions or to the man who killed four women. And we hope that somewhere this guy makes a mistake.'

She nodded and looked back to Wade's letter. 'Wade says *he* didn't kill Alicia. At that point, why would he lie? So if he didn't, and Fulmore didn't, then who did?'

'It's a good question,' Talia said. 'I've talked to seven of the twelve surviving rape victims and they all tell the same story. If Simon and his friends raped Alicia and left her alive like they did all the others, but she was dead when Fulmore found her in the ditch, what happened in between?'

Next to her, Alex felt Daniel tense when Talia mentioned the twelve victims, but his expression didn't change. She filed it away. She'd ask him later.

'Whatever happened, Alex, you saw something,' Dr McCrady said, 'and it had to do with the blanket Alicia was found in. If you're up to it, we need to find out what you saw.'

'Let's do it,' Alex said. 'Now, before I lose my nerve.'

Mary gathered her things. 'I'll get ready. You'll come when the meeting is finished?'

Daniel nodded. 'We will. Chase, have we informed all the women at risk?'

'There were a few we couldn't reach. A couple were out of the country. A couple aren't answering their phones. But the ones we did talk to will be smart if they just stay home with all the doors locked.'

'And their guns cocked,' Alex muttered.

Daniel lightly smacked her knee. 'Sshh.'

'I'm going now,' Talia said. 'I'm leaving early in the morning to drive to Florida to talk to two of the victims who have moved.'

'Thanks,' Chase said. 'Call me if you find anything

new.' When she was gone, he turned to Daniel. 'We got Lisa Woolf's cell phone LUDs. No calls from anyone she hadn't been receiving calls from for months.'

'And her roommates?' Daniel asked.

'They say she went to a bar last night to unwind. She never made it home. But they did find her car about five blocks from the bar.'

Everyone at the table seemed interested by this. 'What?' Alex asked.

'None of the other cars have been found,' Daniel said.

'What kind of car?' Chase asked.

'She was a grad student with no money,' Chase said with a shrug.

'She drove an old Nissan Sentra. It's being brought down here on a flatbed so we can take it apart. Maybe we'll get lucky and find something he left behind.'

Daniel considered it. 'Janet had her Z, Claudia a top-of-the-line Mercedes, and Gemma drove a 'Vette. None of those have been found, but he ditches the Nissan.'

'The boy likes fancy cars,' Luke said.

'We processed the scene at Alex's bungalow,' Ed said. 'Lots of prints to work through. It was a rental property, after all. Nothing on the bathroom window or sill. The bowl of dog food had a very high concentration of tranqs. If your dog had a normal digestive tract, Daniel, he'd be barking with the choir eternal right now.'

'I stopped by the vet on my way in from Bailey's,'

Daniel said. 'Riley will be okay and now we know they were likely looking for the key that Bailey sent to Alex.' He looked at her. 'Don't forget to call your ex.'

'I won't.'

'Then until tomorrow,' Daniel said and started to get up.

'Wait,' Alex said. 'What about Mansfield? I mean, I understand how you have to be careful not to show your hand, but the man can't be allowed to simply roam free.'

'We've got him under very close surveillance, Alex,' Chase said. 'We started setting it up minutes after Hope picked him out of the photo array. Try not to worry.'

She huffed out a breath. 'Okay. I'll try.'

'Then until tomorrow,' Daniel repeated and started to get up again.

'Wait,' Luke said. He'd been typing on his laptop during much of the conversation. 'I eliminated all the minorities and dead people from our list of graduates.'

'Right,' Daniel said, then caught his breath. 'But there was one other that was killed "for the secret."'

Luke nodded. 'Still taking out the minorities, there have been five deaths among the Dutton males graduating within a year of Simon, not including Simon, Wade, and Rhett.'

'Check them out,' Chase said, 'along with their families.'

Daniel looked around the table. 'Anything else?' When nobody said yes, he said, 'We're sure? Okay then. We all meet back here, tomorrow, eight a.m.'

They all stood, then Leigh poked her head in the door. 'Daniel, you have a visitor. Kate Davis. Garth Davis's sister. She says it's urgent.'

Everyone sat down again. 'Show her in,' Daniel said. He looked at Alex. 'Can you go and wait with Leigh in the outer office?'

'Of course.' She followed Leigh to the front where a young woman in a trendy suit waited. Alex searched her face and the woman met her gaze unflinchingly. Then Leigh took her back to the room while Alex settled in one of the chairs to wait.

Chapter Twenty-one

Atlanta, Thursday, February 1, 5:45 P.M.

According to Luke's speed-of-light Google, Kate Davis was a bank manager in her uncle Rob's bank. She was barely a year out of college, but her eyes looked old.

Daniel rose when Leigh brought her to the door. 'Miss Davis. Please sit down.'

She did. 'My uncle's grandson was killed last night.'

'Yes, Atlanta Homicide is handling the investigation,' Daniel said evenly.

'He was a sweet boy, a little slow. Not the kind to mastermind any plot.'

'We didn't say we thought he had,' Daniel said. 'What can we do for you?'

She drew a breath. 'I got a call from my sister-in-law an hour ago. She's somewhere out west with my two nephews.'

Daniel lifted his brows. 'Not a vacation, I take it.'

'No. She ran because she was scared. She called

me because she wants this to be over, because she wants at some point to be able to come home. Garth and my uncle Rob argued this morning. Garth's done something that's made him a target. He's been sitting down the street from my house for the last two nights, watching me. I saw him both times. I thought it was sweet. You know, he's my big brother, and he cares.'

'But?' Daniel asked.

Her chin lifted a fraction. 'My sister-in-law said Garth received a threat on my life with a demand for money. Garth wired a hundred thousand dollars from his sons' college fund. She wanted to go to the police, but Garth wouldn't let her. He said Rhett Porter was executed because he said too much. This doesn't surprise you.'

'Go on' was all Daniel would say.

'Then Garth said Jared O'Brien had also been eliminated.' Her eyes narrowed. 'That does surprise you.'

Daniel glanced at Luke. Luke typed, then shook his head. 'He's not dead.'

'He's not been declared dead,' Kate corrected. 'He disappeared more than five years ago. I was still in high school at the time. I'm sure you all can dig up the old police reports. Unless, of course, it was investigated by Loomis's department.'

Daniel wanted to sigh. Instead he kept his voice even. 'Explain, please.'

'Garth asked my uncle if he would go to the police. Rob said, "Not in this town." Then Garth threatened to report Rob for bank fraud if he said a word. My sister-in-law said she'd put up with Garth's affairs for years, but wouldn't allow him to jeopardize the safety of her sons.'

'Do you know where she was?'

'No, and I didn't ask. I suppose you could subpoena my phone records if you really wanted to trace it. She used her own cell phone. She asked me to come and talk to you if I wasn't afraid. If I was afraid, she said she would call you herself. But she said she wanted me to know that Garth was afraid for my life.'

'Are you not afraid?' Daniel asked softly.

'I'm terrified. I'm afraid I'll end up like Gemma or Claudia or Janet. Or Lisa.' Sadness swept over her face. 'And I'm afraid for my family. Both Garth and Rob have enough ammunition to ensure the other's silence. That terrifies me most of all.'

'You've taken a risk coming here,' Daniel said. 'Why?'

Her lips trembled and she firmed them sternly. 'Because Lisa and I were friends. I used to borrow Gemma's nail polish during lunch. Claudia helped me pick out my prom dress. They were part of my childhood and now they're all gone and part of my life is gone with them. I want whoever did this to pay.' She rose. 'That's all I have to say.'

*

Alex stood at the end of the hall outside Leigh's outer office, next to a window where she could get decent cell phone reception. And a little privacy. Her toe tapped and she realized she was nervous as the phone rang on the other end.

'Hello?' a female voice answered, and Alex wanted to sigh. She'd been hoping Richard would answer. Instead she was talking to Amber, Richard's wife.

'Hi, this is Alex. Is Richard available?'

'No.' The word came too quickly. 'He's not here. He's at work.'

'I called the hospital. They said he was at home. Please. It's important.'

Amber hesitated. 'All right. I'll get him.'

A minute later she heard Richard's voice, quiet and awkwardly formal. 'Alex. This is a surprise. What can I do for you?'

'I'm in Dutton.'

'I heard. I . . . saw the reports on the news. Are you all right?'

'I am. Bailey sent me a letter. I think it came to the house. Can you check?'

'Hold on.' She heard him moving things around. 'Here it is. It's got a key in it. I can feel it through the envelope.'

Alex drew a breath. 'Look, I know this sounds totally crazy, but I want you to only handle it by the corner and open it with a letter opener. It may become evidence.'

'Okay.' She heard him rummage in a drawer. Then, 'You want me to peek inside?'

'Carefully, yeah. And if there's a letter, read it to me.'

'There is. You ready?'

No. 'Yes. Read it, please.'

'*Dear Alex, I know this letter will come as a shock to you after all these years. I don't have a lot of time. Please take this key and put it someplace safe. If something happens to me, I want you to take care of Hope. She's my beautiful daughter and my second chance. I've been clean and sober for five years now, all because of her. And you. You were the only person who believed in me when I hit rock bottom. You were the only one who cared enough to try to get me help. But I want you to know I got help and Hope is healthy and normal. A million times in the last five years I've wanted to call you, but I know I burned my bridges that last time and I couldn't face you again. I hope you'll forgive me and if not, then please take care of Hope anyway. You're the only family I have left and the only one I trust with my daughter.*

'*Hide the key. Don't let anyone know you have it. If I need it, I'll call you.*' Richard cleared his throat. 'It's signed, *Love, your sister, Bailey,* with a little cartoon of a sheep.'

Alex swallowed hard. 'A lamb,' she whispered.

'What?'

'Nothing. I'm going to need to ask the police what they want you to do with the key. If they ask, can you FedEx it to me tonight?'

'Of course. Alex, are you in any danger?'

'I had a narrow miss a few days ago, but, um . . . I'm

in good hands down here.' Her voice had changed, softening as she said the last words.

'What's his name?'

She smiled. 'Daniel.'

'Good. You've been alone too long,' he said gruffly. 'Even when you were with me.'

Tears unexpectedly sprang to her eyes, burning her throat. 'Tell Amber if I call again it's just to get the letter, okay?'

'Alex, are you *crying*?'

She swallowed hard. 'I seem to be doing that a lot lately.'

'You never cried. Not once. I used to wish you would.'

'You wanted me to cry?'

'I wanted you to let go,' he said so quietly she almost didn't hear it. 'I thought if you cried, you might be able . . .'

Alex's heart clenched so hard it hurt. 'To love you?'

'Yeah.' The one word came out sad. 'I guess so. Good luck, Alex. Have a good life.'

'You, too.' She cleared her throat and wiped her eyes. 'I'll call you about the letter.'

Atlanta, Thursday, February 1, 6:00 P.M.

When Leigh had escorted Kate Davis from the building, Daniel turned to the group. 'Six down, one to go?'

Luke looked up from his laptop. 'Jared O'Brien is the right age. He graduated the same year Simon did, from the private school.'

'So far we have Garth and Jared who went to the private school,' Luke said, 'Wade, Rhett, and Randy who went to the public, and Simon who attended both.'

'If O'Brien was a drunk, he could have been a liability,' Chase said. 'Let's get a profile on him, as discreetly as possible. Until then, we don't approach anyone in his family. I don't want to tip anyone off. We still need to find the other living man, so find me connections. See if anybody else has withdrawn a hundred grand from their kids' college fund recently.'

'She said he had affairs,' Ed said suddenly. 'Kate Davis. She said that her sister-in-law said she could ignore Garth's affairs, but not endangering her children. Didn't Bailey's friend say she thought she was seeing a married man?'

'Bailey could have been waiting for Garth that night,' Luke agreed. 'I can see Mansfield beating her up long before I see Garth Davis doing it.'

'If Garth Davis and Bailey were having an affair, I'd expect to find his prints somewhere in that house,' Chase said. 'If he came in to attack her, it's less likely. It would be nice to know which is guilty of assault versus garden-variety infidelity.'

'We took prints from the bathroom and the kitchen,' Ed said. 'But none of them came up in AFIS.'

'Neither Garth nor Randy have a record, so I wouldn't expect their fingerprints to be in AFIS,' Chase said. 'But both are city employees, so they have to have prints on file somewhere.'

'I'll check, or we could just ask Hope, right, Daniel? Yo. Daniel.' Ed snapped his fingers.

Daniel was still thinking of Kate Davis's final words. 'Whoever killed these four women is attacking a place in time. Kate said her childhood was gone.'

'So?' Chase asked.

'I don't know. It just nags at me. I wish there was someone I could trust to tell me how things really were then.' He stilled. 'Maybe there is. I saw my old English teacher my first day back in town. He said something about only fools thinking they could keep secrets in a small town. He told me not to be a fool. I was so busy thinking about bodies and Woolf and the paper, I didn't listen. I think I'll pay him a visit tomorrow.'

'Discreetly,' Chase warned.

'Excuse me.' They all turned to find Alex standing at the door. 'I saw Leigh walk Kate Davis out, so I thought it was okay to come back.'

She'd been crying. Before Daniel knew it, he was on his feet, his hands on her shoulders. 'What's wrong?'

'Nothing. I just talked to my ex. He has Bailey's key. What do you want him to do with it? He says he can FedEx it if you want.'

'We want,' Chase said from the table. 'Leigh can give you the address.'

She nodded and slipped from Daniel's hands. 'I'll call and tell him.'

He watched her go, feeling unsettled and unhappy about it. *Focus, Vartanian.* He sat back down and made himself think. 'Wade had a key,' he said.

'What was it to?' Chase asked.

'I assume it was to wherever they'd hidden the pictures,' Daniel said. 'But Simon had the pictures, in my father's house. That's how my father found them. What if Simon also had a key?'

'Was a key found with Simon's things when he died?' Luke asked.

'Not the first time, but my father might have found it first. If Simon took it with him, maybe it's with all the things they found in his house in Philadelphia. I'll call Vito Ciccotelli and find out.'

Dutton, Thursday, February 1, 7:00 P.M.

'Alex, just tell me.'

Yanked from her thoughts, Alex looked over at Daniel, who stared at the highway before them. His hands clutched the wheel and his face was set more sternly than she'd seen in days. 'Excuse me?'

'We're nearly to Dutton. You haven't said a word since you talked to your ex and you'd been crying. He must have said something more than "Yes, Alex, I have the key."'

His tone was so harsh she blinked. 'What do you think he said?'

'I don't know.' His words were spaced deliberately. 'That's why I asked.'

She stared at his profile, briefly lit by passing headlights. A muscle ticked in his jaw.

'Are you going back?' he asked before she could formulate an answer.

'Back where? To Ohio?' Understanding dawned. 'Or to Richard?'

His jaw tightened further. 'Yes. Either.'

'No, I'm not going back to Richard. He's married.'

'It didn't stop him from cheating before.'

'No.' Alex was starting to get annoyed. 'But I wouldn't do that, even if he would. What kind of person do you think I am?'

He exhaled. 'I'm sorry. I was out of line.'

'Yes, you were. And I'm not sure if I'm royally pissed or flattered.'

He touched her arm with his fingertips. 'Be flattered. I like that better than pissed.'

She sighed. 'Okay, but only because being pissed takes more energy than being flattered. I told him about you. He was worried about everything that was going on down here. I told him I was in good hands.'

She hoped she'd see him smile, but he did not. 'You never said if you were going back to Ohio.'

It was what had had her deep in thought. 'What do you want me to say?'

'That you'll stay here.'

She drew a deep breath and held it. 'Part of me wants to say yes, because you're here. Part of me wants to run in the other direction, and that part has nothing to do with you. My worst memories are here, Daniel. That scares me.'

He was quiet for a moment. 'But you'd consider staying?'

'Would you consider going?'

'To *Ohio*?' He said it like it was Outer Mongolia and she chuckled.

'It's not a bad place. You can even get grits.'

One side of his mouth lifted. 'Scrapple, too?'

She made a face. 'If you insist, I know a place that serves it. But that's just nasty.'

He smiled then, and her heart lifted. 'I agree. I would consider it.'

Again she held her breath. 'Scrapple or Ohio?'

His smile faded, his expression becoming sober. 'Yes. Either.'

A full minute of silence passed. 'That feels good, and right. But I don't want to make you any promises until I'm firm on my feet again.'

'All right.' He squeezed her hand. 'I do feel better now.'

'I'm glad.'

They passed Dutton's Main Street and Alex's stomach began to churn. 'We're almost there.'

'I know. Whatever it is, whatever you remember, we'll deal with it together.'

Dutton, Thursday, February 1, 7:30 P.M.

'This house is a steal at four-fifty.' Delia Anderson patted her bouffant-do. 'It won't last long in this market at that price.'

He opened a closet, pretended to care. 'My girlfriend buys out the store every time she goes shopping. This would never be enough closet space for her.'

'I have two more listings,' Delia said. 'Both have enormous walk-in closets.'

He gave one last turn. 'But this house does have . . . something,' he said. 'It's so cozy and private.'

'That it is,' Delia agreed a shade too eagerly. 'There aren't many houses available with this much property.'

He smiled. 'We like to have parties. Sometimes they get a little wild.'

'Oh, Mr Myers.' She giggled, an unattractive sound coming from a woman her age. 'Privacy is such an underrated consideration in the purchase of a new home.' She paused at a mirror that hung in the foyer and again patted her helmet-head of hair. 'Why, this place is so private, you could have an open air rock 'n' roll show in the backyard and no neighbors would complain about the noise.'

He stepped behind her and smiled into the mirror. 'Exactly my thoughts.'

Her eyes widened in alarm and her mouth opened to scream, but too late. Quick as a wish, he had his knife to her throat. 'In case you haven't guessed already, my name is not Myers.' He leaned in and whispered his name in her ear and watched her wide eyes glaze over with horror as recognition seeped past all that hairspray. 'Let me introduce you to a new concept, Miz Anderson. Accrued interest on an unpaid debt.'

He pushed her to the floor and quickly bound her hands behind her back. 'I sure hope you like to scream.'

Dutton, Thursday, February 1, 7:30 P.M.

'So did Simon have a key?' Ed asked from the back of the surveillance van.

Daniel slipped his phone into his pocket. 'Yeah. Vito Ciccotelli said there were five keys found in Simon's things. He's sending them all first thing tomorrow. Now if we can only figure out what they open.' A movement on Ed's screen had him straightening. 'Looks like Mary is ready.'

'Mary had me set up the camera in Alex's old bedroom,' Ed said. 'Since we found her ring there, we thought it made sense.'

His hands clenched, Daniel watched as the door opened and Mary led Alex in.

'What time is it?' Mary asked her.

'Late. It's dark and there's lightning. Thunder and lightning.'

'Where are you?'

'In bed.'

'Sleeping?'

'No. I'm sick. I have to get up to go to the bathroom. I'm sick.'

'So what happened?'

Alex was standing at the window. 'Someone's there.'

'Who?'

'I don't know. Maybe it's Alicia. She sneaks out sometimes. Goes to parties.'

'Is it Alicia?'

Alex leaned toward the window. 'No. It's a man.' She flinched. 'It's Craig.'

'Why did you flinch, Alex?'

'The lightning is bright.' She grimaced. 'My stomach hurts.'

'Is Craig still out there?'

'Yes. But now there's someone else. Two people, carrying a bag between them.'

'Is it heavy or light?'

'Heavy, I think.' She flinched again, then sucked in a breath. Then stared blankly.

'What is it? More lightning?'

Alex nodded. Hesitated. 'He dropped it.'

'He dropped the bag?'

'It's not a bag, it's a blanket. It fell open.'

'And what do you see in the lightning, Alex?'

'Her arm. Her hand. It just fell out onto the ground.'

She was worrying the ring finger on her right hand, tugging as if a ring were there. 'I can see her hand.' She relaxed slightly. 'Oh, she's just a doll.'

Daniel felt a chill slide down his back and remembered Sheila sprawled like a Raggedy Ann doll in the corner of Presto's Pizza.

'She's a doll?' Mary asked.

Alex nodded, her eyes blank, her voice eerily matter-of-fact. 'Yes. She's just a doll.'

'What do the men do?'

'He grabs her arm, puts it back in the blanket. Now he's got it again and they're running around the house.'

'What's happening now?'

She frowned slightly. 'My stomach still hurts. I'm going back to sleep.'

'All right. Come with me, Alex.' Mary led her to a folding chair and began to bring her out of it. Daniel could tell the moment she was cognizant of her surroundings. She blanched and hunched her shoulders.

'It wasn't a doll,' she said tonelessly. 'It was Alicia. They were carrying her in the blanket.'

Mary crouched in front of her. 'Who, Alex?'

'Craig and Wade. Wade was the one who dropped his end. It was her arm. It . . . it didn't look real. It looked like a doll.' She closed her eyes. 'I told my mother.'

Mary glanced into the camera, then back at Alex. 'When?'

'When she was in bed crying. She kept saying "a sheep and a ring." I thought I'd had a dream. A premonition, maybe. I told her about the doll and she got upset. I told her it was "just a doll, Mama." I didn't know she'd seen the blanket, too.' Tears began to seep from Alex's closed eyes. 'I told her and she told Craig and he killed her.'

'Oh, God,' Daniel whispered.

'She's felt guilty all this time,' Ed said softly. 'Poor Alex.'

'It wasn't your fault, Alex,' Mary said.

Alex was rocking, a barely discernible movement. 'I told her and she told him and he killed her. She died because of me.'

Daniel was out of the van before she finished the sentence. He ran to the bedroom and pulled her into his arms. She came willingly, almost bonelessly. *Like a doll*.

'I'm sorry, honey. I'm so sorry.'

She was still rocking, a terrifying little keening sound coming from her throat. He looked up at Mary. 'I need to get her out of here.'

Mary nodded sadly. 'Be careful on the stairs.'

Daniel urged Alex to her feet and again she came willingly. He put his hands on her shoulders and gave her the smallest of shakes. 'Alex. *Stop it*.' At the crack of his voice, her rocking stilled. 'Now, let's go.'

Atlanta, Thursday, February 1, 10:00 P.M.

'Your aim was better tonight,' Daniel commented as he pulled into his driveway.

'Thank you.' She was still subdued, still numb. Only when he had taken her to Leo Papadopoulos's target range had she regained some measure of control. The paper target had suffered as it became everyone she'd come to hate over the last few days. Craig most of all, but also Wade and Mayor Davis and Deputy Mansfield and whoever had stirred all this up to begin with by viciously murdering four innocent women.

And even her mother and Alicia. If Alicia hadn't snuck out that night . . . And if her mother hadn't lost control . . .

And, and, and . . .

She had aimed better. She'd held that gun steady and she'd fired until the magazine was empty. Then she'd reloaded and done it again and again until her arms were sore.

'I'll get your shopping bag out of the trunk,' he said when the silence had become too great. 'You can hang your new clothes in my closet if you want.'

She hadn't bought that much today, just a few blouses and a few pairs of slacks. Still, hanging them in his closet felt too intimate . . . too *much* when she was so raw inside. But he looked expectant, so she nodded. 'All right.'

He popped the trunk and she expected he'd shut it quickly, but he didn't. The trunk stayed up as thirty seconds became a minute. She got out and sighed. Frank Loomis stood in the shadow of the trunk lid and he and Daniel were engaged in fierce whispers.

'Daniel,' she said, and he whipped around to look at her.

'Go up to the house,' he ordered. 'Please.'

Too numb and weary to argue, she did as he asked and from his front porch watched the two men argue. Finally Daniel slammed the trunk closed loudly enough to wake the entire neighborhood and Frank Loomis stalked back to where he'd parked his car and drove away.

His shoulders heaving with the furious breaths he drew, Daniel turned and came up the sidewalk, a dark cast to his face. With jerky movements he opened the door and shut off the alarm. Alex watched him, remembering how they'd come together against that door the night before.

But Daniel only locked the door, reset the alarm, and started up the stairs, not even looking back to see if she followed. His command to do so was implicit in his body language, so she did. When she got to his bedroom her shopping bags were on his bed and he stood at his dresser, yanking at his tie.

'What happened?' she asked quietly.

He shrugged out of his coat and his shirt, flinging them to a chair in the corner, before turning, bare-chested, his fists on his hips. 'Frank is being investigated by the state attorney's office.'

'As well he should be,' she said, and he nodded.

'Thank you.' His chest expanded and fell. 'He's angry with me. He blamed *me*.'

'I'm sorry.'

'I don't care.' But it was obvious he did. 'What made me mad is that he used our friendship to try to get me to influence the SA. *Friendship*. Biggest crock of bullshit I've heard in years.'

'I'm sorry,' she said again.

'Stop saying that,' he snapped. 'Stop saying *thank you* and *I'm sorry*. You sound like Susannah.'

His sister, who had her own pain, he'd said. 'You talked to her?'

'Yeah.' He looked away. 'I talked to her. For all the damn good it did.'

'What did she say?'

His head whipped up and his eyes bored into hers. '"I'm sorry, Daniel. Good-bye, Daniel."' Pain flashed in his eyes, so intense she felt it press against her own chest. '"You were *gone*, Daniel,"' he added in a snarl, then dropped his head, and his shoulders sagged. 'I'm sorry. I shouldn't be yelling at you of all people.'

She sat on the edge of the bed, too tired to stand. 'Why not me of all people?'

'Everywhere I turn, I see lies and betrayal. The only one who's done neither is you.'

She didn't agree, but wouldn't argue the point. 'Who did you betray?'

'My sister. I left her in that house. Where we grew up. I left her with Simon.'

Understanding dawned, and with it a pity and tenderness that made her ache for both Daniel and his sister. 'Not all Simon's victims went to the public school, did they?' she asked, remembering how he'd tensed at Talia's words in the afternoon meeting.

Again his head shot up. He opened his mouth. Closed it. 'No,' he finally said.

'You didn't do it, Daniel. Simon did. It wasn't your fault any more than it was my fault my mother decided to take on Craig herself. But we think it's our fault, and that's not going to be easy for either of us to get through.' He narrowed his eyes and she shrugged. 'Shooting lots of bullets at that paper man gives a person a certain clarity of thought. I was only sixteen, but my mother was an adult who'd stayed with Craig Crighton entirely too long to begin with. Still, I gave her information that pushed her to the edge. Logically, it's not my fault, but for thirteen years I told myself it was.'

'I wasn't sixteen.'

'Daniel, did you know Simon was involved in the rapes of all those girls?'

He hung his head again. 'No. Not when he was alive. Not until he died.'

'See? You didn't find the pictures until he died, less than two weeks ago.'

He shook his head. 'No, when he died the first time.'

Alex frowned. 'I don't understand.'

'Eleven years ago my mother found those pictures. We thought Simon had been dead a year.'

Alex's eyes widened. *Eleven years?* 'But Simon wasn't dead. He'd left home.'

'True. But I saw the pictures back then. I wanted to tell the police, but my father burned them in the fireplace. He didn't want the bad publicity. Bad for his judgeship.'

Alex was starting to see. 'How did you find them in Philadelphia if he burned them?'

'He would have made copies. My father was a careful man. But the point is, I didn't do anything about it. I didn't tell a soul. And Simon went on unchecked for years.'

'What would you have told, Daniel?' she asked gently. '"My father burned some pictures, so I can't prove anything"?'

'I suspected for years that he was dirty.'

'And he was a careful man. You really wouldn't have been able to prove anything.'

'I still can't prove anything,' he snapped. 'Because men like Frank Loomis are still covering their own asses.'

'What did you say to him tonight?'

'I asked him where he'd been all week. Why he wouldn't answer my calls.'

'And where was he?'

'He said he'd been looking for Bailey.'

Alex blinked. 'Really? Where?'

'He wouldn't tell me. He said it didn't matter, that she wasn't in any of the places he checked. I told him if he wanted to make things right, he'd help us find her versus running around half-cocked himself. I told him that if he really wanted to prove himself, he'd make right what he did thirteen years ago. He'd set the record straight on Fulmore and come clean on who he was protecting back then. Of course he denied he was protecting anyone, but that's the only way I can square what he did in my mind. Frank set a man up for murder. That whole trial was one colossal cover-up.'

'And you'll show that, when you get all Simon's friends in a room and they all start pointing their fingers at each other. It'll fall like dominoes.'

He sighed, most of his rage spent. 'I can't get them to turn on each other until I know who's doing this killing now. And I can't move on that person without giving a warning to Simon's group of degenerates. I'm in a catch-22 from hell.'

She went to him then and smoothed her hands across his chest and up his back. 'Let's sleep, Daniel. You haven't had a full night's sleep in almost a week.'

He rested his cheek on the top of her head. 'I haven't had a full night's sleep in eleven years, Alex,' he said wearily.

'Then it's time to stop blaming yourself. If I can, you can.'

He leaned back and met her eyes. 'Can you?'

'I have to,' she whispered. 'Don't you see? I've lived my life just skimming the surface, never digging deep enough for roots. I want roots. I want a life. Don't you?'

His eyes flashed, intensely bright. 'Yes.'

'Then let it go, Daniel.'

'It's not so easy.'

She pressed a kiss against his warm chest. 'I know. We'll deal with it tomorrow. For now, let's go to sleep. In the morning you'll be able to think clearly. You'll catch this guy, then you can put all Simon's friends in a room and let them tear each other apart.'

'Will you stitch them back together after they tear each other apart?'

She lifted her chin and narrowed her eyes. 'No way in hell.'

He smiled his half smile. 'God, you're sexy when you're ruthless.'

And that quickly she wanted him. 'Let's go to bed now.'

His brows lifted, detecting the change in her voice. 'To sleep?'

She wrapped her arms around his neck. 'No way in hell.'

Atlanta, Thursday, February 1, 11:15 P.M.

Mack lowered his camera with its telephoto lens when the shade on Vartanian's bedroom window came down. Damn, just when it was starting to get interesting. He wished he could have heard the conversation between Vartanian and Alex Fallon, but his listening device had a range of only a hundred yards and didn't let him listen through walls. Two things were clear – Vartanian was still furious with Frank Loomis and Vartanian and Fallon were about to be joined at more than the hip.

The evening had been most illuminating. Mack hadn't expected to see Frank Loomis waiting in front of Vartanian's house. Apparently, Vartanian hadn't expected to see Loomis there either. Loomis was under investigation and worried about it. So worried the high and mighty sheriff had swallowed his pride and asked Daniel to intercede on his behalf. Mack rolled his eyes. Daniel, of course, was too ethical to do such a heinous thing, but he was just loyal enough to have been tempted.

As intelligence went, it didn't come much more valuable than this. Between the botched hit-and-run and the ransacking of her house, Fallon was on her guard and Vartanian wasn't letting her out of his sight. *So I'll bring them to me.* He now knew exactly how he'd bait his trap. Desperation plus a little loyalty, mixed with the hint of Bailey was a combination they'd find irresistible.

He looked over his shoulder to where Delia Anderson lay in the back of his van, wrapped in a blanket and ready for disposal. He'd dump Delia, then get some sleep before he had to hit his delivery route. Tomorrow was going to be a very busy day.

Chapter Twenty-two

Atlanta, Friday, February 2, 5:50 A.M.

The phone woke him. Beside him, Alex stirred, burrowing her cheek into his chest, her arm hugging his waist. It was an incredible way to wake up.

Daniel squinted at the clock, then at the caller ID, and his heart began to race as he reached across Alex's warm body for the phone. 'Yeah, Chase. What is it?' Alex slid off him onto her side, blinking quickly to full alertness.

'The tail we put on Marianne Woolf called. She pulled out of her driveway and flipped him the bird. She's off somewhere, alone in her car. He's right on her bumper.'

A spurt of fury burned inside his chest. 'Dammit, Chase. What part of stay inside and lock your doors and windows did one of these women miss? And what's Jim Woolf thinking, letting his wife do his dirty work for him? How the hell can they jump when this guy snaps his fingers? He murdered Jim's sister, for God's sake.'

'Woolf may not know his wife's on the move. He's still in lockup. He doesn't get his bail hearing until this morning.'

'She could just be going out for a jug of milk,' Daniel said without much conviction. 'Or having a clandestine affair.'

Chase grunted. 'We should only be so lucky. Get moving. I'll have the tail call you.'

Daniel leaned over Alex to hang up the phone, then leaned in to kiss her mouth. 'We have to go.'

'Okay.'

But she was warm and fluid and responding to his simple morning kiss, so he took another, blocking out the world for another few minutes. 'We really have to go.'

'Okay.'

But she was lifting to him, her hands in his hair, her mouth hot and hungry, and his heart was suddenly thudding to beat all hell. 'How fast can you get ready?'

'Including a shower, fifteen.' She surged against him, impatient. 'Hurry, Daniel.'

Pulse pounding in his ears, he drove himself into her wet warmth and she climaxed with a low, startled cry. Three hard thrusts later he followed, shuddering as he buried his face in her hair. Her hands stroked up his spine and he shuddered again. 'Are you sure they have grits in Ohio?'

She laughed, a sated, happy sound, and he realized he'd never really heard her laugh like that. He wanted to hear it again. 'And scrapple,' she said, then stretched around him and smacked his butt. 'Up with you, Vartanian. I want the shower first.'

'I am up,' he muttered, unwilling to withdraw yet, needing another minute before facing what he feared he'd find in yet another ditch. But he lifted his head and saw her sober smile and knew she understood. 'I have two showers. You take the master and I'll take the one in the hall and we'll see who's ready first.'

Warsaw, Georgia, Friday, February 2, 7:15 A.M.

He'd been ready first, but not by much. He'd only been waiting at the front door for three minutes when she rushed down his stairs, perfectly coordinated, light makeup on her face and her wet hair in a neat French braid. She would have been faster, she'd insisted, if she hadn't had to pull all the price tags off her new clothes.

Now Daniel threw a backward glance over his shoulder as he walked from his car to the ditch where Ed already waited. From the front seat of his car Alex gave him a little wave and an encouraging smile and he felt like a first-grader on his first day of school.

'Alex looks better this morning,' Ed said.

'I think so. I took her to Leo's target range after we left Bailey's and let her take it all out on a paper target. That and a good night's sleep seem to have helped.'

Ed lifted a brow. 'Amazing what a good night's sleep will do for you,' he said mildly, and Daniel met his eyes with a half smile.

'That, too,' he acknowledged, and Ed nodded once.

'We moved Marianne Woolf back past the police tape,' Ed said, pointing to where the woman stood snapping pictures with her husband's camera. 'We made sure we strung the tape really far back.'

'What did she say?'

'Unprintable. That woman's a piece of work.'

Marianne lowered her camera, and from more than a hundred feet away, Daniel could feel her glare. 'I don't understand that woman.' He turned his attention to the ditch. 'I don't understand this perp.'

'It's the same,' Ed said. 'Blanket, face, key, hair around the toe, everything.'

It was a shallow ditch and Malcolm Zuckerman from the ME's office was well within earshot. 'Not everything,' Malcolm said, looking up at them. 'She's older. She's had a face-lift and collagen injections to her lips, but her hands are wrinkled and tough.'

Daniel frowned and crouched at the ditch's edge. 'How old is she?'

'Fifties, maybe,' Malcolm said. He pulled the blanket away. 'You know her?'

The woman had well-teased yellow-blond hair. 'No. I don't think so anyway.' Daniel looked up at Ed in consternation. 'He broke pattern. Why?'

'Maybe he tried to get at all the younger ones and

they were too careful to be caught alone. Or maybe she's important to him.'

'Or both,' Daniel said. 'Go ahead and bring her up, Malcolm.'

'Daniel?' Alex asked from behind him.

Daniel abruptly turned. 'You don't want to see this, honey. Go back to the car.'

'I'm sure I've seen worse. You look upset and . . . I got worried.'

'It's not Bailey,' he said, and she relaxed a little. 'It's an older woman this time.'

'Who?'

'We don't know. Stand back, they're bringing her up.'

Malcolm and Trey lifted the stretcher out of the ditch and laid the body on the open body bag they'd stretched on the gurney. Behind him, Alex gasped.

Daniel and Ed turned in unison. Alex was standing rigidly still. 'I know her. It's Delia Anderson. She rented me the bungalow. I recognize her hair.'

'At least we know where to deliver the bad news.' He looked at Marianne Woolf. She'd once again lowered her camera, but this time in shock. 'And we need to keep Marianne quiet.' He lifted Alex's chin and studied her face. 'Are you all right?'

She nodded brusquely. 'I have seen worse, Daniel. Not often, but I have. I'll go back to the car and wait for you. See you later, Ed.'

Ed was thoughtful as they watched Alex walk back

to Daniel's car. 'I'd ask if she had a sister, but that would be in really bad taste.'

Daniel managed to choke back what would have been a startled laugh. It was one of those moments civilians didn't understand. When the burden got so heavy, dark humor was the only non-addictive, non-destructive release. '*Ed*.'

'I know.' Ed glanced at Marianne. 'You deal with the bitch, I'll deal with the ditch.'

This time Daniel couldn't hold back the chuckle, but dropped his head so nobody could see him smile. When he looked up he was serious.

'I'll go deal with *Mrs Woolf*.'

'Yeah, yeah,' Ed was muttering when Daniel walked away.

Marianne was crying. 'Marianne, what the hell are you doing here?'

Marianne's eyes flashed fury despite the tears. 'That's Delia Anderson.'

'How do you know?'

'Because I've sat next to her at Angie's Beauty Shop every Thursday for the last five years,' Marianne snapped. 'Nobody has a bouffant like Delia.'

'We'll have to confirm her identity,' Daniel said. 'Why are you here, Marianne?'

'I got a text tip on my cell.'

'You've been in communication with a killer.' Daniel said the words slowly, hoping by some miracle they'd sink in. 'The killer of your husband's sister.'

She sneered. 'I don't know that. He never said, "I killed them, go see."'

'Just "Go see where there happens to be a freshly killed body."' Daniel rolled his eyes. 'I don't see the difference, Marianne.'

Her chin lifted. 'No, I guess you wouldn't.'

'Why are you and Jim doing this? Please help me understand.'

Marianne sighed. 'Jim's dad ran that paper for years. It was his life – a sweet little small-town paper where the biggest news was the high school football scores. Jim always dreamed it could be more, but his father wouldn't let him try. When his father died, Jim took over, retooled everything. I know you think it's stupid . . .' Again her chin lifted. 'But it's his dream. He got offers from some big-city papers for this story, and it's a story that needs to be told. He's in jail, so I'm telling it until he's out.'

Daniel wanted to shake her. 'But you're letting a killer *use you*.'

She lifted her brows. 'Aren't you? You can't say that this case and this killer haven't gotten even more attention because you've been investigating.' Her voice became grand. Mocking. 'The great Daniel Vartanian, son of a judge, brother of a serial killer. But Daniel has risen above it all, sworn protector of truth, justice, and the American way.' She cocked her jaw. 'It's enough to bring a tear to your eye.'

Daniel stared at her, stunned. 'What about Lisa?

Don't you think she deserves more than this?'

Marianne actually smiled. 'Lisa would be the first one cheering me on, Daniel.'

He stared, completely taken aback. 'I don't understand you.'

'No, I suppose you don't. I guess that's why it's a good thing we still have the Bill of Rights.' She popped the memory card from her camera and glanced up at the barrel-chested agent who'd been her tail. 'I'll go with Tiny here and make you guys a copy of the pictures. It's what Jim told me to do if I got caught.'

'Can you at least refrain from printing anything until we've notified the Andersons?'

Marianne nodded, her disdain gone for the moment. 'Yes. On that we can agree.'

Atlanta, Friday, February 2, 8:50 A.M.

'So how does this woman connect?' Chase demanded. Ed had stayed at the crime scene, Talia was interviewing rape victims, and Hatton and Koenig were still at Peachtree and Pine searching for Crighton. Luke sat next to Daniel at the team room table, absorbed in whatever was on the screen of his laptop.

'She used to work at the Davis Bank in Dutton,' Luke said. 'It's on her real estate website. She lists Davis Bank as a lender for qualified home buyers.'

'That doesn't seem motive enough to kill her,' Chase

said doubtfully. 'What have you found out about Jared O'Brien's family?'

'Only what I was able to glean from the Internet,' Luke said. 'But you're gonna like it. The O'Briens used to own the Dutton paper mill. Larry O'Brien had two sons. Jared was the oldest and went to Bryson Academy. He was the same age as Simon. From the yearbooks it appears Jared was quite the ladies' man. He was homecoming king and prom king during his graduation year.' Luke passed them a copy of Jared's yearbook picture. 'He was a handsome guy. Jared's younger brother was Mack. Mack was nine years younger.' He paused and lifted his brows.

Daniel sucked in a breath. 'Then he went to high school with Janet and the others.'

'At the beginning, yes,' Luke said, 'but if you check the yearbooks, Mack transferred to the public school some time between his junior and senior years. He was too young to be on any of the lists of males Simon's age and he didn't go to Bryson Academy during the years we checked on the murdered women. Larry O'Brien, the father, died of a heart attack about a year after Simon died the first time. Jared, as the oldest son, took over the mill. There aren't a lot of public records, but there seem to have been a lot of people out of work, so it doesn't seem like Jared was a stellar businessman.'

'Kate said he was a drunk,' Daniel said. 'I know he had a record. I had Leigh run him – Jared O'Brien was arrested for DUI twice in Georgia.'

'Jared disappeared the year Mack was a junior in high school,' Luke said. 'The mill goes belly-up because Jared spent all the money, and the mill gets bought out by guess who?'

Chase sighed. 'Who?'

'Rob Davis.'

Daniel's mouth opened. 'No way.'

'Way,' Luke said. 'The father's widow, Lila O'Brien, declares bankruptcy a few months later.'

'And Mack transfers to the public school.' Daniel lifted his brows. 'The timing works. The O'Briens must not have gotten much from the sale if Mack had to transfer.'

'The mill's privately owned, so the terms aren't in the public record,' Luke said, 'but I'd say that assumption is fair.'

'So we may have a motive for revenge against the Davises,' Chase said, 'but the rest of this? How would Mack even know about the "club"? He would have been nine years old at the time. And what about Jared? He disappeared, but nobody's found a body. For all we know, Jared could have come back and started all this.'

'That's possible, except for this next piece.' Luke paused dramatically. 'Mack got arrested for assault and grand theft auto in his senior year of high school. He was already eighteen, so he got tried as an adult and sent to prison. He served four of a twelve-year sentence, then was paroled. One month ago.'

'Whoa.' Daniel wanted to grin, but held it back.

There were still too many gaps they had to fill. 'It all fits, but we need to know why he killed Janet and the others, why he mimicked Alicia's death, and like Chase said, how he even knew about all this.'

'Then let's find him and bring him in for a few questions,' Chase said dangerously. 'You got a photo, Luke?'

Luke slid one across the table. 'That's his mug.'

Daniel studied Mack O'Brien's face. His hair was dark and greasy, his body thin and scrawny, and he had terrible pockmarks on his face from acute acne. 'Doesn't look much like Jared,' he commented. 'Let's get out an APB.'

'I'll contact the parole board for a more recent photo,' Luke said. 'For now, this is better than nothing.'

'What about the rest of Jared O'Brien's family?' Chase asked.

'His mother died while Mack was in prison,' Luke said. 'Jared left a wife and two little boys behind. They live out past Arcadia.'

'You got all this from the Internet?' Daniel asked.

'Dutton's newspaper is online now, up to ten years ago.' Luke shrugged. 'It's one of the things Jim Woolf has done to modernize. Plus the birth and death records are filed at the county seat and Mack's arrest record was on our books. He was sentenced here in Atlanta, by the way. Not in Dutton.'

'Who was the arresting officer?' Daniel asked.

'Guy by the name of Smits, out of Zone 2.'

'Thanks, I'll talk to him.' Daniel looked at Chase. 'We need to notify the Andersons ASAP, but I'd also like to talk to Jared's widow.'

Chase nodded. 'I'll inform the Andersons. We already have both Davis and Mansfield under surveillance. If they try to bolt, we'll grab 'em.'

'Chase.' Leigh ran into the room, Alex at her heels; both were pale. 'Koenig just called. They found Crighton, but he pulled a gun and got Hatton in the shoulder.'

'How bad?' Chase demanded.

'Bad,' Leigh said. 'They rushed him to Emory. He's in critical condition. Koenig's at the hospital now. Koenig was hit, too, but not as bad.'

Chase drew a breath. 'Their wives?'

'Koenig's called them. They're both on their way.'

Chase nodded. 'All right. I'll contact the Andersons, then head over. Luke, I want everything we can get on Mack O'Brien, down to what breakfast cereal he ate as a kid. Get financials on the others – Mansfield, and both Garth and his uncle.'

'I'll call you when I have something.' Luke left, laptop under his arm.

Chase turned to Daniel. 'Crighton can wait. They'll put him in the tank until we're ready to deal with him.'

'You're right. I'll go see Jared's wife.'

'Wait,' Leigh said. 'Your FedExes just came. From Cincinnati and Philly.'

'The keys,' Daniel said. He ripped open the envelopes

and slid the keys onto the table. It was easy to see which of the five keys Ciccotelli had sent from Philadelphia was the right one – it was almost identical to the one Alex's ex had sent. Daniel held up both keys, one in each hand. 'They're not for the same lock, but the keys themselves look like they're from the same manufacturer.'

'Safe-deposit box?' Chase asked, and Daniel nodded.

'I'm betting so.'

'Garth's uncle's bank?' Chase asked, and Daniel nodded again.

'I can't go storming into Davis's bank demanding access to boxes without a warrant, and even when I get one, it's tipping our hand.'

'Call Chloe, get the warrants started,' Chase said. 'Once we get more information, we'll at least have a jump on the paperwork.'

'That's a plan. Alex, you have to stay here. I'm sorry. I can't be worried about your safety and do all of this.'

Her jaw tightened. 'Okay. I understand.'

He pressed a hard kiss to her mouth. 'Do not leave this building. Do you promise?'

'I'm not stupid, Daniel.'

He scowled. 'No evasions, Alex. Promise me.'

She sighed. 'I promise.'

Arcadia, Georgia, Friday, February 2, 10:30 A.M.

Jared O'Brien's wife lived in a house the size of a crackerbox. She answered the door wearing a waitress uniform and a weary expression.

'Annette O'Brien?'

She nodded. 'Yes, that's me.'

She didn't seem surprised to see him, only tired. 'I'm Special Agent—'

'You're Simon Vartanian's brother,' she interrupted. 'Come in.'

She crossed her tiny living room in a few steps, picking up a shirt, a pair of small shoes, a toy truck as she walked. 'You have children,' he said.

'Two. Joey and Seth. Joey is seven. Seth turned five just before Christmas.'

That meant she would have been pregnant with her younger son when her husband disappeared. 'You don't seem surprised to see me, Mrs O'Brien.'

'I'm not. In fact, I've been waiting for you to come for more than five years.' Her eyes shadowed with apprehension. 'I'll tell you what you want to know. But I have to get protection for my kids. They're the only reason I haven't said anything until now.'

'Protection from whom, Mrs O'Brien?'

She met his gaze unflinchingly. 'You know, or you wouldn't be here.'

'Fair enough. So when did you find out what Jared and the others had done?'

'After he disappeared. I thought he'd run off with another woman. I was pregnant with Seth and getting too fat for . . . well, I thought he'd be back.'

Daniel felt anger at Jared and pity for Annette. If Alex were pregnant, she'd still be the most beautiful woman in the world to him. 'But he didn't come back.'

'No, and after a few weeks the bank account was empty and we were hungry.'

'What about Jared's mother?'

She shook her head wearily. 'She was out of the country with Mack. Rome, I think.'

'You had no money for food and his mother was in Rome? I don't understand.'

'Jared never wanted his mother to know how badly he'd messed up his daddy's mill. His mother was used to a certain standard of living and he made sure she had it. We did, too, on the surface. We lived in a big house, drove fancy cars. But we had no credit with the bank and no cash. Jared kept a tight hold on the finances. He gambled.'

'And drank.'

'Yes. When he didn't come back, I started searching all the places he hid money.' She drew a deep breath. 'And that's when I found his journals. Jared had kept one religiously since he was a boy.'

Daniel had to fight to keep from punching at the air in glee. 'Where are they?'

'I'll get them for you.' She went to the fireplace and jostled an interior brick loose.

'Risky place to hide a journal,' Daniel commented.

'Jared hid them in the garage with the spare parts for his 'Vette. My sons and I moved here after we lost everything. Seth has bad allergies, so we never use the fireplace. It's safe enough.' She'd been working at the brick as she spoke and finally pulled it free. Then she sat, pale, openmouthed and staring. 'That's . . . not possible.'

Daniel felt all his glee fizzle away. He walked to the fireplace and looked in the empty hole and suddenly pieces of the puzzle began to slide into place.

'Let's sit down.' When they had, he leaned forward, keeping his expression calm because Annette appeared on the verge of hysteria. 'Has Mack been here to visit?'

The look she gave him was one of genuine shock. 'No. He's in prison.'

'Not anymore,' he said, and she paled further. 'He was paroled a month ago.'

'I didn't know. I swear I didn't know.'

'Have you noticed anything else missing?'

'Yes. My tip money that I keep in a jar in my bedroom disappeared about a month ago. I blamed Joey for taking it.' She covered her mouth with a trembling hand. 'Then two weeks ago it happened again – my tips and the cookies I'd baked for the kids' lunches. I spanked Joey and called him a liar.' Tears filled her eyes. 'Like his daddy.'

'We can deal with that later,' Daniel said gently. 'For

now, can you tell me what you remember from the journals?'

Her eyes had gone glassy with panic. 'Mack was here. My boys are at school. They're not safe if Mack's around.'

Daniel knew he couldn't expect her to be helpful when she was panicked over her kids. He called Sheriff Corchran in Arcadia and asked him to pick the boys up from school, then turned to Annette, who was visibly struggling for control. 'Corchran said he'd let them run his lights and siren. They'll have a ball. Don't worry.'

'Thank you.' She closed her eyes, still very pale. 'Mack is out of prison, the journals are gone, and four women are murdered just like Alicia Tremaine.'

Five women, Daniel thought. Annette O'Brien must have missed the morning news.

She looked at him, her eyes stark and desolate. 'Mack killed those women.'

'You knew him. Could he have done it? Would he?'

'He would and he could,' she whispered. 'My God. I should have destroyed them when I had the chance.'

'The journals?' Daniel asked, and she nodded. 'Please, Mrs O'Brien, can you tell me what you remember from the journals?'

'They had a club. Your brother, Simon, was the president. Jared never mentioned any real names. They used nicknames.' She sighed wearily. 'They were stupid boys.'

'Who raped a number of women,' Daniel said harshly.

She frowned as his meaning became clear. 'In no way am I excusing what they did, Agent Vartanian,' she said quietly. 'Make no mistake about that. This was not a boys-will-be-boys prank. What they did was obscene and . . . evil.'

'I'm sorry, I misunderstood. Please go on.'

'They were boys when it started, fifteen or sixteen. They made up this game, had rules, a secret code, keys . . . It was so stupid.' She swallowed. 'And so horrible.'

'So if Jared didn't mention names, how did you know Simon was the president?'

'They called him Captain Ahab. Simon was the only one in Dutton I knew with a fake leg, so I put two and two together. Jared put in the journal that nobody called him Ahab to his face, just Captain. They were all afraid of him.'

'With good reason,' Daniel murmured. 'What other nicknames did Jared mention?'

'Bluto and Igor. Jared wrote how they always hung around together, and once he slipped and wrote something about Bluto's father being Mayor McCheese. Garth Davis's father was the mayor at the time. I guessed Igor was Rhett Porter.'

'Garth's uncle bought the mill after Jared died,' Daniel noted, and her eyes flared.

'Yes, for pennies on the dollar. We were left with nothing. But you didn't come here for that. The others

. . . Well, there was Sweetpea. I was never sure if that was Randy Mansfield or one of the Woolf brothers. Jared thought it was funny that they called him Sweetpea because the boy didn't like it. It was some aspersion against his manliness. It was how they convinced him to join.' Her lips twisted. '"Have sex with these girls. Prove you're a man." It made me *sick*.'

'You've given me four nicknames,' Daniel said. 'What was Jared's nickname?'

She looked away, but not before he saw the pain and shame in her eyes. 'Don Juan, DJ for short. He was the ladies' man of the group. Jared lured most of the girls.'

'And the other two?'

'Po'boy and Harvard. Po'boy was Wade Crighton. Of that I'm completely sure.'

'Why?'

'The boys had to deliver a girl to the group as part of their initiation. They were divided on whether or not to let Wade in. He was the poor boy. His dad worked in the mill.' Her expression grew grim. 'But Wade had assets. He had three sisters.'

Daniel's stomach lurched. 'My God.'

'I know,' she murmured. 'The club was angry that "Po'boy" refused to bring his real sister, but the consolation prize was twins.'

Panicked bile rose in his throat. 'Wade brought both girls?'

'No. They got mad because they'd been all excited to "do twins" and then Po'boy only brought one. He told them the other was sick and couldn't leave the house.'

'So they raped Alicia.'

'Yes.' Annette's eyes filled. 'Like they did all the others. I . . . couldn't believe what I was reading. I'd married this man. Had babies with him . . .' Her voice trailed away.

'Mrs O'Brien,' Daniel said softly. 'What did they do to the girls?'

She wiped her eyes with her fingertips. 'They'd give them a date-rape drug and take them to a house. Jared never said whose. They'd . . .' She looked up, pained. 'Please, don't make me describe that part. It makes me sick to think about.'

He didn't need her description. He'd seen the pictures in obscene detail. 'Okay.'

'Thank you. When it was over, they'd put the girls in their cars, pour whiskey on their clothes, and leave them with an empty bottle. They'd take pictures to show the girls in case they remembered. They made it look consensual so that the girls wouldn't talk.'

Daniel frowned. None of the pictures he'd seen had incriminated any of the men, and not one looked the least bit consensual. 'Did any of the girls remember?'

She nodded dully. 'Sheila. And now she's dead. I can't get her out of my mind.'

Neither could Daniel. 'Go on,' he said, and she drew herself straighter.

'That night, they left Alicia in the woods when they were . . . finished. In the months before Alicia, Jared had written that he wondered what it would feel like if they were awake.' Annette's eyes were haunted. 'He wanted to "hear them scream." So that night he went back. He waited until Alicia was waking up, attacked her again, and she started to scream. But they weren't too far from the Crightons' house, and Jared all of a sudden realized he didn't want her screaming after all.'

'So he smothered her to make her be quiet.'

'And then he panicked when he realized she was dead. He ran away and left her there, dead and naked in the woods. He wrote all this when he came back from killing her. He was . . . exhilarated. Then the next day, they found Alicia's body in the ditch and Jared was as puzzled as everyone else. He thought it was funny. The others in the club were totally freaked and he alone knew he'd killed her and because that drifter was arrested, he'd get away with it, too.'

And Gary Fulmore had spent thirteen years in prison for a crime he hadn't committed. 'What about the seventh man? Harvard?'

'Again, I always thought that was one of the Woolf brothers. Especially Jim. He was always kind of an egghead.' One side of her mouth lifted sadly. 'After you, of course. You had the best grades.'

Daniel frowned. 'Did I know you back then?'

'No. But everyone heard about you from Mr Grant.'

His old English teacher. 'He talked about me?'

'He talked about all his favorites. He said you memorized a poem and won a prize.'

'"Death be not proud,"' Daniel murmured. 'What happened after you found the journals?'

'I knew that Jared hadn't just run away. I knew they'd disposed of him. In the last few passages, Jared said he was afraid. That when he'd get drunk, he'd talk, and it was getting harder not to talk about what they'd done.'

'He was having remorse?' Daniel asked, surprised.

'No. Remorse was not in Jared's vocabulary. His business was going under. He'd gambled away two family fortunes, mine and his. He wished he could tell everyone what he'd done to Alicia. They'd be amazed. But if he told, the others would kill him.'

'So he wanted to brag.' Daniel shook his head.

'He was scum. So when he died, part of me was relieved, but the rest of me was terrified. I thought, what if the others knew that I knew? They'd kill me, too, and Joey. I was pregnant and I didn't have anywhere to go. I waited, terrified, thinking someone would come into my house in the night and kill me.

'A few weeks passed. The mill went under and Jared's mother had to file bankruptcy. I'd walk down Main Street with my head down. I'm sure most people thought I was ashamed of the bankruptcy, but I was terrified. I knew that some of the men *I knew* had done *those things*. I knew sooner or later they'd see it in my eyes. So I sold what we had left and moved here. I got a job and made ends meet.'

'And you kept the journals.'

'Insurance. I figured if they ever bothered me, I could use them as leverage.'

'What about Jared's mother?'

'Lila tried to get a loan from the bank. She went to the bank and begged.' Her jaw tightened. 'On her knees. She begged Rob Davis on her knees and he turned her down flat.'

'That had to have been humiliating for your mother-in-law.'

'You have no idea,' she said bitterly. 'One of the tellers told everyone she'd seen Lila on her knees in front of Davis.' A hot flush spread across Annette's cheeks. 'The way Delia said it made it seem like Lila was doing something perverted. The very thought . . . Lila never even knew an act like that existed, much less considered doing it to Rob Davis.'

Daniel kept his face neutral, even though he'd tensed inside. 'Delia?'

'Yeah,' Annette said with contempt. 'Delia Anderson, that slut. Everyone knew she was having an affair with Rob Davis. She probably still is. And she had the nerve to spread that lie about Lila. Lila had a bad heart, and after that, everything went downhill. She had to sell everything, too. She had to pull Mack out of Bryson Academy and he was furious. He was wild. He scared me, even before I knew what Jared had done.'

Now the murders of both Sean and Delia made sense. 'Mack was violent?'

'Oh, yes. Mack got into fights all the time, even before the bankruptcy. He never got in trouble. Somehow all the charges would just go away. I thought it was O'Brien money until I found out there wasn't any left. When I found the journals, I knew. All the others had been supporting Jared, giving him enough money to get by, to stay one step ahead of the IRS and his creditors. They must've smoothed the way for Mack, too.'

'That makes sense. I would have come to the same conclusion.'

Her smile was sad. 'Thank you. Most of the time when I thought about telling anyone, I thought they'd think I was crazy. That maybe I'd made it all up. And then . . .'

'And then?'

'Then I'd pull the brick out just enough to prove to myself the journals were still there. And I'd know I wasn't crazy.'

'When was the last time you pulled out the brick?'

'The day they dug up your brother's grave and found someone else buried there I thought, "Now I should tell. Somebody will believe me."'

'Why didn't you?' he asked gently.

'Because I'm a coward. I kept hoping one of you guys would figure it all out. That you'd come and make me tell and that I could tell myself I had no choice. And because I didn't tell, all those girls are dead.' She looked up, her eyes bright with tears. 'I have to live with that for the rest of my life. I don't think you have any idea how that feels.'

You'd be surprised. 'You're telling me now. That's the important thing.'

She blinked, sending the tears down her face, and she wiped them away. 'I'll testify.'

'Thank you. Mrs O'Brien, do you know about any keys?'

'Yes. Simon took pictures of all of the attacks. If one told, they'd all go down, and the pictures kept everyone "honest." Simon kept the pictures as insurance. He never did any of the rapes, he just took the pictures.'

'So what about the keys?'

'Simon kept the pictures in a safe-deposit box at the bank. It was a special box that needed two keys. Simon had one and everyone else had copies of the other. That way it balanced the power. When Simon died the first time, Jared was terrified it would all come out, but time passed and no key was found. Why, do you have it now?'

He let the question pass and asked one of his own. 'Did you find Jared's key?'

'No, but he did have a picture of it in the journal. A drawing, like he'd traced it.'

'Did Jared say under which name the safe-deposit box was listed?' he asked, and held his breath until she nodded.

'Charles Wayne Bundy. I remember being horrified.

And I remember thinking that would be an important detail to keep inside my head in case I ever got pressed to tell. That maybe that would buy protection for my children. But you've already promised me that, so . . . there you are.'

Charles Manson. John Wayne Gacy. And Ted Bundy. It all fit. Simon had had a fascination with serial killers as a teenager, copying their art. Susannah had been the one to find the art he'd hidden under his bed all those years ago. *This was gold.* If Simon had taken incriminating photos of the rapists to ensure their compliance, Daniel would have all the proof he needed once he got the contents of that box.

'Do you have any idea of where Mack might hide?'

'If I did, I'd tell you. I know he's not in his old house. It was torn down while he was in prison.'

Daniel raised his brows. 'Why?'

'Someone broke in and ripped everything up. The walls, the floors. What was left wasn't worth saving.'

Daniel thought of Alex's bungalow. 'They were looking for the key.'

'Probably. Rob Davis benefited. After the house was gone, he bought the land dirt cheap and put in a warehouse for the mill. I can't see Mack hiding there. It's used daily.'

He'd check it out anyway. They had to find Mack O'Brien before he killed again. And he was a warrant away from identifying the final member of Simon's club. *Charles Wayne Bundy's safe-deposit box awaits.*

'Thank you, Mrs O'Brien. You've been more help than you know. Let's go get your boys and we'll get you someplace safe. We can send someone for your things.'

Annette nodded and followed him out the door, and she didn't look back.

Chapter Twenty-three

Arcadia, Georgia, Friday, February 2, 11:35 A.M.

'It fits,' Luke said over the speakerphone in Chase's office.

Daniel was on the phone in Sheriff Corchran's office, relating Annette O'Brien's story while he waited for an agent to take her and her two sons to a safe house. 'Now we just have to find him.'

'We revised the APB,' Chase said. 'We got his parole file. He's a lot bulkier now than he was when he went in.'

'They usually are,' Daniel said grimly. 'He may also have changed his hair. While we were driving to Corchran's office, Mrs O'Brien remembered that a box of blond hair coloring she'd bought was missing.'

'I'll update it again,' Luke said. 'Here's something else – Mack O'Brien was often put on roadside cleanup while he was in prison. He'd been on crews assigned to every one of the areas where he left the bodies.'

'We need to search the mill property – especially the new warehouse that was put up where the O'Briens' house used to be.'

'I've already dispatched a team,' Chase said. 'They're going in as pest inspectors so we don't raise the alarm too soon. What about a warrant for that safe-deposit box?'

'Chloe's working on it. As soon as we're done, I'm driving to Dutton so I can go right to the bank as soon as she gets it signed by the judge. What about Hatton?'

'He's still in surgery,' Chase said. 'Crighton's lawyered up. Won't talk to us.'

'Sonofabitch,' Daniel muttered. 'I'd so like to get him for Kathy Tremaine.'

'After all this time . . .' Luke said, a shrug in his voice. 'I don't see it happening.'

'I know, but at least Alex could get some closure. Has she asked to see him yet?'

'No,' Chase said. 'She hasn't mentioned him at all. She's pacing the floor over Hatton, but hasn't asked word one about Crighton.'

Daniel sighed. 'She will when she's ready. I'm headed out to Dutton. I'll call as soon as I get inside the box. Cross your fingers.'

Atlanta, Friday, February 2, 12:30 P.M.

Alex stood, pacing the short length of the outer office. 'They should have called.'

'Surgery takes a while,' Leigh said calmly. 'When Hatton's out, they'll call.'

Leigh's face was calm, but her eyes were scared. Somehow that made Alex feel a little less alone. She'd opened her mouth to say as much when her cell phone trilled. It was a Cincinnati area code, but she didn't recognize the number. 'Hello?'

'Miss Alex Fallon?'

'Yes,' she said warily. 'Who is this?'

'My name is Officer Morse. I'm with the Cincinnati police.'

'What's wrong?'

'Your apartment was broken into last night. Your building manager noticed the door was open this morning when she came to bring in your mail.'

'No, I called my friend yesterday to ask her to check my mail. She must have forgotten to pull the door shut.'

'Your apartment was ransacked, Miss Fallon. Pillows and mattresses are slashed, contents of your pantry are all dumped on the floor, and—'

Alex's heart had started to race at *ransacked*. 'And my clothing's been slashed.'

There was a hesitant pause. 'How did you know?'

Trust no one, Wade had said in his letter to Bailey.

'Officer, could you give me your badge number and a phone number where I can call you back after I check you out?'

'Not a problem.' He gave her the information and she promised to call him back.

'Leigh, can you please check this officer's ID? He says my apartment was trashed.'

'Oh my God.' Wide-eyed, Leigh took the information. 'I'll do it right now.'

'Thanks. I need to make a few calls before I call him back.' Alex called the hospital and was relieved to hear Letta answer. She told her to be careful, then asked her to give the same message to Richard, who was on shift.

Leigh was hanging up her phone. 'The Cincinnati cop's legit, Alex.'

'Good.' She called Morse back. 'Thanks for waiting.'

'You were prudent to check. Do you know who could have broken into your place?'

'Yes, kind of. Probably the same ones who ransacked my rental house down here. Can I refer you to Agent Daniel Vartanian? He'll know what information to give you.'

'I'll call him. Do you know what they were looking for?'

'Yes, because I got to it first. It was at my ex-husband's house. If whoever did this realizes that, they might go there next.'

'Give me his address. We'll send someone out to make sure they're okay.'

'Thank you,' Alex said, touched and surprised.

'We have been watching the news, Miss Fallon. Sounds like Agent Vartanian has his hands full.'

Alex blew out a breath. 'That he does.'

Dutton, Friday, February 2, 12:30 P.M.

Daniel looked down at the heavy volume of poetry in his hands. He'd stopped by a bookstore on his way from the Arcadia sheriff's office. Chloe Hathaway was still working on his warrant, so he had some time to kill. He was now parked across the street from the bench in front of the Dutton barbershop. He wanted to talk to his old English teacher, Mr Grant, who sat on the barbershop bench watching with a sharp eye.

Daniel got out of his car. 'Mr Grant,' he called.

'Daniel Vartanian,' Grant called back while the other men looked on.

Daniel motioned Grant to come to him and waited as he shuffled his way to Daniel's car. 'I have something for you,' he said when Grant reached him. He handed the man the collection of poems. 'I've been thinking of your English class,' he said in a normal voice, then whispered, 'I need to talk to you, but I needed to be discreet.'

Grant smoothed the volume with a reverent gesture. 'It's a beautiful book,' he said, then whispered. 'I've been waiting for you to come to me. What do you want to know?'

Daniel blinked. 'What do you know?'

'Probably more than would fill this book, but not much of it pertinent. Ask your questions. If I can answer, I will.' He opened the book and leafed until he found the John Donne poem that had been Daniel's favorite. 'Go ahead. I'm listening.'

'I need to know about Mack O'Brien.'

'Quick mind, but a hot temper.'

'Who did he lose his temper with?'

'Damn near everybody, especially after they lost everything. While he was at Bryson, he fancied himself a real ladies' man. Like his big brother.' Grant tilted his head as if he were contemplating the poem. 'Mack was bad news. He vandalized school property, drove that Corvette of his like he was some hotshot NASCAR racer, got into some major fights.'

'You said he was a ladies' man.'

'No, I said he fancied himself to be a ladies' man. It's different.' Grant turned pages until he came to another poem. 'I remember overhearing conversations some of the female students had after Mack changed schools. They'd chatter, thinking I was busy grading papers. They were laughing that Mack had expected to come to Prom – he no longer went to the school and they scorned him. They said he'd only been tolerable because of his car. Without that, they didn't want to give him the time of day. He wasn't nearly as handsome as his big brother. Mack had terrible acne, and it left him pockmarked. The girls treated him pretty badly.'

'Which girls, Mr Grant?'

'The dead ones. Janet was the worst, as I recall. Gemma laughed that she'd gotten drunk and "done him" in his 'Vette. She said she would have had to have been drunk.'

'And Claudia?'

'Claudia usually went along with the others. Kate Davis was the one who usually told them to stop.'

'Why didn't you tell me this before?'

Grant made a show of examining the book before flipping to another passage. 'Because Mack wasn't anything special. They were cruel to a lot of the boys. I wouldn't have even thought about it if you hadn't mentioned his name. Besides, he's in prison.'

'No he's not,' Daniel said quietly. 'Not anymore.'

The old man's back tensed, then he relaxed. 'Good to know.'

'What about Lisa Woolf?'

Grant frowned. 'I remember Mack missing about two weeks of school before he transferred in his junior year. When I asked what was wrong with him, the girls giggled. They said he'd gotten bitten by a dog. I found out Mack was home recuperating from a fight. Apparently he'd tried to put the moves on Lisa and her brothers beat the snot out of him. He was pretty embarrassed. When he came back, he'd walk down the halls and kids would howl behind him, you know, like they were wolves howling at the moon. He'd turn and glare, but he never knew who was making fun.'

Daniel's cell phone buzzed in his pocket. It was SA Chloe Hathaway. 'Excuse me.' He turned slightly. 'Vartanian.'

'It's Chloe. You are the proud owner of one warrant for a safe-deposit box in the name of Charles Wayne Bundy. Hope this is what you were looking for.'

'Me, too. Thanks.' He closed his phone. 'I have to go.'

Grant closed the book and extended it. 'I've enjoyed reminiscing with you, Daniel Vartanian. It's nice to see a former student turn out well.'

Daniel lightly pushed the book back. 'Keep the book, Mr Grant. I bought it for you.'

Grant hugged the book to his chest. 'Thank you, Daniel. Take care.'

Daniel watched the old man shuffle back across the street and hoped he'd been discreet. Too many innocent people had paid for the sins of a handful of spoiled, willful young men. Some rich, some poor, but all with a flagrant disregard for decency, humanity. The law. If tradition held, the men vacated the barbershop bench for the night right at five o'clock. He'd make sure someone was watching Grant's house. He didn't want to live with more blood on his hands.

He'd pulled away from the curb when his cell phone buzzed again. This time it was the office, and immediately his thoughts went to Hatton. He'd been in surgery when Daniel had called the last time. 'Vartanian.'

'Daniel, it's Alex. Somebody trashed my apartment in Cincinnati yesterday.'

'Hell.' He blew out a breath. 'They were looking for the key.'

'How would they know I had the letter up there?'

'Could Bailey's friend have told them, too?'

'I had Chase check. Nobody's visited her and nobody's called her.'

'There are a lot of ways she could have communicated it if she wanted to.'

'I know, but, Daniel, I was thinking . . . The only other person who knew was Bailey.'

It was a long shot, but he heard the hope in her voice and couldn't bear to shoot it down. 'You're thinking whoever took her finally got her to talk.'

'I'm *thinking* she might still be alive.'

He sighed. She might be right. 'If she is alive—'

'If she is alive, then one of those men knows where she is. Davis or Mansfield. Daniel, please, bring them in and *make them tell*.'

'If they've gone to this much trouble, it's unlikely they'll just tell,' Daniel said, trying to soothe without sounding patronizing. 'It's more likely they'll get nervous and go to her. If it's Davis or Mansfield, we have them under surveillance. I know it's hard, but this is the most critical time to stay patient.'

'I'm trying.'

'I know, honey.' He pulled his car into a metered space along the curb across from the bank. 'Anything else? I'm heading into the bank to ask Rob Davis to give me that box, so if Davis and Mansfield are watching, I'm about to set off a flare.'

'Well, there is one little thing. The vet's office called. Riley can leave.'

Daniel shook his head, perplexed at her timing. 'I can't get him right now.'

'Oh, I know, but I was wondering if the agent watching Hope and Meredith could take Riley to the safe house. Hope's been asking for the sad dog.'

That made him smile. 'Sure. I'll call you later. You stay put.'

'I *am*.' And she sounded none too happy about it. 'You be careful.'

'I am. Alex . . .' He hesitated, a little afraid of the words he wanted to say. It had happened so fast. In the end he decided to keep the words to himself a little longer. 'Tell Meredith not to feed Riley anything other than his dry food. Trust me.'

'I do,' she said, and he knew she wasn't talking about Riley. 'Call when you can.'

'I will. This will be over soon.' Feeling as if he stood at the edge of a precipice, Daniel crossed the street to the bank. As soon as he asked for that safe-deposit box, everyone would know, and whatever shit was out there would hit the fan. *You gotta love small towns*. No, he didn't.

Friday, February 2, 12:45 P.M.

Annoyed, Mack pulled his earphones from his ears as Vartanian drove up Main Street, out of range. *Fancied himself a ladies' man, my ass.* He'd hated Mr Grant – stuffy, arrogant old prick. When he'd finished off the others, he'd come back for Grant and the man would regret talking to Daniel Vartanian.

Daniel knew about him. It gave Mack a kick, knowing the man was probably combing the countryside looking for him while he'd sat just fifty feet away.

But his satisfaction was short-lived. *Vartanian had come alone.*

He never dreamed Vartanian would come alone. He'd just assumed Alex Fallon would be permanently attached to him as she had been for the last five days. He was finally ready for them and Vartanian had come alone.

If he wanted Alex Fallon to be the icing on his cake, he'd have to find a way to get her to come to him. Otherwise his coup de grâce would fall miserably flat and that would be a real shame. And speaking of his coup de grâce, he had invitations to mail.

He'd started up his van when he saw Vartanian walking across Main Street way up by the bank. Interesting. Daniel was finally visiting the bank. Mack thought finding keys tied to the toes of four dead women would have had the man visiting the bank sooner, but at last he was there.

Mack smiled when he thought about the pictures he knew Vartanian would find inside 'Charles Wayne Bundy's' safe-deposit box. Soon the pillars of the community would be humiliated, and at a minimum they'd all be sent to jail.

Of course, if over the next few hours Mack was successful, they'd all be dead.

Atlanta, Friday, February 2, 12:45 P.M.

Alex hung up the phone on Daniel's desk and let her shoulders sag.

'Anything wrong?'

She turned to find Luke Papadopoulos watching her in that thoughtful way he had. 'I have this feeling that Bailey's still alive. I'm so . . . frustrated.'

'And you wish somebody would just do something.'

'Yeah. And I know Daniel's right and that he has all these other people to worry about, but . . . Bailey's mine. It makes me feel whiny and selfish.'

'You're not being selfish or whiny. Come on. I'm taking a break for lunch. Usually I eat food from home, but it seems someone has appropriated my lunch.' He narrowed his eyes in the direction of Chase's office. 'He will pay.'

Alex had to smile. 'Chase *is* quite a character. Leigh said the cafeteria has pizza on Fridays.' And she realized she was hungry. She'd left Daniel's house in such a hurry that morning, she'd skipped breakfast. 'Let's go.' She looked up at him as they left Daniel's office. He was a breathtakingly handsome man, she thought. Meredith's type, actually. 'So . . . you got a girlfriend?'

His smile flashed bright against his tanned skin. 'Why, you tired of Danny already?'

She thought of that morning in Daniel's bed and felt her cheeks heat. 'No. I'm talking about Meredith. You'd like her. She's fun.'

'Does she like to fish?'

'I really couldn't say, but I could ask . . .' Her words drained away and she and Luke stopped in the same moment. Standing at the counter talking to Leigh was a woman with a face she recognized. From the tensing of Luke's body, he recognized her, too.

She was small with sleek dark hair and sad, sad eyes. Her clothes said New York and her body language said she'd rather be anyplace other than where she now stood.

'Susannah,' Alex murmured, and the woman met her eyes.

'You know me?'

'I'm Alex Fallon.'

Susannah nodded. 'I've read about you.' She turned to Luke.

'And you're Daniel's friend. I met you at the funeral last week. Agent Papadopoulos, right?'

'Right,' Luke said. 'Why are you here, Susannah?'

Susannah Vartanian's lips curved humorlessly. 'I'm not entirely sure. But I think I came to get my life back. And maybe my self-respect.'

Dutton, Friday, February 2, 12:55 P.M.

Such a lure could not be resisted. He watched Frank Loomis stop on the police department steps, open his phone, and check the text message. Loomis narrowed his eyes at the darkened windows of the newspaper office, closed today due to a death in the family. Mack had to smile. The Woolfs were grieving and he was the reason. It took a long time to pay a debt sometimes. When enough time had passed, the interest was huge.

He thought killing Woolf's sister was a good start toward making good on that debt. He'd used the Woolfs this week and he'd use them a few more times before this was over. But for now, Frank Loomis was getting into his car and driving in the right direction.

The text message had been concise: *Got anon tip. Know where Bailey C is. Go 2 old O'B mill by river. Find BC + *many* others. Can't follow up – at funl home. Wanted you 2 have 411 before Var beat you 2 it. Good luck.* Signed, *Marianne Woolf.*

Frank was on his way. Soon, Vartanian would join him. Mansfield should already be there along with Harvard, the last pillar to fall. It had taken Mack a while to figure out who he was and when he had, even he'd been stunned.

As for Alex Fallon, he had a few ideas for drawing her out. Alex's entire focus in the last week had been on finding Bailey. *And I know where Bailey is.* Once the dust from the coming events of the afternoon settled, Alex would want to believe Bailey lived. Now that Delia was dead, Mack had no more plans to leave any more bodies in ditches, until Alex, that was. Perhaps the inactivity would lure her into a false sense of security.

Then again, she'd be grieving Daniel Vartanian's death, and grief did make people do some very unwise things. Sooner or later, she'd let her guard down, and then he'd have his final victim. His closed circle.

Friday, February 2, 1:25 p.m.

Mansfield stopped next to his desk. 'Okay, Harvard, here I am.'

He looked up, eyes widening, then narrowing in a fraction of a second. 'Why?'

Mansfield frowned. 'Because you sent for me.'

'I did no such thing.'

Mansfield's heart began to pound. 'I got a text on the disposable. Nobody has that number but you.'

'Obviously someone else does,' Harvard said coldly. 'Let me see it.'

Mansfield handed over the phone.

'"*Come ASAP. DVar knows about the goods. Moving out today.*"' His face darkened. 'Somebody knows, even if Vartanian doesn't. You were followed, you fuck-up.'

'No, I wasn't. I'm sure of it. Initially I was, but I lost the tail.' Technically he'd killed the tail, but Mansfield saw no need to make things worse for himself. 'What do we do?'

He was dangerously quiet for a moment. 'We'll take them on the boat.'

'We can only fit half a dozen on the boat.'

Harvard stood, rage coming off him in waves. 'When you have something to say that I don't already know, then speak. Otherwise keep your mouth shut. You get the healthy ones on the boat. I'll take care of the rest.'

Dutton, Friday, February 2, 1:30 P.M.

Daniel waited until he was outside the Dutton city limits before slamming his fist onto his steering wheel. Swallowing back his temper, he dialed Chase on his cell. 'The safe-deposit box was empty,' he snarled without preamble.

'You're kidding,' Chase said. 'Completely empty?'

'Not entirely. There was one little scrap of paper. It said "Ha ha."'

'Fuck,' Chase muttered. 'Did Rob Davis have a record of who last touched it?'

'Somebody with an ID that said Charles Wayne Bundy. The last time somebody was in the box was about six months after Simon died the first time. I really doubt it was Simon. He wouldn't have dared appear in public like that, and had Davis known he was really alive, it wouldn't have stayed a secret long.'

'But I thought Jared's journal said that Simon had the main key.'

'Either Annette remembered wrong or Jared was mistaken, because somebody else used a copy of Simon's key to get into the box.'

'Could Rob Davis have had a master?'

'Of course, but he seemed pretty stunned when the box was empty.'

'What did Davis say when you opened the box?'

'Before we opened it he was sweating bullets. Afterward he was relieved . . . and smug.'

'Well, relax. Um, I mean, really relax, because someone here wants to talk to you.'

'Tell Alex I'll call her back. I'm too—'

'Hello, Daniel.'

Daniel's mouth dropped open and immediately he slowed his car and pulled to the shoulder. His hands were shaking. 'Susannah? You're here? In Atlanta?'

'I'm here. Your friend Luke told me about the pictures you hoped to get from the safe-deposit box. I take it they weren't there.'

'No, they weren't. I'm sorry, Suze. We could've nailed those bastards.'

She was quiet. 'I know where the pictures might be.'

'Where?' But he thought he knew and his stomach got all tight.

'The house, Daniel. I'll meet you there.'

'Wait.' He clenched his jaw. 'Not alone. Put Luke on the phone.'

'I'll bring her,' Luke said when he took the phone. 'I'll meet you at your parents' house. Daniel, Alex is standing here. She wants to come.'

'No. Tell her to—'

'Daniel.' Alex had taken the phone from Luke. 'You stood by me when I went into my house. Let me do the same for you. Please,' she added softly.

He closed his eyes. His house was filled with ghosts, too. Not in the same way, of course, but ghosts, just the same. And he trusted Luke with his life.

But Alex was even more important than that. And because she was, he needed her there. 'All right. Stay with Luke. I'll meet you all there.'

Friday, February 2, 2:20 P.M.

'Bailey,' Beardsley hissed.

Bailey forced her eyes to open. She had the shakes, real bad. 'I'm here.'

'I'm ready for you.'

In another time, another place, those words could have meant something beautiful. Now, here, it meant they were both going to die very soon.

'Bailey?' Beardsley whispered again. 'Hurry.'

Oh, God, she needed a fix. *Hope needs you*. She gritted her teeth. 'I'm ready.'

She watched as he moved huge handfuls of the dirt he'd dug away over days until there was a hole barely big enough for Hope. 'I won't fit.'

'You have to. We don't have time for any more digging. Get on your stomach and put your feet through.' She did and he began to pull, none too gently. 'I'm sorry. I don't want to hurt you.'

She almost laughed. He kept tugging, angling her this way then that. He put his hands on her hips to turn her body to pull her through, but when he came to her breasts, he stopped abruptly. Bailey rolled her eyes. She was on her stomach, half in, half out, filthy and reeking of God only knew what, and Beardsley picked now to get shy.

'Pull,' she whispered. One of his hands slid up her front, one up her back, and he maneuvered her through until he could reach her shoulders. That was even more painful.

'Turn your face to the side.'

She did, and he helped her wiggle her head through so that she didn't get dirt up her nose. Finally she was on his side of the wall.

And seeing him for the very first time. That he was seeing her for the first time wasn't anything she even wanted to contemplate. She stared down, ashamed of how she knew she looked. Gently he cupped her chin with a dirty hand. 'Bailey. Let me see you.'

Shyly she let him lift her face and even more shyly lifted her eyelids. And she wanted to cry. Under the dirt and the grime and the blood, he was the handsomest man she'd ever seen in her life. He smiled at her, his teeth white against his filthy face. 'I'm not that bad, am I?' he murmured teasingly, and the tears she fought welled and spilled.

He pulled her onto his lap and into his arms and rocked her as she'd done Hope so many times. 'Sshh,' he whispered. 'Don't cry, baby. We're almost there.' It made her cry harder, because they were going to die and she'd never get the chance to show him or anyone else what she could have been. They were going to die.

'We're going to do this,' he whispered fiercely. 'They're moving things. Something's happening. Close your eyes.' She did and he wiped her tears with his thumbs. 'I think I made it worse,' he said lightly, then pulled her back to him for one more hard hug.

'Whatever happens,' she murmured, 'thank you.'

He set her off his lap and rose, tall and strong despite his ordeal. He held out his hand. 'We don't have much time.'

She stood on shaky legs. 'What are we going to do?'

He smiled again, approval in his eyes. His eyes were warm and brown. She'd remember that, whatever happened. He handed her what had been a chunk of rock, about four inches long, its edge sharpened to a razor finish. 'This is yours.'

She stared at it, wide-eyed. 'You made this?'

'God made the rock. I just sharpened it. You hold on to it. You may need it if we get separated.'

'What will you do?'

He went to the corner of his cell and brushed at the dirt until he pulled out a sharpened stone, easily three times bigger than hers. 'Have you slept at all?' she whispered, and he smiled again.

'Catnaps.' He spent the next ten minutes showing her where and how to pierce an assailant's body to do the most damage.

Then a door slammed open in the hall and her eyes flew up to his. He looked grim and she was suddenly more afraid than ever. 'He's coming,' she said, shaking.

Beardsley smoothed his hands over her arms. 'Then he's coming,' he said with finality. 'We're ready. Right?'

She nodded.

'Then go curl up over there in the corner. Make yourself as big as you can. You're supposed to be me.'

'I'd need two of me,' she said, and one side of his mouth lifted fleetingly.

'Three, actually. Bailey, you can't falter. And if I give you an order, you obey me without question. Do you understand?'

He was coming closer now, opening a door, then firing a single shot. She heard screams from where she'd only heard the weeping before. Horrified, Bailey met Beardsley's eyes as more doors were opened and more shots fired. The screaming faded as the voices were silenced one by one. 'He's killing them.'

A muscle twitched in Beardsley's jaw. 'I know. Change in plan. You hide behind the door, I'll stand on the other side. Move, Bailey.'

She obeyed and he took up position next to the door, his big dagger in one hand. A second later the door flew open and she covered her face to keep from being hit. Bailey heard a strangled cry and a gurgle and then a thump.

'Let's go,' Beardsley said. She stepped over the body of one of the guards she'd seen one of the times *he'd* taken her back to the office. Beardsley wiped the dagger against his pants, cleaning off the blood, then he was running, dragging her behind him.

But her knees were weak and her legs so bruised she kept stumbling. 'Just go,' she said. 'You run. Leave me here.'

But he didn't let go, dragging her past one cell, then another. Some were empty. Most were not. Bailey gagged at the sight of the girls, chained and bleeding. Dead.

'Don't look,' he barked. 'Just run.'

'I can't.'

He picked her up and tucked her under his arm like she was a football. 'You're not dying on my watch, Bailey,' he gritted, running around the corner.

Then Beardsley stopped and she looked up. *He* stood

in the middle of the hall and he had a gun. Beardsley tossed her and she landed on her knees. '*Run*,' he barked.

Then Beardsley plowed into him and knocked him against the wall. Bailey made herself get up and run while the two men grappled behind her. She heard the sickening sound of bone hitting the concrete wall, but she kept going.

Until she saw the girl. She was battered and blood oozed from a hole in her side and a second, glancing wound to her head. She'd clawed her way across her cell and had stretched out one arm into the hall. But she was still alive.

Weakly the girl lifted her hand. 'Help me,' she whispered. 'Please.'

Without thinking Bailey grabbed the girl's hand and dragged her to her feet. 'Move.'

Dutton, Friday, February 2, 2:35 P.M.

Daniel stood on the front porch of his family's house, feeling a strange sense of déjà vu. It was here he'd stood, nearly three weeks ago, with Frank Loomis. Frank had told him his parents 'might be missing.' Of course they were already long dead. But Daniel's search for them had led him to Philadelphia and Simon and the pictures. His search for the pictures had led him right back here.

'Déjà vu all over again?' Luke asked softly and Daniel nodded.

'Yeah.' He unlocked the door and pushed it open and found his feet wouldn't move.

Alex slipped her arm around his waist. 'Come on.' She tugged him over the threshold and he stopped in the foyer, his eyes doing a sweep of the place. He'd hated this house. Hated every brick of it. He turned to find Susannah doing a similar sweep. She was pale, but as she had during the entire ordeal in Philly, she was holding up.

'Where?' he asked.

Susannah pushed by him and started up the stairs. He followed, holding Alex's hand as tightly as he dared. Luke brought up the rear, alert and watching.

Upstairs, Daniel frowned. Doors he'd closed the last time he was here were opened and a painting on the hall wall was askew. He pushed open the door to his parents' bedroom. The room had been ransacked, the mattress slashed.

'They've been here,' he said flatly. 'Looking for Simon's key.'

'This way,' Susannah said tightly, and they followed her into what had been Simon's room. It, too, had been ransacked, but there had been nothing in the drawers or under the bed for them to find. Daniel's father had disposed of that a long time ago.

There was, he thought, an evilness hanging in the

air. Or perhaps it was just his imagination. But Alex's face had taken on an uncomfortable cast.

'It has kind of a presence, doesn't it?' she whispered, and he squeezed her hand.

Susannah stood at the closet door, her hands opening and closing into fists at her sides. She was still pale, but she squared her shoulders resolutely. 'I could be wrong. There might be nothing here,' she said, then opened the door. The closet was empty, but she walked inside anyway. 'Did you know this house has hidey-holes, Daniel?'

Something in her voice had the hairs rising on the back of his neck. 'Yes. I thought I knew them all.'

She knelt, feeling around the baseboards. 'I found the hidey-hole off my closet one night when I was hiding from Simon. I'd huddled up against the wall and I must have pushed the right way because the panel opened and I rolled behind the wall.' She steadily worked as she talked. 'I wondered if all the closets had these hidey-holes. One day when I thought Simon was gone, I tried to see if I could open his.'

The flat finality with which she'd said it twisted his stomach. 'He caught you.'

'At first I didn't think he had. I heard him thumping up the stairs and I ran to my room. But he had,' she said, quietly now. 'When I woke up with a whiskey bottle in my hand, it was inside my hidey-hole. He'd stuffed me in there.'

Alex smoothed her hand down his arm and he

realized he'd been holding her hand too tightly. He let go, but she held on, comforting him.

Daniel cleared his throat. 'He knew about your hiding place.'

Susannah shrugged with a matter-of-factness that broke his heart. 'There was nowhere to hide,' she said. 'Later, he showed me the picture he'd taken of me with . . .' Again she shrugged. 'He told me to stay out of his affairs. After that, I obeyed him.' She pushed the panel and it gave way. 'After he died, I just wanted to forget.' She leaned into the hole, then reappeared, dragging a dusty box. Luke took it from her and put it on Simon's slashed-up bed. 'Thank you,' she murmured and gestured to the box. 'I think that's what you're looking for,' she said.

Now that he had them, Daniel was almost afraid to look. His heart beating hard, he lifted the lid. And wanted to throw up.

'Dear God,' Alex whispered beside him.

Friday, February 2, 2:50 P.M.

'Come on.' Bailey tugged the girl's hand, dragging her through the dark hallways. Beardsley had pointed this way. He couldn't be wrong. *Beardsley*. Her heart clenched hard. He'd given up his freedom . . . *for me*. Now he'd die. *For me*.

Concentrate, Bailey. You have to get out of here. Don't let that man have given up his life in vain. Focus. Find the door. After another few minutes, she saw light.

Light at the end of the tunnel. She almost laughed, but dragged the girl harder with a spurt of new energy. She opened the door, expecting a loud alarm or barking dogs.

But there was silence. And fresh air and trees and sunshine.

And freedom. *Thank you, Beardsley.*

And then it all shattered. Standing in front of her was Frank Loomis. And he had a gun in his hand.

Chapter Twenty-four

Dutton, Friday, February 2, 2:50 P.M.

The box was filled with photographs and drawings Simon had made. Some Daniel recognized as identical to the pictures his father had burned, but there were many more. Hundreds more. Grimly, he pulled a pair of gloves from his pocket and began to pull the pictures from the box. These photos showed the faces of the young men as they'd committed their obscenities, and somehow they'd managed to make some of their lewd acts seem consensual, just as Annette O'Brien had said. He tightened his jaw as he shuffled through each handful. He'd known what he would see, but the reality was far worse than he'd imagined. He stared at the boys' faces, horrified and physically ill.

'They're *laughing,*' Alex whispered. 'Goading each other on.'

Rage surged, and with it a pagan urge to choke the life from their vile, despicable bodies. 'Jared O'Brien and Rhett Porter. And Garth Davis,' he said harshly, remembering how concerned the mayor had been that night at Presto's Pizza when he'd demanded answers about the man murdering the women of Dutton. 'Sonofabitch. He was at Presto's. He let Sheila serve him food, all the while knowing what he'd done.'

'Throwing the book at Garth Davis will feel damn good,' Luke said grimly.

Daniel moved to the next picture. 'Randy Mansfield.' He thought about the bad news he'd had from Chase as he'd waited outside the house for Luke, Susannah, and Alex. Mansfield had raped young girls. Now Daniel knew he was a killer, too.

Beside him, Alex flinched when he showed the next picture. Wade. With Alicia.

'I'm sorry,' Daniel said, sliding the picture to the back. 'I didn't want you to see it.'

'I already had,' she said in a low voice, 'in my mind.'

Daniel continued shuffling through the photos, then came to a dead stop when he saw Susannah. Young. Unconscious. Violated. His hands jerked, reflexively flipping it over, and he stared at the back of the hideous photo, his emotions churning.

He'd left her here, alone. Unprotected. With Simon. Who'd done . . . *this*. His roiling stomach heaved. He hadn't known back then. But it didn't change the fact that it had happened. Simon had allowed . . . No, he'd *encouraged* those animals to violate his own sister. My sister. She'd been scared and abused and *I did nothing*.

Bile burning his throat and tears burning his eyes, he slid the picture into his suit pocket, away from the others. He looked away. 'I'll burn it,' he whispered hoarsely. 'I'm sorry. God. Suze.' His voice broke. 'I'm so sorry.'

Nobody said a word. Then Susannah took the picture from his pocket and put it with the others. At the back of the stack, but with the others all the same.

'If I'm going to take my self-respect back, I have to stand with them,' she said with a calm that cut him in two. Unable to reply, Daniel only nodded.

Luke moved to his side and took over the task of sorting through the pictures while Daniel gathered his composure. He and Luke worked on in silence, and by the time they'd finished, they'd identified five young men, monsters all.

'Garth, Rhett, Jared, and Randy,' Alex said quietly. 'And Wade. That's only five.'

'Number six was Simon, who took the pictures,' Daniel said, frustration eating at his control. 'But we still don't have the seventh. *Goddammit.*'

'I thought Annette said they had pictures of everyone,' Alex said. 'That that was how Simon kept control.'

Luke stripped off his gloves. 'Maybe she was wrong.'

'She was right about everything else.' Daniel forced his mind to think, to piece together what he knew. 'But someone else had both keys to that box, or we would have found the pictures in there. The last access to the safe-deposit box was six months after Simon left twelve years ago.' Daniel pointed to the box. 'These pictures have been here all this time, so we have to assume there were at least two sets to begin with.'

Luke nodded, understanding. 'Simon lied about everyone being equally implicated. He had a partner. The seventh boy.'

'Whose name we still don't have,' Daniel said bitterly. 'Dammit.'

'But you have Garth and Randy,' Alex said urgently. 'Bring them in. Get them to talk. Get them to tell you where they put Bailey.'

'I already did,' Daniel said, putting the top back on the box. 'While I was waiting for you to get here, I had Garth's tail pick him up.' He hesitated, dreading what he had to tell her. 'But Mansfield . . . Alex, the agent who was following him is dead.'

Alex paled. 'Mansfield killed him?'

'It looks that way.'

Anger flashed in her eyes. 'Dammit, Daniel. You knew about Mansfield *yesterday*. I *begged* you to pick him up. If—' She cut off the rest of her accusation, but it still hurt.

'Alex, that's not fair,' Luke murmured, but she shook her head hard.

'Now Mansfield knows you know what he's done,' she said raggedly. 'If he has Bailey, he'll kill her now.'

Daniel wouldn't insult her intelligence by denying her words. 'I'm sorry,' he said.

Her shoulders sagged in defeat and his heart clenched. 'I know,' she whispered.

Luke picked up the box. 'Let's get this back to Atlanta and start questioning Garth. He knows who the seventh boy was. Let's get him to roll.'

'I'll give my statement,' Susannah said, glancing at her watch. 'My flight's at six.'

She was following Luke out the door when Daniel got hold of himself. 'Suze. Wait. I need . . . I need to talk to you. Alex, can you give us a minute?'

Alex nodded stiffly. 'Can I have your keys? I've got a migraine coming on and my Imitrex pen is in my purse.'

He could see the pain behind her eyes and wished he could erase the stress that had put it there. Instead, he fished out his keys. 'Stay with Luke.'

Her jaw clenched as she snatched the keys from his hand. 'I'm not stupid, Daniel.'

'I know,' he murmured after she was gone. It didn't change the fact that he worried about her constantly. Like he should have worried about Susannah, back then. Daniel forced himself to look into his sister's eyes. They were carefully blank. She looked delicate. Fragile. But he'd learned that Susannah, like Alex, was neither delicate nor fragile. 'What made you come back?' he asked, and she lifted a slim shoulder.

'The others will testify. What kind of coward would I be not to do the same?'

'You're not a coward,' he said fiercely.

Her lips curved sardonically. 'You have no idea what I am, Daniel.'

He frowned. 'What the hell is that supposed to mean?'

She looked away. 'I have to go,' was all she replied as she turned to go.

'Susannah, *wait*.' She turned back, and he forced himself to ask the question he needed to know. 'Why didn't you tell me? Call me? I would have come to get you.'

Her eyes flickered. 'Would you have?'

'You know I would have.'

Her chin lifted, reminding him of Alex. 'If I'd known that, I would have called. You left, Daniel. You got away. The first year you were at college, you never came home, not once. Not even at Christmas.'

He remembered that first year of college, the overwhelming relief of getting away from Dutton. But he'd left Susannah to the wolves. 'I was selfish. But if I'd known, I would have come back. I'm so sorry.' The last was a helpless plea, but her expression didn't soften. There was no contempt in her eyes, but neither was there forgiveness.

He'd thought he'd needed atonement, to bring justice and closure to Simon's victims. Now he just wanted forgiveness from the one person he could have saved, but didn't.

'It is what it is,' she said evenly. 'You can't change the past.'

His throat thickened. 'Then can I change the future?'

For several seconds she said nothing. Then she shrugged. 'I don't know, Daniel.'

He wasn't sure what he'd expected. He wasn't sure what he had the right to ask for. She'd given him honesty, and that was a start. 'All right. Let's go.'

'Are you all right?'

Alex glanced up at Luke as she found her migraine medicine in her purse. For a few hours, she'd had hope of finding Bailey. Now that hope was dashed. 'No, I'm not. Turn around, Luke.'

His black brows bunched. 'What?'

'I have to shoot this in my thigh and I don't want you seeing my underwear. Turn around.' Coloring slightly, he complied, and Alex lowered her slacks enough to jab the pen in her bare thigh. She adjusted her clothes, then looked at Luke's back. Even from behind him she could tell he was scanning the countryside, alert and watching.

Mansfield was still out there, and he'd killed one man. Maybe more. A shiver ran down her back as the hairs on her neck lifted. It was probably just the house scaring her, she thought. Mansfield was probably miles away. Still, as she'd told Daniel, she wasn't stupid. She looked at Daniel's keys in her hand and knew what she'd do.

'Can I turn around?' Luke asked.

'No.' Alex opened Daniel's trunk, retrieved her gun,

and awkwardly slipped it behind her waistband. She closed the trunk, feeling no safer. 'Now you can turn around.'

Luke did so, giving her a pointed look. 'Keep your eyes open if you need to use it. I'm sorry about your stepsister,' he added quietly. 'So is Daniel. Really.'

'I know,' she said, and remembering the hurt in his eyes, she knew it was true. He'd done his job, but Bailey would be dead just the same. *Nobody wins.* She was spared further reply by the emergence of Daniel and Susannah from the house. She gave him his keys and he locked the front door.

'Let's go back,' Daniel said, his expression flat, and Alex wondered what Daniel and Susannah had discussed – and what they had not.

Friday, February 2, 3:00 P.M.

Frozen in place, Bailey waited for Loomis to give her away. Her heart pounded like a wild thing. So close. She'd come so close . . . Beside her, the girl started to cry.

Then, to her shock, Loomis put his finger over his lips. 'Follow the trees,' he whispered. 'You'll find the road.' He pointed to the girl. 'How many more in there?'

Bailey clenched her eyes shut. *All gone.* 'None. He killed them all. All except her.'

Loomis swallowed. 'Then go. I'll go get my car and meet you by the road.'

Bailey held the girl's hand tight. 'Come on,' she whispered. 'Just a little bit longer.'

The girl still cried softly, but Bailey couldn't let herself feel sympathy. She couldn't let herself feel anything. She just needed to keep moving.

Now that was interesting, Mack thought, watching Loomis point Bailey and the other girl toward freedom. The man was actually doing his job. For once in his life Frank Loomis was actually serving and protecting. He waited until Loomis was a few feet away before stepping into his path. He held his gun steady and Loomis stopped dead.

Loomis's eyes rose to his face, recognition instantly dawning.

'Mack O'Brien.' His jaw tightened. 'I guess it goes without saying that you're not in prison anymore.'

'Nope,' Mack said cheerfully. 'One-third served.'

'So it's been you, all along.'

There was satisfaction in his smile. 'All along. Give me your guns, Sheriff. Oh, wait, you're not a sheriff anymore.'

Loomis's lips thinned. 'I'm being investigated, not tried.'

'Like there's a difference in this town? Give me your guns,' he repeated deliberately. 'Or I'll kill you where you stand.'

'You're going to anyway.'

'Maybe. Or maybe you can help me.'

Loomis's eyes narrowed. 'How?'

'I want Daniel Vartanian here. I want him to see this operation first-hand and to catch them red-handed. If you give him all this and Bailey, that should be enough to influence your trial. I mean, investigation.'

'That's all I have to do? Get Daniel here?'

'That's all.'

'And if I refuse?'

He pointed at Bailey and the girl, picking their way through the woods on bare and bloody feet. 'I raise the alarm and Bailey and the girl die.'

Loomis's eyes narrowed. 'You're a sonofabitch.'

'Thank you.'

Dutton, Friday, February 2, 3:10 P.M.

'How's your headache?' Daniel asked.

'I hit it in time. I'm fine,' Alex said, keeping her eyes on the window where Dutton's Main Street wound by. She should apologize to him, she knew. She'd hurt him when he was just doing his job. But, dammit, she was *angry*. And helpless, which made her even angrier. Not trusting her voice or her words, she kept her mouth firmly closed.

After another few minutes of silence Daniel hissed a curse. 'Could you just yell at me, please? I'm sorry about Bailey. I don't know what else to say.'

The wall holding her fury broke. 'I hate this town,' she gritted from behind clenched teeth. 'I hate your sheriff and the mayor and everyone that should have done something. And I hate—' She broke it off, breathing hard.

'Me?' he asked quietly. 'Do you hate me, too?'

Trembling, eyes burning, she rested her forehead against the car window. 'No. Not you. You were doing your job. Bailey got caught in the cross fire. I'm sorry for what I said. This isn't your fault.' She turned her face so that the window cooled her flushed cheek. 'I hate myself,' she murmured, closing her eyes. 'I should have said something back then. I should have done something. But I curled up into a little ball and hid it all away from the world.'

His fingertips brushed against her arm, then fell away. 'Last night you said we couldn't blame ourselves,' he said.

'That was last night. This is today, when I have to think of a way to tell Hope her mommy's never coming home.' Her voice broke and she didn't care. 'I don't blame you, Daniel. You played this exactly the way you had to. But now I have to go on and so does Hope. And that scares the hell out of me.'

'Alex. Please look at me. Please.'

His expression was one of tortured misery and her heart broke even more. 'Daniel, I don't blame you. Really. I don't.'

'Maybe you should. I'd prefer it to this.'

'To what?'

His hands clenched the wheel. 'You're pulling away from me. Last night it was *we* have to go on. Today you're back to doing it all by yourself. Dammit, Alex. *I'm here* and nothing for me has changed in the last hour. But you're pulling away from me.' He flinched. 'Goddammit,' he swore bitterly and pulled his cell phone out of his pocket, sending plastic gloves everywhere. 'Var*tan*ian.'

He went still and immediately the car began to slow. 'How?' he demanded.

Something was wrong. *More wrong, anyway*. Daniel pulled to the shoulder as she nervously picked up the scattered gloves, tucking them into her own jacket pocket.

'Where?' he bit out. 'No fucking way. I come with backup or I don't come at all.' His jaw cocked. 'No, I don't guess I do trust you. At one time I did. But not anymore.'

Frank Loomis. Alex leaned closer, trying to overhear. Daniel was patting his pockets. 'Can you get me a pen?' he asked, and she dug one from her purse. He pulled his notebook from his shirt pocket. 'Where exactly?' He scribbled an address with a frown. 'I'd forgotten about that place. That at least makes sense. Okay. I'm coming.' He hesitated. 'Thank you.'

He did an abrupt U-turn, making Alex grab for something to hold on to. 'What is it?' she asked, afraid to hear the answer.

He flicked on his lights. His speedometer had already climbed to eighty.

'That was Frank. He said he's found Bailey.'

Alex sucked in a breath. 'Alive?'

Daniel's jaw was taut. 'He says so.' He pressed a button on his phone. 'Luke, I need you to turn around and meet me at . . .' He held the phone to Alex. 'Tell him the address. Tell him it's out past the old O'Brien mill. Susannah will know where that is.'

Which had been what 'at least made sense.'

Alex did and Daniel took the phone back. 'Frank Loomis says he's found where they're holding Bailey Crighton. Call Chase, have him send backup. I'm going to call Corchran in Arcadia. I trust him and he's close by.' He listened and glanced at Alex. 'That's why I'm calling Corchran. He won't get there too much after us. He can take Alex and Susannah.'

Alex didn't argue. He looked too intense. Dangerous. She felt no threat to herself, but grim satisfaction that whoever crossed them would be forever sorry.

He hung up and handed her the phone. 'Find Corchran's number in my notebook and dial it, please.' She did and he quickly brought the Arcadia sheriff up to speed and requested his presence. He hung up again and put his phone back in his pocket.

'I thought you and Chase checked out O'Brien's mill,' she said.

'The new mill, yes. I forgot about the old mill. I haven't been out there since I was a little kid. It was just a pile of rubble even then.' A muscle in his jaw twitched. 'When we get there, please stay in the car with your head down.' He looked at her, his gaze sharp and hard. '*Promise me.*'

'I promise.'

Friday, February 2, 3:15 P.M.

'It's done.' Under the cover of the trees, Loomis pocketed his phone. 'He's coming.'

As if there had been any doubt. 'Very good.'

'Now let me go. I'll go pick Bailey and the girl up and take them to the hospital.'

'No. I need you to stay here. In fact, I need you to move.' He gestured with his pistol. 'Out in the open.'

Loomis's face showed his shock. 'Why?'

'Because even Judas showed up to the Last Supper.'

Stunned realization dawned in Loomis's eyes. 'You're going to kill Daniel.'

'Probably not me.' He shrugged. 'You made the call to Vartanian. If you're not here to meet him when he gets here, he'll leave, and then my fun is spoiled. So move.'

'But Mansfield will see me,' Loomis said, disbelief making his voice high-pitched.

'Exactly.'

'And then he'll kill me,' Loomis said, tonelessly now.

He smiled. 'Exactly.'

'And he'll kill Daniel. You planned to kill him all along.'

'And everyone took you for just a slack-jawed, hick sheriff. *Move.*' He waited until Loomis started to creep to the edge of the woods, then gave his silencer a good twist. 'And just to make sure you don't do something stupid like try to run . . .' He fired once into Loomis's thigh. With an agonized cry, Loomis sank to the ground. 'Get up,' he said coldly. 'When you see Vartanian's car drive up, you walk on out to meet him.'

Friday, February 2, 3:30 P.M.

'We have to go.' The captain of the small boat scanned the landscape nervously. 'I'm not waiting for your boss any longer, not while I'm sitting on this kind of cargo.'

Mansfield tried his cell again, with no answer. 'He was taking care of the ones who couldn't travel. Let me go back and find him.' He leaped to the dock.

'Tell your boss I'm waitin' five more minutes, then I'm gone.'

Mansfield turned, eying the man coldly. 'You'll wait till we get back.'

The captain shook his head. 'I don't take my orders from you. You're wasting time.'

It was true. Nobody took orders from Mansfield. Not anymore. No thanks to Daniel-fucking-Vartanian.

And whoever stirred up all this shit to start with – who, if Daniel had really been as smart as everyone always said he was, should have been caught already. But he wasn't caught because Daniel was as big a fuck-up as everyone else.

Clenching his teeth, he pushed the heavy door aside and walked down the hall, frowning at the dead girls. What a waste. With a little time, they would have been fit for resale. Now they were useless.

His steps slowed as he approached the cell that had held the chaplain. The door was open, a body slumped over the threshold, but something wasn't right. He drew his gun and soundlessly moved forward. *Fuck.* It was one of Harvard's security guys, not the chaplain, as it should have been. Mansfield rolled him over and grimaced. The man had been ripped open, stem to stern.

Wiping his bloody hands on the guard's pants, Mansfield checked the next cell. The door was ajar. And the cell was empty. Bailey was gone. He took off at a run, coming to a dead stop as he rounded the corner and nearly tripped over the body crumpled in a heap on the floor. Mansfield dropped to his knees, checking his pulse. Harvard was alive.

'The boat's leaving in a few minutes. Get up.' Mansfield started to lift him only to have his hand pushed away.

'Bailey got away.' Harvard lifted his head, his eyes bleary. 'Where's Beardsley?'

'Gone.'

'Fuck. They can't get far. Beardsley has a hole in his gut and Bailey's shaking so hard she can barely walk. Find them before they bring the cops on our heads.'

'What about you?'

'I'll live,' he said acidly. 'Which is more than I can say for the two of us if we're found here, with all these bodies.' He struggled to sit up and reached for his gun, but his holster was empty. 'Dammit. Beardsley has my gun. Give me your backup.'

Mansfield pulled his pistol from his ankle holster.

'Now move your ass. Find Bailey and Beardsley and kill them.'

Friday, February 2, 3:30 P.M.

Frank was waiting for them outside what looked like a concrete bunker. The perimeter was overgrown with weeds and the road was pitted from disuse. Daniel checked his watch. Luke and Sheriff Corchran should be here any minute.

'What is this place?' Alex asked.

'It was the O'Brien paper mill back in the twenties. They upgraded to the new mill in my grandfather's day, when the town got a railroad spur.' He pointed beyond the trees to where the Chattahoochee River flowed. 'Before that, they used the river to bring logs in and move the paper out.'

'I thought you said it was a pile of rubble.'

'It was. That bunker's new, and camouflaged well enough that we didn't see it from the air.' He said no more, watching Frank, who was leaning against his squad car, watching them.

'What are you waiting for?' Alex hissed, her voice vibrating like a plucked string.

'Backup,' he said succinctly, not taking his eyes from Frank. 'And Sheriff Corchran to take you to where it's safe.' He heard her indrawn breath and knew she wanted to argue, but he knew she would not and he respected her for it. 'I don't want to get Bailey killed by going in there half-cocked, Alex. If she is in there and she's alive, I want to bring her out that way for you.'

'I know.' The words were barely audible. 'Thank you, Daniel.'

'Don't thank me. Not for this. Shit.' Frank was coming toward them, lumbering almost, and it wasn't until he was a foot away that Daniel saw the dark wet stain on his pants leg. 'He's been hit.' The hackles raised on the back of his neck and he put the car into reverse. Alex unsnapped her seat belt, but he grabbed her arm. 'Wait.'

Alex stared at him. 'We can't just let him bleed to death. He knows where Bailey is.'

'Wait, I said.' Daniel's mind was racing, but indecision kept his brain spinning out of gear. *Trap,* his mind was screaming. But he'd been friends with this man a very long time. He rolled down his window a few inches. 'What happened?'

'Caught a bullet,' Frank gritted, hooking his fingers in the open space of the window, smearing blood on the glass. He leaned in close. 'Turn around and go. I'm sor—'

A shot cracked the air and after a split second of stunned pain and disbelief, Frank slid down Daniel's car door. Daniel was already slamming his foot on the gas, sending them careening backward. 'Get down!' he barked, not looking to see if Alex obeyed.

He wrenched the wheel, prepared to do a one-eighty. Then flew forward, smacking his head against the wheel when he hit something large and solid. From the corner of his eye he saw Alex slide down the dash to the floor in a heap.

Dazed, he looked up into his rearview and saw another Dutton patrol car, then looked right and saw Randy Mansfield standing in front of Alex's open car door holding a Smith & Wesson .40 caliber semi-automatic. Pointed at Alex's head.

'Drop the gun, Danny,' Randy said calmly. 'Or I'll kill her while you watch.'

Daniel blinked, reality congealing in a rush. *Alex*. She was huddled on the floorboard, motionless, and his heart stopped. 'Alex. *Alex?*'

'I said give me the gun. Now.' He held out his left hand. His right still held his Smith at Alex's head.

Where are you, Luke? Keeping his eyes on Mansfield's

gun, he slowly extended his Sig, grip first. 'Why?'

'Because I don't want you to shoot me,' Mansfield said dryly. He slipped Daniel's Sig into the back of his waistband. 'Give me your backup, just as slow.'

'She might be dead already,' Daniel made himself say. 'Why should I do anything you say?'

'She's not dead. She's just playin' possum.' He shoved the barrel of his gun into Alex's head, but she didn't move, and Mansfield looked impressed. 'Either she's really knocked out cold or she's really good at playin' possum. Either way, she's still alive but won't be in about ten seconds unless you do what I say.'

Gritting his teeth, Daniel pulled his backup from his ankle holster. *Dammit, Luke, where the fuck are you?* 'You sonofabitch,' he hissed to Mansfield.

Mansfield took his revolver, then motioned with his head. 'Get out of the car and put your hands on the hood. Nice and slow, you know the drill.'

Daniel got out of the car and looked to where Frank lay, not moving. 'Is he dead?'

'If he's not, he will be soon. Hands on the hood, Vartanian. You, get up.' He shoved the gun at Alex's head again, but from his new position, Daniel couldn't see if she moved or not. With a frustrated huff, Mansfield slid Daniel's backup into his waistband next to his Sig, then grabbed Alex's hair and yanked. Still nothing.

Daniel pushed back his panic. She was probably unconscious. It might be a blessing in disguise.

Mansfield would leave her here, and Luke would find her.

'Pick her up,' Mansfield said, stepping back.

'What?'

'You heard me. Pick her up and carry her inside. I may need her later.' Mansfield motioned impatiently with his gun. 'Do it.'

'She could have a back injury.'

Mansfield rolled his eyes. 'Vartanian, I'm not stupid.'

Gingerly, Daniel lifted her from the car. Her breathing was shallow but steady. 'Alex,' he whispered.

'Vartanian,' Mansfield snapped. 'Move.'

Daniel scooped her into his arms, one arm under her knees, the other clutching her shoulders. Her head lolled like a rag doll and he remembered Sheila, dead in the corner. His arms tightened around her and he flicked a last desperate glance over his shoulder. *Luke, goddammit. Where are you?*

Chapter Twenty-five

Friday, February 2, 3:30 P.M.

From the cover of the trees, Bailey watched the unmarked car race by doing nearly a hundred, its lights flashing. *Police*. Relief had her nearly passing out. The cops were headed toward the compound. Maybe more would come. She had to get to the road.

She shook the girl's shoulder. 'Come on,' she rasped. 'Walk.'

'I can't.' It came out a moan and Bailey knew the girl could go no further.

'Then stay here. If I don't come back, try to get help for yourself.'

The girl grabbed her arm, eyes wide with terror. 'Don't go. Don't leave me.'

Bailey firmly removed the girl's hand. 'If I don't get you help, you'll die.'

The girl's eyes closed. 'Then just let me die.'

Beardsley's voice came to her mind. 'Not on my watch.' She turned to the road and forced her feet to move, but her knees kept giving out. So she crawled. The road was raised and she had to climb an embankment. Her hands kept slipping on the grass, her palms wet with blood. *Move your ass, Bailey. Move.*

She was a few feet from the road when she heard the second car. Picturing Hope's sweet face, then Beardsley's bloodied one, she threw herself forward. The car came around the bend, swerving in a cloud of dust and screeching brakes. She heard shouts. A man's voice. Then a woman's.

'Did you hit her?' the woman asked. She crouched and Bailey could see dark hair and big gray eyes, filled with fear. 'My God. Did *we* do this?'

'We didn't hit her.' The man hunkered down, his touch gentle. 'Oh, shit. She's been beaten and she's burning up.' He ran his hands down her arms, then her legs. His hand stilled abruptly on her ankle, then he gently gripped her chin. 'Are you Bailey?'

She nodded once. 'Yes. My baby, Hope. Is she alive?'

'Yes, she's alive and she's safe. Susannah, call Chase. Tell him we found Bailey and tell him to get us an ambulance ASAP. Then call Daniel and tell him to come back.'

Bailey grabbed his arm. 'Alex?'

He looked up the road and Bailey's heart sank. 'She was in that car? Oh my God.'

His black eyes narrowed. 'Why?'

'He'll kill her. He has no reason not to. He killed

them all.' The pictures flooded her mind. 'He killed them all.'

'Who? Bailey, listen to me. Who did this to you?' But she couldn't speak. She rocked, thinking of the girls, chained to the walls, their eyes wide and lifeless. 'Bailey.' The pressure on her chin increased. 'Who did this to you?'

'Luke.' The woman came back, cell phones in both hands, her face paler than before. 'I called Chase and he's sending help, but Daniel doesn't answer.'

Friday, February 2, 3:40 P.M.

The stage was set. All the players were here. All Mack had to do was sit back and watch the fun, but he'd have to make it happen quickly. They knew who he was now, so any dallying with pretty Alex Fallon would have to be cut short. By morning he'd have left his final blanket-wrapped victim and the circle would be complete.

By noon tomorrow he'd be behind the wheel of Gemma Martin's repainted 'Vette and halfway to Mexico, and he'd never look back.

But for now . . . the rest of the pillars were about to fall.

Friday, February 2, 3:45 P.M.

Alex's head hurt and her scalp burned, but otherwise she was unhurt. She'd been dazed by the crash, but heard every word between Daniel and Mansfield. She'd focused on remaining limp, and it was harder than it looked. But for now, she seemed to have fooled both Mansfield and Daniel. Her heart clenched at Daniel's worry, but for now that's the way it needed to be.

Where was Luke? she thought. He should have been here, long before now.

Daniel had carried her inside the bunker. She'd kept her eyes closed, but she could hear the echo of his and Mansfield's footsteps in the silence. There were no stairs, just a long straight hallway. Then Daniel turned, easing her to the right, through a doorway.

'Put her on the floor,' Mansfield commanded, and gently Daniel laid her down. 'Now sit.' She felt cold as Daniel moved away, taking his warmth with him. 'Put your hands behind you.' She heard the clink of metal and realized Mansfield had just handcuffed Daniel. She'd hoped Daniel would detect the gun she'd slipped in her waistband while he was carrying her, but he hadn't. *So it's up to me.*

'Why did you shoot Frank Loomis?' Daniel asked. 'He called me, just like you wanted him to.'

There was a moment of silence. 'Shut up, Daniel.'

'You didn't know he'd called me,' Daniel said, new

speculation in his voice. 'He wasn't working with you.'

'Shut *up*.'

Daniel didn't shut up. 'What are you doing here? Using the river to transport drugs?'

Alex fought not to wince as she heard the blow, then Daniel's muted grunt of pain.

'Well, whatever you're doing,' Daniel continued a minute later, 'your ship sailed. I saw a boat heading downriver just as you shot Frank.'

There was an abrupt movement and Alex lifted her lashes enough to see Mansfield moving toward the window. She heard a hissed curse.

'You're stranded here,' Daniel said evenly. 'My backup's on the road coming in. You won't get out of here alive if you try to run.'

'Of course I will,' Mansfield said, but his voice was not calm. 'I have insurance.'

That would be me. Straining to see beneath her lashes, Alex looked at Daniel and stiffened. He was looking right at her, eyes narrowed. He knew she was awake, aware.

Suddenly Daniel lunged, chair and all, charging into Mansfield, headfirst. Alex sprang to her feet as Daniel shoved Mansfield into a desk. Alex ran for the door, recognizing Daniel had bought her escape.

But a shot rang out and her heart and feet simply stopped. Mansfield stood with his back to her and Daniel lay on his side, still handcuffed to the chair. Blood was rapidly spreading across Daniel's white shirt from a bullet wound in his chest. His face was rapidly growing pale, but he aimed his gaze right at her. *Move*.

She tore her eyes from Daniel to Mansfield, whose shoulders heaved from the deep breaths he dragged in. He stared down at Daniel, holding his gun tight in his right hand. In his waistband was Daniel's gun. Just one gun.

Mansfield had taken two from Daniel. Daniel's small backup revolver was gone.

Then she forgot all about Daniel's backup when Mansfield kicked Daniel's ribs so hard she heard them crack even over Daniel's moan.

'You sonofabitch,' Mansfield muttered. 'You had to come back. Had to stir everything up. At least Simon had the good sense to stay gone.'

Alex fumbled for the gun at her back, mentally chanting the instructions Daniel had drilled into her head. She released the safety just as Mansfield pointed his gun at Daniel's head. Mansfield whirled around at the sound, and stunned, he stared at the gun in her hand for a split second before lifting his eyes and his gun in the same motion. Without thinking she kept squeezing the trigger until, eyes wide, he fell to his knees, then onto his face. Now *his* white shirt was rapidly growing red.

She kicked the gun from Mansfield's hand and took Daniel's gun from his back and put them on the floor next to Daniel's head before pushing her own gun behind her waistband beneath her jacket. Then she knelt next to Daniel and pulled his shirt away from his chest, her hands briefly trembling when she saw how badly he was hurt.

'I told you . . . to run,' he whispered. 'Dammit . . . *run*.' The rise and fall of his chest was growing shallower and she could hear his breath sucking in and out of the wound.

'You've already lost a lot of blood and probably punctured your lung. Where are the keys to your handcuffs?'

'Pocket.'

She found his keys and his cell phone and forced her hands to still as she found the key to the cuffs, freeing him. She shoved the chair away and gently rolled him to his side, pushing a lock of hair from his forehead, already beaded with sweat.

'That was stupid,' she said hoarsely. 'He would have killed you.'

His eyes slid closed. He was fading fast. She needed to seal his wound and she needed to get him out of here. There was no way she could drag him to the car on her own. She needed help.

She tried his cell phone, but there was no reception. Her heart racing, she looked around the room. It was a bare office, with only an old metal desk.

She yanked open the desk drawers until she found office supplies. 'Scissors and tape.' She breathed a sigh of relief. It was heavy packing tape and would do. She grabbed it and ran back to Daniel, this time not bothering to step over Mansfield. She walked across his leg, dropping to her knees. 'I'm going to seal this wound. Hold still.'

From her pocket she pulled the gloves he'd spilled over the floor of his car earlier, then stretched one of the gloves tight and quickly performed a three-sided seal over the hole in his chest. 'I have to turn you. It's going to hurt. I'm sorry.' As gently as she could she turned him to his side, cut his shirt away from his back and blew out a sigh of relief. It was a through-and-through. No bullets still rattling around in his body. Quickly she repeated the procedure. In a few seconds the sucking grew quieter and her pulse started evening out along with his.

'Alex.'

'Stop talking,' she said. 'Save your breath.'

'*Alex.*'

'He's trying to tell you to look at me.'

Spinning on her knees, Alex's gaze flew to the doorway. And then she knew.

'Number seven,' she said quietly, and Toby Granville smiled. Blood trickled down his face from what across the room appeared to be a blunt trauma to his temple. In his hand he held a small revolver. In his eyes she saw the shadow of pain. She hoped he hurt a whole lot.

'I was actually number one. I just let Simon think he was because he was an unbalanced scary bastard.' He looked at Mansfield with contempt. 'And you were a fuck-up,' he muttered before turning his attention back to Alex. 'Slide Mansfield's gun over here, then Vartanian's.'

She did as she was told, biding her time.

'Wasn't . . . on the list,' Daniel whispered. 'Too old. My age.'

'No, I was Simon's age,' Granville said. 'I skipped a few grades and graduated from Bryson before he got kicked out. We used to joke about having a club, Simon and I, as far back as junior high. Everyone always thought it was his idea, because he was an unbalanced scary bastard. But it was mine. Simon was mine. He did what I said and thought it was his plan all along. Jared could have been mine, too, but he drank too much. None of the others had the nerve.' His movements ginger, Granville bent to pick up the two guns Alex had slid across the floor.

The moment he dropped his eyes, she pulled her gun from her back and fired, hitting the wall the first time. Plaster flew even as her second bullet found its mark, as did her third, fourth, and fifth. Granville crumpled, but he still breathed and gripped his revolver.

'Drop your gun,' she said. 'Or I'll kill you.'

'You won't,' he said. 'You don't . . . have it in you. Murder . . . in cold blood.'

'That's what Mansfield thought,' Alex said coldly. She lifted the gun. 'Drop your gun or I'll shoot.'

'Walk me out the door . . . and I'll drop the gun.'

Alex gave him a look of incredulity. 'You're insane. I'm not helping you.'

'Then you'll never know . . . where I put Bailey.'

Her chin came up and her eyes narrowed. 'Where is she?'

'Get me out . . . and I tell you.'

'He . . . probably has . . . a boat,' Daniel said, grimacing. 'Don't.'

'Bailey,' Granville taunted.

Behind her Daniel's breathing was labored. She needed to get him to a hospital.

'I don't have time for this.' Alex aimed for Granville's heart, but hesitated. Granville was right. Killing a man in self-defense was one thing, but killing a wounded man in cold blood . . . Shooting him, though, she could handle.

Aiming, Alex squeezed the trigger and Granville screamed. Blood now gushed from his wrist, but his hand was open and the gun was on the floor. Alex put it in her pocket and knelt next to Daniel, searching for his handcuffs with one hand and feeling for his pulse with the other. It was weak. Terrifyingly so.

His color was still bad and he still struggled for each breath, but the spread of blood had stopped, at least. 'I have to get help for you and I don't trust him not to hurt you while I'm gone. But I can't kill him. I'm sorry.'

'Don't be. Might need him later. Cuff him . . . behind

his back.' Daniel grabbed her jacket with one bloody hand when she started to get up. 'Alex.'

'Hush. If I don't get you to a hospital, you'll die.' But he didn't let go.

'Alex,' he whispered and she leaned close. 'Love you . . . when you're ruthless.'

Her throat closed and she pressed a kiss to his forehead, then straightened, her expression stern. 'Love you,' she whispered back, 'when you're not a dead hero. Stop talking, Daniel.'

She went back to cuff Granville. It was harder than it looked and she was breathing hard and covered in his blood when she turned him on his back. 'I hope you rot in prison for a long time.'

'You think you know . . . everything.' He dragged in a breath. 'You know nothing. There are . . . others.'

Her head came up and she grabbed her gun. 'Others where?' she asked, alarmed.

Granville's eyes had gone unfocused. He'd lost a lot of blood. 'Simon was mine,' he muttered. 'But I was another's.' Then, dazed, he looked up, his eyes flaring wide in fear.

She started to look over her shoulder but stopped when she felt cold steel shoved against her temple.

'Thank you, Miss Fallon,' a voice whispered in her ear. 'I'll take that gun.' He squeezed her wrist until her fingers opened and the gun dropped to the concrete floor. 'Things wrapped themselves up well. Davis is arrested, Mansfield is dead and . . .' He fired and her stomach wrenched as Granville's head exploded all over the floor. 'Now, so is Granville. The seven are now none.'

'Who are you?' she asked, even though she already knew the answer.

'You already know,' he said quietly, and she knew she'd never known true fear until that moment. He forced her to her feet. 'Now you'll come with me.'

'No.' She struggled and he dug his gun back into her head. 'I just need to get help for Daniel. I won't tell them you're here. You can go. I won't stop you.'

'No, you won't. Nobody will stop me. But I won't let you go. I have plans for you.'

The way he said it made her knees buckle. 'Why? I never even knew you like Gemma or the others.'

'No, you didn't. But you'll die, just the same.'

The sob was building again, but this time it was mixed with terror. 'Why?'

'Because of your face. It all started with Alicia. It'll end with you.'

Alex went cold and still. 'You'd kill me for a *grand finale*?'

He chuckled. 'That and to make Vartanian suffer.'

'Why? He never hurt you.'

'But Simon did. I can't hurt Simon, so Daniel will have to take his punishment.'

'Like you were punished for what Jared did,' she murmured.

'I see you understand. It's only fair.'

'But killing me isn't fair,' she said, trying to stay calm. 'I never hurt anyone.'

'That's true. But meaningless at this point. You'll die, like the others, and you'll scream, loud and long.' He pulled her backward and she fought wildly.

'We called for backup,' she sputtered. 'You can't get away.'

'Yes we can. I hope you don't get too sick in a boat.'

The river. He was going to take her away by the river. 'No. I won't go like a lamb to slaughter. If you want me, you're going to have to drag me by my hair.' He was going to kill Daniel. But when he did he'd have to move the gun from her temple. It would be the only chance she had. The second she felt the pressure against her temple decrease, she twisted, trying to claw his face. Abruptly he loosened his grip and for a moment she was too surprised to do anything.

Then she blinked as a final shot rang out. She had only a moment to look up into the face of . . . the paperboy . . . before he dropped. Stunned, she watched as he went down, focusing on the neat hole in his forehead.

'This is the paperboy.' She shuddered when she realized how closely O'Brien had been watching her, then looked up and sucked in a silent scream. A man with a dirty, bloody face stood holding O'Brien's gun in his hand. He was weaving on his feet.

Alex peered closer. *'Reverend Beardsley?'*

He nodded grimly. 'Yeah.' He leaned up against the

door and slid to the floor, carefully placing O'Brien's gun on the floor beside him.

She looked at the hole in O'Brien's forehead, then back at Beardsley. 'You shot him? How could you shoot him? You were . . . behind him.' She spun around to see Daniel slowly lower his head to the floor. In his hand he held his backup revolver.

'*You* shot him?' Daniel nodded once and said nothing. Alex stuck her head out the doorway and looked both ways. 'Anybody else here with guns?'

'Don't think so,' Beardsley said, and grabbed her leg. 'Bailey?'

'Granville said she was still alive.'

'She was alive an hour ago,' Beardsley said.

'I'll find out. I have to get help now.'

Clutching Daniel's cell phone in her hand, Alex ran until she saw light streaming in through the small window in the outer door. She stopped for a moment, almost blinded by its brightness. Then she opened the door and walked out and dragged in the deepest breath she'd ever breathed.

'*Alex*.' Luke came running. 'She's hit,' he yelled. 'Get the medics.'

She blinked as men came running with a gurney. 'Not me,' she snapped. 'Daniel's been hit. He's critical. He needs to be airlifted to a level one trauma center. I'll show you where he is.' She ran, adrenaline fueling her muscles. 'Bailey escaped.'

'I know,' Luke replied as he ran beside her. Behind

them the gurney squeaked. 'I found her. She's alive. In pretty bad shape, but she's alive.'

Alex knew the relief would hit her once Daniel was on the gurney. 'Beardsley's in here, too. He's alive. He may be able to walk out on his own, but he's bad, too.'

They got to the room at the end of the hall and Luke stopped dead at the three bodies that littered the floor. 'Holy Mother of God,' he breathed. 'Did you do this?'

A bubble of hysterical laugher tickled where minutes before a sob had burned. The medics were lifting Daniel to the gurney and she could breathe again. 'Most of it. I killed Mansfield and wounded Granville, but O'Brien killed Granville.'

Luke nodded. 'Okay.' He nudged O'Brien with his shoe. 'And this one?'

'Beardsley took his gun and Daniel made the head shot.' A grin nearly broke her face in two. 'I think we did good.'

Luke grinned back. 'I think you did good, too.'

But Beardsley didn't smile. He shook his head. 'You were too late,' he said wearily.

Alex and Luke instantly sobered. 'What are you talking about?' Alex said.

Beardsley pushed himself against the wall until he stood. 'Come with me.'

Throwing a backward glance at Daniel, Alex followed, Luke's hand on her back.

Beardsley pulled on the first door to their left. It was unlocked, but not empty. Alex stared in horror. And what she saw would be indelibly etched in her mind forever.

A young girl lay on a thin cot, her arm chained to the wall. She was gaunt, her bones clearly visible. Her eyes were wide open and there was a small round hole in her forehead. She looked about fifteen.

Alex rushed forward, dropping to her knees, pressing her fingers to a thin neck for a pulse. The girl was still warm. She looked up at Luke, overcome. 'She's dead. Maybe an hour ago.'

'They're all dead,' Beardsley said harshly. 'Every one that was left behind.'

'How many were there?' Luke asked, his voice hard with fury.

'I counted seven shots. Bailey . . .'

'She's alive,' Luke said. 'And she got one girl out with her.'

Beardsley's shoulders sagged. 'Thank God.'

'What is this place?' Alex whispered.

'Human trafficking,' Luke said succinctly, and Alex just stared at him, openmouthed.

'You mean all these girls . . . ? But why kill them? *Why?*'

'They didn't have time to get them all out,' Beardsley said tonelessly. 'They didn't want the ones left behind to talk.'

'Who's responsible for this?' Alex hissed.

'The man you called Granville.' Beardsley leaned against the wall and closed his eyes, and it was then that Alex noticed the dark stain on his shirt. It was spreading.

'You got shot,' she said, reaching out to help him.

He put out one hand. 'Your cop is in worse shape.'

'How many did they get out?' Luke asked, and on his face Alex saw the same feral rage that she'd seen the night at the target range.

'Five or six,' Beardsley said. 'They took them down to the river.'

'I'll notify the local police and the water patrol,' Luke said. 'And the Coast Guard.'

Behind them, Daniel was being wheeled out on the gurney.

'Go with him,' Beardsley said. 'I'll be fine.'

Another gurney entered the way they'd come. 'These medics are here for you.' She took Beardsley's hand. 'Thank you. You saved my life.'

He nodded, his eyes flat and cold. 'You're welcome. Tell Bailey I'll visit her.'

'I will.' Then Alex and Luke followed Daniel's gurney out the door, looking at each door as they passed. Five more victims. She wanted to scream, but in the end she moved up to Daniel's side, took his hand, and went out with him into the sunshine.

Chapter Twenty-six

Atlanta, Friday, February 2, 5:45 P.M.

'Alex.' Meredith came to her feet as Alex rushed through the emergency room doors. 'Oh my God, Alex.' She threw her arms around Alex and Alex held on tight.

'It's over,' she murmured. 'They're all dead.'

Meredith pulled back, visibly shaking. 'You're hurt. Where are you hurt?'

'It's not my blood. It's Daniel's and Granville's mostly. Did they bring Daniel in?'

'The helicopter got here about twenty minutes ago.'

Alex went to the nurses' station, Meredith at her side. 'I'm Alex Fallon. Can you—'

'This way,' the nurse interrupted as a crowd of reporters surged around her. She led them back to a small waiting room. 'Agent Chase Wharton told us you'd be coming. He wants to talk to you.'

'I want to talk to Daniel Vartanian's doctor,' Alex insisted. 'Bailey Crighton's, too.'

'The doctor's in with Mr Vartanian now,' the nurse said kindly, then looked at Alex more closely. 'You were here a few days ago, visiting the nun who died.'

'I was.' Alex was pacing the small room, her nerves jangling.

'You're an ER nurse.' The nurse's brows lifted. 'Now it makes sense. That was one hell of a field job you did on Vartanian.'

Alex stopped pacing and looked the woman in the eye. 'Was it good enough?'

The nurse nodded. 'Looks that way.'

Alex let out a sigh of relief. 'Can I see Bailey?'

'Come with me.'

Alex held Meredith's hand hard as they followed. 'Where is Hope?'

'With Agent Shannon and Riley, still at the safe house. We thought it best not to bring her to see Bailey until she's cleaned up. Alex, I saw Bailey when they brought her in. She's in really bad shape.'

'But alive,' the nurse said. She gestured to the exam room. 'Just a few minutes.'

Despite the preparation, Alex winced when she saw Bailey. 'Bailey, it's me, Alex.'

Bailey's eyelids fluttered as she struggled to open her eyes.

'It's okay,' Alex soothed. 'You need to rest. You're safe. Hope's safe.'

Tears seeped from Bailey's swollen eyes. 'You came. You saved my baby.'

Alex gently took her hand, noting the bruises and the nails broken well past the quick. 'She's a beautiful little girl. Meredith's been taking care of her.'

Bailey forced her eyes open, looking from Alex to Meredith. *'Thank you.'*

Meredith's swallow was audible. 'Hope's fine, Bailey. She misses you. And Alex never gave up hope that you were alive.'

Bailey licked her dry, split lips. 'Beardsley?' she croaked.

Alex dabbed Bailey's mouth with a wet cloth. 'He's alive. He saved my life, too. He told me to tell you he'd come to see you. Bailey, the police found your father.'

Bailey's lips trembled. 'I need to tell you. Wade . . . did some horrible things. My father knew.'

'I know. I finally let myself remember. Craig killed my mother.'

Bailey flinched. 'I didn't know that.'

'Do you know about the pills I took that day? Did Craig give them to me?'

'I think so. I don't know for sure. But Alex . . . Wade . . . he . . . I think he killed Alicia.'

'No, he didn't. He did a lot of other horrible things, but he didn't kill her.'

'Rape?'

Alex nodded. 'Yes.'

'There are others.'

Alex shivered. Granville had said the same thing.

'You mean the letter Wade sent you? We found it, with Hope's help.'

'There were seven. Wade and six others.'

'I know. Except for Garth Davis, they're all dead, and Garth's been arrested.'

Again Bailey flinched. 'Garth? But he . . . Oh, God, how stupid I was.'

Alex remembered Sissy's phone call and the man Bailey was supposed to have met the night before she was taken. 'You were having an affair?'

'Yes. He came to see me after Wade died, offered his condolences as mayor.' She closed her eyes. 'One thing led to another. And Wade warned me, too. *Trust no one*.'

'Did Garth ask about Wade's belongings?' Meredith asked quietly.

'A few times, but I didn't think anything about it and I hadn't gotten Wade's letters yet. I was so happy to be treated nice by someone in the town . . . Garth was looking for that damn key, just like him. That's all *he* kept asking for. That damn key.'

'Who kept asking for the key?' Alex asked, and Bailey shuddered.

'Granville.' She said it bitterly. 'What did the key open?'

'A safe-deposit box,' Alex said. 'But it was empty.'

Bailey looked up in devastated bewilderment. 'Then why did he do this to me?'

Alex looked at Meredith. 'That's a good question. Daniel and Luke thought the seventh man had another set of keys, but I guess Granville didn't.'

'Or he would have taken the pictures from the box himself,' Meredith said.

'He may still have done that,' Luke said from the doorway. 'Granville may have taken the pictures years ago. We don't know yet. But Simon's turning up alive after all those years had them all nervous. If Daniel had Simon's key and Bailey had Wade's key, they would have started asking questions, and Granville didn't want that.' He stood next to Bailey's bed. 'Chase wants to talk to you, Alex. How are you feeling, Bailey?'

'I'll be okay,' Bailey said fiercely. 'I have to be. How is the girl I found?'

'Unconscious,' Luke said.

'That's probably for the best,' Bailey murmured. 'When can I see Hope?'

'Soon,' Meredith promised. 'She had a terrible trauma seeing you beaten. I don't want to scare her again. Let's get your hair washed and try to hide some of the bruises before we bring Hope in to see you here.'

Bailey nodded wearily. 'Alex, I told Granville I sent you the key. Did he hurt you?'

'No. This blood on my shirt is mostly his. He's dead.'

'Good,' Bailey said harshly. 'Did he suffer?'

'Not enough. Bailey, who else did you see while you were being held?'

'Just Granville and sometimes Mansfield. Sometimes their guards. Why?'

'Just asking.' Alex would wait to tell Bailey that Granville said there were others, just as she'd wait to tell her Craig had murdered Sister Anne. 'Sleep now. I'll be back.'

'Alex, wait. I didn't want to tell him you had the key. He . . .' Her eyes filled with tears as she pointed to the fresh needle marks on her arm. 'He shot me up.'

Alex stared at the needle marks, horrified. 'No.'

'I was clean for five years. I swear.'

'I know. I talked to Desmond and all your friends.'

'Now I have to quit again.' Bailey's voice broke, breaking Alex's heart.

'You don't have to do it alone this time.' Alex kissed Bailey's forehead. 'Sleep now. I need to talk to the police. They're going to want to talk to you about the girls.'

Bailey nodded. 'Tell them I'll help all I can.'

Atlanta, Saturday, February 3, 10:15 A.M.

Daniel woke up to find Alex sleeping in the chair next to his bed. He tried to say her name three times before he could get enough volume to wake her up. '*Alex*.'

She lifted her head, blinking to immediate attention. 'Daniel.' Her shoulders sagged and for a moment he thought she'd cry. Panic snaked through him.

'What?' The single syllable tore a chunk from his throat.

'Wait.' The ice chip she slipped in his mouth felt like

heaven. 'They took out your breathing tube, so your throat will be sore for a while. Here's a pad and pen. Don't talk.'

'What?' he repeated again, ignoring her. 'How bad am I?'

'You'll be out of the hospital in a few days. You were lucky. The bullet didn't hit anything vital.' She kissed one corner of his mouth. 'You won't even need surgery. Your wound had already started to seal itself. You'll make a full recovery and be back to work in a few weeks, a month at the outside.'

Something was still very wrong. 'What happened to Mansfield and Granville?'

'Mansfield, Granville, and O'Brien are all dead. Frank Loomis, too. I'm sorry, Daniel. He was probably dead a few minutes after he was shot. But Bailey's alive.'

'Good.' He said it as fiercely as he could. 'What happened back there, Alex?' he asked hoarsely. 'You and Luke . . . I heard you talking. Something about girls.'

'Granville was into something horrific,' she said quietly. 'We found the bodies of five teenaged girls. He'd been keeping them prisoner. Beardsley said he thought there were maybe a dozen in all. Granville began to move them, but he didn't have time to move them all. He killed the ones he left behind.'

Daniel tried to swallow, but couldn't. Alex slipped another ice chip in his mouth, but this time it didn't help. 'One of the girls got away, with Bailey's help. She's unconscious, so we don't have any details yet. Luke said he recognized one of the dead girls from the work that he was doing before.' She sighed wearily. 'I guess he can't forget their faces any more than you could forget the faces in Simon's pictures. One of the girls we found was featured on one of the child-porn sites Luke's team shut down eight months ago.'

Daniel's stomach rolled. 'God.'

'We were an hour too late.' Alex stroked his hand lightly. 'Daniel, before he died, Granville said he taught Simon, that there were others, then he said, "I was another's."'

'Who were the others?'

'He never said.'

'Mack O'Brien?'

'Chase's team found where he'd been living.'

'At the warehouses Rob Davis built on O'Brien land?'

'You're half right. He'd been living in one of the warehouses the printer of the *Review* used for storage. Delia's car was equipped with GPS and Chase's people followed the signal and found all the other cars Mack kept. Luke found e-mails on Mack's computer. He was planning to sell Delia's Porsche, Janet's Z, and Claudia's Mercedes. He'd repainted Gemma's 'Vette. Apparently he was going to keep it.'

'Wait. Mack was in a warehouse where they stored copies of the *Review*? Why?'

'He worked for the *Review*. Daniel, Mack was the

paperboy. He stood on my front porch talking to me Tuesday morning, just as pleasant as you please.'

Daniel's gut tightened at the thought of Mack O'Brien that close to her. 'Shit. And nobody recognized him?' he asked hoarsely.

'Marianne hired him. She did all the admin for the paper. She'd never met him. Mack would have been just a little boy when you all were in high school. He delivered the papers when most people were asleep, and the rest of the time he just drove around in Marianne's delivery van, watching. Mack did a lot of watching.'

'Who?'

'He watched all of them. He's got pictures of Garth going into Bailey's house, Mansfield delivering girls to Granville's bunker, Mansfield—'

'Wait. Mansfield was involved in *that*?'

'Yeah. We don't know how yet, but he was part of Granville's business.'

Daniel closed his eyes. 'Fuck. I mean . . . God, Alex.'

'I know,' she murmured. 'For what it's worth, it looks like Frank wasn't. He got a text message yesterday morning telling him where he'd find Bailey. He thought it was from Marianne, but it was from Mack's cell phone.'

'But Frank still falsified evidence in Gary Fulmore's murder trial.' His voice was a dry croak, and Alex fed him another ice chip with a look of reproach.

'Use the pad and pen. Yes, Frank did falsify

evidence then, but I don't think he meant to betray you yesterday. Bailey said Frank helped her get away.'

There was some comfort in that, Daniel supposed. But still . . . 'I wish I knew *why*. I need to know *why*.'

'Maybe he was protecting someone. Maybe he was being blackmailed.' She smoothed a hand over his cheek. 'Wait until you're strong again. You'll investigate and hopefully come up with some answers.'

Hopefully. Daniel knew he might never know Frank's reason, but he had to believe Frank had one. 'What else?'

Alex sighed. 'Mansfield hired Lester Jackson, the guy who ran me down and who killed Sheila and that young Dutton officer at Presto's Pizza. Chase found a disposable cell in Mansfield's pocket. The phone number matches the incoming calls to Lester Jackson's cell phone the day he tried to kill me.'

'Journals?'

'Chase found them with Mack's things. And with the journals they found a bag with strands of hair.' She drew a breath. 'Alicia's hair. Anyway, everything Annette O'Brien said was right. Mack had been following Garth and Rob Davis and Mansfield for a month. I think he wasn't sure who the seventh guy was either, because he had pictures of a lot of the men in town at the beginning. But then he saw Granville standing outside the bunker and from then on, all the pictures were only of Toby, Garth, Randy, and Rob Davis. Rob was having an affair with Delia, so I guess Mack figured killing her was a double bonus. He got revenge on Delia for maligning his mother and hurt Rob Davis even more.

'Mack had pictures of Mansfield killing Rhett Porter.' She hesitated. 'And he had pictures of me and of us.' Her face heated. 'He was outside your house Thursday night in his van. He took pictures of us, through your window. It doesn't appear that he uploaded them. Or anything.' She shrugged. 'He wanted me to close the circle.'

She said it so matter-of-factly, while Daniel's temper boiled. 'Sonofabitch,' he said through clenched teeth, and she rubbed his hand. 'Safe-deposit box?'

'If Rob Davis knows, he's not saying. Garth has lawyered up. Eventually they may give some answers, but it'll be in exchange for favor with the SA's office.'

'Hatton?'

She smiled. 'He's going to be okay. He might not come back as a field agent any time soon, but he'll live. He said he was close enough to retirement anyway.'

'Crighton?' he asked, and her smile faded.

'They found his bloody prints in Sister Anne's room, in her blood, so they have enough to arrest him for her murder. Chase has told me that if Craig doesn't confess, we can't get him for killing my mother or for conspiring to hide a crime with Wade.'

'The pills you took?'

'I may never know. I don't plan to beg him for an answer.'

'Have you seen him?'

She tensed. 'No.'

'I'll go with you,' he said. She relaxed, and he knew she'd been afraid to go alone.

'Bailey thinks he and Wade forced me to take the pills, based on some things Wade said back then, but we have nothing definitive.'

'Bailey's awake?'

She nodded. 'I've been hospital-room-hopping,' she said with a little smile. 'You and Bailey and Beardsley and Hatton and the girl Bailey saved. Bailey said that the one thing she did remember about the night Alicia died is that Alicia put something in my soup at lunch to make me sick. She knew she was going to a party that night and she didn't want me tagging along. She was still mad at me about the tattoo and telling the teachers about our switching for tests. Her being pissed probably saved my life.'

He tightened his hold on her hand. 'Hope?'

'She knows Bailey is alive, but hasn't seen her yet. Bailey still looks bad. Daniel, Granville injected Bailey with heroin to get her to talk.' Alex's voice trembled. 'She'd been clean for five years. Now she has to go through all that again. He was a doctor.'

'He was a cruel bastard.' Daniel forced out the words.

She sighed. 'That, too. Bailey was having an affair with Garth, but it's not clear if he knew Mansfield and Granville had kidnapped her or not. Like I said, Garth has lawyered up. Luke's been trying to question him, but so far Garth's not talking. That's pretty much it.'

'Suze?'

'She's still here. She's been sitting with you and Jane Doe.' When he lifted a brow, she added, 'The girl Bailey helped. We don't know her name. Daniel, I've been thinking.'

A wave of dread filled him. Then he brushed it away. She might leave eventually, but she wouldn't leave him now. Of that he was confident. 'About?'

'You. Me. Bailey and Hope. You're going to be fine when you get out, but Bailey . . . she's got a long road to walk. She'll need help with Hope.'

'Where?' he asked.

'Here. Her friends are here. I'm not going to take her away from all that. I'm going to stay here. I'll need to find a house for me and Bailey and Hope, but—'

'No,' he rasped. 'You stay with me.'

'But I'll need to watch Hope while Bailey goes into rehab.'

'You stay with me,' he repeated. 'Hope stays with us. Bailey can live with us as long as she needs to.' He started to cough and she put a cup of water to his lips.

'Slow,' she ordered when he would have gulped. 'Just a little sip.'

'Yes, ma'am.' He lay back and met her eyes. 'You stay with me.'

She smiled. 'Yes, sir.'

He didn't drop his gaze. 'I meant what I said, back there.'

She didn't falter. 'So did I.'

He breathed out a sigh of relief. 'Good.'

She pressed her lips to his forehead. 'Now you know everything you need to know. Stop talking and go to sleep. I'll be back later.'

Atlanta, Saturday, February 3, 12:30 P.M.

'Bailey.'

Her eyelids fluttered at the familiar voice and her heart sank. She was back *there*. Getting away had been just a dream. Then she felt the softness of the bed beneath her back and knew the nightmare was over. One of them anyway. Her addiction nightmare had started up all over again.

'Bailey.'

She forced her eyes open and her heart stuttered. 'Beardsley.' He sat in a wheelchair next to her bed. He was clean now. Bruised, with a big gash on the side of his face, but clean. His hair was sandy brown, cut army-short. He had strong cheekbones and a sturdy jaw. His eyes were brown and warm, like she remembered. His lips were cracked, but firm and proportioned. Everything about him was firm and proportioned. 'I thought you died,' she whispered.

He smiled. 'No. I'm a little tougher than that.'

She could believe that. He was truly wider than three of her. 'I saw Alex.'

'Me, too. She's been making the rounds, checking on us. You have a very strong stepsister, Bailey. And she has a strong stepsister, too.'

His compliment warmed her. 'You saved my life. How can I thank you?'

He lifted his sandy brows. 'We'll come back to that later. How do you feel?'

'Like I've been held prisoner for a week.'

Again he smiled. 'You did good, Bailey. You should be proud of yourself.'

'You don't know what you're saying. You don't know what I've done.'

'I know what I've seen you do.'

She swallowed. 'I've done terrible things.'

'You mean the drugs?'

'And other things.' Her lips curved sadly. 'I am not a girl you'd take home to Mother.'

'You mean because you were a prostitute and had affairs?'

She opened her eyes, stunned. 'You knew?'

'Yes. Wade told me about you before he died. He was so proud that you'd turned your life around.'

'Thank you.'

'Bailey, you aren't understanding me. I know. I just don't care.'

She met his warm eyes, nervous again. 'What do you want from me?'

'I don't know yet. But I want to find out. We weren't thrown together for no reason and I want you to know that I'm not going to walk away now that that phase is done.'

She didn't know what to say. 'I have to go back into rehab.'

His brown eyes flashed anger. 'And for that I'd gladly kill him again.'

'Beardsley, he . . .' The word stuck in her throat.

He clenched his jaw, but when he spoke, his voice was gentle. 'I know that, too. Bailey, you walked through that door today on your own two feet. Don't look back.'

She closed her eyes and felt the tears seep down her face. 'I don't even know your first name.'

He covered her hand with his. 'Ryan. Captain Ryan Beardsley, US Army. Ma'am.'

Her lips quivered up into a smile. 'It's nice to meet you, Ryan. Is this where we say it's the start of a beautiful friendship?'

He smiled back. 'Isn't that the best place to start?' He leaned forward and kissed her cheek. 'Now sleep. And don't worry. As soon as you're ready, they're going to bring Hope to see you. I'd like to meet her, too, when you're comfortable letting me.'

Atlanta, Saturday, February 3, 2:45 P.M.

'How is the girl?'

Susannah didn't need to look to know Luke Papadopoulos was standing behind her. 'She woke up for a little while, but slipped back under. I suppose it's her way of dodging the pain for a while.'

Luke came into the little ICU room and pulled up the other chair. 'Did she say anything when she woke up?'

'No. She just looked at me like I was God or something.'

'You brought her out of the woods.'

'I didn't do anything.' She swallowed. Truer words had never been spoken.

'Susannah. You did not cause this.'

'I don't happen to agree.'

'Talk to me.'

She turned to look at him. He had the darkest eyes she'd ever seen, blacker than night. And right now they seethed with turbulent emotion. But the rest of his face was composed. He could have been a statue for all the emotion she saw on his face. 'Why?'

'Because . . .' He lifted a shoulder. 'Because I want to know.'

One side of her mouth lifted in what she knew had been labeled a sneer by many. 'You want to know what, Agent Papadopoulos?'

'Why you think this is your fault.'

'Because I knew,' she said flatly. 'I knew and I said nothing.'

'What did you know?' he asked rationally.

She looked away, fixing her gaze on the girl with no name. Who'd looked at her like she was God. 'I knew Simon was a rapist.'

'I thought Simon didn't do any of the rapes, that he only took the pictures.'

She remembered the picture Simon showed her. 'He did at least one.'

She heard Luke's indrawn breath. 'Did you tell Daniel?'

She whipped around to glare at him. 'No. And neither will you.'

There was a fury within her. It boiled and bubbled and threatened to escape every day of her life. She knew what she had done, and what she had not. Daniel had seen only a glimpse of pictures in which no rapists were identifiable. She could not say the same. 'I only know that if I'd said something, this might have been avoided.' She ran her hand lightly over the rail on the hospital bed. 'She might not be here right now in this hospital.'

Luke was quiet for a very long time, and together they sat watching the girl breathe, thinking their own thoughts. Susannah could respect a man who knew when to respect the quiet. Finally he spoke. 'I recognized one of the bodies back there.'

She turned to look at him again, stunned. 'How?'

'From a case I was working eight months ago.' A muscle twitched in his cheek. 'I failed to protect that girl. I failed to bring a sexual sadist that preyed on children to justice. I want another bite at the apple.'

She studied his face, the set of his mouth. She didn't

think she'd ever seen a more serious man. 'Granville's dead.'

'But there's another. Someone who was pulling the strings. Someone who taught Granville how to be very good at his job. I want him.' He turned to meet her eyes and she nearly backed away from the power that emanated from him. 'I want to throw him into hell and throw away the key.'

'Why are you telling me this?'

'Because I think you want the same thing.'

She turned back to Jane Doe, the rage inside her bubbling higher. Rage at Simon, at Granville, at this mysterious whoever . . . and at herself. Then, she'd done nothing. As of today, that changed. 'What do you want me to do?'

'I don't know yet. I'll call you when I do.' He got up. 'Thank you.'

'For what?'

'For not telling Daniel about Simon.'

She looked up at him. 'Thank you for respecting my decision.'

They held each other's eyes for a long moment. Then Luke Papadopoulos gave her a nod and walked away. Susannah turned back to the girl with no name.

And saw herself.

Atlanta, Monday, February 5, 10:45 A.M.

It had been three days since Mansfield had shot Daniel, sending the dominoes toppling. It had been three days since Alex had killed a man and watched two more die before her eyes, and it still hadn't sunk in. Or maybe she just wasn't sorry.

Alex was leaning toward the second one.

She pushed Daniel's wheelchair through the doorway at the justice center into the small room where their meeting was to take place. 'This is a waste of time, Daniel.'

Daniel pushed himself from the chair and walked to the table on his own two feet. He was thinner and still pale, but recovering well. He pulled her chair out, then sat next to her. 'Humor me. You might not think you need closure, but I do.'

She stared at the wall. 'I don't want to see him.'

'Why?'

She moved her shoulders, uneasy. 'I've got things to do, productive things. Like getting Bailey into rehab and getting Hope to preschool every day and finding a job.'

'All very important things,' he agreed affably. 'So what's the real reason?'

She turned to glare at him, but the tenderness in his eyes made her swallow hard. 'I killed a man,' she murmured.

'You're not feeling guilty about Mansfield.' It was more statement than question.

'No. The opposite, actually. I'm glad I killed him. I felt . . .'

'Powerful?' he supplied, and she nodded.

'Yeah, I guess that's it. Like for that moment I was in charge and fixing something that had gone horribly wrong with the universe.'

'You did. But that scares you.'

'Yes, it scares me. I can't go around shooting people, Daniel. Craig won't talk to me and I'm going to feel helpless. I'll wish I could shoot him, too, and I can't.'

'Welcome to my world,' Daniel said with a wry smile. 'But avoiding him isn't the answer, honey. All avoiding the truth got you was screams and bad dreams.'

She wanted to argue, but knew he was right. Then forgot about arguing when the door opened and a guard led Craig Crighton into the room, his arms and legs shackled. The guard pushed Craig into a chair, chains jangling.

It was a full minute before Alex realized several things. She had her head down, staring at her hands, just as she'd done that day in the hospital, so many years before. No one had spoken. And there was no screaming in her mind, only bone-chilling silence. Daniel covered her hands with his and squeezed lightly, giving her the strength to lift her eyes and then her chin until she looked Craig Crighton full in the face.

He was old. Haggard. Years of drug use and living

on the streets had dulled his eyes. But he stared at her just as Gary Fulmore had, and Alex realized he was seeing Alicia. Or maybe even her mother. 'Craig,' she said evenly, and he jumped, startled.

'You're not her,' he mumbled.

'No, I'm not. I know what you did,' she said, still evenly, and Craig's eyes narrowed.

'I didn't do anything.'

'Agent Vartanian.' Alex looked over to where a young man in a blue suit sat next to a stylish blonde in a black suit. The young man had spoken. Alex recognized the blonde as state attorney Chloe Hathaway from the times Hathaway had visited Daniel in the hospital. Alex's assumption that the young man was Craig's defense attorney was quickly confirmed. 'What are you hoping to get from this meeting? My client has been charged with the murder of Sister Anne Chambers. Surely you aren't expecting him to implicate himself in another murder.'

'Just to talk,' Daniel said easily. 'Perhaps to clear up a few points from the past.'

'I know your client killed my mother,' Alex said, proud her voice didn't tremble. 'And while I'd like to see him punished, I know he won't admit it. I would like to know, however, what happened next.'

'You took a bottle of pills,' Craig said coldly.

'I don't think so,' Alex replied. 'If you gave them to me, I'd like to know.'

'If he gave them to you,' Craig's attorney said

smoothly, 'that would have been attempted murder. You can't expect him to admit to that either.'

'I won't press charges,' Alex said.

'You wouldn't have a choice,' Chloe Hathaway said. 'If Mr Crighton tried to kill you by giving you an overdose of pills, I'd have to prosecute.'

'But you could work something out, couldn't you, Chloe?' Daniel asked.

'Reduced charges on the nun?' Craig's lawyer asked cagily and Alex's temper blew.

She stood up, trembling now, but from rage. 'No. Absolutely no. I will not sacrifice justice for Sister Anne just to soothe my pride.' She leaned across the table until she was eye to eye with Crighton. 'You killed my mother and your son raped my sister. He tried to rape me and you never did a thing to stop him. If I did take those pills, I'm not ashamed. You took away everything I loved then. You won't take my self-respect now.' She looked at Chloe Hathaway. 'I'm sorry you were bothered to come, but we're done.'

'Alex,' Daniel murmured. 'Sit down. Please.' His large hand covered her back, tugging her until she sat back down. 'Chloe?'

'Immunity on the attempted murder charge, but nothing on the nun's murder.'

Craig's lawyer laughed. 'So this is basically a good deed? No thank you.'

Daniel was giving Craig his coldest stare. 'Consider it penance for killing a nun.'

They sat in silence until Alex could bear it no longer. She stood up. 'My mother didn't kill you when she had the chance. Call it fear or panic or mercy, the result is the same. You're here and she's not, because you were afraid your secret would be found out. But guess what? It would have come out sooner or later anyway. Secrets have a tendency to do that. I lost my mother, but you lost, too. You lost Bailey and Wade and your life as you knew it. I have my life. Even if your attorney manages to get you out of here someday, you'll never get your life back. Knowing that will be enough.'

She'd walked to the door when Craig stopped her.

'You didn't take the pills. I gave them to you.'

She turned around slowly. 'How?' she asked as neutrally as she was able.

'We ground them up, put them in water. When you came to, we made you drink it.'

'We?'

'Wade and I. He didn't want to, for what it's worth.'

Alex walked back to the table to face him. 'And the pills you put in my hand the day Kim came to take me home?' she asked, and he dropped his gaze.

'I hoped either you'd take them or Kim would find them and turn me in. That's all.'

It was enough. 'If you ever get out, you stay away from Hope and Bailey.'

He nodded once. 'Take me back.'

The guard took Craig away, his lawyer following. Chloe Hathaway gave Alex an appraising look. 'I wouldn't have given him an inch on the nun. Just so you know.'

Alex smiled thinly. 'Thank you for the immunity. It's good to know the truth.' When the SA was gone, Alex turned to Daniel. 'And thank you for making me come. I really did need to know.'

He stood and put his arm around her. 'I know you did. I wouldn't have cared either way, but you needed to know. Now all the secrets that were, aren't. Let's go home.'

Home. To Daniel's house with its comfortable living room, the pool table and the bar with *Dogs Playing Poker*, and the bedroom with his big bed. It would be the first time Daniel had been home since he'd been shot, and heat spread within her at the thought of no longer sleeping in his big bed alone.

Then she remembered the state in which she'd left his house and winced. 'Um, as long as we're baring truths, I have a small confession. Hope fed Riley.'

Daniel groaned. 'Where?'

'In the living room. I called Luke's mama and she's sending Luke's cousin. He has his own carpet-cleaning business. It should be clean before we get back.'

He sat in the wheelchair with a sigh. 'Any more secrets or confessions?'

She laughed, the sound surprising her. 'Nope, I think we're good. Let's go home.'

About the Author

Karen Rose is an award-winning author who fell in love with books from the time she learned to read. She started writing stories of her own when the characters in her head started talking and just wouldn't be silenced. A former chemical engineer and high school chemistry and physics teacher, Karen lives in Florida with her husband of twenty years, their two children, the family cat, Bella and their dog, Loki. When she's not writing, Karen is practicing for her next karate belt test! Karen would be thrilled to receive your e-mail at karen@karenrosebooks.com.

Die For Me

Karen Rose

A SECRET CELLAR

A multimedia designer is hard at work. His latest computer game, *Inquisitor*, heralds a new era in state-of-the-art graphics. But there's only one way to ensure that the death scenes are realistic enough . . .

AN ISOLATED FIELD

Detective Ciccotelli's day begins with one grave, one body and no murder weapon. It ends with sixteen graves, but only nine bodies and the realisation that the killer will strike again . . .

A LIVING HELL

When it's discovered that the murder weapons are similar to those used in medieval torture, Ciccotelli knows that he's up against the most dangerous opponent of his career – let the games begin . . .

A killer obsessed with the past, victims tortured to death, and all in the name of a game – *Die For Me* is Karen Rose's most chilling thriller to date.

Acclaim for Karen Rose:

'Karen Rose's *Count To Ten* takes off like a house afire. There's action and chills galore in this non-stop thriller' Tess Gerritsen

'Rose delivers the kind of high-wire suspense that keeps you riveted to the edge of your seat' Lisa Gardner

978 0 7553 3706 4

headline